SLIDE

SLIDE

MICHAEL DAY

PAN BOOKS

First published 2003 by Pan Books
an imprint of Pan Macmillan Ltd
Pan Macmillan, 20 New Wharf Road, London N1 9RR
Basingstoke and Oxford
Associated companies throughout the world
www.panmacmillan.com

ISBN 330 49224 1

A CIP catalogue record for this book is available from
the British Library.

Typeset by SetSystems Ltd, Saffron Walden, Essex
Printed and bound in Great Britain by
Mackays of Chatham plc, Chatham, Kent

For Susan, Emma and Jessica – you gave so much

Acknowledgements

I owe a debt of gratitude to many kind and generous people, but especially to Judy Smith, who gave me the initial determination to write this story; my parents and parents-in-law, who supported me so enthusiastically and then without a moment's hesitation selflessly helped finance the time to research and write; Joan Hayes and Michael Morrish, who recognized the importance of the project and never failed with support when it was most needed; Sara Fisher, my agent at A. M. Heath, whose unfailing enthusiasm and dedication kept me going through the darkest of days, and without whom this story could never have been told; and my editor at Macmillan, Peter Lavery, for whose professionalism I have the deepest respect. You are fine and very special people, all of you.

Fact

Towards the end of the Second World War, the New Zealand army experimented secretly with an extraordinary idea – how to create a tsunami wave and turn it into a weapon of war. During an operation code-named 'Seal', trials were conducted off Whangaparaoa, near Auckland. Special underwater explosions were set off in order to trigger miniature tidal waves, but before the tests could be completed, the war ended.

Then, between 1962 and 1974, the US Navy and the US Weather Bureau joined forces to try and tame the power of Atlantic hurricanes. This was Project Stormfury, which seeded the eye wall of a number of storms with varying degrees of success. Stormfury later planned to move its operations to the island of Guam in order to concentrate on Pacific typhoons, but the People's Republic of China, fearing that seeding would be used as a weapon to steer typhoons deliberately towards their shores, protested, and the Project was quietly abandoned.

At about the same time, the United States flew a total

of 2,602 sorties over Vietnam, injecting 47,409 canisters of seeding agent into monsoon rain clouds in an attempt to change the climate and significantly affect the delivery of supplies to the Communists along the Ho Chi Minh trail.

Aware of the growing danger posed by these new geophysical weapons, members of the United Nations signed the Environmental Modification Treaty in 1977. It prohibited any modification of the environment as a weapon of war, at a time when member states felt that a growing interest in the field would make their agreement increasingly important in the future.

And now, that future has come . . .

*'It's not something I would want to confront.
200 m.p.h. winds, over thirty feet of water
sucked up and driven onshore,
torrential rain . . . a great swathe of destruction
over thirty miles across. It's a terrible weapon,
a destroyer of cities!'*

Dr Cyrus Kuls, Los Alamos National Laboratory, New Mexico

Southeast Asia *showing places in the story*

Prologue – Jakarta, Indonesia

Lukman edged carefully into the ransacked bedroom and stared down at the charred corpse.

He knew what had happened: the man had been torched.

It was obvious.

He was a 'firecracker'.

Someone had filled his pockets with jumping jacks and doused him with petrol. Then they'd released the cords and set him alight. Probably laughed as he crashed around the room, screaming in agony, arms flailing at the roaring bush of fire that he'd become.

He must have been rich.

They only torched the rich . . .

. . . and the Chinese.

Lukman stared at the corpse. He was fascinated by how it had warped and twisted in the searing heat of the flames. He reckoned that if he gave it a nudge it would just fall apart. He peered more closely and saw how the face had melted, saw how the arms had charred into blackened twigs. Saw how the muscles had shrunk, drawing up the limbs, tightening the fingers into stiff claws like those of a dead bird.

But it was the shoes that gave it away.

They'd somehow fallen off as the body curled and crisped at temperatures of over 2,000°C. They were a man's shoes, scorched on one side. Nice ones, with beautifully tooled leather uppers. Only the Chinese could afford shoes like that.

Lukman lounged up against the wall. Dressed in black, his lean frame seemed to merge into the charred fabric of the room. His smooth brown skin was stretched finely across the neatly chiselled features of his Malay face, and a thin black moustache decorated his upper lip. As his intelligent gaze slid carefully around the room, he missed nothing.

Lukman took a long pull on the stub end of his cigarette – a *kretek*. The cloves glowed and crackled in the sudden rush of oxygen, then he casually flicked the fag end into a corner of the room. He'd been smoking steadily all morning, trying to blot out the uneasy mixed stench of sweet petrol and acrid burned fat that pervaded the city.

He kicked lazily at the debris on the floor, tracing out shapes in the fire-ash with the toe of his right boot. After several nights of rioting, large areas of central Jakarta resembled a nightmare. He'd seen gutted buildings and rubble-filled streets, looters silhouetted against the flames, luxury goods spilling out onto the pavements. He'd heard the familiar sharp crack of M16 semi-automatic rifles as the President's troops had tried to wrest control from the marauding gangs of Islamic students and yobs.

Indonesia was once again on the verge of collapse, mass frustration seething feverishly.

Lukman smiled thinly.

A helicopter clattered noisily overhead. He checked his watch, and knew it was time. His moment had come.

Carefully stepping over scattered furniture and broken glass, he worked his way towards the bedroom window. Seven floors up, in the Skyline Hotel, he had a clear view of his 'killing ground'. He had chosen the large open space where the broad sweep of the six-lane Jalan Thamrin crossed the Hasymin Road. It was ideal: there were no obstacles in his field of fire. Kartini would soon be down there; the RRI media crew would see to that – the 'Tiger' had paid them well for their loyalty.

The radio resting on the bed briefly came to life. A burst of static, then: '*Tiger yellow. Tiger yellow.*'

Lukman moved smoothly into action. Standing on a chair, he reached up with a screwdriver and dropped down a large air-conditioning grid from the ceiling. From the recess he slid out a heavy rectangular green plastic case, and flicked up the catches. Inside, snugly embedded in its yellow foam packing, gleamed a deadly PSG-1. Four feet of the best German sniper technology. He knew the weapon well: beautifully machined, reliable, accurate over long distances. He'd prepared it for this occasion weeks ago, cleaning and oiling the working parts before hiding it away. Now it felt alive in his hands, eager to go, eager to unleash its deadly load of 7.62mm-calibre metal.

Picking up the rifle and two five-round magazines, he carried them over to the window. He set the gun down on its little bipod and tucked himself down behind it. He needed to check the range. A fireman was visible on the opposite side of the junction, picking his way through the burned-out remains of the Hard Rock Café. Lukman pulled the cheek pad firmly against his face, and squinted down the scope. He focused the cross-hairs on the man's back. Just a few light touches on the range adjuster were all that was needed.

Relaxing his breath, Lukman reached out to prop a mirror up against the window jamb. He positioned it carefully, so that he could see a short way back up the street.

Then he waited.

He waited a long time.

A light breeze wafted against his cheek, bringing with it the sharp scent of burning wood from forest fires that raged uncontrollably in the searing drought a thousand miles to the east. The sun beat down through the smog, casting an eerie coppery glow across the devastated city. Somewhere behind the building, a helicopter banked hard, its blades slapping the air with their steady beat. A stolen armoured car raced down the street, tyres whining on the tarmac, the slipstream of its passage blowing hundreds of plastic carrier bags into the air from a pile that had spewed out from a ransacked department store. Islamic fighters sprawled across its sloping armour plate – wild and masked, looking for trouble, pushing their country to the edge of destruction, preparing the way for the Tiger.

The radio gave another burst of static: '*Tiger black.*'

Lukman glanced into the mirror. He could see people gathering at the end of the road. A police motorcycle drew up, lights flashing, followed by an army lorry. Soldiers jumped down and took up position on either side of the highway.

Then, at last, what he had been waiting for: a big white limousine with blackened windows, a miniature flag of Indonesia fluttering on its bonnet.

Bakorstanas agents swarmed around the car as an aide opened the door. Lukman could feel his heart thumping in his chest, strong and painful, beating against the floor where he lay.

He waited, but nothing happened.

An age seemed to pass.

Then the media people arrived, a collective fuss of TV cameras and reporters, and at last the man himself stepped out: Kartini, elected President of Indonesia – Lukman's target. A dumpy little man with rounded shoulders. Dressed casually in a blue batik shirt and grey slacks, belly straining against his clothing. Heavy gold spectacles on his smooth round face, a small round black *peci* hat perched on his fat head. He surveyed the devastation around him, his lips twisted into a disdainful smirk.

This was the man who had finally brought Indonesia to

5

her knees. The most hated man in the country: a pimp, who prostituted the country's wealth, taking bribes and favours on a grand scale while his own people starved. The man who'd presided over broken deals and false promises. The man who'd stubbornly disregarded the climatic chaos now engulfing his country; who'd disregarded the suffering of his people – the devastating storms, the darkening shadow of famine.

This was the man who was going to die.

Lukman's seventh-floor lair was like an oven, baking hard in the searing late-morning sun that flared down through a thick haze of pollution. A tiny bead of sweat trickled out from one of his armpits and ran across his chest. It irritated him. He rubbed it away, then squinted back through the scope at the road junction. Lines of soldiers were starting to cross, each one turning round slowly as he walked to check the side roads. Lukman knew that Kartini couldn't be far behind them.

And at last he came, surrounded by a huddle of grey-suited *Bakorstanas* and white-shirted aides.

The media people did their job well. They stopped Kartini right in the middle of the road junction, making him a perfect target. Someone approached the camera with a little clapperboard, and the RRI reporter started her interview.

Even from this distance the *Bakorstanas* – the Indonesian Secret Service – were looking edgy. The place was too open. They fidgeted, aware of the danger.

Lukman held the rifle hard against his shoulder. He

slowly let out his breath, his right finger curling around the trigger. He took up the slack, and slowly lowered the scope until Kartini's head filled the sights. He centred the cross-hairs on the President's podgy right temple.

Kartini was talking to the cameras. He was trying to convince the world of his control over the city, of his authority over this vast scattering of islands. He was convincing himself of his own invulnerability.

Lukman flexed his finger . . . and fired.

A sharp *crack* reverberated around the tall buildings.

Lukman's shot was good. The bullet entered neatly just above Kartini's right ear. It passed through the brain and erupted out of the lower left jaw, leaving behind a fist-sized exit hole of shattered bone and torn flesh. Kartini looked startled for a moment. He swayed, then dropped heavily like a slaughtered animal.

But Lukman wanted to make sure; he dared not face the consequences of failure. He hurriedly looked back through the scope, saw Kartini on the tarmac, saw the bodyguard who shielded him. He fired a second shot. The bodyguard slumped away. He fired a third, fourth, fifth round, in quick succession; each shot kicked the rifle back into his shoulder. The bullets burned neat holes through Kartini's outer flesh before flattening into white-hot slugs that tore and ripped at the vital organs inside.

Lukman's gunfire brought chaos to the street. The camera crew had fallen to the ground, terrified by the zip and crack of passing bullets. Someone was squealing in pain: a hideous animal noise.

The *Bakorstanas* agents panicked. They now ignored Kartini completely, his life steadily draining away in a spreading pool of dark red blood. They were looking up, trying to spot the sniper among the confusion of windows. Guns waving, they yelled orders to one another. They were frightened by their failure, frightened of what might happen to them.

Lukman moved fast. The whole area would soon be cordoned off. Abandoning his equipment, he made for the door. But, stepping over the blackened corpse, something made him hesitate. He looked down at the charcoaled remains of the face, saw again the sagging lips and the empty eye sockets, and gave the burned body a savage kick. The corpse rolled stiffly like a fallen branch. A piece of blackened jewellery popped away from the charred flesh and slipped to the ash-laden floor. He stared down at the dulled metallic surface, realized the wealth in the pitted stones set into heat-stained filigree, and his hand moved to take it . . .

Then stopped.

Why bother? Why bother when he was already much more than just a dollar man?

He didn't need that. Not now.

It was time to go.

Lukman slipped out of the ruined hotel and entered the familiar maze of little paths that led through the shattered *kampung*, his exit route through the stink and filth of the shanty town having been carefully planned long ago. He had an intimate knowledge of this, his home territory, and knew his route well. He was confident of his escape.

SLIDE

No one followed him.

No one caught his fleeing shadow.

And no one could foresee the evil that would follow in the wake of his assassin's bullet.

Part One: ROLLING DICE

Indonesia Wrecks Vital Ocean Experiment

The United Nations was informed yesterday that ocean-research ships from both the United States and the United Kingdom have been refused permission to enter Indonesia's Exclusive Economic Zone – a 200-mile strip of water that, under United Nations law, entails certain rights of ownership. Now a set of ocean temperature figures, vital to the world's understanding of the likely effects of global warming, will no longer be collected. The Indonesian stand is clearly illegal, and will be discussed at a special meeting of the UN Security Council tomorrow.

In defence of his actions, President Rahman, the new self-styled 'Tiger of Asia', claimed last night that the research measurements were only being taken in order to gather information that would enable foreign submarines on secret missions to escape detection. The Indonesian Navy has since issued a warning that they will take direct action should the ban be violated in any way.

This latest incident underlines the West's growing concern about instability in South-East Asia. Last year, China's dramatic pre-emptive strike against the Spratly oilfields brought the region to the brink of all-out war. Now, as Indonesia appears to slide away from democracy, Rahman's new and aggressive hardline Islamic government poses yet another threat to peace in this increasingly volatile area of the world.

The Times, 3 January

Chapter One – first week in January: Straits of Malacca, off the south-west coast of Thailand

The long, narrow sampan headed straight into the path of the advancing storm, its sharply pointed bow cutting through the choppy waves. Sheets of spray whipped back over the prow, repeatedly drenching the tiny figure who sat hunched, gnomelike, in the middle of the boat – a Chinese girl, no more than five or six years old, her head buried deep inside the pixie hood of her blue quilted anorak. In her arms she cradled a naked doll, its plastic head cuddled protectively against her chest.

Her father stood on a wooden platform at the back of the boat, his head turning anxiously to spot any pursuing planes. The rising wind gusted around him, so that sometimes he caught the hot smell of the roaring engine. He had little protection against the weather, and had pulled the brim of his black salt-stained cap, with its fading Mercedes-Benz star, low over his forehead. His face was gaunt and unshaven, reddened by wind, sun and salt.

Lightning flickered across the flat wall of cloud that hung dark and heavy on the horizon. When the storm came, it hit the boat hard. The rain became torrential. The Chinese man shouted to his little girl, and pointed urgently to something lying in the bottom of the boat. She turned and reached down, lifting up a small red rucksack with its precious cargo, which she placed carefully on the seat beside her. Her father watched her, and could see how her tender skin had bled in places, leaving brown patches of scab. For a moment, her two dark little eyes stared back at him. Then she bent to pick up a tin, and began to bail out the growing puddles.

As the towering thunderhead moved off eastwards, the rain eased and then stopped abruptly. Strong sunlight streamed down through breaks in the overcast. The little girl stopped bailing, and put her tin down carefully. Details of the Thai coast became clearer. A cluster of small islands slowly appeared, overhung with fragments of wispy cloud. Mangrove swamps fringed the blue-grey coastline, their dark mass broken only by the occasional thin white line of a sandy bay.

The boat sped on through the water. The man and his daughter were grateful for the strong heat of the sun as it dried out their sodden clothes.

Then he saw it.

A silent black dot wavering just above the horizon. Something flying low, a long way to their left. He had no doubt about what it was – an Indonesian plane, pushing into Thai air space, hunting, searching. They'd been caught, just as he'd known they would be. Caught in the open: an obvious target, a dark spot on the pale aquamarine of the sea.

He leaned into the slipstream, urging the boat forward, running for the safety of the islands, the narrow 'V' of their tell-tale wake creaming away to either side. The plane began to turn gently towards them. Thoughts raced through the man's head as fear grabbed at his heart. Had someone spotted something? A smudged blip, maybe, on a radar screen? They had to get off the water, safeguard the rucksack.

Rounding the nearest island, he swerved sharply into a little cliff-lined cove. Revving the motor hard, he brought the boat to a sudden halt. He manoeuvred it under the welcoming cover of a jagged overhang and cut the motor. His ears sang in the unaccustomed silence. He pulled the boat close in against the rock, cutting his hands as he scrabbled for a grip on the sharp-edged limestone. Their dramatic entrance had created waves in the cove that slapped at the sides of the sampan, rocking it, making it difficult to hold.

He waited, listening.

A bird screeched and flapped away through the jungle canopy, sending leaves pattering to the ground.

The little girl looked back, and said something to him in Mandarin. She was hungry and thirsty. She looked like she might cry. He held a finger to his lips to quieten her, and smiled at her, encouragingly.

Now he could hear the plane approaching, the distinctive whine of powerful turboprops rising steadily as it

17

closed the distance. He stooped lower in the boat, pulling it hard against the protective cliff. The little girl's face began to crease. Then, overcome by her father's fear and uncertainty, she let go a pitiful sobbing wail.

Suddenly the plane was upon them. It flashed low overhead. He caught a glimpse of a big grey twin-engined aircraft, its long thin wings streaked with oil, bright orange pods beneath. Then it was gone, the powerful roar of its engines dropping an octave before fading altogether behind the protecting wall of rock. The air slapped and roared in the plane's wake, and a strong smell of kerosene drifted down from its close passage overhead.

The man didn't move. He waited for the plane to return, listening carefully for the note of its engines. But there was only silence. Only then did he know for sure that they'd escaped. His arms and legs shook as he released the boat from its rocky embrace.

The little girl struggled back towards him, making her way over wooden seats and a clutter of ropes and petrol cans, clutching the little red rucksack in one hand, her plastic doll in the other. He knelt down and took her into his arms, wiping away her tears with a grimy thumb. He spoke softly to her: 'Nearly there, little one, nearly there. Tonight we stop the boat, and find our friends. Then you can sleep, and eat, and you will feel better.'

He stroked her straight black hair, and held the little body close, so tiny and slim in his strong arms.

Chapter Two – later the same day:
the Philippine Sea

The officer of the watch stood on the ship's bridge, staring out into the blackness of the sub-tropical night, and yawned. The crisp white uniform of the New Islamic Indonesian Navy fitted his slim frame well, giving him a commanding presence and an air of authority beyond his years.

He was bored.

He'd hoped, when he'd joined the *Ibn Battuta*, that a tour of duty on an oceanographic ship would have been an adventure. He'd imagined long voyages to distant oceans, the excitement of exotic ports. But, so far, all that he'd done had been navigate from one location in the Philippine Sea to another, while the Russian scientists on board bobbed up and down through the sea in their bright orange submersible.

A loud electronic chime broke through the hushed rhythm of bridge procedure. He reached forward and picked up the handset.

He spoke in Indonesian, his voice crisp and formal: 'Officer of the watch.'

He'd expected a routine reply, and was surprised when an anxious female voice answered, shrill with distress. 'Oh, thank God! Would you come down to the labs, please – quickly! Something's happened. There's been some sort of accident. I need help.'

The officer considered for a moment, his eyes narrowing. The request was out of the ordinary. He wasn't quite sure how he should deal with it. 'I'll try and be with you as soon as I can,' he finally replied.

He replaced the handset thoughtfully, then picked up the ship's mobile and punched in a number. 'Dr Hendra?' He hesitated for a moment. 'Officer of the watch here, sir. Sorry to disturb you at this hour. I've had a call from one of your technicians in the main lab . . . No, sir, I've no idea what the problem is. She just said it was urgent.' He nodded in agreement to an instruction. 'Right, sir . . . I'll meet you down there, straight away, sir.'

Dr Jazid Hendra, technical wizard of Rahman's new Islamic-style government, was a wealthy entrepreneur. A strange and rather cold man. The *Ibn Battuta* was essentially his ship, built to contract in a Malaysian shipyard with no expense whatsoever spared.

The laboratories were central to Hendra's design. State-of-the-art, very high-tech, they made other contemporary research vessels look like relics of the Victorian age. But behind those white-painted doors, with their prominent black and yellow radiation hazard signs, was a closely guarded secret. And people soon learned not to ask questions or show too much interest. You would be under suspicion as an enemy of the state – and a target for the unsavoury attentions of the *Bakorstanas*.

Dr Hendra and the young officer arrived outside the lab together. Hendra nodded curtly, and briskly passed over a little radiation patch dangling from a silver crocodile clip. 'Fasten this to your lapel, young man, before we go inside.' The officer did as he was instructed.

Hendra was small in stature. Heavy gold-framed glasses rested on a neat, square Malaysian head and his dark hair was greying slightly at the temples. He had an icy presence, and a reputation for ruthless efficiency. The young officer was not surprised to see his superior fully dressed at such an early hour.

He watched as Hendra placed the thumb of one hand onto a small optical reader, and wiped his security card through a magnetic slot with the other. Electric bolts clacked open, and the doors slid back smoothly, with a slight hiss.

'Airlock. Shut the door behind you, please – green button.' Hendra's voice was cold and smooth, like folding silk. The young officer did as he was told. Momentarily, they were both bathed in a weak orange light. Then the second door slid open.

Immediately a stench of rotten eggs poured into the airlock. The young officer gagged, but Hendra kept his composure. A young Indonesian technician stood in front of them. She fiddled nervously with her hands. Her face, framed by an officially issued Islamic headscarf, was pinched and pale with shock. 'My God, girl – what have you done?' enquired Hendra icily. 'How many bottles have you broken?'

The girl cringed, and watched silently as Hendra walked swiftly across the lab to punch a red button on a panel. The faint whisper of the ventilation system rose to a roar as powerful fans began to pump away the foul air.

'I'm sorry, Doctor,' she mumbled. 'I wasn't sure what to do.' The girl wore the light green cotton shirt and trousers issued to all his lab staff. Small tears crept from the corners of her eyes, and her anxious gaze darted around the room as if looking for a means of escape. 'I think it must have been some sort of accident,' she stammered.

'Well, go on!' demanded Hendra. His powerful presence filled the room, making him seem taller than he really was. 'Tell me!'

She gestured vaguely towards a door that stood slightly ajar on the other side of the lab. 'Over in the cold store – where we keep the biological samples.'

The young officer turned to look, and saw a pool of pale fluid oozing from under the door. It glistened in the harsh lighting. The girl's eyes still betrayed her shock at the memory of some horror that lay inside the storeroom. He waited nervously as Hendra strode across the lab.

Hendra pulled the door fully open, and for a moment just stood there, his shoulders a square silhouette against the harsh light flooding out from the store.

Overcome with curiosity, the young officer moved forward to see more clearly.

The body of the marine must have tumbled out of the

cold store as soon as the young female technician had opened the heavy doors. No doubt the corpse had collapsed towards her with a sickening wet thud. Fine wire, pulled tight and cutting deep into the flesh, had been wrapped around its neck. An obscene sulphurous stench rose from the undersea samples now strewn soggily across the tiles.

The young officer wrenched his head away from the sight and puked, then rested his arm and head shakily against the adjacent wall.

Slowly, Hendra retrieved a handkerchief from his top pocket, and neatly shook it out. Carefully bringing it up to his mouth, he stepped back a pace. Something crunched underfoot – a small, white, deep-ocean crab, its entrails now bursting from its body. Wiping his foot on the floor to rid himself of this foul mess, Hendra turned and stalked away, his leather shoes clicking precisely on the tiled floor. He plucked a telephone handset from the wall.

'Hendra here. Have the captain come down to the labs. Yes, right away!' he barked. 'And I want the head of security, too.'

The lights in Hendra's cabin burned brightly. A steady stream of deliciously cool air flowed gently from the air-conditioning vents, a welcome contrast to the sticky sub-tropical night outside.

The cabin was austere, devoid of everything except bare necessities. The walls were white and a single square of rich blue carpet covered the beautifully polished wooden floor. Carefully centred upon it was an antique mahogany desk with brass drawer-handles. The only ornament in the room was an exquisite china figurine in the shape of a dolphin.

Two pictures hung on the wall. The larger one was a view of Hendra's ship, its rakish lines cutting through a dark Pacific swell. The other showed an ocean vent, three thousand metres down in the crushing blackness of the deep. The camera flash had revealed a 'black smoker': an underwater volcanic spring, its grotesque chimneys belching out scalding clouds of black mineral-rich fluid.

Together, these two photographs told the story of Dr Jazid Hendra's rise to power, of how he'd discovered an El Dorado, a cornucopia of mineral treasures – possibly the source of unbelievable wealth. Careful sampling by his oceanographic team had revealed that billions of dollars' worth of precious metals were precipitating out from around these vents, creating giant outcrops of mineral ores, sometimes as much as four storeys high: gold, silver, copper, zinc – all down there for the taking.

And then they'd discovered something else.

Something far more interesting, something far more precious.

Uranium.

Stitched into the very fabric of the chimneys by metal-fixing bacteria that lived in the scalding water of the vents.

And with the Indonesian economy tottering, and the military threat from China growing daily, President Rahman hadn't needed to think twice. He had begun to invest heavily in Hendra's deep-ocean mining project.

Which was good, because Hendra knew about something else that lurked down there.

Another mineral.

A rather strange rock.

A rock streaked with marbled layers of rusty orange and green, flecked with specks of gold.

But Hendra had stayed quiet about this new find. Kept a sample of it in one of his desk drawers. Had the habit of taking it out at night to let his gaze slide wonderingly across its surface. And he told no one about it . . . except the one man he needed to make his scheme work. Lukman.

Because Hendra knew that what he'd found had the potential to make him billions of dollars.

It was his insurance in a fragile world.

Behind Hendra's desk hung a large portrait of 'The Tiger', the New Islamic President of Indonesia. Rahman had deliberately softened his image for the artist, discarding his customary gold-braided uniform for an open, dark grey waistcoat worn over a white mandarin-collared shirt. But his middle-aged Malayan face still gazed down sternly into the cabin.

The portrait was a good one. It captured Rahman's imposing demeanour and transported his presence right into the room, commanding attention and respect from any of those assembled there. And late at night, when Hendra took out his little piece of rock to examine it, he always cast a furtive eye over his shoulder, as if the great and dangerous man was watching his every move.

On this particular evening Hendra had arranged for a small private meeting to take place beneath the portrait. As he sat behind the desk in his customary hard leather chair, before him were the ship's security officer and the captain of the *Ibn Battuta*. The atmosphere was tense.

'Do we know what was taken yet?' asked Hendra sharply.

'Only a computer disk,' replied the security officer hesitantly, 'showing mineral-sample readings.'

Hendra's fingers pinched at a bulge of skin under his chin. His sharp eyes narrowed. 'Which site?' he enquired sternly.

'*Krakatau*, on the Palau Ridge.'

The security officer watched a shadow pass across Hendra's face and guessed at once that whatever was on that stolen disk, it must be important. He tried to head off Hendra's impending wrath. 'Of course, the disk itself will be of no value to anyone, Dr Hendra,' he said hurriedly. 'The data's all coded, and without the necessary software it simply cannot be read.'

Hendra nodded imperceptibly. 'But since your electronic wizardry failed to detect these intruders,' he answered smoothly, 'how can you be so sure about the security of your other systems?'

The security officer fidgeted. There was silence for a moment.

'Did they take anything else?' demanded Hendra sharply.

'Not as far as we can tell. Only a mineral sample . . .' He paused. 'And we can't locate another disk – from the *Halimun* site.'

For a moment Hendra did nothing. He just stared at his security officer.

Halimun!

The word jarred. Shreds of fear fluttered and sliced at his belly.

'What did you say?' he demanded quietly.

But already his fists were bunching on the table in front of him, while inside his head a nightmare was unfolding – a nightmare in which his secret was suddenly revealed, his greed exposed to the world like a snail plucked naked from its shell.

'We can't locate one of the other disks,' repeated the security officer nervously.

'You fool!' hissed Hendra. 'Those disks are highly classified. They hold special information . . . information vital to the future of this nation . . . to the President . . . to *me*!' His eyes bulged. 'My God! How could you have been so stupid, to let this intruder through your fingers like some slippery eel?' He was breathing deeply, snorting the air through his nostrils. 'Let me remind you. This is a secure scientific mission. We have Navy people on board.

We have some of the best geological minds, all experts in their fields. We need these professionals in order to be successful. But you . . .' He slowly pushed his face close up to the security officer, until he could see the grease-filled pockmarks in the man's skin. 'But you, I think, we can do without. You are inadequate . . . incompetent . . . and defective.'

The security officer blinked. He could see how Hendra's body was trembling with rage. He'd never seen him like this before. Never seen such fury.

'So, who was this intruder, hmm? Chinese?' Hendra's hand thumped down onto the desk, as if trying to extract an answer from it. 'American?' Hendra thumped again. The dolphin figurine rattled. 'Well?' He paused, expecting a reply. 'I will make you pay for this. I will make you pay for this very dearly – with your life.' He slapped a trembling palm against a button. A guard entered, weapon held at the ready.

Hendra stood up.

'Take this man!' he ordered, his vibrating finger now pointing at the security officer. 'And dispose of him.'

It was over an hour later when Hendra finally put down the telephone. He passed a handkerchief through the beads of sweat gathered on his brow. Despite the air-conditioning, his cabin felt unbearably close and sticky in the overheated night air. He flung open a window.

Hendra had used a direct satellite link to contact the

President. Rahman had been typically calm, and very polite – but had left him in no doubt as to the danger Hendra was in. He'd been warned that his blunder might have blown apart the whole operation, jeopardized all their plans for the future.

And when General Rahman was displeased, Hendra knew there would be consequences: imprisonment, the stripping away of his wealth . . . maybe something worse.

Hendra's gut tightened, and he felt a cold stab of fear. Events were quickly spiralling out of control. If Rahman discovered what he'd been hiding, he was finished. Rahman would never forgive him for such treachery. It would all be over.

His trembling hand wiped his face again. Somewhere out there, the secret of his work – those computer disks and the rock sample, the treasures so carefully culled from the deep – were being passed into the wrong hands.

But *whose* hands? Those of the Chinese? Of the Americans? Where should he start looking?

Hendra slid open a desk drawer and began to finger the strange piece of rock that held so much promise. He glanced up nervously at Rahman's portrait, and saw the eyes staring down at him. He hastily slipped the sample back into the drawer and pushed it shut.

He was walking a tightrope. He had to get that information back.

At any cost.

Chapter Three – three days later: Bangkok

Unshaven and unkempt, his clothes dirty from sleeping rough, the Chinese man wandered down a narrow, frenetic street in Bangkok's China Town. Clutched tightly to his chest was a small red rucksack, smeared with mud. A little girl trailed beside him, one hand hooked into his, a naked doll hanging loose from the other.

The man stopped at a street corner, eyes raw from the stinging haze, and dug deep into his pocket. He pulled out a tatty sheet of paper on which he'd scribbled an address in pencil. The man was searching for the offices of the Poh Tek Tung – a Thai volunteer organization that, in the absence of any city ambulance service, preyed on the scenes of car accidents, to take away the dead.

In the offices of the PTT worked a man who he knew would help him. A man who represented the last link in the fragile human chain that had hooked him out of Indonesia with his precious cargo. A man who would exchange the contents of his rucksack for money.

The offices of the PTT weren't difficult to find: gaudy

blue and red neon strips spelled out the initials. A row of PTT cars was drawn up outside, all flashing lights and bright door badges. Shuffling in through the swing doors, pleased to be out of the heat and noise of the city, the Chinese man and his little girl made their way to the enquiry desk. Behind the desk sat a uniformed officer, large red shoulder-flashes sewn proudly onto his dark blue uniform. The officer's expression filled with suspicion as the two of them approached. 'Yes? Can I help you?'

The Chinese man put down his little rucksack, and fished around in its zippered front pocket. He produced a dirty name-card and showed it to the officer. He pointed. 'I would like to speak with this man: Somchai Jornpaison.'

The PTT man studied him, catching a whiff of unwashed flesh. A flicker of contempt passed across his face.

'Tell Somchai Jornpaison that I've come from Jakarta,' urged the stranger. 'Tell him that I have news.'

A little gust of stale breath washed over the desk officer as the Chinese man spoke, making him recoil in disgust. Boat people! Bloody Indonesian refugees. Sodding Chinks. 'Somchai's not on duty,' he said through gritted teeth. 'Come back again next week . . . when you've had a wash.'

The Chinese man ignored the suggestion, and glanced back at the tatty name-card. 'No, you must be mistaken,' he persisted. 'Somchai works here full time. I would like to see him, please. I know he's here.' His little girl stared fixedly up at the desk man, her black eyes like two shining marbles just above the level of the table top.

The desk man became angry. 'I've told you, he's not here. Somchai – is – not – here, understand? Now piss off!' He waved his hands dismissively, as if trying to flap the miserable pair away.

Anger welled up inside the Chinese man. He wouldn't be treated like this. Blood pulsed through the facial artery on the side of his head. He leaned over and grabbed the PTT man by his lapels, wrenching him out of his seat and pulling him bodily across the desktop. Papers slid off and scattered to the floor. The telephone crashed off the edge and hung by its cord.

'Listen to me, you bastard!' The Chinese man's jaw was clamped tight with anger, the stubble standing out on the taut flesh of his chin. 'I don't care what you say, or what you think. I haven't come all this way to be pushed around by some shit in uniform. Now – I want to see Somchai, understand? Go and tell him that I'm here, OK?' He slowly let go of the PTT man, who slid back into his seat.

Alerted by the commotion, another man appeared on the stairs at the rear of the foyer: a short, barrel-chested man, calmly smoking a cigarette. He peered down at the scene below, and a commanding voice echoed through the room: 'Did I hear you asking for Somchai Jornpaison?' He studied them carefully, his air one of superiority. Then he drew heavily on his cigarette, holding on to the smoke before exhaling it in a steady stream. Then, dropping its remains onto the floor, he ground the fag end noisily into the concrete stairway with the toe of his shoe.

'I am Somchai Jornpaison,' he said imperiously. 'Come this way, please.'

Somchai sat down in his tiny office on the second floor. He was a powerfully built elderly man with a sweep of grey hair fringing his round and balding head. His broad Chinese face had a polished, almost translucent skin texture, and his eyes glinted with intelligence.

There was almost nothing on his dark rosewood desk except a large fan that ineffectually wafted the hot, smog-laden air around the room. A blind had been pulled down over the window, but its slats were open to let in the anaemic light of a thin yellow sun trying to pierce the thick haze of pollution outside.

Somchai took the rucksack from the Chinese man and unfastened it. He peered inside and pulled out a bubble-wrapped package fastened with a fat elastic band. As he fingered the package curiously, he could make out a small cylinder of rock, tinged an unusual orange, and what he assumed were two computer disks.

'Where did you get this?' he demanded.

The Chinese man shrugged. 'They told me to get it to you. They said it was important.'

'Who? Who told you this?'

The visitor's eyes stared back at him, blank and empty of emotion. 'Dissidents. Underground people.'

Somchai nodded. He fingered the package again, before placing it carefully on the desk in front of him.

A dirty hand clamped down onto his: 'They told me there would be a reward – something in it for me if I acted as courier. They said that there would be money.'

Somchai looked at him, studying the fatigue in his eyes. 'You will be well paid for your work.'

Slowly, the dirty hand was removed.

'Tell me, how is it for the Chinese in Indonesia now?' Somchai asked.

'Bad.'

'Muslims?'

The Chinese man spat noisily into a corner of the room. 'Bastards!'

Somchai nodded slowly. 'And the *Bakorstanas*?'

The man paused before replying softly, 'Everywhere now. On the streets, in the shopping malls, in the schools. Watching, listening.' He spat again, noisily. 'You know how it is. Please, the money – my little girl, I need food for her. We need to rest.'

'I understand.'

Somchai passed back the empty rucksack. He eyed the fading star embroidered on the man's cap. 'Did you work for Mercedes?'

'A dealership, in Jakarta. I lost it.'

Somchai nodded slowly. 'How?'

The man drew in a ragged breath. 'My business partner disappeared. He was found dead in a Glodok canal. Then I lost my garage . . . in the race riots.'

'And your wife?'

The Chinese man looked down at his little girl. '*She*'s my future now.'

Somchai stared into the man's haunted eyes.

The Chinese man paused, as if remembering something, then gathered himself together. 'The hate . . . you have no idea. Christians, Chinese – separated, herded. I've seen things . . .' The small bead of a tear began to gather in the corner of one eye. 'Atrocities . . .' He shook his head.

Somchai opened a drawer in his desk, and pushed a crisp brown envelope across the table. 'You and your little girl, you're safe now. We've paid you well for your work, Mercedes man. Go now, sort yourself out. But remember, this struggle is just beginning. We may need your services again. Perhaps in the future?'

The man looked up. 'Yes. I'll be ready.'

They shook hands solemnly before the office door closed behind them with a squeak of its well-worn hinges.

Somchai pushed up a segment of the half-open window blind, and watched thoughtfully as the Chinese man and his little girl trudged off into the stifling heat of a Bangkok afternoon. Then he let the blind go, and stared down at the little package lying on his desk.

He'd been waiting for this delivery. There was something important here. Evidence, information about what Rahman had found on the ocean floor. Now it was Somchai's turn to run the gauntlet, to carry this information back to England and have it analysed. And *Bakorstanas* were no doubt sniffing at its trail right now. He'd have to move fast.

He picked up his telephone and dialled a special number. It was a long number.

He waited for some time.

Finally he spoke his message, clear and simple. 'Tell Malcolm: his uncle's coming home.'

Then with one swift movement, he replaced the receiver and swept the package into his safe, which he locked firmly.

That same evening, Somchai carefully sealed the rock sample and the computer disks into a padded brown envelope, and left the PTT offices to catch a night flight to the UK. But instead of taking a PTT car, he hired a taxi, thinking it would be better not to attract too much attention.

It was late by the time his taxi pulled away. The sky over Bangkok had become a gloomy, dirty orange as the lowering sun filtered through the layers of smog, buildings glowing a dull copper in the refracted evening light. The pale green Mercedes moved steadily through the chaotic rush-hour traffic. It came to a halt at the traffic lights beside the little hexagonal watchtower at Pan Fah. Masked pedestrians, sweating in the overheated air, stared into the car with envy. Pigeons flocked over the wall from the gardens opposite, wings flapping as they got ready to roost.

A motorbike drew up alongside the taxi; an off-road

bike, riding high above the ground on its knobbly tyres. As the masked rider looked in, Somchai stared blankly back. The bike's exhaust rasped as its rider revved the engine, spewing out a plume of hot oily-grey smoke.

The lights changed and the bike accelerated down the road.

Somchai glanced down at his briefcase, wondering exactly what information might be locked inside the package. How valuable it might be. Whether it was really worth all this time and effort – and risk.

He stared moodily out of the window.

The traffic thinned as they headed north. They hit the expressway leading to Don Muang airport, and the Mercedes gathered speed. Somchai noticed the same motorbike again, just ahead of the taxi. It was braking gently, and the taxi driver pulled out to overtake it.

But then a powerful sports bike slid alongside, boxing them in, so the Mercedes was bracketed. Somchai could hear the harsh note of both engines, the off-road bike in front, the sports bike edging forward until it was level with the car's front window. Just kids, he assumed, racing the taxi.

Then the sports-bike rider pulled a pistol.

Sweat broke out on the neck of the taxi driver. He started to pull over. The rider kept the pistol trained on him. The other bike stayed resolutely in front, blocking any chance of a quick getaway.

Highway robbers!

Somchai opened his briefcase and desperately began to

stuff the package down the back of the seat. Then he took out his wallet.

The car stopped. The two riders stayed on their bikes. The one on the sports bike leaned down to open Somchai's door. Through the visor Somchai could see the soft features of a woman. He stretched out his hand, offering her his wallet. But the woman didn't take it, waving her pistol at him instead. My God, she wanted him to step out!

Suddenly, there was a flash of metal followed by a terrific bang. Another car had clipped the woman's bike from behind, catapulting it high into the air to sail right over the bonnet of the taxi. The bike was already disintegrating as it hit the outer edge of the tarmac. It slid a short distance before slamming into the crash barrier, sparks cracking bright orange in the gathering darkness. The tank split. Fuel spilled out in a spreading pool and seeped under the shorted battery leads. There was a dull thump, and the bike debris was quickly engulfed in a mass of flame. Black smoke boiled across the reddening sunset.

Ahead of Somchai, the car responsible braked hard in a cloud of burned-rubber smoke. The off-road bike began to spin round, turning to face the taxi. Somchai crouched down behind the driver's seat, reaching under his jacket for his handgun – a SIG P226, given to him by the British but never used in anger. His hands shook as he chambered a 9mm round. He peered over the front seat to see what was happening.

The car ahead was reversing at high speed, white tail lights shining in the gloom. It hit the back of the off-road bike hard, bulldozing it straight into the front of the taxi. Somchai was thrown into the footwell by the impact, the gun knocked from his hand. He lay there for a moment, badly shaken. He could hear the taxi driver struggling to get out of his vehicle, banging on the door, yelling for help. But the door had been buckled and wouldn't open. The driver placed his feet up against it, pushing and kicking with all his strength.

Then there was someone else at the passenger door. 'Somchai! Quick! Get out!'

The Mercedes man! How had he got here?

'Didn't you see them?' he was shouting. 'Didn't you see the bastards going after you?'

The other traffic on the expressway was coming to a halt. People were gawping at the debris littering the road, the plume of oily smoke, the flames licking around the burning bike. Some were getting out of their cars, hesitating, not sure what to do.

Somchai walked unsteadily round to the front of the taxi and saw the tangled mess there, the wisps of steam rising up from the shattered radiator. He kneeled by the rider who was hanging head-down out of the wreckage, and ripped open his jacket. A medallion slipped across the man's chest and dangled over his face. A silver medallion embossed with a tiger's head.

Fear stabbed at Somchai's heart.

Bakorstanas – Rahman's Secret Service. Murderers and torturers.

They'd followed him. Rahman's men had followed the

package out along the network and here into Thailand. His cover was blown.

Somchai turned and yelled at the Mercedes man. 'The package, quick! Get the package you gave me!' The Mercedes man looked vague, not comprehending. Somchai ran round to the back of the taxi and reached in. He pulled the packet from behind the seat, and ripped it open.

'We've got to get this to the British. It's vitally important. They know it's coming. Look, I'll split the contents, make it more difficult for them.'

The Mercedes man looked uncertain and peered down at the package.

Somchai pulled out the piece of rock and thrust it into his hands. 'Take this to the docks,' he ordered. 'You know, the docks by the river – where you came in. Find an old schooner, a Bugis ship – it'll be the only one there. Give this to a young Frenchman called Jean. Say it's from Somchai. Tell him to get it out through Sulawesi – he'll know what to do, he's my son. Go on, go! Before the police get here.'

Already Somchai could hear the wail of approaching sirens. The Mercedes man nodded, climbed back into his car and eased it forward. Metal ripped as the bike pulled free. Then he drove off, accelerating fast, scattering the people gathering by the scene, bits of bodywork waving in the slipstream.

Somchai leaned heavily on the bonnet of the taxi. He was shaking and his legs felt weak. The taxi driver was still behind the wheel, vomiting noisily. Someone was using a fire extinguisher to put out the flames that had by now engulfed the bike wedged under the crash barrier.

Looking around, it occurred to Somchai that just for a moment he'd become invisible. No one was now paying him any attention. Instead, people were fussing over the injured driver. Someone was covering the corpse of the bike rider, others were just standing, staring at this spectacle of death. Somchai was left on his own, another bystander, the opened packet with its two computer disks still clutched in his hand.

His mind suddenly locked into gear. He shoved the packet into his pocket, swung his legs over the crash barrier, and dropped into the rice field beyond.

Then he simply walked away, allowing himself to be quickly swallowed up by the gathering dusk.

Somchai crunched along a farm track, its white limestone chippings easily showing him the path as they shone in the late-evening gloom. Behind him, the carnage on the expressway receded slowly into the distance. He'd escaped. He'd evaded the *Bakorstanas*. For a moment he felt elated, strengthened by his survival. He walked fast, putting distance between himself and the scene of the attack.

But half an hour was all he could manage. His legs shook from delayed shock, and he sweated and panted in the hot and sticky night air. Mosquitoes swarmed out of the rice paddies to either side. He was being badly bitten and he scratched at the hard lumps forming on his face and arms. Ahead of him he could make out the silhouette of a rice store against the skyline, a flimsy thatched hut on spindly legs. He flopped down beneath it, and lay back gratefully on a patch of bare earth – exhausted.

Though his body rested, his mind churned. The *Bakorstanas* would be back, he knew that. They would hunt him down – relentlessly. He had to get those disks out of the country quickly, but the airports, the post – any normal lines of communication – they would all be watched. So he had to be clever, cleverer than they were. He had to use whatever resources were left to him.

He stared up at the thick blanket of stars spread across the night sky, and slowly it came – a plan, a devious plan, to lure someone into the country who would act as his courier.

He had connections he could use, people who would understand what he needed, people who would be efficient and discreet.

But he also needed someone very close to him. Someone he hadn't seen for a very long time.

Someone he loved very deeply.

His daughter.

Chapter Four – second week in January: Kettla oilfield, North Atlantic

Some 800 metres below the waves of the North Atlantic, the heavy yellow hatch cover dropped down from the roof of the deep-ocean habitat with a hiss of gas struts and a solid thump. A faint smell of clean oil and hot electronics drifted down from the submersible docked above.

Below the hatch stood two figures, both dressed in white overalls. Radio headsets dangled from their hands. One, a short stocky man, had the name *Glyn* embroidered in neat blue italic writing across his left breast pocket. The other, a small slight figure, had her name handwritten onto torn masking tape: *Nicole Tai-Chung*.

Glyn unhooked a shiny aluminium ladder from the bulkhead wall. Reaching up, he hung it neatly from two slots cast into the rim of the open hatch. He rested the rubber feet on the metal decking below.

His voice was gentle, almost rhythmic. There was a touch of Welsh lilt. 'OK, Nicole, I'll go up first and get some lights on. Try not to touch the seals on the hatch as you go past – even a slight scratch can be fatal at this depth.'

Nicole imagined the thousands of tons of cold sea water pressing down on top of them, and remembered being told how it could work away at a weakened seal, then pierce it, creating a needle jet with enough force to laser through a man's hand.

She pulled herself easily up through the hatch and worked her way forwards. Slipping carefully into the right-hand observer's seat, she waited patiently while Glyn finished his checks.

Looking around, she thought of the tiny primitive craft she'd piloted back in her postgraduate days. She remembered the cold clamminess of her first trips down to the Mid-Atlantic Ridge, condensation beading on the sides of the crude living sphere; three bodies sprawled on a mattress barely big enough for two, a tangle of cramped arms and legs. This was totally different.

Multifunction displays came to life around her. She started to fumble with the unfamiliar safety harness. Glyn leaned across helpfully, and tried to reach down to bring up the straps for her. But Nicole politely pushed his hand away, preferring to work it out for herself.

She pushed the metal blades into their sockets with a satisfying click, then gazed out of the vast armour-acrylic observation dome whose inner surface was in front of her. Her image was reflected back from the solid blackness of the deep Atlantic as in a mirror.

Despite her family name – Tai-Chung – there was very little about the small willowy figure staring back at her that suggested she was Chinese. Rather, she owed her beauty to her aristocratic French mother. With her pleasant open face, long dark hair, and a hint of Asia, she was physically very attractive.

But looks could be deceptive. Behind that soft and rather fragile face was a capable and resourceful young woman with an iron determination and an inner strength honed from years of loneliness and disappointment.

The thin whine of gyros and cooling fans began to rise to a new pitch. Glyn seemed uncertain about some of the switches, and had to glance often at his checklist. Then the CO_2 scrubbers started up with a muffled roar. He indicated to Nicole that it was time to put on her headset.

'Can you hear me?' His voice sounded synthetic over the earphones. She nodded in reply.

He pressed a button on his side-stick to contact the controller. 'Kettla One to Seaflame, permission to launch, over.'

The answer came back swiftly. 'Seaflame. Permission to launch, Kettla One. Have a nice day. Look after Nicole, keep her nice and warm for us. Out.'

Nicole was irritated by their words. She was a fully qualified sub pilot herself, and she deserved more respect – but sensibly she held her council.

Glyn doused the cockpit lights and her reflection abruptly vanished. Now her stare plunged straight into the darkness of the Atlantic. In the sweep of powerful flood-lights she could see the gentle curve of Number One Habitat sprawling over the ocean floor, its far end disappearing mysteriously into the gloom. Two powerful hydraulic manipulator arms cradled the scene, their square-section titanium glinting metallically in the artificial light.

'Final checks,' warned Glyn. 'Hatch secured, oxygen level – OK, CO_2 level – OK, ballast – OK. Stand by to launch.'

He reached down and grasped a large red handle.

'Launch!'

His arm jerked. Behind them, the steel jaws of the docking latch disengaged with a clang. A little shock wave reverberated through the submersible. There was a hiss of compressed air, the machine rocked slightly – and they were free. Nicole appreciated the slick manoeuvre. Not bad for a rookie pilot.

They drifted slowly away from the habitat.

Nicole could see countless pinpoints of light traversing the darkness. There was intense activity all around them. Kettla Field was a technological miracle of the new millennium. They were going after a special type of gold trapped in the huge sedimentary basin lying deep beneath Rockall Bank. Black gold.

Oil.

Enough oil to encourage the greedy money markets to reach deep into their pockets. And that was why Nicole was here, to write an article about this developing technology for a major science journal.

Glyn kept the submersible low, skimming just twenty feet above the ocean floor.

A pipeline came into view in their powerful lights, much bigger than Nicole had expected. It was a good six feet in diameter, round and fat, encased in concrete to protect it against the tremendous pressure of the deep ocean.

Then Charlie Station loomed out of the darkness. A fluorescent red marker flag stood out, printed with a large white letter C. By its side was a steel-wire cage, containing unidentified equipment.

'Here we are. This is what we want to show you – our new high-pressure welder.'

Nicole wasn't encouraged. She waited patiently for Glyn to start his demonstration.

Listening to the roar of the scrubber fans in the cockpit, she could feel rather than hear the deep rumble of some machine at work out there on the ocean floor.

Glyn hooked one of the manipulator arms into the welding machine and took it out of its wire basket.

The rumbling seemed louder now. A steady vibration in Nicole's ears. She worried about not recalling any mention of equipment in their vicinity at the briefing.

Glyn caught her concern, but carried on operating the controls as he carefully set up his demonstration. 'Don't worry,' he said distantly. 'The seabed's full of machinery in this area. Don't forget, sound travels a long way down here.'

Nicole listened carefully to the sound again, listened to it as it slowly turned into a deep-throated roar, a definite vibration against the acrylic dome.

'I still think you should contact Seaflame,' she urged. 'Just to be certain.'

Glyn turned to her. 'It's OK, we're quite safe.'

But she wouldn't be put off. 'Contact Seaflame now, Glyn! There's something out there, and I think it's very close.'

Glyn began to operate the thrusters, reversing the submersible away from the cage. Nicole looked down instinctively to monitor the ocean floor – to watch it drift backwards beneath the observation dome. As she stared more closely, she could see what looked like a fine rain of mud drifting down.

She looked up, found the dome being rapidly covered in a thin layer of sediment.

'Glyn . . .!' she warned.

But he lacked confidence, and pretended not to notice.

'Glyn!' she repeated.

Suddenly there was a loud reverberating clang. The craft jarred to a sudden halt and Nicole was jerked back in her seat, banging her head against the restraint. Glyn swore under his breath as the submersible began to pitch nose-up.

There was another heavy jarring as they locked against something solid, then the loud thump of an explosion. Everything jolted inside the cabin and dust rose from the floor. Alarms began to chime. Rows of orange and red warning lights flashed on the pilot's console.

The submersible continued to lift, its nose high. Nicole gripped the sides of her seat, while Glyn was shouting into the mike: 'Seaflame! Seaflame! This is Kettla One. We have a problem here.'

Nicole looked across at the centre console and noticed

that their two oxygen tanks were both in the red – one completely empty, the gauge for the other dropping fast. She recognized immediately the desperate nature of their situation. If the tanks had been holed, they might be leaking into the submersible. If so, then even the simple action of throwing a switch could turn their cockpit into a raging inferno.

'Glyn,' she said carefully, 'I think we're losing oxygen into the cabin.'

One of the alarm chimes changed to a strident warning klaxon. Glyn reached out and pushed the override button. The din stopped, but he seemed uncertain of what to do next, as if mesmerized by the noise.

Procedures came quickly to Nicole's mind. She knew their priority was to turn off the oxygen. She looked across at Glyn's console, identified the master switch and tried to push it with her thumb. But she found it difficult to reach with the submersible's nose pitched so high, and missed.

She tried again.

The radio came on, loud in her ear. 'Seaflame. What is your position, Kettla One? Over.'

Glyn didn't answer.

'Charlie Station,' yelled Nicole, 'we've had a collision – losing oxygen fast. We're going to surface.'

She punched Glyn's frozen hand away from the controller, then leaned back, tightening her harness, grasping the side-stick beside her own seat. They were almost vertical now, sitting on the submersible's tail, locked firmly against whatever machine they had collided with.

She worked carefully at the lever, bringing the nose down little by little. The craft shuddered, metal shrieked as it twisted and sheared . . . then the vibration suddenly stopped and everything went smooth.

They were free.

Nicole looked back down onto the ocean floor from the cockpit of the nose-high submersible, and saw a gigantic machine below them. Tracked, bright yellow, as big as a house – a huge trenching machine.

Someone had messed up badly.

It shouldn't have been there.

She inched the side-stick forward. Thrusters pushed down hard against the inertia of the submersible, bringing it down onto an even keel.

'I'm going to surface,' she shouted to Glyn, 'Check harness! Brace! Brace!'

Glyn sat there, white-faced, impassive.

Valves clacked open and something hissed furiously. The sub shuddered as she dropped ballast . . . then they were rising fast. Nicole felt a steady push from beneath her seat. The chimes stopped. There was silence now, except for the sound of water rushing past the canopy in a steady roar. The colour of the water began to lighten visibly, the darkness of the deep ocean retreating, the sea becoming first dark blue, then pale blue as visibility increased near the surface.

Nicole looked at the instruments. '150 metres. Brace for surfacing.'

She looked up and for a moment caught a glimpse of the Atlantic's surface looming far above them. Huge waves churning silently, air bubbles streaming – this was going to be rough.

The sub rocked slightly as it felt the bottom motion of a wave, then it burst through. Nicole was thrown upwards by the violence of their deceleration, banging her knee hard on the instrument panel, cutting straight through the fabric of her overalls. Blood welled from the wound.

There was a moment of confusion as they floundered on the surface. Then the first Atlantic wave hit.

The submersible rolled badly, like a sickening roller coaster, and broached. At the top of the first crest it rolled dizzily, threatening to capsize before righting at the last minute – only to drop sickeningly into the next trough. Spray and foam whipped back over the half-submerged acrylic dome.

Nicole looked across at Glyn, whose body was rolling with the motion of the submersible. His face looked pale and shocked.

Fired by adrenalin and very angry, she suddenly let her feelings go. 'What the hell's the matter, Glyn? Don't you know any of the procedures? Don't they train sub pilots any more? You could have had us both killed!'

Glyn was still deathly pale. 'You won't . . . you won't . . .' he faltered.

'What? Tell the others?' Nicole studied his face. He seemed so young, so frightened. She looked past him at the heavy seas rolling outside, then thumbed her transmit button. 'Seaflame, this is Kettla One. On the surface and requesting assistance.'

She looked back at Glyn and saw the tortured look of panic and jealousy on his face.

And knew that she'd just made an enemy.

Chapter Five – three days later: London

Nicole put down the phone and stared, puzzled, at the large looped letters of her handwriting scrawled across the pad. Something was wrong.

Marie, her housekeeper, was busy stacking lunch plates into the dishwasher. She sensed Nicole's disquiet and looked up. 'Bad news, Ms Tai-Chung?'

Nicole peeled off the sheet and pocketed it. 'They want me to go out straight away,' she said. Her gaze was distant.

Marie looked puzzled. 'Who do?' she demanded.

Nicole sighed. 'The agency, the people who commissioned this article.'

'Then you tell them, Ms Tai-Chung,' insisted Marie in her thick Filipino accent. 'You tell them you got family. You not want to go right now.'

'I can't afford to turn it down, Marie. It's good money.' Nicole hesitated for a moment before continuing. 'I wonder why they want me out there so quickly?' A frown creased her forehead. 'It doesn't make sense.'

'What about Peter?' warned Marie. 'He got his evening at school, I think.'

For a moment, Marie's words tugged at Nicole's conscience. But she couldn't afford to turn this assignment down. Not with the money they were offering. Not when the money could buy the very thing that Peter needed most – his future.

'I'll be back soon,' she answered lamely.

Marie gave her a reproachful look. 'So, you go gallivanting off again, heh?'

Nicole reached up for a clean coffee cup, biting her lower lip, knowing that she had to do just that. 'Yes – Indonesia. On an oil rig, somewhere in the Java Sea.' She spooned in some coffee. 'A Chinese rig. They want me to do a piece about that oilfield – you know, the one that's always in the news.'

Marie tutted loudly, and turned to pick up some plates. 'Indonesia! That why they pay you so much.' She began to wipe the table top. 'I think they want you out there quickly before you change your mind. And you say "No" if you have any sense.'

Nicole cradled the coffee in her hands. Marie was wrong; she had to do this. 'It's only a few days, Marie. And Indonesia's not so bad at the moment. Besides,' she added brightly, 'the company's Beijing Global. My father once worked for them.'

Marie looked up from stooping over the dishwasher controls. 'Your father!' She spat out the words, 'Ha! He no good to you. When you last see him, eh? When he last write to you? We on our own here, we look after each other.'

Nicole smiled as water began to hiss into the dish-washer.

'Anyhow, you don't really need *me*, Ms Tai-Chung,' continued Marie. 'You very strong woman.' And she busied herself wiping pots and pans.

Nicole laughed, and wandered off in the direction of her living room. She called back casually over her shoulder: 'When did Peter say he would be back?'

'He phone from friend's house, a half-hour ago,' answered Marie. 'Said he would come soon. He good boy!'

Nicole smiled. Yes, Peter was a good boy. She couldn't even think of doing the work she did without his patient understanding.

Peter was precious to her, perhaps too precious. He was all that she had since the rest of her family had become so distant. There was Jean, her brother. They'd been insepar-able as children, then he'd gone off to university and joined their father's company as a geologist. They'd drifted apart, as siblings sometimes do, finally losing touch altogether. Last thing she'd heard he was somewhere up in the moun-tains of Kalimantan, prospecting for minerals.

And then there was her mother, hiding away in her big mountainside chateau in France, still playing the role of the injured diplomat's daughter years after being dumped by their father. Still bitter and getting more and more crippled with arthritis.

And what of her father? He'd been kind and soft when

she was a child and Nicole still loved him, missed him terribly. She'd almost forgiven him for abandoning them. He'd always been surrounded by a delightful air of intrigue and mystery. It had swirled around him like autumn mist. He'd disappeared for long periods of time, made secret telephone calls, and had strangers coming and going in the dark hours of the night.

Nicole sank down into the comfortable sofa with her coffee and watched the light from a pale sun drift silently in through the windows of her living room. A domestic sound of clattering cups and cutlery came in from the kitchen.

Her gaze fell on the mantelpiece, stacked with the bric-a-brac of fractured memories. In pride of place stood a large framed photograph of a rugged young man with thick dark hair. He was squatting down amongst tall reeds, cradling an expensive camera. Alongside was a younger Nicole, one arm hooked into his. They were both dressed in loose combat fatigues, and behind them, grinning cheekily for the camera, were two little Arab boys.

A dark shadow passed across her heart.

Al Hammar, the great marshland of southern Iraq. She'd been the only one who'd returned from that assignment. And she'd never had the chance to tell him that he'd lived on – deep inside her, in his son's budding flesh.

Al Hammar.

A dark place.

The place of Saddam's terrible chemical slaughter of the Marsh Arabs. Chemicals that now stalked through the innocent veins of their son, choking his young body, clotting it with malignant cells.

The specialist hospitals had never given him long to live. But he was still here. Still living. Still fighting.

Now each day had become a precious gift.

It made Nicole love her son intensely. He was all that she had, all that she wanted, and she couldn't bear to think of losing him. She longed for a miracle cure, something to give him back his future. Something to recover her family from its wreckage strewn around the world.

She got up and took another picture in her hands. A colour photograph of herself surrounded by a group of scruffy young men, arms pressed around each other's shoulders. All standing together on the deck of a yellow submersible that wallowed in a calm and impossibly blue sea.

Hawaii! A smile played on her lips. Her postgraduate dissertation. Studying the huge landslides that had roared off the sides of Molokai Island in the ancient past. Looking for evidence of tsunami impact. Nicole remembered the wild parties they'd held on the beaches of Oahu, and sighed. Things that might have been . . .

The front door slammed. 'Hi, Mum!'

Peter burst into the living room, fresh-faced, perspiring from his bike ride, skin glowing from the cold wintry air. He flopped down onto the settee.

'Hi!' she said, turning. 'How are you?'

Peter looked up, his face innocent. 'Fine!'

'No headaches, not feeling sick?'

'Don't fuss, Mum. I'm fine.'

She gave him a cuddle. 'I know you are.'

Peter smiled at her from within the embrace of her arms, then glanced down at the photograph she was still holding. He fingered its frame, then looked up.

'Are you going away again?' he asked, suddenly serious.

Nicole sighed. 'Yes, but only for a short while.'

Peter was crestfallen. 'Where?'

'Indonesia,' she said, then added quickly: 'I have to go out to an oil rig, in the Java Sea.' She brightened a little. 'It's one that belongs to your grandfather's company.'

'Why?' he demanded.

Nicole smiled tolerantly. 'Because it's my job. It brings in money – you know, pays the bills, for Marie, your schooling, this house . . .'

'Yeah, I know all that.' He fiddled with the fastening of his jacket. 'I mean . . . why do they want you?'

'Well, I spent a lot of time in Malaysia when I was your age, and Indonesia's such an interesting place right now . . .'

His big eyes stared up at her again. 'You won't be going down in a submersible this time, will you?'

She remembered the Kettla fiasco, thought of her responsibilities, remembered Peter's fears for her safety. She wondered what would have happened if she hadn't come back to him. How long he would have survived without her.

Nicole drew a deep breath, trying to stuff those swaying serpents of guilt back into their vipers' nest.

She had to do this. To get some money. To help him.
She knew of no better way.

'No,' she said quietly. 'No submersibles, not this time. I
promise.'

Chapter Six – third week in January: Utara oilfield, Java Sea

Nicole sat facing the rear of the helicopter, her ears assaulted by the roar of the twin turboshaft engines. Her body shook to the steady rhythmic beat of the heavy rotor blades. Seven other passengers were packed in tightly around her, trussed up in dayglo-orange survival suits, lap-strapped to rows of flimsy seats. Most had headphones clamped over their ears – there was little to do except sleep, read, or simply stare. Oilmen, all Asians, on the weekly shift-change out of Surabaya.

The morning sun blazed in through the square windows. The high collar of Nicole's immersion suit, with its heavy brass zip, began to chafe at the soft skin beneath her chin. The heat from her perspiring body funnelled out past her nose, releasing a cocktail of past odours: hot rubber, sweat, the sour stench of someone else's vomit.

The little island of Masalembur slipped by in an almost solid haze lifting off the superheated sea. Nicole knew they couldn't be far now from the Utara oilfield. She fretted over the absence of her reporting equipment. She wished especially for her camera. She had a wonderful picture here: Asian roughnecks, packed shoulder to shoulder in the cramped and noisy cabin, the low morning sunlight casting hard-edged shadows across the rugged landscapes of their faces. It could have made a dramatic magazine cover, and would have been another feather in her cap; all frustratingly wasted. She'd argued with the flight line officials, of course, but had got nowhere. Her camera and laptop had had to be packed away with the rest of the gear. 'Safety rules,' they'd insisted. 'Computers and camera motors interfere with the helicopter's navigation equipment.'

But Nicole guessed it really had more to do with security issues. Ever since former President Kartini had sold Indonesia's oil to the Chinese in order to line his own greedy pockets, the Utara field had become a potential source of conflict between the countries. Now Rahman was threatening to reclaim the oil, and eject the Chinese by force.

As if to emphasize this, they passed low over a small group of warships. But whether they were Chinese or Indonesian, Nicole couldn't tell.

Her neighbour jabbed her sharply in the ribs. A rugged Malay face grinned at her, gold tooth shining brightly in the sunshine. Unable to speak through the frantic racket, he jabbed downwards with a finger, then pointed across to the left. Nicole gazed out of the vibrating window.

From this distance the rig looked very small: an orange metal box on spidery steel legs, with two large red and white cranes slung out over the water. She could just see the name of the company painted on the side in large white letters: Beijing Global.

Soon the helicopter settled onto the tiny helipad perched high above the sea. The door slid back noisily, and an orange-suited crewman, grubby ear-defenders around his neck, began to pull their baggage from the hold and heave it across the tiny deck. The roughnecks pulled off their headphones, and began to dismount.

Nicole was met at the bottom of the short stairway by a tall Chinese oilman in red overalls. Underneath his white plastic safety helmet, his face was long and sour, his skin tinged with grey. He shouted to her above the noise of the helicopter.

'Miss Tai-Chung? Welcome to Beijing Global. My name is Zhou, Zhou Yew-Ming.' His English was very good. He shook her hand formally. 'We've been expecting you. Come this way, please. I've asked for your baggage to be left in your cabin.'

Nicole followed him as he clattered down a steep metal stairway and onto the main deck of the rig. The noise of machinery was everywhere: the steady drone of a generator, the despairing moan of a winch as it strained at a cable. There was a heavy oily smell about the place, and a saltiness that caught at the back of her throat. As she hurried along behind Yew-Ming, she could feel the whole rig shaking beneath her feet with the motion of the drilling.

Yew-Ming ushered Nicole into a tiny office and slammed the door, staunching the worst of the noise. The cabin had no windows, but was lit instead by two bright fluorescent tubes. Geological maps covered the walls and littered the workbench. A PC sat at one end, its screen covered with an array of figures. The floor was cluttered with wooden boxes, each one holding a set of carefully labelled core samples. Yew-Ming cleared a space on the dusty workbench and they sat facing across it on stools.

'I thought we'd start here. This is where it all happens.' Yew-Ming picked up a plastic cup, and filled it with fruit juice from a large jug on the work surface. He passed it across to her. 'You'll need this after your flight. You dehydrate very quickly in those conditions.' He paused while Nicole downed the cup thankfully. She watched his face. It seemed so dour, so completely without humour.

'I'm sorry,' he continued, 'I haven't been told. What paper are you from?' She could smell stale onion on his breath.

'None. I'm freelance.' She passed her cup back. 'If I'm in your way, I'm sure I can get round the rig on my own.'

His long face stared at her. Not a muscle twitched, nothing moved to give away what he was thinking. 'That won't be necessary,' he said. 'Tell me – what is it that you'd like to know?'

'Everything! I'm writing a feature article for a big international magazine.'

Yew-Ming took off his plastic safety helmet and placed it carefully on the workbench. Nicole noted how it had flattened down his hair and left a red mark on his forehead. He fingered his own plastic cup, studying Nicole's face, his eyes pebbly and cold.

'Before we start, I think you need to get one or two things straight.'

Nicole stiffened inwardly at his rudeness, but kept her cool, not willing to antagonize him.

'These might be Indonesian waters,' he continued, 'but this is Chinese oil. Not everybody appreciates that. I don't want you stirring up trouble.'

'I'm not stupid,' she replied. 'I know what's going on here.'

Yew-Ming sipped at his drink, looking at her carefully over the rim of the beaker. 'I'm afraid that's not enough assurance, Miss Tai-Chung. We're under constant threat of invasion. I need to be clear about your loyalty.'

Nicole bridled at his pompous attitude. 'My father used to be a director of Beijing Global,' she announced. 'I doubt that you have anything to fear from me.'

'I know who your father is.'

Nicole was instantly wrong-footed. How would he know that?

'Sometimes, as a journalist, you must pick up information,' he continued, 'particularly sensitive information. What do you do then, Miss Tai-Chung? What do you do with that sort of information . . .?'

But Nicole was puzzled. 'How do you know about my father?' she demanded.

'Just answer my question.'

'Not until you tell me what you know about him.'

Yew-Ming paused, his face still deadpan beneath

hooded eyes. 'I worked for him when he was a director of this company.'

Nicole stared into his face and saw something whispering there, something behind that blank mask. Had she stumbled upon something? Was there perhaps a purpose to his bizarre line of questioning? She proceeded to answer his earlier question carefully, hoping to tease more out of him.

'I'm a professional, Yew-Ming. It's my job to inform people.'

But Yew-Ming wasn't drawn. He tossed his empty cup into the bin. 'What would you do if, during your stay here, you were passed something – something that you suspected might be significant to another power? What would you do with that?'

Nicole's mind was instantly alert, poised like a cat. Was he offering her something? For money, maybe?

Or was this a trap?

She thought quickly, pitched her answer carefully. 'I'd have it analysed, find out what it contained . . .'

'In London?' interrupted Yew-Ming.

She was surprised at the question. 'Yes, in London.'

This answer seemed to satisfy Yew-Ming. He got up abruptly from his workbench and turned to his PC, clicking the screen free of its table of numbers. 'Thank you, Miss Tai-Chung, that is all.'

She was surprised. 'I'm free to go?'

'Tread carefully, Miss Tai-Chung.' He had his back to

her now, tapping at the computer's keyboard, bringing up new rows of figures that he scrolled down the screen. 'Trust no one.'

Bemused, Nicole made for the door. She pulled it open against its stiff spring, then let it slam shut again, shaking the flimsy fibre walls of the geology lab. She found that her presence in the corridor was drawing stares.

She asked directions from a passing crewman who, fortunately, knew where her cabin was, and gratefully retreated into it.

The room turned out to be very cramped, about nine feet by twelve. The colour scheme was the same tacky brown quarry tiles and pale blue steel walls found everywhere. It was almost completely filled by two iron-framed double bunks and four pressed-steel lockers. A solitary plastic stacking chair sat in one corner. She had a window, but someone had taped newspaper over it – probably as a 'blackout' to sleep more easily during the day. The painted walls were covered by tape marks, no doubt where pin-ups had been removed. Her bag had been slung onto one of the lower bunks, along with her laptop and aluminium camera case.

Nicole sat down opposite the bunk, still wondering about her strange exchange with Sour-Face. She rummaged in her camera case, and loaded a new film. Time was limited and she was keen to get started.

Then, her camera slung over her shoulder, she confronted the next problem – a lock on the door, but no key. She paused for a moment, thinking about all that expensive gear lying on the bunk bed.

Then she shrugged and went on out, slamming the door shut behind her.

That night a sound knifed through Nicole's dream and woke her instantly. It was the sharp, unexpected squeak of the automatic closing arm on her cabin door as it slowly retracted.

She was instantly alert, eyes open, not moving a muscle.

Damn – no key! she thought.

She held her breath, listening. Perhaps she'd imagined it.

There was a soft thud and a click as the door pushed shut against the frame.

She lay very still, waiting, trying to decode every tiny creak and rustle.

He was moving across the floor towards her. The bastard, who did he think she was? Some whore in Jakarta?

For a moment she imagined a warm rough hand on her belly, sliding up towards her breasts.

No! Not that!

She reached out slowly with one hand, and with her fingertips felt for something on the bedside chair. She imagined his leg coming over her, a great weight mounting her, his hands pushing down on her shoulders.

No!

Her hand touched the hard outer casing of her travel clock. She shuffled it carefully into her grasp. Sensed him closer now. Could almost guess where he was. The plastic of the clock felt smooth beneath her fingers.

Now!

'BASTARD!'

Uncoiling like a spring, the tension in her releasing in one explosive reaction, she hurled the clock with all the force she could muster. Reaching up behind her for the light, she yanked it on and slid off the bed in the opposite direction. She heard the clock strike a steel wall and clatter to the ground in pieces. She crouched down behind the bunk, breathing heavily, heart pumping, waiting for the two neon strips to flicker into life.

The room flooded with a cold pale light.

It was Sour-Face.

He stood sheepishly just a few feet from her bunk, fully dressed in red overalls and a white hard hat. His boots were off. Nicole noticed a small hole in one of his socks. He was blinking under the harsh glare, hands held away from his body, palms outward in submission. In his left hand was a small package, its bubble-wrap glistening in the light.

'Christ, Yew-Ming, what are you doing? Get out of here!'

The man was embarrassed, and took a pace backwards. 'Miss Tai-Chung, I'm sorry ... it's not what you think, I ...' He cleared his throat nervously. 'I have something here for you.'

Nicole kept her naked body hidden below the level of the lower bunk. 'What do you mean?'

Again he held the package towards her, like a small child handing over a present. 'This is from Somchai, Somchai Jornpaison. He especially asked me to give it to you.'

Nicole was puzzled. 'Somchai? Who the hell are you talking about?' Her legs were getting cramped and she shifted her position. 'I don't know any Somchai! Now get out, Yew-Ming, or I'll have you busted from the company.'

'Please, Miss Tai-Chung, Somchai knows you. He knows you very well. He wants you to take this back to England. He trusts you and says you will know what to do with it.'

'Is this some kind of joke?' she demanded.

'No – no joke. Just take it. It's very important. You're a journalist. You take it.'

Nicole stared at Yew-Ming. He seemed far less threatening now in the harsh lighting, incongruous in his work clothes and holed socks. 'Just put the packet on that bunk over there, then get the hell out of my room, OK? Go on, get out!'

Yew-Ming did as he was told, and backed slowly out of the room. 'Thank you, Miss Tai-Chung, thank you.' He was almost bowing. 'Please, keep the package safe. Take it back to England – for Somchai.'

The door shut slowly as he walked away.

Nicole stood up slowly from behind her refuge. She

rummaged inside her bag and pulled on her tracksuit with shaking hands.

Then curiosity overcame her. She dragged the other double bunk over to the door and shoved it into place as a barricade. Scooping up the bits of her travel clock, she dropped them loudly into the metal waste bin.

In her job you were only ever passed something for one good reason – *information.*

Taking the bubble-wrapped package back to her bunk, she lay down and examined it, feeling its contents with her fingers. Inside she could clearly see a computer disk. She tried to prise off the tape, but it was tough. Reaching into her soap bag, she used nail scissors to hack at the covering.

Slowly she turned the disk over in her hands. It had been professionally labelled with a string of alphanumeric codes that meant nothing to her. There was also a brief description: PALAU RIDGE – HALIMUN.

She lay back and stared up at the ceiling, thinking. *Halimun?* That name – there was something there, a distant memory.

Of course: Halimun! A volcano, high up in the mountains of western Java. She'd been there as child, climbed its rain-sodden flanks with her father. And Palau? Her Malaysian served her well – *palau* meant 'island'.

Islands and volcanoes. Code words?

She reached for her laptop, set the machine up on the chair beside her bunk, and kneeled down at the keyboard. She waited for the system to boot up. Her palms were sticky and she had to wipe them on her tracksuit. She inserted the disk into the drive slot. It loaded immediately. Success!

Then she was asked for a password.

Damn! Of course there'd be a password. The small cabin felt hot and stifling. She clenched her fists, banging them against her thighs, wired up with tension. She felt a trickle of sweat work its way down her temple.

OK . . . Password . . . Password.

She thought for a moment. She typed PALAU. That failed. She typed HALIMUN. That failed too. She typed RIDGE, MALAY, ISLAND, JAVA, SUMATRA, INDONE-SIA, CHINA . . . all useless. She stared blankly at the little screen, frustrated. So close. So close to what was on that disk, yet the information remained enticingly shielded, locked away from her prying eyes.

She slipped the disk into the laptop case and carefully hid the computer away, stowing it safely under her bunk. It would be easy to smuggle the disk back to England, then she could have it looked at properly. She knew people who could break the code. She switched off the light and lay back, staring up at the ceiling.

Memories came back strongly in the dark. Somchai? Yes, she remembered a Somchai now. Somchai Jornpaison. A scene passed before her eyes, difficult to grasp at first, then more sharply focused. She was a little girl, playing with Jean, her brother. They were in the huge company house on the edge of Kuala Lumpur. Big fans rotated in the ceiling of her bedroom. She heard the elegant voice of her mother calling them, her French accent as strong and sweet as ever. Nicole smiled. Then other memories. The violent rows, when she'd hidden under the bed, hands over her ears, warding off the sounds of the blows. And how Somchai was always there for her, her father's servant. She'd called him Aslan, not Somchai, after the Narnian lion – so inappropriate for a scrawny old man from the Bangkok slums with a lump on the side of his head like half a plum. But he was strong, and gentle, and he'd taken care of her when her parents' rows spilled over into violence.

Then her father had left them.

Nicole sat suddenly upright on the bed. That was why she'd been asked to come here. That was why it had all been arranged so quickly. She wasn't on the rig to write a story at all. She was here to collect this disk from Yew-Ming – and from 'Somchai'. Not the real Somchai, of course – that was ridiculous, he would be dead by now – but from someone calling himself Somchai. Who? Her father, using the old man's name? Knowing that she would still remember?

But in the stifling darkness of the room that idea seemed altogether too fanciful. Why on earth would her father get involved in this subterfuge? If he wanted to give her the disk, he'd have simply posted it.

So who was this Somchai? Who would think to use that name? Her brother, maybe? No, he was in Kalimantan. He didn't even know that she was out here.

But whoever it was, they were right! She couldn't refuse

to take the disk – professionally or otherwise. She was too much of a journalist.

Whatever it was, it was something important that they wanted her to find out.

And Nicole had every intention of doing just that.

Chapter Seven – two days later

The silence woke her.

Nicole looked at her watch, pushing in the little button to make its light work – 4.06. She lay there for a moment. The room was in darkness, except for a small glimmer creeping under the door from the corridor.

The drilling had stopped. The familiar rumble and constant vibration that had been with her throughout her time on the rig had died. There was complete silence, as if no one was there any more.

She sat up and turned on the strip lights. They flickered into action, revealing the familiar blue walls and quarry-tiled floor, the empty metal bunk jammed up against the door. She switched off the light, crossed the room and peeled away the blackout. It was dark outside. The rig lights were still on, but she couldn't see anybody. She went back to bed and lay looking up at the ceiling.

She dozed, wondering why the drilling had stopped, what problem there might be.

Time passed. Her mind drifted – around Jornpaison, around the disk, Yew-Ming . . .

CRASH!

Her thoughts splintered as something heavy was rammed up against her cabin door. Another tremendous crash – she was jolted fully awake. Another crash – the flimsy door handle flicked off its mounting and went spinning across the floor. The bunk bed was forced back into the room, its metal legs squealing on the hard tiles.

Light flooded in from the corridor.

Silhouetted against the glare was a nightmare figure. A figure dressed in full combat gear, his stubby machine gun levelled straight at Nicole's chest, night-vision goggles lowered over the eyes, the lenses protruding forward like the eye-stalks of some demented insect.

A microphone was positioned across the mouth – a thin, mean mouth. The armed intruder uttered something, paused for a moment as if listening – then advanced on Nicole.

The ferocity of his attack took her completely by surprise. She staggered back in her bunk, trying to get away, limbs shaking from the sudden surge of adrenalin. Gloved hands moved out towards her. She yelled, screamed. But the scream was stifled by one of the massive hands. Sticky tape was strapped across her mouth. She could scarcely breathe. A thick nylon pad went across her eyes. She could hear the Velcro fasten at the back. A buckle was pulled tight, too tight. She fought back, striking out with her legs, but nothing was there. She boxed with her fists, connecting with bits of soft clothing and the hard metal edges of equipment. She was picked up, turned over, and dropped violently onto her stomach. Her hands were yanked up behind her back and held in a vice-like grip. She heard the rasp of tape as it was wound round and round her wrists.

She lay there for a moment, cocooned, immobilized. She couldn't get enough air – she thought she was drowning. She forced herself to keep calm, to control her breathing, slow down her pulse rate.

Nicole was lifted violently off the bunk and dropped to her feet. A hefty kick to her ankles got her walking. She was propelled out of the room at speed and along the corridor, becoming confused, disorientated by the twists and turns. Forced up a steep metal ladder, she tripped and fell forwards, hitting the front of her face on a metal riser. The metallic taste of blood flooded into her mouth, making her choke. Her lips felt thick and lumpy.

Then the hustling stopped. Her knees were kicked from behind, and a large hand pushed down on her head to force her to the floor. She was left alone.

Slowly she calmed, and the panting grew less. She began to take in her surroundings and felt a cool breeze on her face. The ground was rough and gritty beneath her knees – it felt like asphalt. There was a shuffling sound as someone shifted position by her side. Someone else moaned – there were other people here. Nicole listened carefully, and became aware that she could hear the sound of waves far below. She guessed they were perched somewhere high up on the rig, probably on the heli-deck. Too dangerous to get up and walk about. She had to stay still and think.

They were Indonesian soldiers; she'd caught sight of the shoulder flash just before she'd been blindfolded. They must have invaded the Chinese rigs – all of them.

The disk! Yew-Ming's disk! It must still be in her cabin, concealed inside the computer case. What if it was discovered?

The sharp *crack-crack-crack* of a rapid-fire rifle made her jump. It sounded as though it was close. She couldn't tell where the shots were coming from, or what was happening. There was something else that sounded like a pistol firing. A scream, then a moment's quiet, followed by the brief rattle of a machine gun. Some of the people on the deck began to whimper with fright. From far away she could hear whistles and catcalls. Then the rig went quiet again.

Her legs were becoming numb with pins and needles from kneeling in one position. She shifted around, her arms still aching from being tugged up savagely behind her back.

Then Nicole began to worry about Peter.

And suddenly the vipers' nest was there again, the terrible guilt sapping her confidence. A picture formed in her mind, and it wouldn't go away: a picture of her kitchen. She could see Peter bolting down his breakfast cereal, frantically packing his bag for school, dashing off for the school coach. Christ! What was she doing? Putting her own life at risk like this, when Peter needed her so badly.

The soft sound of rubber-soled boots approached along the deck, followed by a conversation in Malay.

'Is this her?'

'That's the bitch. Found her in one of the cabins.'

'Nice, eh? You didn't do her, did you?' A coarse laugh. Someone spat heavily and noisily.

'Nobody said anything about a bitch on the rig.' A boot connected violently with her thigh. She cried out at the sharp, hot pain. The bastard – some feeble shit all charged up on adrenalin.

A strong hand grabbed Nicole under one arm. She found herself being dragged to her feet, yelping as pain stabbed through her thigh. Another kick to the back of her legs and again she was propelled forward. She hobbled as fast as she could, a leg muscle seizing, guided once more through a maze of twists and turns. No time to think: it was all she could do to keep upright, to stop herself from tripping over. They were going too fast, it was difficult to keep her balance.

She was pushed into a room. She could hear the door swinging shut behind her. The shoving stopped.

Silence, except for the sound of breathing.

Then papers shuffled on a desk. She was leaning deliberately to one side, trying to take the weight off her damaged leg.

'Ah! The female.' The voice was Malay, soft and well spoken. 'Would you remove the tapes for me, please?'

First the tape was peeled roughly from her mouth, stinging her skin as it was pulled away and forcing open the wound on her lip. Nicole cried out involuntarily. Then a steel blade sliced at the tape around her hands, and finally the blindfold was removed from her face. The sudden light was enough to make her squint. She felt giddy, disorientated, had to rub her hands together to restore circulation.

She'd been dumped in some sort of office. There were maps of the Java Sea pinned to the wall, with blue lines dividing off the various oil concessions. A brown and cream filing cabinet stood in one corner. To her right, under armed guard, stood a line of oilmen – all of them Chinese. Sour-Face was among them, dressed in a grubby vest and shorts. She tried to make eye contact, but he looked straight ahead, ignoring her.

Through the window in front of her, she could glimpse the cold yellow light of an early dawn. In front of the same window was a desk. All the maps and documents previously covering it had been pushed to one side. Behind it lounged a young Indonesian soldier, slowly swivelling from side to side in the office chair. He had a thin and neatly trimmed moustache. His eyes were bright and intelligent under his red beret. He wore his authority like he wore his immaculate camouflaged uniform, with ease and confidence.

'Are you Miss Nicole Tai-Chung?' he asked slowly in excellent English.

She wasn't going to answer. She hated his smug face and she was angry. Angry at the way she'd been treated. Angry with herself for not being in control of the situation. She resented being pushed around – she resented feeling so helpless. So she said nothing.

'OK – shall we start another way? My name is Lukman. Major Hari Lukman, of the *Kopassus* – Indonesian Special Forces Regiment. Now, perhaps you'd care to introduce yourself.'

He waited. Nicole saw the contents of her holdall spread across his desk. Her heart froze. Lying there were her camera and laptop. What if he'd already found the disk? What if he recognized what it was? That it was stolen? She glanced again at Yew-Ming, but he ignored her.

The young officer repeated his question, impatiently this time: 'I said, "Are you Nicole Tai-Chung?"'

Still she said nothing.

The young officer sighed and began to rummage through her possessions, looking for something to corroborate her name. His hands seized upon the black computer case and he began to unzip it.

'No!' cried Nicole.

Lukman raised his eyebrows.

God! She couldn't believe the mistake she'd just made.

Again she looked at Yew-Ming. He was looking at her now. He was signalling something with his eyes – but it was subtle, too subtle, and she didn't understand. She turned back to the young officer.

'Who the hell do you think you are?' she demanded. 'You have no right to mistreat me in this way. I'm a British citizen, a freelance journalist. I demand to be treated correctly.'

Lukman eyed her quizzically, then he laughed. 'Miss Tai-Chung, I don't give a damn who you are.'

He nodded to the soldier standing at her side. The man lifted his gun and worked the bolt, sliding it back and then letting it slam forward as it pushed a round into the chamber. Then the man pointed the gun at Nicole.

'Now, we're looking for something rather special, Miss Tai-Chung. Something stolen from our research vessel.'

My God! The disk?

Lukman began to reach once more into the black computer case . . .

There was a blood-curdling yell off to Nicole's right. Yew-Ming had twisted to one side, aiming a powerful kick at one of their guards. He'd lifted his foot high into the air in a great swinging arc. It connected with the soldier's face and there was a sickening crack. The soldier looked startled, then screamed with pain as he staggered to one side, groping at his lower jaw.

For a moment time seemed to stand still. Then the reaction was instantaneous. The other soldiers jumped on Yew-Ming and threw him to the ground. They were shouting and yelling obscenities at him. A big bastard came up and kicked him powerfully in the ribs, again and again. Nicole could hear Yew-Ming sobbing, taking the impacts, unable to draw breath. She turned and screamed at the officer, telling him to make them stop, leave the man alone.

Lukman jerked quickly to his feet, tipping over the desk as he rose, scattering its contents all over the floor. He drew his pistol and, holding it with both hands, pointed its barrel at Yew-Ming, ordering his men to back off.

Nicole looked down at her possessions spread across

the floor. She could see her black computer case, its lid partly unzipped, and the laptop sprawling out of it. She hesitated, looked around. Yew-Ming was sobbing from the vicious blows to his body.

Lukman was coming out from behind the overturned desk. He started to pull Yew-Ming to his feet. Nobody was paying Nicole any attention now. The Chinese stood submissively in line, some of them looking at her, wondering what she was about to do.

She dived forwards and went onto her hands and knees, scrabbling at the computer case. She plunged her hand inside, feeling for the little disk compartment. There were three disks in there. She grabbed them all, hoping to God she'd found the right one. She slid them all into the waistband of her tracksuit, then stood up, meekly waiting, her mind working furiously. It had taken only a brief moment.

Yew-Ming was on his feet now, but he couldn't stand and had to be held upright by two of the soldiers. His face was badly battered, cuts and splits everywhere. Blood seeped from some of the wounds. His legs were puffy from the kicking, large dark discolourations already beginning to show. Nicole looked at him, wanting to reassure him, tell him that she'd got the disk, that it was safe with her. But his head just hung down loosely. He coughed – and blood sprayed onto the floor.

A young soldier reached down and pulled the desk back into its former position. Then he heaved all the items from the floor back onto it.

Yew-Ming was groaning from the pain. Lukman barked an order in Indonesian. Another soldier bundled Nicole to one side. She'd suddenly become a piece of discarded baggage, no longer of any interest to them.

Lukman turned his full attention to the row of Chinese oilmen standing dejectedly along one wall of the office. His whole manner had changed as anger and outrage coursed through him. The oilmen shrank back as he began to strut up and down in front of them, berating them in Bahanese. They flinched as he shouted at them, working himself up into a frenzy. He wanted their hands clasped upon their heads. He began slapping at them to make them understand, aiming kicks at them. Then, seizing their hands, he forced them up onto their heads.

Nicole stood and watched this ghastly performance of ethnic hatred. It sickened her – the way he treated the Chinese like animals, demeaning them, beating them down physically and psychologically.

Finally Lukman ran out of steam. He was sweating profusely and wiped spittle from his chin as he stepped back. He ordered one of his men to search Yew-Ming as he hung, slumped, between two of the Indonesian soldiers, his mouth slack, lips moving soundlessly. Nicole couldn't tell whether he was even fully conscious.

The soldier began to run his hands around Yew-Ming's vest and shorts. His hands stopped over a pocket. He'd found something! Ripping the pocket away from the fabric, he shouted to Lukman as he held up a computer disk.

Nicole's eyes widened. From where she was standing

the disk looked just like her own. Why did Yew-Ming have another disk sewn into his shorts? Was it a copy? Who was it intended for? What the hell was going on here? What was she getting herself involved in?

As the disk was passed to Lukman, the young officer read the label carefully. He looked at Yew-Ming, then at Nicole, and a big smile spread across his face. He'd clearly found what he was looking for. He unbuttoned one of the top pockets of his overalls and slid the disk inside, patting it into place.

'Well!' he said. 'An interesting day. I must say I'm looking forward to reading your story in the English papers, Miss Tai-Chung. I'm only sorry that you will not be able to stay with us any longer.'

They were going to let her go!

'You were, of course, very well treated, as were all our prisoners here.' He smiled at her, a sickly-sweet smile. Then he abruptly turned to his soldiers and, pointing to Yew-Ming, barked out an order: 'Take this bastard up to the heli-deck, and dispose of him.'

Nicole desperately tried to save Sour-Face. She attempted to keep Lukman's attention. 'What will happen to the other men on the rigs, Major Lukman?' she blurted out. 'All the Chinese workers? Will you shoot them as well? Or will you send them off to one of your gulags to rot?'

'That's enough!' Lukman's voice was harsh and commanding. 'You're a guest in my country, and you'll remember that. Don't insult us. There are no gulags here, only in your imagination.'

SLIDE

A single pistol shot sounded loudly above them, its noise reverberating within the metal walls of the cabin.

Lukman stared at Nicole for a moment. Then a thin smile stretched slowly across his face as he watched her sickened reaction. 'Enjoy your flight to Singapore, Miss Tai-Chung. I don't think we shall meet again.'

Chapter Eight – the following day: the Java Sea

Four hundred miles to the west of the Utara oilfield, a colourful three-masted *pinisi* schooner bucked through the heavy swell of the Java Sea. Its steeply raked bow, decorated with green and red geometric patterns, plunged through the waves.

A young man in T-shirt and jeans clung to the battered bowsprit. He was lost in thought, watching the steady progress of waves breaking beneath him. Behind, the great brown lateen sails hummed and vibrated in the wind – a wind that pummelled his face, bringing with it the rank smell of salt, and leaving a stinging taste on his lips.

He scanned the horizon frequently. Indonesian ships and aircraft had been moving around them all day, and their activity made him uneasy.

As he made his way back to the rickety cabin perched on the stern he had to clamber awkwardly across the untidy cargo of planks covering the broad thirty-foot-wide deck. Inside the cabin it was dark, and the air was pungent with burning charcoal from the cooking fire.

The crew of six were settling down to their early-evening meal. Dressed in a variety of dirty T-shirts, sarongs pulled high up their legs, they sat cross-legged in a circle on the bamboo floor. They began to scoop their hands alternately into piles of white rice and a communal mound of spiced squid set down on a large square of banana leaf.

They were Bugis people, seafaring gypsies, friends of the Indonesian Chinese. Despite being staunchly Muslim, they were fiercely independent, incensed by Rahman's attempts to regulate their trade, a trade that had served the people of the Indonesian archipelago for over a thousand years.

Jean Tai-Chung took his place within the circle, squatting next to Adji, the grizzled elderly captain of the schooner. He put down the small blue Adidas sports bag that never left his side, and turned to the old man. 'Why are they showing so much interest in us, Adji? What are they looking for?'

Adji shrugged. He took a long noisy slurp of tea from his chipped glass tumbler, and wiped his lips with the back of his hand. He spoke with slow deliberation. 'I don't know, Jean. This is normally an empty part of the sea. Perhaps is nothing.'

They ate in companionable silence for a while, listening to the gentle creak of the schooner's timbers as she rolled in the Java Sea swell.

Adji looked down at Jean's blue sports bag. 'Known your father long time, Jean. A good man. Given you best gift any *bapak* can give – he trust you.'

Jean nodded. 'How many days now, Adji?'

'Two – maybe three – depends on the winds. We lucky, monsoon winds blow strongly this year. At other times . . .' He shrugged his shoulders. 'Nothing, then very slow.'

Adji chewed noisily on a ring of rubbery squid, a fleck of rice bobbing on his stubbly chin. 'What will you do with that rock when you reach Ujung Pandang?'

'Take it home, back to England; have it analysed.'

Jean reached down and unzipped his bag. He took out the small cylinder of rock, unpacked it from its bubble-wrap, and held it between his hands. It was roughly six inches long, with broken ends. Not for the first time, he wondered at the strange marbled layers of rusty orange and grey. He fingered the slight fluting on the otherwise smooth surface of the cylinder.

Adji leaned across and peered at it with suspicion. 'You be careful, Jean. That rock, I can feel its power. That rock is not of this earth.'

Jean laughed. 'Well, it must have come from some-where, Adji. It looks quite earthly to me.' He pointed with his fingers. 'See these flutes? It's been cut with a drill. It's a core sample.' Jean frowned. 'I've been a geologist for over ten years now, but I still don't recognize this rock. Such an odd colour.' He weighed the cylinder in his hand. 'Quite dense, too. This represents something very important, Adji, something the Indonesians have found.' He caressed the fluting thoughtfully with his thumb. 'Proper analysis in a laboratory will reveal it. I've no idea myself what it might be, but I know my father felt it was important enough to risk his life.' Jean slowly rolled the rock backwards and forwards between his fingers.

'They are looking for that rock, Jean, that's why your father passed it to you. Maybe they look for you too. You be careful. I tell you, I sense evil in that stone, it's not of this world.'

'Oh, it's of this world, all right, and in any case—'

The distinctive rush of a cannon shell tore through the air outside, followed by the crash of an explosion. The ensuing pressure wave deafened them slightly for a moment. Jean leaped up, dropping the stone back into the sports bag. Fighting for space at the door with the rest of the crew, he raced on deck.

He saw a bright orange flash on the horizon. A second shell tore through the air. A plume of water rose from the sea ahead of them. Then came the delayed thud of the gun firing.

Adji shouted orders. The crew jumped into action, letting down the great sails. The boat began to slow in the water. 'Gunboat!' yelled Adji.

Already Jean could make out the rounded grey outline of a patrol boat. It was coming in fast, water creaming back from the bows, the front turret swivelling purposefully towards them.

'They'll come on board and search us. They probably think we've been pirating. Hide, Jean, you must hide!'

Jean raced back to the cabin, and began to stash all his belongings into his sports bag, pushing them down on top of the rock sample. Back on deck, he searched frantically for somewhere to hide. He found a narrow space running for some distance into the cargo of roughly stacked planks, and began to worm his way inside.

The resinous scent of the recently cut wood was powerful in the early-evening air. Its roughness grazed Jean's hands and face. Sharp splinters dug into his flesh.

He paused for a moment, trying to catch his breath. He could tell from the muffled shouts of the crew that the gunboat had come alongside. He heard the muted rumble of its powerful diesels, felt the schooner rocking gently in the swash of its arrival. He looked back down the long tunnel of planks and could still see light and movement at the end. He wasn't far enough in – he would easily be discovered.

Desperately, Jean began to crawl forward again, but the space was getting tighter. His bag dropped down in front of him. A hole! He felt around with his hands. The cavity led back beneath him into another crevice. He had to get down there, out of the way of probing torches. He started to use his hands to pull himself forwards, but in the darkness he wasn't sure which way to go. Then he became stuck – there wasn't room to turn his body. Frantically, he clawed at the surrounding timber, trying to twist himself out of its grasp. He freed himself, slipped, then caught his grip again. He scrabbled and twisted until at last he'd managed to double back upon himself, and gratefully dragged his body into the velvety blackness of the lower passage.

It ended in a wedge-shaped space. He could crawl no further, but at least he was safe from the boarding party in his timber cave. He lay there, clutching his sports bag, panting, listening to the muffled sounds of activity on deck: the deep throbbing of the gunboat's diesel engines; the heavy boots of the marines; orders being given; the sound of hatches being opened, then dropped back with a bang. He was too frightened to think of the great weight of timber above, which might shift and crush him at any moment.

'Jean!' The name entered his consciousness, filtering through his dream.

'Jean!' It came again, persistent, demanding his attention.

'Jean, you OK? You awake?' He opened his eyes. It was dark, he could see nothing. His neck was stiff, his back hurt, and he was cold.

'Jean? You OK? You must come out now.'

Jean couldn't move in the cramped confines of his timber cave, there wasn't enough room. Everywhere he stretched, something blocked him. He had to get out, he desperately wanted the freedom of space around him. Panicking slightly, gasping for breath, he scrabbled against the wood as he tried to get back down the awkward tunnel. Then he checked his anxious movements, forcing himself to move more slowly, to keep calm.

'OK, Adji, I'm coming out.'

His limbs were stiff. They ached from the awkward position he'd been lying in. He scraped his knees and legs, and felt a sharp splinter enter the soft pad of his hand. His hands became sticky with a congealing mixture of sap and blood.

Then, at last, he was out.

It was dark. He found Adji crouching behind the pile of timber. 'Keep down,' Adji whispered. 'The gunboat's on our port side, they're watching us. You must come quickly, back into the cabin.'

'What do they want?'

'Drugs? Guns? Who knows? They stop all of us. Bugis are no friends of the Indonesians – you know that. Now, come, get back into the cabin! They must not see you.'

Keeping low, Jean and Adji crept back into the cabin's shelter. A hissing butane lamp hung from the roof of the cabin, swaying in the gentle swell. Some of the crew were now asleep in rickety bunks arranged along the wall, but two of them were sitting on the bamboo floor. There was a delightful aroma of strong sweet tea. One of the men offered Jean a glass almost too hot to hold. Adji added a thick layer of condensed milk from an open can on the floor. Jean stirred it in gratefully with an old bent spoon. 'Where are we heading?'

Adji sucked in air through his front teeth. 'Sunda Kelapa.'

Jean was startled. 'Jakarta! They're taking us to Jakarta?'

'I'm sorry, Jean.'

'Damn!' Jean muttered under his breath. He cupped the glass of hot tea and watched the pale brown liquid slowly spin around just below the rim. 'Why? Why are they taking us to Jakarta?'

Adji waved his hands apart, and shrugged – an empty gesture, a gesture of apology. 'They found drugs.'

'Drugs? Adji! You're a Muslim, for God's sake. Drugs are forbidden to you. You shouldn't have any drugs.'

'I know.' Adji hung his head. 'The Bugis never take drugs, but sometimes . . . we trade a little.'

'But you've jeopardized everything, Adji. What am I supposed to do with this now?' He indicated the sports bag. 'Why ever did you take the risk?' Jean was quiet for a moment, and then added: 'You've let my father down.'

Adji didn't answer. He studied the bamboo floor, and his spoon clanked rhythmically against the side of his glass as he stirred his tea.

In the chill of early dawn, the schooner, escorted by Indonesian marines in a powerful inflatable, eased its way into the narrow confines of the Great Canal, seeking out the cramped timber wharves of Sunda Kelapa harbour. As they tied up, Jean could see the docks bristling with troops. A row of drab army trucks had been parked on the dock road, and soldiers were searching the long line of schooners nosed up against the wharf.

Jean became increasingly anxious. He knew that he

mustn't stay on the boat any longer. He must escape through the docks, and into the old city of Batavia. He must move fast before the marines boarded the boat.

'Hey, mister, you come here now.' Adji, his brown face weathered and grizzled beneath a battered straw hat, beckoned him back into the cabin. 'You put these on, and then you look like dock worker.'

He passed Jean a pair of stained shorts, a ragged shirt and a torn jungle hat. The old shirt smelled badly of stale sweat. He grinned at Jean's distaste. 'Somchai tell me to look after you – so, I look after you!'

Jean stripped off his own clothes, and began to drag on the old ones. 'I can't take my sports bag, it's too obvious.'

Adji rummaged in a corner and returned triumphantly with a battered straw bag. Jean was about to place the rock sample in it when the old man caught his arm. 'Always travel a child away from its mother, to keep the family safe.'

Jean looked blank.

Adji took the rock gently out of his hand, and unwrapped it. He placed it carefully on one of the hearth stones by the fire, then, searching noisily in a tool chest to one side of the cabin, he produced a battered and rusting hammer. He brought it down sharply on the lump of rock, and with a sharp crack, a fragment flew off, rattling away between the lengths of bamboo flooring. Adji picked up the small piece and passed it to Jean. 'Put this in your shirt pocket, to be safe.'

Adji placed the rest of the rock sample inside Jean's

bag. Then, reaching down, he picked up a plastic bowl and tipped a slippery pile of day-old fish on top of it. He looked Jean in the eye, his face slowly splitting into a toothy grin. 'Tell Somchai that Adji remembered his promise. Now go, and may Allah be with you.'

Jean felt uncomfortable in the old and dirty clothes. He walked slowly down the narrow gangplank from the bows and then along the quayside, past the line of schooners.

Already the morning sun had considerable strength. It brought out the spicy smell of wood shavings and the odours of rubber and oil from a row of ancient cargo trucks. Dock workers shouted orders to one another, and heaved sacks and planks into the backs of lorries. A group of soldiers sauntered along the road towards him. They were dressed in camouflage uniforms, rifles hanging loosely at their sides, and were casually checking the piles of timber. They ignored him as he walked past.

Jean felt conspicuous, glaringly obvious amongst the dockyard activity.

At the end of the road, two army lorries had been drawn up to form a barrier. Soldiers were checking papers as the workers filed past. Jean knew that he had to ignore them. He wanted to run – he had to force himself to keep slouching along at the same pace. He knew that he had to melt away into the background, slip away unnoticed.

Slowly the checkpoint drew nearer. Jean walked on, head down, studying the tarmac, watching the potholes pass steadily beneath his feet. He started to count every step.

Now he could hear the murmur of voices, the scrape of boots on gravel, the questions of the soldiers as they inspected documents.

Still Jean walked on, the rhythm of his feet marking out the passage of time with agonizing slowness. Ahead, he could see a gap between the wall of a building and the huge metal fender of an army truck – and without any fuss, he slipped through it.

Now the road into the city stretched out ahead of him, the road to freedom. The excitement of his escape had heightened his senses. He became aware that the air was tainted with the sharp smell of fresh fish. He heard the cries of market sellers, saw the familiar shape of the old Dutch lookout tower reaching up above the surrounding jumble of buildings.

He was free! It had been so easy, so simple.

'Hey, you! Your papers!'

His steps faltered for a moment. Walk on! Slouch along the road like a tired shift worker. Pretend you haven't heard. Perhaps it wasn't him they meant, perhaps it was someone else.

'Hey! You!'

Booted footsteps came pounding along the tarmac behind him. The city was so near, he could easily hide among its confusion of buildings. He couldn't stop – not now! Without warning, his nerve gave. He bolted, running for cover, his bag swinging on the end of his arm.

A shot rang out, the sharp crack deafening him slightly. Jean saw a puff of dust as the bullet struck the wall in front of him. He dodged to the right, trying to put the soldier off his aim.

Another crack. A red-hot pain speared into his leg. It collapsed under him, sending him tumbling to the ground. For a moment he smelled the dust on the hot asphalt, then another sharp pain made him cry out. Further shots – heavy hammer blows to his body.

He lay quietly in the gutter, watching in surprise as a pool of blood spread out across the black tarmac, following the line of his outstretched arm. People gathered at a safe distance to stare at his body as it lay by the side of the road, one leg twisted awkwardly. Soldiers appeared, pushing the onlookers away. Slowly, grey mist drifted in from the sides, shrinking the scene, all sounds slowly dying away. Then came a pleasant, gentle feeling: a silent blackness. And then . . . nothing.

The young lieutenant in charge of the roadblock came running up. He crouched down by the body on the road; just a dock worker, his bag of fish spewed across the tarmac.

'He went through the checkpoint, sir. Ran off when I challenged him.' The young soldier was nervous. He'd never fired in earnest before.

The lieutenant searched the man's clothing and found nothing. He scooped up the bag and tipped out the rest of the fish. They spilled onto the road in a slippery pile – a little package rolling after them. The lieutenant was puzzled and reached out to pick it up. Squatting on his haunches beside the dead man, he turned it over in his fingers and began to peel off the bubble-wrap. Inside was a cylinder of rock: a strange rock, layers of rusty orange and grey flecked with white and gold. Why would this man have such a thing in his bag of fish? Why would he want to hide a lump of rock?

For a moment he hesitated, almost throwing the rock back into the gutter. Then he stood up, ordering his men to keep the people away, and reached for his radio.

The bespectacled Department of Defence official was hard at work behind his desk. It was getting towards midday and, not for the first time this month, the struggling air-conditioning system had broken down. He had all the windows overlooking Merdeka Square wide open, and the steady noise of traffic drifted up from the packed Jakartan street below, punctuated by the annoying screams of youngsters playing football on the large grassy open spaces between the rows of palm trees. The air was hot and unbearably sticky, and although the big fan in the ceiling wafted steadily round and round, it was doing nothing to help. Then the sound of the *azan*, the Islamic call to prayer, began to wail from the loudspeakers in the minaret of the mosque standing just behind the National Museum.

The official was about to give up. He yawned, and flicked dust off his papers.

SLIDE

There was a gentle knock at the door and one of his secretaries came in. Soberly dressed, her Islamic headscarf dutifully in place, she placed a large manila envelope on his desk, and then quietly left. The door clicked to behind her. The official was grateful for any sort of distraction. He wiped the beads of sweat from his face, picked up the packet and sliced it open with an intricately patterned letter opener. Inside was a large colour photograph of a cylinder of rock. It rested on a pale blue background, and a black and white scale-bar had been placed beside it.

The official stared at the photo for a moment, then reached for a ruler. He measured the length of the rock, and checked it against the scale-bar. He got up from behind his desk and frowned, flicking at the corner of the print. Then he bent back to the table and searched inside the envelope for anything else it might contain. Finding a flimsy pink report form, he read it carefully – twice. Then he glanced again at the photograph.

He thought for a moment. He knew there was a reward for the recovery of this rock. One of Dr Hendra's young scientists had been to see him and had told him it wasn't worth bothering the President with such a trifling matter. Had palmed him a big rupiah note to keep him quiet. Asked him what he would like if he ever recovered the sample. A car, perhaps? A Mercedes?

That was a big bribe for something the President must not know about.

The official flicked nervously at the photograph. The President or Hendra? Who would give him the most?

He hesitated, then decided. He reached for his telephone, and asked for the Presidential Palace.

Soon, one of the Palace secretaries came on the line.

The official requested that an urgent message be sent ... to Dr Jazid Hendra.

Chapter Nine – the same day: thirty miles south of Jakarta, Rahman's Palace, Bogor

The deliciously cool water smacked against Amir Rahman's scalp as he plunged into the pool. He arched his body as the fluid surged around him, letting the full force of the dive carry him back to the surface. With a rush, he broke through the surface, water streaming down his face.

General Rahman took pride in his body. Fifty-six years old, thickset, as strong as a man less than half his age, he enjoyed his early-morning swim. He pitched over and began to plough steadily up and down the pool, his powerful muscles rippling beneath the surface of his smooth brown skin.

Rahman towelled himself down, and donned an elegant dressing gown. A small, wizened Palace official, resplendent in his blue-turbaned uniform, entered discreetly to leave an ornate silver tray by the side of the pool. It contained a cut-glass goblet of chilled pineapple juice with slices of star fruit slotted on its rim. Rahman took the drink and, going out through sliding glass doors, stepped onto the broad terrace of the Presidential Palace.

He breathed in deeply, savouring the cool crispness of the early-morning mountain air. Then he leaned on the balustrade and gazed down at the landscape spread out before him. A broad swathe of parkland drifted down towards a great lake, sunlight glistening on its surface. A gentle breeze sighed through the palms, bringing with it the scent of cloves and nutmeg. Perched in the foothills of the mountainous backbone of Java, Rahman's palace could have been a million miles from the oppressive and over-heated stink of Jakarta.

Rahman soon retired to his bedroom and had himself dressed in his military uniform. His gold braid and medal ribbons gleamed impressively in the morning light streaming in through the window. Then, taking the wide curve of the Palace staircase two steps at a time, he went buoyantly down to breakfast.

His wife, Thameena, was already at the table. She was a tall, handsome woman, elegant in her long patterned dress, dark hair pulled back and kept in place with an ornate silver pin. She looked up from behind her newspaper. 'I see you're in a good mood this morning, Amir,' she said. A pleasant enough greeting, yet somehow edged with customary coolness.

Rahman ignored her and sat down at the dark, well-polished colonial dining table. He placed a heavy cloth napkin on his lap. A palace servant came forward to offer some coffee.

Thameena's superior voice continued, spilling acidly

from behind her paper: 'I suppose you're aware that you've stirred up yet another hornets' nest of international protest?'

'Good!' said Rahman perfunctorily, lifting the coffee to his lips.

Thameena sniffed. 'Neither China nor ASEAN seem very keen on your recent actions,' she persisted. Rahman watched as she folded the newspaper carefully onto the table. He thought about ASEAN – the Association of South-East Asian Nations – a powerful group of countries that sought political stability in the region, countries that would oppose his actions just to maintain the status quo.

Thameena looked at him down her long elegant nose, and continued: 'Murdering innocent oil workers in the Utara field is hardly a sensible strategy for an aspiring world leader.'

'Murder, Thameena?' enquired Rahman with forced politeness.

'Then are these lies that I am reading here?' She held up the newspaper so that he could read the headline.

'That!' Rahman laughed. 'All nonsense, the ravings of *The Indonesian Times*. The paper's run by a Chinese immigrant, as well you know. It's just gossip – rumour.' He sipped his coffee again, then added quietly under his breath: 'And I think it's time we put a stop to his subversion.'

Thameena tapped irritatingly at the newspaper. 'And your death camps, Amir, are they gossip, too?'

Rahman clenched his jaw. He was tired of his wife's

constant needling. 'Don't be ridiculous, Thameena! There are no death camps,' he muttered.

But she wouldn't let go. 'So – more rumour. I do declare this country runs on rumour . . .'

The delicate silver cutlery bounced on the table as Rahman jerked to his feet, dumping his heavy napkin. 'This country does *not* run on rumour, Thameena!' he shouted. '*I* run this country.'

Thameena's dark eyes flashed with hatred. 'Then, if you run this country, Amir, why do you need to spill so much blood? Why are there so many atrocities? Why do you care so little for your own people?'

Rahman leaned forward, supporting the weight of his body on the palms of his hands. His eyes smouldered. 'Because that is the way with power, Thameena. And what would *you* know of that with your privileged background? My country is in chaos: Muslim against Christian, Malay against Chinese. We need stability, unity – and if that means casualties, if a few Chinese parasites die on the way, well . . . what of it?'

There was silence for a moment, the air between them charged with tension.

'I despise you for what you have become, Amir Rahman,' hissed Thameena. 'You commit these atrocities in the name of Islam, when that very word means peace. You are a traitor – to me, your country, your religion . . .'

'You dare to defy me?' Rahman's voice was full of dark threat.

'What? You'll have me shot? Make me disappear, like all the rest?' Her laughter echoed clearly around the high-ceilinged room. 'Now that's one thing you'll never do. You'd make me a martyr.' Her voice hardened. 'You didn't marry me for love, Amir. You married a convenience, a conduit to those above you, a way to the influence and power that you crave. And I was stupid, wasn't I? Stupid enough to fall for all your lies.' Her dark gaze smoked with hate. 'Go back to the gutter, Amir Rahman. Go back to the stinking slums of Sumatra from whence you came. Leave this country alone . . .'

Rahman swung his hand in a wide and powerful arc, the palm smacking hard against the side of Thameena's face.

She stopped, startled, eyes wide.

Slowly her hand came up to feel the pain caused by the stinging blow.

Rahman glared at her, eyes like steel. 'You choose to defy me, woman. Well, that is your mistake. If you stand in the way of my plans, then, believe me, you will disappear, like all the other traitors I've had to squash into the dirt of this wretched country.'

He spun swiftly on his heel and stalked away.

Some hours later, Rahman stood once more on the Presidential Palace terrace, searching impatiently for signs of his official jet. He looked up at the overcast sky and saw clouds that threatened to spill rain later in the day. The air now was hot and oppressive.

He made an effort to put his differences with Thameena behind him, forced his mind to concentrate on the present as he calmed his smouldering anger. After all, today was an important day – his first meeting with APOS.

APOS – the Alliance of Pacific Ocean States, Rahman's latest political creation, a carefully engineered chance for him to step more prominently onto the world stage.

APOS was a new initiative. It partnered Indonesia with two other island groups lying to the north-east – the tiny independent republics of Palau and Micronesia, both doomed by the steadily warming global climate. Standing just a few feet above the waves, the rising waters of the Pacific threatened to swamp the little islands into extinction. Already, high tides and powerful typhoons had demolished sea walls, flooded homes and poisoned good farmland with salt. The islanders felt abandoned by the world. Even the United States, ravaged by environmental and security problems of its own, had turned its back on its former friends, and the United Nations seemed paralysed by mutual recrimination and self-interest.

Rahman hoped to seize his chance. He would build new sea defences for the threatened islands – at a price.

And that price was to be territory.

Thousands of square miles of it. Deep beneath the surrounding ocean.

All of it valuable real estate, rich in minerals.

And with the islands in such a desperate state, it would be as easy as stealing sweets from a baby.

Rahman scanned the skies, and at last caught the soft whistling sound of his little Lear jet. He watched as it flew gently over the Palace, the two escorting MiG-29 fighters peeling off to the right, trailing faint plumes of smoke across the grey overcast.

Rahman walked back through the Palace and out onto the top of the imposing columned steps at the front. Brokering a deal was good for him. It was like hunting, when the biggest kick came at the kill.

He smiled, enjoying the occasion. He was putting on a show. No detail had been left to chance. Behind him he could hear the nervous babble of the one hundred or so guests already installed in the dining room – specially chosen soldiers, diplomats, and top engineers. The military band was looking splendid in its blue and grey livery, brass instruments polished and shining. Long red and white Indonesian flags draped the columns, drifting gently in the breeze. Military police stood guard in their olive-green uniforms and round white helmets.

At last, the black Presidential Mercedes arrived, the band began to play, and the soldiers stood to attention. Rahman watched as his Minister for Technology, Dr Jazid Hendra, gently led the Presidents of Micronesia and Palau up the short flight of steps.

'*As-salaamu alaykum*, peace be upon you.'

Both Presidents grinned back nervously, not used to such attention. They exchanged formal pleasantries with their host, then, along with a hovering retinue of aides, Rahman led them slowly into the Palace.

The dining hall had been arranged for a magnificent banquet. Huge ornate golden chandeliers hung from the dark-planked ceiling. Carpets had been laid upon the parquet floor, and on each one stood a beautiful table surrounded by a circle of round-backed rattan chairs. Each table was laden with traditional cuisine – dishes of curries, vegetables, sambals, and exotic fruits. In one corner, a gamelan orchestra sat cross-legged behind their richly carved percussion instruments, entertaining the guests with a gentle flow of soft rhythms and melodies.

Thameena was there too, looking splendid in her long flowing robes, a lotus blossom woven into the swirl of dark hair beneath her elegant lace veil. But she was already up to her tricks. Standing at the side of the President of Micronesia, she pitched her voice unnecessarily high above the sound of the music and milling guests, her words drifted pointedly across the dining room: 'I think you can see, sir, that my husband is keen to demonstrate his new power.'

'Indeed I can, madam,' the President replied. 'And in such a magnificent building too, in the best possible tradition of colonial architecture. Early nineteenth-century Dutch, I believe?'

Rahman saw the need to intervene, and moved swiftly

towards them. 'Oh, more than just a magnificent building,' he said. 'Much more. But come, let us sit at the centre table. We have much to talk about.'

The meal was long and convivial, full of laughter and conversation, and the making of new friends. Rahman played gently on the naivety of the two Presidents, flattering them, inflating their sense of their own importance. Carefully laying the foundation for the deal to come.

Towards the end of the banquet, blue-liveried Palace functionaries brought in beautiful round silver pots from which arose the delightful aroma of freshly prepared Indonesian coffee, thick with the tang of ginger.

Outside, the afternoon storm had gathered its skirts, and through the large windows could be seen lightning, flickering soundlessly over distant mountain peaks. Rahman, who had an eye for the theatrical, sensed his moment. He put down his empty cup and invited the two chief guests and their aides to move towards the library, already organized for their convenience.

But Thameena had other ideas. She rose: 'One more thing before you begin your long and arduous discussions.' Rahman felt anger and irritation rise within him as she led his small party through the other guests towards a column at one side of the dining hall, forcing Rahman to trail behind.

Against the column's white plaster hung a framed photograph, turning sepia with age. The picture showed an Indonesian couple, obviously of the privileged classes. He was stiff and formal in a Western-style dinner jacket; she was petite and demure in a white lace jacket and matching sarong, her arm hooked formally into his. Rahman guessed what was coming.

'This is Raden Ajeng Kartini – my heroine,' fawned Thameena. The two Presidential guests looked on dutifully. 'Her face appears on our rupiah notes, and we have a statue of her in Jakarta. She had a brilliant mind, a European education, and very modern views. It was she who won freedom for Muslim women throughout Indonesia.' She paused for effect. 'It is my vision that one day we will win freedom, too, for *all* the peoples of Indonesia.' She looked sharply across at her husband. 'Not for just a few!'

The Presidents fidgeted, smiling nervously, uncertain of her innuendo. Rahman suppressed his anger, wondering quickly how he might precipitate the business of the day, how he might shut Thameena up.

'But there was another Kartini, of course,' Thameena continued loudly. 'The weak puppet who lost his life in the economic chaos, corruption and bloodshed that resulted in my husband coming to power. *That* worm only held on to power through bribery and torture.' Rahman saw her quizzical look. 'And bribery and torture have, sadly, not yet gone away.' She paused dramatically. 'We must all be careful where we place our loyalties today.'

There was a hushed silence.

The President of Micronesia coughed politely.

Rahman stiffened visibly, intensely angered by his wife's

deliberate intervention. She was a menace, a loose cannon. He had to find a way to pluck her out – like a thorn.

Jazid Hendra, too, sensed the danger of the occasion. Sipping from his coffee cup, he placed it carefully back on its saucer and beamed. 'Come now, sirs,' he said in his silky voice. 'I do believe that we've feasted enough today. Let us take our leave of these people, and of Amir's beautiful and charming wife, and talk of the future of your islands – together, as friends.'

Rahman smiled, grateful for Hendra's intervention. He doubted Thameena had done much damage. At the end of the day, it would be money that talked. And that was what he was offering – in modest amounts, of course.

A Palace official preceded the small retinue out of the dining room and into one of the side wings of the great house.

Outside, the darkening sky finally gave birth to its storm. A strong wind gusted around the Palace complex, sending the palms into a tossing frenzy. Swollen raindrops lashed against the window-panes, making the sodden flags and streamers outside cling to the stonework.

They entered the quiet warmth of the Palace library, where Rahman had arranged for them to sit round a large wooden table, seated in large leather easy chairs. Hendra fussed around, offering them coffee and *kreteks* from a little wooden box. By the door, stiff in the smart dress uniform of the *Kopassus*, stood Rahman's personal bodyguard – Major Hari Lukman.

Rahman carefully took in the body language, noted the relaxed postures of the two Presidents, and knew that this was going to be easy.

By late afternoon, the meeting was over. The deed was done – the deal struck, the two Presidents flown skilfully away into the still-active storm.

Now the library was hot and oppressive despite the air-conditioning, and the sky outside remained dark and angry. Lightning flashed, shimmering its hard electric whiteness against the dark ranks of leather-bound books. The Palace buildings shook with the massive detonations of tropical thunder.

Rahman stood by the window, watching the storm, his hands deep in his pockets. 'That went rather well, don't you think?' he offered.

Hendra leaned forward and took a small round peppermint from an ornate dish on the table. He held it delicately between thumb and forefinger, inspecting it. 'Very successful, sir,' he replied silkily. 'We seem to have secured a huge increase in our resource base . . .' He paused to pop the sweet carefully into his mouth. 'And for a minimal effort.' He sat back slowly, wiping his fingers on his napkin.

'We've committed ourselves to a lot of expenditure,' cautioned Rahman. 'On sea defences – sea walls, that sort of thing.'

'True!' replied Hendra. He smiled a thin smile. 'But we

don't have to move too fast on that, do we? Not for a few rather unimportant islands, with virtually no population.'

Another huge detonation rocked the Palace.

Rahman nodded thoughtfully. 'A successful deal, then.'

He turned from the window, a flash of lightning momentarily silhouetting his powerful frame. His eyes gleamed in the dim lighting of the library.

'What about uranium, Jazid? Do you think you'll find more of it deposited around their islands?'

Hendra sucked thoughtfully at the peppermint, then carefully wiped a slight wetness from his mouth. A jewelled finger blazed briefly in the soft lighting. 'I'll be sending the *Ibn Battuta* out there straight away, sir, to carry out a proper survey of the ocean floor. Yes, I would say there's a good chance of finding uranium. Certainly enough to bring our reserves up to the required strength.'

Rahman grinned smugly and returned to the table. He sat down in his chair and leaned back comfortably. 'I want to take this opportunity to assess our current position, Jazid. Arguni, the uranium refinery – I trust our security is still good?'

Hendra swivelled round towards Lukman. 'I believe that's the major's responsibility, sir.'

Lukman eased himself away from his position by the door. 'There's been no compromise of our security at Arguni. The whole operation's well hidden underground. As you know, the submarine pens open directly into deep water . . .'

'Yes, of course!' Rahman cut him off with a wave of his hand, and turned back to Hendra, leaning forward in his chair. 'Tell me, Jazid. More importantly, how is the uranium refining going?' Rahman had the suppressed excitement of a child, his eyes glinting in the soft light of the library. 'How close are we getting to our first weapon?'

Hendra replied in a hushed, dry tone: 'Well, we're rapidly building up stocks of enriched uranium. I think we may be close to testing. Our technology's good – old but well proven. We've drafted in more scientists from the Islamic southern states, most with experience of Soviet weapons construction.' He paused to reach out for another peppermint and nibbled at it, examining its contents as Rahman looked on eagerly. 'Basic labour is still a problem, though,' Hendra added.

Rahman's eyes darkened. 'I thought we'd agreed to use our Chinese – keep them out of trouble.'

Hendra sniffed. 'The attrition rate's running very high, sir. Maybe . . .'

'Then feed them more!' Rahman glared.

'But we can barely feed some of our own people. We've already lost much of our crop land due to flooding and drought. The climate's warming fast, we're fighting a major environmental crisis . . .'

'If you want this project to succeed,' hissed Rahman, 'I suggest that you follow your only option.'

Lightning strobed again and another sharp detonation of thunder rocked the building. Rain lashed against the window, cascading down the glass like a miniature waterfall.

Hendra's answer came back slowly and deliberately. 'You must understand, sir, that life expectancy on the refining floor is very low. It might eventually cost us more in human lives than you realize.'

'You have my orders,' snapped Rahman. Dismissing any further discussion of the matter, he flipped open a blue document in front of him and carefully studied it for a moment. 'Major Lukman – what about the missile system? How much further have we got?'

'The first four sites are now operational, sir,' replied Lukman. 'Numbers three to six on your diagram.'

Rahman flipped through the document, found the right page, studied the plan, and grunted his approval. 'What about security? Have we been compromised in any way?'

'No, sir. We're shipping the technology out through Vladivostok – labelled as machine parts. The port's in chaos because of the Korean famine so I don't think anybody's had much time to worry about it.'

'Good, good.' Rahman formed his hands into a little steeple. 'It's most important that we get the missiles onto the Pacific sea-mounts as soon as possible.' A malevolent gleam appeared in his eyes. 'Once our defensive ring is complete, we can take advantage of climatic disarray, increase our interests in Asia, become a far more significant force in the world. It will be Indonesia's dream come true!'

He motioned to Lukman, who was still standing by the

door. 'Sit down, Major. Come on, relax. No one will disturb us here.'

Lukman sat down neatly next to Rahman, and reached onto the table to take a *kretek* from the little wooden box that lay there.

'You told me that you had another idea, Major Lukman,' Rahman prompted.

Lukman sat back, placing the cigarette in his mouth.

'I've been thinking, sir,' he began. 'Command and control, for the missile system – wouldn't it be better if we set it up away from Arguni? I don't think it's wise for us to have, as they say, all our eggs in one basket.'

Rahman stared across at him, pleased with this suggestion. 'That's good, Major . . . very good. Tell me, what are you suggesting?'

Lukman drew on his *kretek* to light it, then snapped shut the lid of his gold lighter and pocketed it. The sweet scent of burning cloves drifted into the library. 'Palau, sir, lies 400 miles to the east of the Philippines. It's right in the path of the big typhoons. Means we could build our first flood defences there without arousing any suspicion. Then we section off part of the flood control centre, make it secure, and use that as cover for our missile command and control.' He paused. 'I don't think the President of Palau would need to be unduly involved, or alarmed. It would just be our little secret.'

A broad smile swept across Rahman's features. 'Excellent!' he boomed. Then he fixed Lukman with a stare, his eyes taking on a manic gleam. 'We need a cover story for

Arguni as well, Major Lukman. It's obviously much more than just a copper mine.'

Hendra moved forward in his seat, his silky voice steady and controlled. 'I think you'll find that Major Lukman and I have got that well in hand, sir. We think Arguni should be redefined as a Centre for Deep-Ocean Studies. A perfect excuse for developing deep-ocean technology, don't you think? Arguni's remoteness is still its greatest asset. And with most of its facilities underground, it's secure against satellite passes.' He paused reflectively. 'But one thing still bothers me, sir. Some of our technicians, their skills are not necessarily oceanographical. Might I suggest that we develop another more transparent project – a parallel one? I'm suggesting that we design a fuel-cell car as a little sideline. It would tie in so well with what we are doing at Arguni. Cobalt motors would make use of our deep-ocean resources. It would appear to the world as if we were building a pollution-free car to run in our cities. That might have a distinct appeal to a world under environmental threat.'

Rahman sat back and looked at Hendra like a proud father gazing upon his son. 'Jazid, that's such a splendid idea!'

Outside, the storm had at last started to abate, and a thin cold light began to seep into the room.

Hendra gained confidence from this triumph. 'Sir, there is just one last thing.'

Rahman looked up, a questioning expression on his face.

'The lady Thameena, sir. Your wife . . .'

'My wife?' demanded Rahman in surprise.

'Yes, she has become . . .' Hendra hesitated. 'Well, I believe . . . rather outspoken in her views . . . a little headstrong, perhaps even a security risk. I was wondering, whether you felt the need . . .'

Rahman was staring at Hendra, his expression incredulous, his eyes round with astonishment. 'Security?' he hissed severely. '*You* talk to *me* about security?'

Hendra persisted. 'Security is important, sir, if we are to become the supreme power within the entire region . . .'

'Dr Hendra, I take it you have not yet recovered either of the disks or the core sample that you so carelessly misplaced?' said Rahman sarcastically.

Hendra stiffened visibly in his seat. That harsh reminder ran like cold steel through his body. 'I have every confidence in my men, sir. I'm sure they will be recovered soon.'

'Then perhaps I need to remind you of the cost of failure,' suggested Rahman, his face darkening further. 'Fail me,' he growled, 'and I will make sure that you pay the price.'

Rahman got up from the table and began to shuffle his papers into a neat pile. As he stood by the door, he looked back at Hendra. 'In a programme as ambitious as ours, Dr Hendra, there is no room for incompetence.'

And with that, he swept out of the room.

*

'You should be careful, Jazid,' said Lukman from his chair. 'It's never wise to criticize the President's wife.'

'The woman has a sharp tongue. She needs to be controlled . . .'

'I think the President is only too well aware of his domestic situation,' Lukman snapped back.

Hendra bit his tongue. Lukman was Rahman's hench-man. He had links right into the inner sanctum, which made Hendra uneasy. Lukman was an intelligent man, a man whose loyalty could be bought but never relied upon. And Hendra knew that he still needed that loyalty.

He opened his briefcase and took out a large manila envelope. 'I think we might have had some good news at last, Hari,' he said.

He slipped a photograph from the envelope, a large glossy colour print of a photograph showing a cylinder of rock resting on a blue background. He passed it over to Lukman.

As he watched Lukman study the photograph, he was certain that he saw a shadow move uneasily across the man's face. It both surprised and puzzled him.

'This is good news, Jazid,' said Lukman silkily as he passed the photograph back. 'Now the core sample's been recovered, we just need the two disks. Where was it found?'

'On a courier, down by the docks. I'm stepping up our searches; the two disks can't be far behind.'

Lukman stubbed out his *kretek* and smiled thinly. 'Maybe nearer than you think, Jazid. Oh by the way, my men brought someone in this morning – someone we think knows about those disks.'

Hendra was startled. 'You've interrogated him?'

'No,' said Lukman with a sneer. 'We thought we'd leave that to you, knowing how much you enjoy that sort of thing.'

Hendra saw the smug look on Lukman's face.

And hated him for it.

Chapter Ten – first week in February: Sukapura bonded warehouses, north-east Jakarta

It was a humid equatorial night, and the sultry air, heavily scented with frangipani, hung lazily over the blocks of floodlit warehouses. A sleek black Mercedes nosed quietly into the factory estate, its engine whispering gently in the stillness. Under the slowly moving tyres, a stone cracked and scuttered away into the darkness. The car eased its way between the warehouses, until finally it turned and the harsh glare of its headlights bounced off the scratched and battered metal doors of a loading bay. The horn sounded: a single sharp tone.

The car waited.

With a sudden shriek of tortured metal, the door began to rattle up into its housing. The chauffeur blipped the engine and, with a soft roar, the big limousine eased gently inside the warehouse. The large door shuddered back into place, hitting the ground with a solid thud.

Hendra looked out through the tinted glass of the rear passenger window. All was quiet inside the building, except for the ticking of the cooling exhaust.

The door of a little cabin suspended high up the warehouse wall swung open. A man, his T-shirt a vivid scarlet against the dark grey background, clattered down a short metal stairway to meet Hendra. 'Jazid! It's good to see you. I'm glad you were able to come at such short notice.'

It was Lukman.

Hendra smiled briefly and eased himself out of the rear seat. He reached back into the Mercedes and took out a slim black case. 'Has he said anything yet?' he asked cautiously.

Lukman grinned slyly. 'No – as I said the other day, he's your man, Jazid.' His sharp-eyed gaze slid over Hendra's face. 'We haven't touched him yet.'

Lukman led Hendra through the towering stacks of Malaysian imports. Reaching the far end of the building, he pulled back the handle of a red-painted door, and held it open against a strong spring to let him through. Now they were in a floodlit yard at the rear of the warehouse, filled with rows of huge articulated trucks and with containers stacked two and three high.

Lukman approached one, an old rusting hulk. He felt for a handle in the shadows and wrenched open the locking pins. The door was heavy and swung slowly, its unoiled hinges groaning in protest.

A sharp stink of stale urine flooded out, assaulting Hendra's nostrils. He plucked hastily at his top pocket and placed a carefully laundered handkerchief to his nose. Then he peered into the interior.

SLIDE

In the gloom, barely relieved by a single light bulb dangling on a cable, he could see a man suspended from the ceiling, trussed like a snared rabbit. His hands, tied together, were held in a loop of rope above his head. The same rope then wound tightly around his neck, before following the curve of his spine to his ankles, which had been pulled up slightly behind him in order to buckle his knees, forcing him to teeter on his toes in unremitting pain. There was a cotton bag over his head, and every time he shifted, the rope threatened to strangle him.

Hendra stepped further into the container, the sound of his leather shoes echoing harshly off the metal walls. In the centre were a small rickety desk and two battered canvas-backed chairs. Lounging in one of them was a scruffy Indonesian – his white T-shirt covered with the stains of manual labour. The man stood up and spat a fat red globule of saliva and betel-nut juice onto the floor.

Hendra took the chair that the Indonesian had been sitting on and perched neatly behind the desk. Placing his black case on the desktop, he studied the prisoner carefully. He had taken a great risk coming here. If Rahman managed to get even just a hint of this, it would be Hendra swinging in the ropes, not the prisoner. He felt compelled to finish the job quickly and efficiently, then leave.

Lukman and the Indonesian cut the man down, then dragged him noisily across the floor and dropped him into the chair opposite Hendra. The prisoner sat motionless, head hanging to one side. He smelled of sweat – and fear.

Hendra put away the handkerchief, felt around in his

suit pocket, and popped a small white peppermint into his mouth. He sucked thoughtfully, staring at the captive, studying the raw and bleeding wounds where the rope had cut into his wrists.

'Would you remove the bag, please,' he said at last.

The Indonesian slid the cotton bag off the man's face, revealing a mass of cuts and dark yellow bruises. Hendra examined the prisoner carefully. An old man – Chinese, stocky, round-faced, thinning hair, going bald. His eyes were unaccustomed to the light, and he screwed them up. Hendra pondered what he might know, what answers might be locked up in that old and battered head.

Lukman and the Indonesian watched silently, waiting to see what Hendra would do.

Hendra took off his glasses, and tapped his lips thoughtfully. He found this sort of thing distasteful, preferring to leave it to people like Lukman.

'This must be a very unpleasant experience for you,' he began. His voice was gentle, almost silky.

The man didn't react.

'I expect you'd like to have a wash, somewhere to lie down,' Hendra continued.

He paused. Still no reaction.

'I can arrange all that for you, if you wish.'

Again, Hendra paused. The prisoner remained slumped, head lolling, eyes staring at the floor.

'What is your name?'

The rheumy eyes finally blinked.

Over to one side, Lukman pulled a chair out from the

wall; the sudden hard scraping of steel on steel jarred the silence.

'Somchai Jornpaison.'

The man had spoken in such a low whisper that Hendra missed it. 'I'm sorry?'

'Somchai Jornpaison.' The lips hardly moved.

Hendra looked across at Lukman, but Lukman gave an exaggerated shrug. Hendra turned back to the prisoner.

'Come now, your real name, please,' he said kindly.

'Somchai Jornpaison.' The voice was dry and cracked.

Hendra paused for a moment. This was getting nowhere.

'What organization do you work for?'

No answer.

Hendra repeated the question, more harshly. 'I said: "What organization do you work for?"'

'No one.'

'Do you work for the Chinese?'

'No.'

'But you are Chinese.'

'Yes.'

'Then you work for them.'

'No.'

'But I thought you Chinese always stuck together.'

The man said nothing. Hendra fished in his pocket for another peppermint. He sucked thoughtfully for a while. 'Do you know why we Indonesians hate the Chinese?' He pondered his own question for a moment. 'Because you're parasites. Because you've sucked this country dry for years

– until there's nothing left for us.' The old man stared back at him, eyes blank, face totally devoid of expression. 'And you know what we do with parasites, don't you?' continued Hendra as he sucked steadily at his peppermint. 'We exterminate them.'

The man just sat there like a mannequin, casting his gaze back to the floor. This was becoming irritating. Hendra leaned forward in his chair to get closer to him. 'You realize the only reason I have you in here is because you know something. Something which is very important to me. Tell me what I want to know, and you're free to go – anywhere you want.' He tapped the plastic arms of his glasses against his teeth. 'So, tell me! Tell me what you did with those two computer disks. The ones that were stolen from the *Ibn Battuta*.'

The prisoner continued to stare at the floor. He began to rock steadily in his chair. 'My name is Somchai Jornpaison, I am Chinese; my name is Somchai Jornpaison, I am Chinese . . .'

This wasn't going well. Days in captivity had hardened the man. He wasn't going to talk. Hendra felt the onset of panic. A twinge of fear speared through him. He *needed* the information inside this man, and he needed it now. He was under pressure; he could feel Rahman close behind him, could feel his breath raising the hairs on the back of his neck. He had to connect with this prisoner. He had to make him talk.

Hendra stood up suddenly, knocking his chair back with a clatter. He reached across the table and pulled the prisoner's face tight up against his. The sharp stone on his finger caught at the man's cheek, struck a vivid scarlet line across the dry yellow parchment of his skin. Even then the man didn't react.

Hendra stared into the captive's face and played his first major card.

'Listen, Chinese, we already know who gave you the disks. We just want to know what you did with them. That's simple enough, isn't it?' His voice took on a steely tone. 'If you continue refusing to tell me, I can offer you a simple choice. Either I can ask that man over there to snap the ligaments in your joints one by one, until the pain runs through your body like liquid steel ... or I can have you shot, and immediately terminate your miserable life.' For a moment they stood there, locked together in Hendra's grip. The Chinese man's eyes averted, his gaze cast down to the floor, Hendra's stare boring into his cheek.

Over to one side, the Indonesian guard grinned sadistically, his teeth stained red. Lukman looked on impassively, surveying the scene through hooded eyes.

Hendra let the man slump back into his seat. 'So go on, make the sensible decision. Tell me what you know.'

'My name is Somchai Jornpaison, I am Chinese; my name is ...'

Hendra sat still for another moment. This was hopeless. The whole approach was clumsy, and it wasn't him. It lacked intelligence. It lacked finesse. This man had survived in his own private little hell for days with no light, no food, just hanging there from his hook like a butchered carcass.

Yet still he remained strong and wilful: he wasn't going to break now, not for anybody, not for anything.

Hendra played his second card. 'I've already retrieved the core sample from your courier.' He paused briefly, looking for a reaction. 'We shot him down, at the docks.'

The man stopped his chanting, just for a brief moment. Then he continued.

So! thought Hendra. *You* do *know something.* This was his man, all right, and if he knew the courier found at the docks, he should be known to the *Bakorstanas*.

Hendra reached down for his black case and slipped out a laptop. He plugged it into his mobile phone, switched on, and waited for the system to boot up. As it gave a small electronic beep, he tapped at the keyboard, using his personal code to access the Government National Security Database. The familiar first page came up on the screen. Hendra typed in his password, and selected SEARCH. He began to enter the man's physical details – racial characteristics, estimate of height, facial dimensions and so on. He pressed ENTER.

There was a pause.

Lukman came across and looked over his shoulder. The hour-glass symbol went off, the cursor blinked steadily.

127 entries – far too many.

Lukman jabbed at the screen with his finger. 'Try SPECIAL DISTINGUISHING MARKS.'

Hendra looked up at him. 'We'll need to look him over, see if we can find anything.'

Lukman signalled to the Indonesian. Together they

advanced on the prisoner and, putting their hands under his arms, began to heave him to his feet.

Then the prisoner took them completely by surprise. Pulling his legs up sharply from the floor, he suddenly rolled off his chair. Caught off balance, the Indonesian teetered for a moment, then fell, cracking his head on the edge of the steel table. The prisoner twisted round, and with his hands clasped together, brought them down hard on the Indonesian's neck. The man yelped with pain, and then lay still, blood oozing from the gash on his forehead.

Lukman moved swiftly. He yanked the prisoner to his feet and propelled him at high speed into the side of the container. His head slammed into the wall, the solid *clang* reverberating strongly inside the metal box's interior. Lukman got a grip on the man's neck and hair and began to smash his forehead hard against the wall, again and again. Finally he let go. The prisoner collapsed slowly onto the floor, buckling into a ragged heap. Lukman stood still, breathing hard, air hissing through his nostrils. Then he looked across at Hendra.

Hendra nodded.

Lukman ripped the shirt from the man's back. There, on the right shoulder blade, Hendra noticed something they could use – a faint whitening of the skin, a small triangular scar. He came over and peered at it in the gloom of the dim lighting, then returned to his desk and clicked the relevant boxes in the database. Again he went to SEARCH. This time it narrowed to just two possibilities.

He clicked the first. A colour mugshot and a personal

biography appeared on the screen – the man in the photo was Chinese, all right, but his face was also badly scarred down the right-hand side.

Wrong one.

Hendra drew a tight breath, and clicked the second possibility. This time he received a black and white three-view; a round Chinese face, slightly balding. He clicked BIOGRAPHY.

Dr Lim Siang Tai-Chung: b.1944. Dissident.

He looked across at the ragged heap of the prisoner lying on the floor, and then at Lukman. 'It's him. We've got him.'

Lukman hurried across and studied the screen. He thumbed the tracker pad, pulling the cursor down the scanty details.

1975 – daughter, Nicole. 1978 – son, Jean.

Lukman stooped and pointed at the screen. 'Now that is *very* interesting.'

His point was lost on Hendra. 'What is?'

'Nicole Tai-Chung. That was the girl on the oil rig. You know, the reporter. The one I told you about.'

In Hendra's mind, jigsaw pieces fell rapidly into place. He nodded at the prisoner slumped against the wall. 'You think that's her father?'

'Yes, I do.'

Hendra stared straight ahead for a moment, sniffing at the possible trail like a bloodhound. 'So what happened to her, Hari?'

'We deported her. Sent her back to Singapore.'

'Was she working for someone?'

'An agent, you mean?' Lukman shook his head. 'I doubt it. They probably just used her as a courier.'

Hendra looked across at Lukman. He'd got so close to her on the rig, how had he missed her involvement? If he thought she had the disks, why hadn't he taken them? He searched Lukman's face, saw the shadow again – something the man was concealing. This man was a snake, could never be trusted. Perhaps he had the disks already. Perhaps he'd taken them from the girl. But why do that? What was he up to? Hendra knew that he must move carefully.

'Of course, she might still have the disks,' Lukman continued. 'She's a journalist, she won't pass them on. She'll try and find out what's on them.'

Hendra quit the database and switched off his machine. 'I want those disks back, Hari.'

Lukman nodded. 'Of course.'

'And I want the girl, too. I need to find out what she knows.'

Lukman looked at the old man still slumped on the floor. 'What about him?'

'Him? He's an engineer. Give him back to the *Bakorstanas*, let them put him to work.' Then a thought struck him. 'Wait, if that's her father ... we could use him as bait.' He paused for a moment, thinking a plan through in his mind. 'Why don't we send him out to Arguni, and make sure that she gets to know about it? Then she'll come to us. It'll make it so much easier to get her, so much tidier.'

He picked up the laptop and placed the chair back under the table. He began to walk swiftly towards the container door, but a feeling at the back of his mind persisted – an uneasy feeling that Lukman knew something and wasn't telling. Something about the disks – and about that girl.

The Indonesian got up groggily and moved to open the door for him, blood still oozing from the gash on his head. Hendra turned and fixed Lukman with a commanding stare. 'I want that girl back, Hari. But alive, and with those disks. It should be simple enough, even for you – a small blackmail operation.'

Then, without waiting for Lukman's answer, he stepped outside, letting the door bang shut against the metal frame of the container.

As the slam of the door echoed and drummed around the harsh empty space, Lukman sat down at the rickety desk. Ignoring the Indonesian, he took out a packet of Djarum and thumbed it open. A small flame flared briefly from his gold lighter as he lit a *kretek*. He exhaled slowly, letting the scented smoke drift lazily up towards the bare light bulb, where it curled and twisted in random air currents. He watched the spiralling patterns, and let them work on his mind, taking him back to the rig.

He smiled. He'd struck gold that day.

He'd thought he might have, at the time.

He remembered the single disk he'd found on the

Chink geologist. He'd guessed it must have been one of Hendra's secret disks, and he'd been right. Well, that was his insurance policy now: a wild card to be played in the event of Hendra's greed getting out of control. Or Rahman's ambition spiralling the whole nation into oblivion.

He sucked thoughtfully at the *kretek*, listened to the comforting crackle of the burning cloves. Both men were powerful, and both could take him close to the top. But both, regrettably, were flawed, and so would ultimately fall.

They stood in his way.

Lukman drew again on the *kretek*. He remembered how the girl reporter had watched him, saw again in his mind the hatred that had twisted the features of her lovely face. He remembered her black bag hitting the floor with a bang, the computer sliding out. Of course she had the other disk. He was quite sure of that now. The bitch had hidden it. And he'd missed it. Bad mistake, that. He hated himself for it.

He took another long drag at his cigarette.

She'd never get into it, though. It was locked solid, electronically, for good. But she had been a witness to his guilt: she'd seen him take the other disk. Her awareness had been written all over her face. The bitch was a liability. She'd have to go.

Hate began to curdle the blood in his veins. He dropped the half-finished *kretek* on the floor and ground it out with his foot. Then he picked up the mobile and punched in a number. Waited for a short while.

'Get the team together,' Lukman said quietly. 'We're going to London. We have a little unfinished business.'

Chapter Eleven – second week in February: London

It was a dark wintry evening. Nicole drove the big grey Mitsubishi Shogun slowly up the gently undulating rise towards her home, the heavy beat of the big V6 reverberating along the line of neat suburban houses. Rain lashed at the windscreen, the wipers working hard to keep it clear.

At the top of the rise, Nicole swung the heavy vehicle expertly onto her gravel drive and pulled up in front of the porch. The security light snapped on. Golden threads of rain streaked through its powerful beam. Scraps of vegetation blew in front of the vehicle. Nicole cut the ignition and pushed the door open against the pressure of the wind. She got out. Gusting rain lashed at her body, quickly drenched her, even through her coat. She yanked her silver camera case out of the back and made a dash for the front door.

It was calmer in the porch. She struggled to find the keys in her handbag. She pushed the brass Union into the lock . . .

And froze immediately, her hand motionless.

Instead of standing firm, the door had yielded, swinging back beneath her hand, its draught excluder rubbing gently on the carpet.

The wind eddied around her feet, sending a pile of dead leaves spinning sharply against the porch tiles. Nicole's heart beat strongly. She looked down, saw marks – fresh white scars gouged into the dark-stained wood, where something hard had levered against the doorframe.

Her thought was immediate. *Peter! Is he all right?*

She eased the door open and stepped quietly inside, half expecting a figure to leap at her from the shadows. The wind gusted powerfully again, roaring through the trees. Another scatter of leaves rattled into the house.

She reached for the light switch. A soft click – nothing. She tried again – nothing. She stood still for a moment, trying not to breathe, just listening – only the sound of the storm outside, and the unlatched door banging gently against its frame. She stood at the bottom of the stairs and looked up into the unaccustomed darkness, her heart beating painfully in her chest.

She called out urgently: 'Peter?'

A lump was forming in her throat. Where was he? And where was Marie?

'Peter! Answer me!' A note of desperation in her voice.

Nothing – just the rising sound of the wind.

Nicole began to mount the stairs, then changed her mind and walked swiftly across the carpet to pick up the phone. She pushed three nines – waited. Nothing. She pushed again, more urgently. Still no response.

She crashed the receiver down, suddenly feeling very cold and alone.

Panic threatened.

She scrabbled desperately for her mobile, switched it on with her thumb, punched in the numbers – but even before she'd finished, a high-pitched screech began to pour from the earpiece. She switched off and tried again. The same result.

She looked around. In the quietness of her home, shadows were beginning to close in on her. She turned and, imagining the worst, began to make desperately for the stairs . . .

Hard steel jabbed firmly into the soft flesh beneath her jaw. She opened her mouth to cry out in pain, but a gloved hand clamped across her lips and forced her head back.

A hand that smelled of sweet leather.

She kicked out backwards, as hard as she could. She missed, her heel connecting painfully with a sharp wooden edge. Something tumbled and smashed loudly onto the floor. There was an answering shout from upstairs. *More than one!*

She kicked again, this time to one side, caught her attacker on the shin. He grunted, yanked her head further back, jabbed the pistol in closer. He shouted something to his friend in a foreign tongue. It was a type of Malay she recognized – Indonesian.

Someone else rushed downstairs, feet beating an urgent rhythm on the treads. There was a hurried whispered conference. They'd been disturbed; they hadn't expected her to return so soon.

They dragged Nicole into the living room and flung her face-down on the floor. Her arms and legs were kicked wide apart. She heard the distinctive ratchet sound of a metal slide being pulled back and let go as a pistol was cocked, pushing a round into the chamber.

'Where is the disk, Miss Tai-Chung?' The voice was harsh, heavily accented.

The question took her by surprise, and for a moment it didn't register. *The disk? My God, the disk!* They wanted the disk from the oil rig. She didn't have it. Not here. She'd kept it safe, in another place.

Feet shuffled in the dark.

'The disk, Miss Tai-Chung.' The voice was steady and confident, sounding very much in control.

Nicole's anxiety was all for Peter. 'What have you done with my son?' she demanded, her voice muffled from having her face pressed into the floor. 'Where is he?'

The soft click of the safety catch.

'The disk, Tai-Chung.'

'I don't know what you're talking about.'

A shoe pushed menacingly up against her side. Then another voice, softer this time and more cultured. 'Miss Tai-Chung, we don't have much time. We know you have the disk. Now, please, tell us – where is it?'

Her heart thumped strongly. She knew that voice. She'd heard it before.

'I don't have the disk. I gave it to the police.'

She lied. It was a mistake.

The shoe gave a sudden, vicious kick. Nicole gasped at the sickening pain in her side, drew her legs up involuntarily, and retched. 'Come on, Nicole,' urged the cultured voice. 'You can do better than that.'

Then, above her nausea, another voice. 'Why not kill the fucking bitch? You want her dead, don't you?'

Outside, the storm still gusted violently. Debris scuffed against the window-pane, and Nicole felt a change of air pressure as the front door swung open again, letting in a surge of wind. Then it slammed violently back into place ... followed by a splintering crash as a pane of glass cascaded out of the frame.

There was a sudden loud report, deafening in the small room. A strong whiff of gunsmoke. Nicole's ears sang.

'Now!' said the cultured voice, firmer this time. 'For the last time, the disk.'

She tried to keep calm, knew she mustn't panic. Knew she must stay alive for Peter. Knew they wouldn't kill her, that they needed her.

'What have you done with my son?' she asked again, voice wavering slightly, her limbs shaking.

There was a little laugh. 'Nice boy! Nice manners!'

'What have you done with him?' She managed to speak more loudly this time. 'I want to see my son!'

'He went for a walk – with your fat Filipina. Couldn't keep him here, could we? Not with what we wanted to do. Couldn't let him see us. Fancy you leaving him all alone, with just that fat cow to look after him, nice boy like that.'

Desperation raged inside Nicole. She wanted her son back. Wanted him safe. There was another savage kick to her side. Searing pain lanced through her body. She doubled up in agony, retching emptily onto the carpet.

'Come on, bitch, the disk. Tell us about the disk . . .'

'Or we might just try a little experiment with your boy.'

There was silence as Nicole tried to recover her breath.

'She's not going to talk,' came the same voice. 'Maybe she's passed it on. We'll take her for a little ride, sharpen up her memory.'

From the darkness came a suppressed giggle of anticipation, then she was yanked violently to her feet. An arm locked around her neck, and a gun was prodded painfully into the back of her head. She was propelled into the hall, her mind confused. Where were they going now? What were they doing?

Someone shouted loudly in her ear: 'Your keys! Give us your fucking keys!'

For a moment, Nicole faltered; she didn't understand. What keys? A hand slapped across her face; her cheek stung. Her handbag was shoved in front of her. 'Your fucking car keys – now, get them!'

She groped in the handbag with her free hand. Her hand closed automatically on the keys. She withdrew them. The handbag was dropped to the floor, the keys snatched away. She was pushed through the door, her feet crunching across the broken glass.

Outside, the wind tore at her hair. She yelled out, hoping someone would hear her above the din of the storm, but a gloved hand suddenly clamped down across her mouth.

She was pushed into the back of the Shogun. Keys jangled in the ignition, and the engine roared into life. Her head was forced down hard onto the seat. She felt the vehicle surge backwards, heard gravel spraying up into the wheel arches. They came to a sudden halt, the gear lever was thrown forward, and the Shogun accelerated hard.

Almost immediately there was a sudden yell, and the driver hit the brakes. The vehicle slewed violently . . .

A jolting crash.

Nicole was flung forwards into the footwell. Glass sprayed out onto the bonnet. There was chaos inside the vehicle. Men were shouting outside.

She felt the vehicle reverse. Struggled to get back up into her seat, to see what was happening. The vehicle was accelerating forwards again . . .

She got her head up.

There was a police car blocking her entrance way. In the glare of the headlights she could see it clearly – blue lights strobing, front caved in, one headlight shining up through the rain, glass glinting on the gravel. The doors were open, two patrolmen leaping from their seats.

The big Shogun smashed into the patrol car again. Once more Nicole was flung forwards, her face banging violently on the front seat. Again the driver threw the vehicle into reverse. One of the policemen was hammering at the window now, shouting at him to get out.

The Shogun lurched forward yet again and, with another crash, the battered patrol car was pitched out into the road, giving them space to accelerate into the avenue.

A truncheon smashed the side window; the driver's door was yanked open. The policeman was hanging onto the windscreen with one hand, grabbing at the steering wheel with the other, fumbling for the ignition keys. The driver tried to knock him away. They drove erratically down the street, the policeman scrabbling for the keys, still trying to pull them out. The man in the back seat let go of Nicole and leaned forward to punch him away from the vehicle. The driver slammed on the brakes and the copper lost his grip, fell to the ground and rolled away like a rag doll.

The Shogun accelerated again, rapidly going up through the gears. Another patrol car rounded the corner ahead of them, slewed to a halt across the road, blue lights strobing over darkened houses. Two more policemen leaped out, yellow jackets shining in the headlights. A hand was held up high to stop them.

The Shogun braked hard, its tyres protesting loudly. One of the Indonesians leaned out of the front window, both hands holding a pistol. *Crack! Crack!* A window crazed on the patrol car as the policemen jerked down.

Then, in all the confusion, Nicole suddenly saw her chance.

She realized that, just for a moment, the Shogun was merely coasting. She grabbed at the door handle and half fell out of the vehicle. Hanging by her feet from the seat belt, fingers scrabbling for grip on the wet hardness of the tarmac, she made a bid for freedom. But at the same moment, the driver put his foot down. The tyres spun and started to drag Nicole along the road. Then the heavy vehicle hit the corner of the police car, jolting it sideways, and with the impact, Nicole suddenly found herself rolling free.

The Shogun roared away from her. There was a brief glare of red lights as it braked for the corner of the avenue, then silence.

She lay face-down on the wet tarmac, dazed.

It was suddenly beautifully quiet and peaceful. Nicole turned her head painfully and, in the dim orange of the street lighting, thought she could make out two figures in blue uniform running down the road to where she lay. And as she gathered her wits, a great feeling of despair for her son began to course through her dirty and bruised body.

A doctor in white overalls and and latex gloves patched up the cuts and bruises on Nicole's head and hands. She could feel his delicate touch, caught the distinctive smell of disinfectant on his fingers. As nurses clattered away the stainless steel bowls and antiseptic wipes, there came an urgent bleeping on the doctor's pager and he hurried off, taking his leave with a flurry of kind words.

Outside, a uniformed policeman stood guard.

Nicole sat there quietly; clinging to her mobile phone, waiting for the call, the call that would tell her Peter was safe. *Willing* it to come. The police had been very kind to her. Had promised they would find him. Had told her that they had a trace on her stolen vehicle; that they would do all that they could to get her son back safely.

So she clung on to that – clung on to hope, clung to her phone.

She sat there numb, waiting, willing Peter to be safe.

After a long time, Nicole heard footsteps coming down the corridor. Precise steps, confident, one after the other, marching, getting nearer. Was someone coming to see her with news? About Peter?

The steps stopped outside. Her heart raced.

She became aware of an affected voice in quiet consultation. Then a tall figure appeared in the doorway – dark suit, snow-white wavy hair. He stood there looking in, surveying her with cold grey eyes, his mouth tight and thin-lipped.

'Good evening!' His accent was Oxbridge, well rounded, the delivery clipped. 'Are you Miss Tai-Chung?'

'Yes,' she answered anxiously. 'Where is my son?'

He ignored her. 'My name is Simes,' he said. 'Foreign

Office.' He began to take off his heavy black overcoat, raindrops shining like beads on the shoulders. Drawing up one of the cheap plastic hospital chairs, he arranged his coat neatly over the back and started to sit down.

'Where is my son?' asked Nicole urgently. 'Do you have any news?' Her eyes were pleading, full of hope.

Simes raised his eyebrows. 'Your son?' He seemed to consider the question for a moment. 'Yes, I believe we might know where he is . . .'

'Then where is he?' she demanded. 'I want to see him!'

Simes sat down carefully, slowly crossing one leg over the other. He lifted up a black leather document case and placed it precisely across his knees.

'You'd like to see him?' he mused. His cold grey eyes glinted at her in the harsh hospital lighting. 'Not yet, I'm afraid. Not until we've had our little chat.'

'What do you mean, "not yet"?' she said sharply. 'He's my son! Why not? What's wrong with him?'

Simes stared at her for a moment, bewildered by her little outburst. 'Oh, he's quite safe. You'll see him soon . . .'

'I want to see him *now*!'

'I'm afraid that won't be possible.'

Anger and frustration surged wildly within Nicole. 'Now, look here!' She got up suddenly, felt dizzy, had to grab for her chair. 'You can't keep me from my son.'

Simes sniffed, looked at her sharply, his face a stony mask. 'Miss Tai-Chung, I don't think you quite understand your position. I'm not *asking* you to stay here – I'm *telling* you.'

Nicole ignored him and began to make for the door.

Simes twisted in his seat and clicked his fingers. The duty policeman appeared in the doorway, feet apart, blocking her exit, and quietly folded his arms.

She stopped, stunned by this action. Then she rounded on Simes. 'Who the hell *are* you?'

Simes gave that little sniff again. 'I told you: Foreign Office.'

Nicole's mind worked swiftly. 'Is this about the disk?'

'It might be,' said Simes pedantically.

'If I tell you all that I know, will I be able to see my son soon?'

'Once you've told me, you can do what you like.'

She sat down and met his haughty gaze with an icy stare of her own.

'Good!' he said. 'That's better. Now, we need some information.'

'I'll tell you everything that I know,' she answered quickly.

Simes eased back the brass zip on his document case and shuffled out some papers. 'Tell me, have you ever heard of a man called Somchai?'

Nicole was startled by the question. Her mind swept back to the night on the oil rig, to the matter of who she thought Somchai might be – to her father. She hesitated slightly before replying. 'Yes.'

Simes looked surprised. 'Why did you hesitate?'

'I didn't expect the question . . .'

Simes tapped thoughtfully at his lower lip with a long

and well-manicured finger. 'Interesting! Tell me, when did you first hear his name?'

An image flooded into her mind, of 'Sour-Face' invading her cabin, looking startled in the bright lighting, talking nervously about 'Somchai'. 'A few weeks ago,' she answered.

'Not before that?' demanded Simes sharply.

'It was also the name of my father's manservant – when I was a child. When we lived in Malaysia.'

Simes nodded, as if confirming a suspicion. He produced a slim manila folder and slid out a large glossy black and white photograph. 'And what about this man? Have you ever seen him before?'

Nicole took the photo, and recognized the face straight away as that of Yew-Ming.

A trolley rattled noisily along the corridor outside.

'Yes,' she said, passing it back. 'His name was Zhou Yew-Ming.'

'And where did you last see him?'

'On an oil rig – in the Java Sea.'

'Did he pass something to you?'

Irritation at Simes's increasingly imperious manner began to harden the edge of Nicole's voice. 'Yes.'

Simes fixed her with an icy stare. '*What* did he pass to you?' he asked.

'A computer disk.'

'Do you still have those disks?'

Nicole caught the plural, hesitated. 'No . . . I said *one* disk. Yew-Ming only passed me one disk.'

Simes looked up for a moment, his eyes pale, cold, unblinking. 'Two disks, Nicole. I think he gave you *two* disks.'

'There was only one.'

'But you were asked to courier *two* disks for "Somchai".'

Nicole looked at him aghast, colour reddening her cheeks. 'My God! You know all about this, don't you?'

'Of course!'

Nicole's mind was confused. She was finding it difficult to grasp what Simes was saying. Jigsaw pieces began to fall into place; pieces that she'd first tried to fit together back on the oil rig. 'Look – who exactly is this Somchai?' she suddenly demanded.

Simes's look mocked her. 'Don't you know?'

'My father?'

He looked down sharply at his notes. 'Let's just keep to my questions, shall we.'

Then Somchai *must* be her father! What had he done? What was he muddled up in?

She suddenly remembered the scene in the geologist's office, remembered the disk falling to the ground as they dragged Yew-Ming forward. 'The other disk,' she said, 'the one you've been talking about – Yew-Ming kept it. He didn't pass it to me, he kept it. A soldier took it, the one in charge. I think his name was Lukman.'

Simes nodded encouragingly. 'Then perhaps you have the rock sample?'

Nicole looked blank.

'A core sample,' explained Simes patiently. 'A small

cylinder of rock about six inches long, numbered in red ink. Do you have it?'

'I told you, I was only given a computer disk.'

Simes was watching her carefully now, gauging, measuring. 'Tell me, Nicole, do you know what's on that disk?'

'No, I don't. It's password-protected.'

'We need that disk. It may be very important.'

'You can have it – with great pleasure.'

'Where is it?'

'In a bank safe.'

'Can I have the number?'

'Will I see my son then?'

'Of course.' Simes began to shuffle his stuff back into his document case. He gave her a cautious look. 'Before I collect the details, I think you should know that you may be in considerable danger.'

'I can handle myself!'

'Miss Tai-Chung, I don't think you understand. The men who came looking for you, who tried to take your son; they're *Bakorstanas* – Indonesian Secret Service. They're ruthless. They'll kill to get what they want.'

A chill ran through Nicole's body. 'This hasn't got anything to do with me, Simes. I'm not involved.'

'You *are* involved, Miss Tai-Chung, whether you like it or not.'

'Then I want protection,' Nicole demanded.

'Of course!' Simes paused for a moment. 'But we can't guarantee your safety for ever.' He gazed at her, his face blank of all expression. 'Tell me,' he said, 'have you ever considered working for us? For the interests of the Crown?'

Nicole stared back incredulously. 'I'm sorry ... *what* did you say?'

'Perhaps if you agreed to go back to Indonesia for us, make contact with this "Somchai" – retrieve the missing data. Then it would be a *fait accompli* as far as the *Bakorstanas* were concerned. You would be left alone.' His thin lips quivered as he spoke. 'I thought it might help you.'

'I'm not interested.'

Simes sniffed again. 'Such a pity. You're a very talented person.'

'You don't know me, Simes.'

'Oh, I do,' said Simes with faint amusement. Then he stood up, tucking his briefcase under his arm, and looked down at her. 'You know, you really should consider cooperating with us, Miss Tai-Chung.'

'For God's sake, Simes, I've got a child! Can't you understand that? He's got cancer!'

For a moment Simes faltered. Then he scribbled a number on a card and passed it to her. 'If you have cause to change your mind, do contact me. It's a protected line.'

Nicole stared up at him. Saw the glassy coldness within his eyes.

'Take your disk, Simes,' she said. 'Then go to hell!'

Chapter Twelve – third week in February: Bouches-du-Rhône, France

The big Armée de l'Air base at Istres on the southern end of the Crau Plain lay empty and lifeless beneath a grey blanket of wintry overcast. A cold mistral blew down from the north. It scythed across the open airfield, forcing a small group of mourners to huddle protectively against its unexpected bitterness. Nicole turned up the collar of her thick black coat and held down the black veil that tugged irritatingly across her face. Through its flapping tracery she watched the distant Transall C-160 turn off the runway and commence its long taxi run towards them, lights blazing against the bleak flatness of the aerodrome.

Two cars were drawn up in front of the hangars – both Citroëns, both black. One was a big diplomatic limousine, the other a hearse. The drivers waited by their cars, rubbing their hands against the cruel slice of the wind.

With a steady roar, the big transport plane taxied onto the apron. Slowly it turned round, the propellers sending hot blasts of exhaust-scented air across the group – a welcome warmth in the bitter wind. The engines cut, and the propellers wound down to a stop. Hydraulic pumps whined as the rear loading ramp was lowered to the tarmac.

Nicole felt anxious. Inside the dark fuselage of the plane was the body of her brother, Jean. She'd been told only the day before that he was dead, that they were bringing him home. But she found this fact difficult to accept. She hoped, indeed she believed, that at any moment he would come walking down that ramp, that the officials who had informed her on the telephone had got it all wrong. She would see him walking across the tarmac towards her with that stupid grin all over his face. '*Hi, Nic!*' he would say.

Instead, two men in olive-drab flying suits emerged, carrying a polished chromium frame mounted on large trolley wheels. There was something about the contraption that reminded Nicole instantly of hospitals. 'Oh God!' she thought. 'It's true. It's really him.'

The two crewmen disappeared back inside the plane. Then, slowly, walking in step, four men in combat fatigues came down the ramp, an aluminium coffin supported on their shoulders. They placed it gently on its stand and drew up in a line to one side. They came to attention and waited.

Nicole stood still, unwilling to go forward. The wind flapped encouragingly at her clothes. The black-suited official at her side was very kind. 'I'm afraid you must identify the body, Miss Tai-Chung,' he said in French. 'Take your time. You have as long as you need to prepare yourself.'

'I'm ready,' she answered. 'I'll go now.'

She walked slowly up to the coffin, her slim body stiff

and unwilling, her mind numb and detached. She looked down at her own distorted reflection in the polished frame of the trolley, trying to find some meaning in its twisted image. Last week she had had a brother. Now he was dead.

Gunned down in Jakarta.

Why? He shouldn't even have been there.

Past events crowded in on her – the trauma of the oil rig, the violence of the Indonesian Secret Service, her recent interrogation by Simes. And somehow, weaving it all together, the shadowy figure of her absent father.

And now this – the telephone call from the embassy, the flight down to her mother's chateau in the middle of the night. She felt that she was sliding. She felt clinging threads dragging her down into someone else's world – a world she didn't want to be part of. She had to resume control, get a grip on her life.

A harsh snap interrupted her thoughts. She looked up. One of the soldiers had unlatched the coffin and was gently easing back the lid.

Nicole looked down and stared at Jean's face. It was exactly as she remembered it – yet somehow it wasn't Jean any more. There was no intelligence in the set of his features, no emotion. Just a lifeless mask of wax.

Jean was dead.

The official was at her side again. He spoke gently: 'I'm sorry, Miss Tai-Chung, but I have to ask you, are you able to identify the body? Is this man Jean Tai-Chung?'

Through her quiet grief she heard herself answer. 'Yes, it's him. It's Jean.' But, as she said it, her gaze drifted across the rest of his body and caught sight of the old and badly stained shirt, the ragged pair of shorts. They didn't look right. They weren't the sort of clothes that he would ever wear. Why was he wearing them? Who had dressed him like that? Nicole's mind became full of uncertainty.

As the official led her back to the car the soldiers closed down the lid, then carried the coffin carefully to the back of the hearse. The official said that he would accompany her; after all, it wasn't too far. They would sign the official papers back at the chateau, after she'd had time to recover.

It was warm in the back of the Citroën. Nicole sat in the comfort of the leather upholstery and watched the familiar scenery of the Baux valley speeding past. She'd travelled this way many times as a child. Dense hedges of bamboo swayed drunkenly beside deep irrigation ditches, bent over by the strength of the mistral. Occasionally the wind would catch the Citroën and try to push it across the carriageway.

Nicole brooded about Jean, fretted over those clothes he'd been wearing. Slowly her anxiety grew, until her curiosity became insatiable and she could wait no longer: 'Why was Jean dressed like that?' she asked abruptly.

The official turned to her. 'I'm sorry?' He looked a little startled.

'My brother,' she demanded. 'Why was he wearing those filthy clothes?'

The man looked at Nicole, eyebrows slightly raised. 'Because they're his, maybe?'

Nicole shook her head. 'Jean took great pride in his

appearance. He wouldn't wear anything so filthy, so ragged.'

'He was caught looting, Miss Tai-Chung. He'd got muddled up in some sort of race riot.' He gave Nicole a pitying look. 'I know it's difficult. Death is always difficult.'

Nicole stayed quiet then. She knew that it wasn't at all like Jean. He wouldn't do that. Something was wrong. The last time she'd heard from him he was prospecting for minerals in the mountains of Kalimantan, working for Beijing Global. He shouldn't have been anywhere near Jakarta. What had he been doing there?

Nothing seemed to add up any more.

The little convoy turned off the D5 and began to climb a narrow, twisting mountain road leading into the Alpilles. Stark limestone crags stood out against huge grey banks of rain-washed cloud. It had been an unusually harsh winter. Patches of snow lay on the higher peaks. It began to rain, lashing at the windscreen in great bursts.

Her mother's family chateau lay on the bleak southern slopes of the mountain, squat and sullen on its great promontory of rock. The two black Citroëns swung onto the gravel drive, entering through huge wrought-iron gates. They halted in the paved courtyard, the sound of their engines echoing against massive stone walls. The coffin was taken solemnly through great oak doors and placed in a small ante-room just off the hallway. The interior of the chateau was dark and silent, as if in sympathy with the occasion.

The official accompanied Nicole inside, and they sat

down at a large heavy table surrounded by robust antique chairs. Logs spat and blazed in the huge fireplace. In their flickering light, the man opened his case, spreading the documents before him. He produced a pen and asked Nicole to sign – *here*, and *here*. Nicole took off her gloves and did as instructed. After exchanging pleasantries, he excused himself and was gone.

For a moment, Nicole was left alone with her thoughts.

There was a rattle in the passageway, and a thin, pale woman appeared, pushing herself along in a wheelchair. Her face was drawn down with illness, but her back was ramrod straight. She too was dressed in black.

'Have they gone, Nicole?' she demanded.

'Yes, Mother, they've gone.'

She brought her wheelchair up to the table and studied the documents. 'Damn official papers, look at them all!' She waved her hand dismissively.

Nicole began to tidy the documents nervously. 'They've put Jean into that little room beside the hall. Would you like to see him?'

Her mother snorted. 'Why? When did he ever come to see me?'

Nicole pleaded with her. 'You ought to at least take a look at him, Mother. It's important.'

'No!' She was emphatic. 'Always was your father's boy. Now look what he's done – brought disgrace upon the family, dragged our name into the gutter. A thief! A common little thief – my own son!'

'Oh, come, Mother, you don't really believe all that, do

155

you? Surely you don't think Jean would do a thing like that!'

Her mother sat still for a moment, her jaws working angrily. Then she spun her wheelchair round, presenting her back to Nicole. 'Why not? Your father betrayed his family.'

'How? By running away? Maybe he did the right thing.'

Nicole stopped herself before she went too far. She stared at the fire, watching the small flames flicker and spurt around the charred blocks of timber. Her mother was so unyielding, so unforgiving. Would she now simply shut the memory of Jean out of her life, like she had their father?

'I tried to telephone Father last night – about Jean. I couldn't get through.'

Her mother spun sharply in her chair. 'Oh, why worry about him?' she spat. 'He wouldn't care. He won't even want to know. And when did *you* last see your father, hmm? How many years ago? He abandoned me here, Nicole, don't you ever forget that. Left me on my own, shut up in this great place, trapped in this crippled body. You tell your father . . .'

'Mother!' Nicole gripped one side of the wheelchair. 'Will you listen to me? Please?' She placed her hands softly on her mother's. 'Something's wrong. I don't think you're right about Jean.'

'Aren't I?'

Nicole fiddled with the armrest of her mother's chair. 'Jean's body, it's dressed in somebody else's clothes. I don't understand. Why would anyone do that?'

Her mother took one of Nicole's hands and rubbed it gently. 'Nicole, he was caught stealing, looting. He was shot in a riot. We're lucky even to have his body back. Who knows why he was dressed the way you say he was? Does it matter? He's dead, and that's that. This is a chapter of our family history that's closed – for ever.'

But Nicole didn't want the matter closed. She wanted to voice her suspicions. That her father worked for the British government, that maybe Jean had too. She turned to her mother, but recognized the iron set of her lined face in the red glow of the flames. She sighed, and decided to let it go, knowing that she ought to be content that her mother was simply holding her hand here, before the fire on this bitter wintry day – and that perhaps there never would be anything more.

Nicole spent the rest of the afternoon making the necessary arrangements for her brother's funeral. The priest came round and spent some time with them. Nicole mentioned her concern about the strange clothes; there was talk of a post-mortem. But her mother was adamant. She didn't want any of that; she wanted Jean buried, the whole sad incident forgotten.

Later, when the undertakers came, they handed Jean's clothes to Nicole in a sealed white plastic bag. She dumped them in her bedroom.

After dinner, Nicole felt increasingly restless. She wanted to get back to London. She sat on the edge of her bed and phoned her son, Peter. She missed him badly. She worried in case the stress of the last few weeks had made his illness worse. She worried about his security, wanted to check that someone was with him.

She was so pleased to hear his voice when he answered. He talked excitedly about his official protection, about the nice police lady who was looking after him. For him it was all one big adventure. Nicole told him that she would be back home soon, that there wasn't much else she could do at Grandma's – but not that she felt that she didn't belong at her mother's place any more.

She put the mobile back on the bed and began to gather up her few things, putting them into her case. She would return in a few days' time for the funeral. She picked up the plastic bag containing Jean's clothes and dropped it on the bed. Then, with idle curiosity, she pulled open the seal and began to take the garments out one by one. The state of them worried her. It was something that wouldn't go away. She pulled out his underclothes and laid them out next to his badly stained ragged shorts.

They didn't match. The underclothes were of a decent quality, brand-name items; but the shorts – they were definitely not his.

She pulled out the shirt and held it up by its arms, examining the stains and the rips. She sighed, and let it drop.

Surprisingly, it hit the floor with a sharp crack and something rattled out of sight across the floorboards.

Nicole looked down, trying to spot whatever it was. She

got up from the bed, and groped around in the darkness beneath bits of furniture. At last, underneath a bookcase, her hand closed on something small. She retrieved the object carefully and examined it under the bedside light.

It was a fragment of rock. As she rotated it in the light the chipped ends sparkled with little flecks of gold. There was part of a number on one edge, hand-drawn in red ink. She thumbed away the dirt. Some sort of code? Part of an old core sample, perhaps? Something Jean had drilled in Kalimantan?

A memory crept forwards in her mind. Something that Simes had said the night the Indonesians had raided her home. A core sample. *Had she been passed a core sample, coded in red ink?* Could this be it?

For a moment her feelings were confused. It no longer surprised her that Jean might be mixed up in this mess, but she desperately wanted to protect him, to allow him to be buried in peace – not branded as a thief or a looter. Perhaps this strange object might clear his name, make his memory more precious to their mother.

Nicole thought for a moment, turning the rock fragment over and over in her hand.

Then she reached for her mobile and thumbed the miniature keyboard, searching the directory for a telephone number.

And soon, six hundred miles away in a darkened office in London, the phone on Simes's desk began to ring.

Chapter Thirteen – early May:
London

Malcolm Simes strode purposefully along the Victoria Embankment, his shoes squeaking on the dry Saharan grit that dusted the pavement. He halted at the RAF Memorial, standing expectantly at the roadside – a tall, prim figure in his expensively tailored city coat.

He glanced at his watch. He was a little early, and he found that irritating. It was important to have a well-organized life, to be absolutely punctual, neither too late nor too early. Time should not be wasted.

Simes idly watched the passing traffic.

It was hot, too hot for late spring. The sun felt strong as it beat down out of a cloudless azure sky, and he felt uncomfortable in his heavy coat. The weather seemed all wrong these days. He'd been to the Barbican the evening before, and the opening theme of Rachmaninov's Second Piano Concerto still played steadily in his head – a passionate and sombre melody. The music took him back to the Cotswolds of his childhood, to a more gentle climate and the tantalizing smell of rain on hot tarmac after a summer storm.

A dark green Jaguar limousine slid to a halt beside him. Simes noted with disapproval the road-stained flanks of the car, and looked hard at the grey-uniformed chauffeur, trying to catch his eye reproachfully. A second car slid in behind the first – halting a little too fast, its bonnet bouncing down on the front suspension, the tyres squealing on the tarmac as they momentarily locked. Simes ignored the fuss and let himself down into the back seat of the leading car.

'Good morning, Malcolm. Another hot day.'

'Good morning, Prime Minister,' replied Simes. 'Yes, indeed it is.'

As the car accelerated powerfully away from the kerb, Simes fastened his seat belt and settled back. The interior of the car was cool and satisfyingly British – beige upholstery, leather, a touch of dark polished walnut. The chrome and black of an elaborate communications console sat discreetly between them. The Prime Minister laid aside the papers he'd been working on and folded away his glasses. 'Now, Malcolm, I hope this won't take too long. I have to speak to the House within the hour.'

'No, Prime Minister, I wouldn't drag you away from your desk unless I thought it strictly necessary.' Simes unzipped his leather document case and pulled out a sheet of paper. 'But I thought you should see this.'

The PM put on his glasses and scanned the document for a minute. 'Where did you get this?' he enquired.

'From our man in Indonesia,' pronounced Simes in his rather affected voice. 'Came out via a courier. It's the analysis of a computer disk.'

'Yes, I can see that,' said the Prime Minister. He pursed his lips thoughtfully as he read. 'So you think this is why the Indonesians closed off their territorial waters back in January?'

'I think it might be.'

The Prime Minister passed the document impatiently back to Simes. 'So, they've discovered metal deposits at the bottom of the Philippine Sea. Is that all?'

'With respect, Prime Minister, don't you think—'

'Malcolm, people have known about deep-ocean metal deposits for years!'

'Yes, but there's more, Prime Minister. We've recovered one of their core samples. I sent it to Southampton for analysis, to their Department of Oceanography. They got very excited about it. It seems that the Indonesians have stumbled upon a rather unusual deposit.' Simes was now looking a little smug.

The PM looked across at him: 'Well! Go on!'

'Uranium,' announced Simes triumphantly.

'Uranium?'

'Yes!' Simes was looking very pleased with himself. 'Because of metal-fixing bacteria – in the hydrothermal vents. And, what's more, it's not the usual 238, either. This stuff's rich in 235.'

The PM peered at Simes over the top of his glasses. 'I don't follow you.'

'Bombs, Prime Minister,' explained Simes darkly. 'Uranium 235 is used for making atomic bombs.'

The Prime Minister's jaw dropped. 'Oh!'

'Yes,' Simes was warming to his theme, 'and I'm afraid it gets worse.'

'Good God, you think they've built a bomb?'

'No, they've probably still got a long way to go – but we think they might be using cobalt.'

'Cobalt?'

'As part of the bomb-making project.'

The Prime Minister looked blank.

'Cobalt bombs, sir. It was William Baker, my number two, who made the connection. He remembered reading about work done by the Americans back in the 1960s, at the height of the Cold War. You wrap a cobalt jacket around an atomic bomb and when the bomb goes off the cobalt turns into a powerful emitter of gamma radiation. It's a real killer, a very dirty bomb.'

There was a pause as the PM took in Simes's momentous news. '*Reductio ad absurdum*,' he muttered.

Simes recognized the implications of the Latin instantly. 'A doomsday machine, Prime Minister? Well, maybe, but I don't think that's on their minds—'

The Prime Minister suddenly snorted. 'Oh come on, Malcolm, you're pulling my leg. This whole idea's preposterous! Surely the Indonesians don't yet possess the technology to make such a thing.'

Simes looked a little shocked. 'I assure you, Prime Minister, I am being *very* serious.'

'But to make such a bomb, it's so difficult.'

'On the contrary, it's far too easy. It's not bomb-making that's the problem; it's getting hold of the uranium. And when you get it, you have to refine it – by centrifuging out the heavy 238 isotope. It's painstaking work, can take years.' He leaned towards the Prime Minister. 'But in this case it's very different. Not only have the Indonesians got their own supply of uranium, it also requires far less centrifuging – because it seems to have been naturally enriched.' Simes sat back, a look of self-satisfaction on his pampered face. 'They're on a fast track.'

'Why didn't I know about this before?' demanded the Prime Minister.

'With respect, sir, I'm telling you now.'

'Do the Americans know?'

'The CIA? Oh, I doubt it,' scoffed Simes. 'They didn't even know that India and Pakistan had the bomb back in '99. Too much technology and not enough people on the ground. Most ineffective!' Simes sounded very disapproving.

'But this stuff – your uranium – it's at the bottom of an ocean. Who the hell's going to pay to get it all up? And why would they want to make such a ghastly thing in any case?'

'To win a war, I should think, Prime Minister.'

'Oh come off it, Malcolm! Not even the Indonesians would be stupid enough to plan on actually using it.'

'With respect, sir, they don't have to use it. The power of the atom bomb lies in its possession, not in its use.'

The PM stared out of the window, watching the London

traffic as it snarled up in front of some traffic lights. He turned back to Simes. 'Is there a weapons-building programme?'

Simes looked a little uncomfortable. 'I'm afraid we don't know, sir. But I think the data speaks for itself . . .'

'You mean you know he's digging out uranium, but you don't actually know whether he's building a bomb?'

'Well, strictly speaking that's correct, but—'

'I'm sorry, Malcolm, I can't go any further with this. Look, at the end of the day, Rahman's just another tinpot Asian dictator.'

'With respect, sir, you shouldn't dismiss him like that. There's a lot of technology in Indonesia – more than enough for a weapon of this sort. It's potentially very dangerous. We must protect our interests in the region. He must be stopped.'

'No, I'm sorry, Malcolm, I don't buy it. It's too far-fetched.'

'Perhaps the Americans ought to know . . .'

'No! . . . Look, Malcolm, I'm not going to scare the pants off the Americans with some cock and bull story about doomsday weapons in Indonesia. It's all *maybe*. There's no fact. For Christ's sake, it's the bloody election in just a few weeks! Imagine what a field day the press would have if this leaked out. You'll need more evidence than just a hunch to get things moving, Malcolm – much more evidence.'

*

William Baker was waiting for Simes as he came in through the doors of his club. For Simes, his club represented a bastion against the advancing proletarianization of life, a place where standards still existed, where he could feel secure.

Baker looked up as Simes approached the table he'd reserved for lunch. 'Well, did he go for it?' he asked.

Simes sat down, the waiter helping him to push his chair nearer to the table.

'No, his mind's full of the damned election,' muttered Simes. 'I don't think our friend in the Muslim Brotherhood bothers him a bit.'

'But Rahman's ruthless; he's capable of anything. Didn't the PM grasp that?'

'I'm afraid not. To the PM, Rahman's just another fanatic. He doesn't understand the potential of the situation, and he certainly doesn't want to panic the Americans. Not with an election around the corner. Indonesia's a hell of a long way from his mind right now.'

'So he's simply stuck his head in the sand.'

'Bill, he's stuck his head in so far his bloody arsehole's showing.'

Simes poured his grinning colleague a drink from the bottle of chilled Californian Sauvignon. 'You know, a thought did occur to me,' he said. 'It might not be Rahman behind this at all. It could actually be Hendra, his technology minister. I know someone who went to Cambridge with young Jazid Hendra. Bet you didn't know we educated the bugger. They classed him as a bit of a weirdo even in those days. Read a lot, very Muslim, didn't drink, no sex – you know the sort of thing.'

'You think Hendra might be pushing Rahman?'

'Maybe.'

'And you think they're going to build this bomb?'

'Why not? For some reason Rahman can't stand the Chinese.'

'Have they got what it takes?'

'Aldermaston think so. Within about three years, what's more – given their naturally enriched uranium ore, and assuming they've got the centrifuge array to purify it up and running.'

'But where's all the bloody technology coming from?'

'Russia, I expect. Hendra's probably got Muslim connections all though the Islamic states on the southern borders of the Federation. The Russian Ministry of Atomic Energy has been leaking like a sieve for years.'

Bill raised his eyebrows and whistled. 'That bastard's developing the potential to destabilize the whole region. If we leave it too long, the consequences of anyone having a go at him in the future become unthinkable. Why doesn't the Atomic Energy Authority investigate?'

'Got no reason to. He's not buying uranium from anybody, and there's no evidence that he's trying to purchase equipment. They need a good excuse to go in with an inspection team, and they haven't got one. It's a nonstarter.'

'So where do we go from here?'

Simes sighed. 'We need more information, Bill, much

more. Unfortunately we've lost Somchai. Either he's gone to ground, or he's been carted off to some gulag – or he's dead. And we've lost his boy, too – got himself shot down in Jakarta. Whole bloody network's falling apart.'

'Do the Indonesians know about our interest?'

'I don't think so. They blamed their security breach on Chinese dissidents.'

Their meal arrived, formally served. Simes squeezed a little fresh lemon onto his salmon and spread little rolls of butter carefully over his new Jersey potatoes. He looked across at Baker. 'I've been thinking about the Tai-Chung girl.'

'Yes, she's really got herself caught up in all of this, hasn't she?'

'Very much so, poor thing. Did you know the old boy used her as his courier?'

'No! So much for family. I heard the *Bakorstanas* have since paid her a visit.'

'They certainly did. Handled herself well, by all accounts – quite a toughie.' Simes pushed his fork into a well-buttered potato. 'They were looking for some of their missing stuff. We're keeping a very close eye on things at the moment – very discreetly, of course.'

'Does she know who "Somchai" is?'

'She's a bright girl. She has her suspicions.'

Baker sliced some of his salmon away from the bone. 'Would she agree to work for us?'

'I've been thinking about that. I had a look at her file. She would be very good, you know.' Simes savoured some of his salmon. 'Rather nice!' He chewed appreciatively. 'Did you know she was once a submersible pilot?'

Baker looked up, surprised. 'Really?'

'Trained at Southampton when she was studying ocean-ography for her degree. Even did some work around deep-ocean hydrothermal vents in the Atlantic.'

'Good God, she's tailor-made for the job! We could get her right inside Rahman's little mining operation.'

'And she speaks Malay of course. Family used to live out there before they split up.'

'She's ideal, then. Would she be interested?'

'There's a catch: family ties – got a boy. Suffers from cancer of the pancreas.'

'Oh!'

Baker placed his cutlery carefully to one side of his plate and dabbed at his mouth with a stiff white napkin. He put the crisp cloth unfolded back onto the table.

'Terminal?' he asked.

'Probably.'

'Could be a lever, though,' added Baker, 'if we picked the right moment.'

'I agree. And "Somchai" would be, too – if he's still alive. Blood runs thicker than water, and all that.'

'Yes, I'm sure you're right,' Baker mused. 'Shouldn't be too difficult to come up with something to convince her.'

Simes sipped his Sauvignon, savouring it for a moment.

'I could have another word with her, to try and get things moving. Start upping the pressure a bit . . .' His eyes focused brightly on Baker. 'You know, if you think about it, she really *has* got to work for us. It's the only way we'll ever get to know what's really going on out there.'

'Do you think you could manage to persuade her?'

Simes studied the colour of his raised glass carefully against the light.

'Bill, in a situation like this, I'm prepared to be an absolute bastard.'

Chapter Fourteen – early June:
Woburn, Bedfordshire

The little falcon came in fast on its long scythe-like wings, a feathered bullet sweeping low over the heads of the audience. Nicole ducked as it shot by within inches of her head, leaving just a hint of disturbed air in its wake. It plunged dramatically into the arena. The audience gasped. The falcon racked round in a steep turn, its wing-tip zipping audibly through blades of grass as it swept in to attack the lure swinging in long lazy arcs from the falconer's hand. Claws extended forward, the falcon made a swipe at the lump of fresh meat, its curved beak stabbing down at the feather-wrapped flesh. But the falconer jerked the lure away, forcing the bird to break off. With short, rapid beats of its long narrow wings it climbed away behind the audience.

'Good morning, ladies and gentlemen – and welcome to Joey.' The commentator's voice boomed around the arena. 'Joey is a hobby, a bird of prey found across large parts of Europe and Asia. Until recently there were very few . . .'

Nicole looked down at Peter sitting beside her as the magnified voice of the commentator swirled around them. She noticed how he sat hunched forward to watch the show, alert and intelligent. He must have sensed her gaze, and looked up, smiling, swinging his legs gently above the staging.

A deep cut sliced across Nicole's heart. Peter needed her now more than ever. To Nicole he was the bravest boy alive, and she was so proud of him. He'd come through his latest major surgery with few complications, just some mild jaundice – but deep inside his body there still lurked a tiny twisted knot of malignant cells, lodged in the lining of a pancreatic duct.

It was a knot that so far they hadn't dared to touch.

It was a time bomb.

Nicole's instincts had never been more fully alive. She was here to protect his young life – her life, her dead lover's reincarnation. She was here to see Peter through the dangerous times ahead. That was what really mattered.

Only that.

She gave Peter's hand a squeeze. 'It's time for lunch. I'll go back to the car and sort out the picnic. I won't be long.'

Peter grinned and nodded.

She stepped down off the staging and slipped out of the arena, the booming voice of the commentator following her into the nearby field where the cars were parked. She could see the big wine-coloured flanks of her new Shogun rising high above the others.

The bodywork felt hot in the sunshine as she opened

the rear door. A draught of hot air wafted out, bringing with it that new-car smell of hot plastic and fresh carpet. Nicole took out a large blue cooler box, and shifted a heavy sports bag onto her shoulder. Then she slammed the door shut and plipped on the central locking. She set off between the cars, searching out the picnic table they'd selected earlier.

Adjusting her load, she looked up. A man was standing at the end of the row of cars. A tall man, Asian, athletic, clothed in a grey T-shirt and black tracksuit bottoms. His head was closely shaved, and a gold ring dangled from his right ear. Arms folded, he was watching intently as she approached.

'Miss Tai-Chung?'

Nicole faltered.

Oh God, no! Not the Bakorstanas. *Not again.*

She felt trapped between the rows of cars. Looked around. Where was her protection? They were supposed to be here. Supposed to be looking after them both.

She stood there, cooler box in one hand, the other holding the strap of the sports bag. She kept her voice low, carefully in check: 'Get out of my way. Leave me alone.'

'We would like to speak with you.' The man looked menacing, the sun behind his back silhouetting the folded muscle on his arms.

Nicole turned abruptly and began to walk back the way she'd come. She could shout, she could scream, she knew she'd be safe – there were too many people around for him to do anything to her.

'Wait!' His deep resonant voice rang out.

She kept walking, forcing herself not to break into a run. 'Go away, leave me alone!' She felt in her pocket for her mobile.

'Tai-Chung. Stop, please!' The commanding voice ricocheted along the corridor of cars. 'I'm not here to harm you. We have news of your father.'

Nicole halted in her tracks. For a moment she stood there, disbelieving. She turned back towards him. 'What did you say?'

'I said we have news of your father.'

Nicole's heart thumped in her chest. Thoughts raced through her mind. Just who was this? What did he know?

'You must speak with us. Please, give me your bags.' He put his hand out.

Still Nicole hesitated. 'Who *are* you?'

'My name is Gomez. We have a mutual friend, a Mr Simes.'

Simes! My God, he was hounding her, even out here. Suddenly she felt angry. Angry at being stalked like this. She wanted to be free of the past. She wanted to finish this nonsense, end it once and for all.

She stepped quickly back along the row of parked cars.

Gomez led her to a big grey BMW parked discreetly amongst the other vehicles. Its engine was ticking over quietly, the air-conditioning humming. He politely opened the passenger door for her.

Simes was sitting inside. He put down his newspaper. 'Good morning, Nicole. How nice to see you again.'

'My son's on his own!' she answered.

'Not any longer,' Simes assured her. 'He's in good hands. I won't keep you long.'

Nicole hesitated, before slipping into the back of the car. Gomez shut the door from the outside, then moved forward to guard it from the front. It was pleasantly cool inside.

'I'll listen to what you have to say about my father – nothing more.'

Simes slipped a manila envelope out of his case and extracted a scruffy tabloid newspaper. He passed it to Nicole. 'This is a copy of *Bu Shi*,' he said in his polished voice, 'one of the Chinese underground papers currently peddled in Jakarta.'

Nicole took the newspaper. It felt cheap and rough between her fingers. Among the Chinese characters printed untidily across the front page was a large grainy photograph. It showed a line of people queuing to get into the back of a lorry; they looked ragged and dejected. She read the caption: 'The final destination for many of our race – Rahman's concentration camp on the remote island of Arguni.'

Nicole passed the paper back to Simes. 'I know what's going on in Indonesia, Simes. I read the newspapers and watch the TV like everybody else.'

He looked Nicole straight in the eye. 'Your father's there, in the photograph, Nicole.'

A pang of emotion stabbed at her – a sharp arrowhead of guilt.

She snatched the paper back and studied the line of figures. 'How do you know? How can you be so sure?'

'Because we've had the photograph enhanced.' He slipped a glossy black and white photograph out of the manila envelope and handed it to her. His finger tapped the image. 'Look at that man – the one in the middle.'

Nicole peered at the photograph. Simes had indicated a short man dressed in a ragged vest and baggy shorts. His body was thin and emaciated, the bones of his joints protruding through his skin. The muscles of his arms had wasted to thin little strips, and loose skin was hanging down like empty flaps. He was completely bald, his eyes hollow.

'Is that really my father?'

Simes nodded.

'Are you sure?'

'We're sure.'

She peered intently at the image again. Now she could see a likeness in the structure of his face. She was instantly shocked; this wasn't the man she remembered! What had happened to him?

'Where is this place?' she demanded.

'Arguni's an island off the northern coast of Papua. It's an Indonesian labour camp.'

Nicole fiddled with the photograph. 'Why have they got him there?'

'We don't know. He's there with over a thousand others; some are scientists and engineers, they're all male, and all of them are Chinese. Officially, the place is a copper mine, but a copper mine doesn't need such a large number of technocrats. We think it's a cover for some sort of engineering project.'

'Making what?'

'We don't know.'

Nicole stared at the photograph, numbed by the mindless horror of it all. 'Slave labour?'

'Almost certainly.'

'If that's my father, I have to get him out. I can't leave him in such a place.'

'Arguni is very remote, Nicole. The nearest major airport is at Jayapura, two hundred miles to the east. The roads are virtually non-existent. Miles of mangrove swamp and thick jungle cover everything. You could die out there on your own. The only way onto the island is by company ferry, or helicopter.'

'Then that's something I'll have to risk.'

Simes laughed cynically. 'The place is sealed off by Rahman's troops: red berets – *Kopassus* – the very best. In any case, if the malarial mosquitoes don't get you first, the local tribes probably will. You wouldn't stand a chance. They're still virtually in the Stone Age – some of them are headhunters!'

'So why are you telling me this? What's the point, if you don't think I can get him out?'

A man with a little boy strode past the car. The child hung back on his father's arm, staring at Simes. Then he stuck his tongue out. Simes ignored him.

'Are you prepared to listen to what I have to say, Nicole?'

She bit at her lower lip, still studying the photograph with its ghastly evidence. She didn't answer.

'We want to strike a deal with you. We'll help you get onto the island. In return, you must find out what's going on there. Do this for us, and we'll use all our resources to get your father safely back home.' Then he added quietly, 'After all, he is one of us.'

Nicole put down the photograph. 'What did you say?'

Simes's cold eyes stared straight back at her. 'Oh, come on, you must have realized! He's a sleeper. Has been for years. A very loyal one.'

Nicole felt numb. So she'd guessed right. Her father, 'Somchai', was working for the British. Why hadn't he ever said anything? Why hadn't she known?

'Is it a deal, Nicole?'

'No! Look, why me, Simes? Why send *me*, when he got me into this mess in the first place? I don't owe him anything. If he's one of your agents, then he's *your* responsibility. Send out one of your own people!'

'Because you're uniquely suited to this job, Nicole. You speak fluent Malay and Mandarin. You're a very intelligent and resourceful young woman.'

'Don't bother to flatter me! Those qualifications are hardly unique!' she scoffed.

Simes cleared his throat. 'You're right, of course. There is something else. You're ideal for the job in another way. Let's just say that you have . . . well, let's call it a significant additional qualification.'

Nicole turned to Simes, a look of disgust shaping her face. 'What qualification? Tell me!'

'I'm afraid I can't.'

'Then forget it!' She made a move for the door. 'You're trying to blackmail me. Get someone else to do your dirty work; it's what they're paid for.'

'You're condemning your father to a horrible death, Nicole. You can't get him out on your own.'

'Don't blackmail me, Simes. Like I said, he's *your* responsibility.'

Nicole reached for the door handle. She was finding the whole thing ridiculous, quite preposterous. Her father had abandoned his family, got her into this mess. She didn't owe him anything. They couldn't use her in this way.

'Look, Simes, right now my son's dying of cancer, so you know where my loyalties lie. I don't think you're asking the right person, do you?' She swung her legs out of the car. 'Don't bother to find me again!'

'We know about your son,' Simes called after her. 'We can organize a cure for him.'

Nicole paused. Then she turned. 'How?'

'We could send him out to California, to Dr Natasha Yuvchenko at the Pescadero Cancer Institute. They've made enormous advances in cancer treatment there recently, something to do with genetic fingerprinting. It might be his only chance.'

Nicole faltered. A chance that Peter might live? 'I'll take him out there myself,' she replied quickly. 'I can afford to.'

'Money won't buy you access to Yuvchenko, Nicole. There's a very long waiting list . . . and you're running out of time.'

The bastard!

She knew well enough that Peter might die soon. Knew, too, that without him she would be alone in the world. She had to do the best for her son; she owed it to him. It was his only chance.

She narrowed her eyes. 'Why should I trust you, Simes?'

'Because you have no choice.'

Nicole stared across the rows of parked cars. He was right, damn him, there was no choice. But to leave her son like this, to go off on an assignment that was so dangerous, it was asking too much.

'I'll think it over,' she said, and slammed the door shut. She snatched her belongings from Gomez and made her way back to the showground.

As she stalked away, she knew that Simes had played his game well. How could she turn down the chance that he was offering her, the chance to see Peter grow up into a fine young man? If her father was left alone in the labour camp, he too would surely die. She couldn't refuse. Could never live with the guilt if she failed them now. She clenched her fists in desperation, knowing that she'd been trapped.

Sitting down at a wooden picnic table Nicole watched little pedalos splashing their way around a boating lake, the sun glinting off their miniature wakes, a gentle breeze carrying the light sound of children's laughter. If she did this thing, she would have to leave Peter behind. She'd done it before, of course, but never for so long – and never for anything so dangerous.

Someone came up behind her, feet brushing gently through the grass. She guessed it was Simes. The table rocked slightly as he sat down, blocking her view of the lake. He retrieved his wallet from the inside pocket of his suit and pulled out a creased black and white photograph, its chemicals browning with age. He placed it carefully on the table between them.

'You're not the first, Nicole,' he said. His voice was kind – he seemed to have mellowed.

'What do you mean?'

'This is Yvonne – or rather, that was her code name. She was a mother, too; two girls and a boy. In 1941 she volunteered to work for the SOE – Special Operations Executive – against the Nazis. They dropped her into occupied France. She organized a resistance group during the preparations for D-Day.'

'What happened to her?'

'The SS captured her in 1944. She was tortured – and executed.'

'What happened to the children?'

'The two girls were killed in a V2 attack, towards the end of the war.'

A slight breeze ruffled Nicole's hair. 'And the boy?'

Simes looked at her, and said nothing.

Realization dawned. 'Oh, my God! I'm sorry.'

Nicole took the passport-sized photo. Saw a full-faced

young woman with smooth skin looking back at her – heavy features, a shock of dark permed hair. The woman was dressed in a military uniform.

'You see, sometimes it's necessary to look beyond the immediate, beyond yourself: to make a huge sacrifice for the common good, for your family, maybe for your country. It's a kind of . . . maturity.'

Perhaps he was right. Maybe she was being selfish, indulging in all this heartache.

Simes retrieved the photograph and slipped it carefully back inside the folds of his wallet. 'Peter's father – I believe he died when you were both on assignment. In Iraq?'

Memories flooded back. 'We both worked for the same magazine, covering a story about the Marsh Arabs after the Gulf War. The Iraqis were putting poison in the canals. People were dying by the thousand.'

'Did the poison kill him?'

'They drank the water. They had to. You couldn't see the poison. A huge growth developed on his head. It came up in days, like a big purple blister. He wasn't the only one; they all got it, especially the children. We couldn't get help to him in time. We were being herded by the helicopter gunships, kept on the move.'

The screams of children playing on the boating lake drifted back to them in the breeze.

'Why weren't you affected?'

'I was – I got out, just in time.'

'And chemicals often cause genetic damage?'

Nicole looked up at him, guilt written across her face. 'Why do you think Peter is like he is?'

Suddenly she knew – with utter certainty. Knew that she had to do this ghastly thing. That this was the miracle she'd been waiting for. But it had come with a price attached.

'I think you'll find that Rahman's just as evil, Nicole,' Simes said gently. 'A similar breed. A man from a lowly background, climbing fast, hungry for power. A bully.'

'His treatment of the Indonesian Chinese shows that,' she said flatly.

'And this is probably just the start. We think he's trying to provoke a war, force his way to becoming *the* major power in the Far East.'

Nicole gazed at all the happy people around her, the smiling faces, the parked cars, the children splashing in the lake. None of it seemed real now.

'That disk you gave us, it told us something. We know he's developing a nuclear weapon. He didn't think twice about pushing the Chinese out of the Java Sea, and they didn't retaliate. Maybe they already know something.'

Simes paused for a moment, then continued. 'Rahman's strong, Nicole. Strong, and immature. We need to know what he's planning. We need to know what's going on at Arguni.'

'And you want me to be part of that?'

'I think you're already a part of it, don't you?'

Simes put the wallet back carefully into his inside

pocket, then drew out a letter. He placed it on the table between them, his fingers holding it down against the stiff breeze. She looked, and her eyes caught sight of a blue-winged airmail logo, a pair of American stamps with 'San Francisco' on the franking. The letter was addressed to her.

She took it uncertainly, then pushed her thumb under the flap, tearing at the flimsy paper.

There was a quiet moment as she read.

'It's the only place with the right sort of expertise,' Simes urged. 'It could save Peter's life.'

She placed the letter on the table where it fluttered in the breeze, threatening to blow away.

Simes put his hand down again to hold it. 'Well?' he asked quietly.

Nicole held his gaze. There was no backing out now. This was Peter's chance, and she had to seize it.

'What would I have to do?'

'Go out to Arguni, find your father – and report back on what's happening there. You're the best person we know for this. You can handle a submersible, and that means you can get right into the heart of the Indonesian operation without arousing suspicion. You would be trained, of course, and you would have another agent to protect you.'

'When would I need to start?'

Simes looked at her for a moment, his cold eyes betraying no emotion.

'Soon,' he said quietly.

Nicole faltered. 'How soon?'

'In a few days – enough time to give you a chance to settle Peter into California.'

Only a few days! But she had so much to say to him. 'I must see him,' she said urgently, 'on my own, before I go. I want to be with him. I have to talk to him, explain all this to him. It's going to be difficult.'

Simes nodded. 'Of course.'

She looked past Simes and let her eyes travel the expanse of the boating lake. She watched as it seemed to expand into a huge ocean, a great expanse of water that had the power to separate lives.

Lives that, until now, had been closely intertwined.

Part Two: AND TIGER'S ROAR

CNN News Broadcast:
from our Asia Correspondent

15 November

'We are coming like thunder. We will set up an Islamic union, build a powerful nation. The West is dying, the stink of decay hangs on every street corner. And the Chinese dragon? Why, he's slunk back into his lair to lick his oily pride. We are becoming a powerful people again. We have the power of Islam behind us. We are a force to be reckoned with . . .'

That was President Amir Rahman of Indonesia, speaking last night at a huge political rally in the city of Yogyakarta. Empty rhetoric? Well, as with most dictators, a set of over-inflated half-truths might be a more accurate description.

The reality is that, since Rahman came to power, over a million Indonesian Chinese are thought to have disappeared. Many have probably been sent to concentration camps, and there are suggestions that some are being used as forced labour – but where, and to build exactly what, have never been disclosed.

Yet whilst Rahman's record on human rights is open to question, his ability to develop and exploit new technology and astound the rest of the world is not. First there was his rapid exploitation of the ocean floor, using imported Russian high technology. Now sources in Jakarta have leaked the fact that Rahman is building a new type of automobile at a secret location far to the east, one that they claim will be technically advanced and totally non-polluting. There is certainly a huge market for such a vehicle. It would satisfy both the demands of the environmental lobby and the desires of the performance-directed motorist at a single stroke. And as the world slides inevitably towards climatic chaos, anything that can drastically reduce pollution and yet maintain people's comfortable lifestyles is going to be an immediate winner – and a turning point for this fledgling Asian economy.

Chapter Fifteen – November: Camp Victoria, Belize

Once Peter had been safely placed at his Californian clinic, Simes flew Nicole out to Camp Victoria, a spy school run jointly by the CIA and MI6 – remote, camouflaged, well hidden among the damp, craggy, rainforest-clad mountains of Belize.

Here she was drawn slowly into a new world: a dark world of espionage and arduous training.

There were other people, of course. She saw them when their paths crossed, mostly British or American. But they were kept well apart and rarely had a chance to speak to each other.

She felt isolated. Longed to be back with Peter, to feel his touch, to hear his laughter.

The discipline in the camp was strict, almost military. They organized an intense fitness programme, punctuated with lessons in tradecraft. Nicole had to sit in darkened rooms to focus her attention, was lectured to by experts, or found herself huddled one-to-one over the latest espionage equipment.

And so it went on, day after day, week after week. Survival skills, weapons training, communications, unarmed combat, psychology.

And all the while a picture filled her mind, an image of a boy smiling gently, legs swinging above wooden staging. It was a picture that haunted her. It was also a picture that drove her on.

She received his letters, of course, in bundles sent on from London. She wrote back almost every day. But she couldn't tell him where she was, or what she was doing – could only talk about their memories. Sometimes she received postcards too. They were beautiful pictures, which she pinned up above her bed. Pictures of the sea breaking on a rugged Californian coastline, of dark forests of giant redwoods, of a cluster of low modern buildings crouching on a cliff top, surrounded by attractive landscaped gardens.

Letter or card, they always said the same – that he missed her, was confused about why she'd gone away. And, in the suffocating heat of the night, his words stole her sleep, left her tossing and turning until the cool of the morning. But she had to be strong, had to deal with the pain.

She didn't dare fail him, not after she'd come so far.

Towards the end of Nicole's training her lessons became more focused and she found they now had the power to command her attention. She began to get a taste of what might lie ahead – the country of Indonesia, nuclear weapons technology, delivery systems. They helicoptered her out to the USS *Peleliu*, a specially modified assault ship. On board was a small team of US Navy SEALS who gave her a rigorous refresher course on submersibles and allowed her to pilot one of the most up-to-date machines from the Navy's Deep Flight programme. And they even gave her a holiday, too, chasing giant manta rays through the deep waters of the Caribbean and watching turtles cruise among spectacular coral reefs.

In the end, some fourteen weeks later, they decided Nicole was ready.

They called it the 'lake house'.

It stood on spindly wooden legs, fifty feet out from a rocky shore. Constructed from dark wooden planks, it had a steeply pitched roof and a wide veranda with an ornately cut balustrade. A large white umbrella flapped and spun over a pair of lounging chairs, and a small palm in a terracotta pot provided the only relieving splash of colour.

As Nicole walked along the little wooden causeway towards the house, a stiff breeze tugged at her hair and flapped her grey overalls. An osprey circled silently overhead, its long narrow wings fingering the wind for lift. Through the narrow slits in the planking beneath her feet, the dark aquamarine lake water seemed to shift and squirm uneasily.

At the end of the causeway she read the sign that arched overhead: '*By failing to prepare, you are preparing to fail.*'

Abraham Lincoln's famous grim reminder – a widely held maxim at Camp Victoria.

A pair of wooden doors creaked open on dry hinges. A Secret Service man took her into a large square entrance hall, where the hot sun warmed the timbers. A strong resinous scent of teak pervaded the building.

Another door was held open for her. She crossed the hall and entered.

The room was dark and pleasantly cool – air-conditioned. There was a thick carpet, and sounds were muted. All around her she could hear the faint hiss of static from speakers. She stood for a moment, watching a narrowing triangle of light recede slowly as the door swung gently shut. Then she was in total darkness, and all was still.

'Good morning, Miss Tai-Chung.' Nicole was startled by the synthetic voice booming from the speakers. 'Please, do sit down.' The lights brightened to reveal a small modern desk and two comfortable office chairs. The wall in front of her contained a large display screen.

She sat down.

'I am responsible for briefing you on your mission. I apologize for this rather impersonal routine – it is, of course, better that we do not actually meet.'

There was a pause and a gentle hiss of static. Nicole wasn't sure whether she was supposed to say something. She shifted uneasily.

'To protect you and your family, we've asked you to operate under a false identity. Please would you tell me your name?'

'Annabelle Luard.'

There was a moment's hesitation. 'Good. Now please confirm that you have established a legend.'

'I'm French. I live in Fougères, Rue de la Pinterie, overlooking the Nançon. I work for IMCOP, the International Marine Commission on Pollution, based in Nantes. I'm a submersible pilot.'

Again that slight pause. It intrigued Nicole: a time delay? Was she talking with someone thousands of miles away, possibly in London? The voice continued.

'Good. Please confirm the steps you have taken to establish your legend.'

'I have all the papers. I've been accepted by IMCOP, and will begin a short familiarization course in a few weeks' time.'

A slight pause.

'I am going to brief you on your mission. You may not write *anything* down. You must remember everything that I am about to say. Do you understand?'

'Yes.'

Pause.

'Certain recruitment advertisements for submersible pilots have been appearing in the specialist press.' The screen in front of Nicole flickered into life. It showed a small block advert offering adventure – and a London freephone number for further information.

'Once you've completed your course at IMCOP, you will break contract and apply for one of these posts. The advertisements are known to be a front for the Indonesian government. They are recruiting small numbers of suitably qualified submersible pilots to work on a special oceanographic project based at Arguni, a small island off the northern coast of Papua. As you know, the region is very remote. It lies over 2,000 miles to the east of Jakarta, at the furthest extremity of the Indonesian archipelago.'

Slight pause. The gentle hiss of static.

'Would you please put on the virtual-reality glasses that you will find located in the top drawer of your desk.'

Nicole pulled the drawer open; it slid easily on its nylon runners. Inside were a pair of glasses, but instead of clear lenses they had thin dark grey plastic shields that wrapped around the eyes. A tiny electrical lead dangled from the end of one arm. She put the glasses on.

'Are you ready, Annabelle?'

'Yes.'

Pause.

'Please insert the end of the lead into the socket on your desk.' Nicole lifted the glasses slightly to see more clearly, and pushed in the connector. Something flickered in front of her eyes . . .

She was suspended miles above an island floating in a surreal dark blue sea. The virtual reality was impressive. She grabbed at the sides of her chair, seized by a slight vertigo as she watched the computer-generated surf break convincingly against the rocky cliffs far below.

She could see that the island was volcanic. The central part had been blasted away long ago in a cataclysmic explosion. Now only a horseshoe remnant sheltered a central lagoon. The southern coast was badly scarred by a deep grey-coloured depression – a huge opencast mine. The tailings had been dumped unceremoniously into the sea, and were staining the water around it. Between the mine and the entrance to the lagoon was a complex of buildings. The rest of the island was covered in dense rainforest.

'Arguni Island is just one of several islands lying between Cape D'Urville and Jayapura. It's been the location of a huge copper mine for some years, but there's growing evidence that the mine is actually a cover for some other activity.

'This settlement, here' – a small red arrow appeared over the simulated island – 'is ostensibly for transmigration workers – people the Indonesian government have shipped away from overcrowded Java to try and relieve the growing pressure on the land. We estimate the population of the camp to be in excess of a thousand people, far more than is needed by any mining operation. In reality it's a concentration camp, a gulag, containing Chinese slave-workers for a huge and as yet unidentified construction project. These ventilation towers' – again the arrow – 'would seem to indicate some sort of underground complex. We also believe that many Chinese intellectuals are being held in the camp – probably scientists and engineers.'

Pause.

'Do you have any questions so far?'

Nicole shook her head. She was thinking about her father, one of those intellectuals. She remembered the photograph Simes had shown her, the skeletal frame of her father's emaciated body.

'Have you any questions, Annabelle?'

'Sorry – no, no questions.'

Slight pause.

'Good. Now, once you are established as a submersible pilot at Arguni, we want you to infiltrate the underground complex. We have evidence that the Indonesians are mining uranium from the seabed, and we think this is the most likely base for their operation. Your mission is, one, to identify the Indonesian nuclear weapons-building programme, and, two, to determine how advanced the project is.'

Pause.

'Will you take off your glasses, please?'

Nicole did as she was told, blinking as her visual perspective shifted back into the close confines of the briefing room.

'We're especially interested in a boat called the *Gajah Mada*.' An image flashed onto the screen. 'It's a large ship, red-hulled with a grey superstructure, and a tall black central drilling tower. She's a mining ship, cruising regularly in the waters off Micronesia in the West Pacific. We know she's extracting manganese nodules from the ocean floor – quite legally, of course, since Rahman recently dealt himself into their territorial waters. We think the Indonesians may be refining strategic minerals like manganese, titanium, cobalt, nickel – probably for weapons-building.

'The *Ibn Battuta* is also a regular visitor.' Another image flashed onto the screen. 'She's a state-of-the-art oceano-graphic ship, equipped with Russian submersibles. We would like to know what her role is in this operation. We believe she may be responsible for bringing up the uranium ore, probably from around geothermal vents, where it's being deposited in the chimneys by metal-fixing bacteria.

'On your arrival, you are to meet up with this man.' Another picture. 'His name is Alexander Rykhlin. He's an American agent working for the CIA.' Nicole studied the face – rugged features framed by a rather unruly mop of dark hair, a naval-style beard, eyes sharp and intelligent.

'He will arrive slightly ahead of you. You will work together as a team. He's there for your protection; you will have no other support at Arguni. Your only equipment will be a means of communicating with your case officer in London. This will help to protect you and your family should the Indonesians become suspicious. Rykhlin will report directly to the DDO – Deputy Director of Oper-ations – in Washington. He will have surveillance equip-ment, which you are also authorized to use. When we wish to extract you from the island, you will receive a message: '*Keep strong*'. Then you will act according to Rykhlin's orders. Do you have any further questions?'

Nicole did. 'Yes: this is a deal, an arrangement. I want you to confirm that whatever happens to me, you will continue with my son's treatment for cancer; and that you are prepared to rescue my father, a British agent who is currently being held on that island.'

Pause.

'We are fully aware of our obligations.'

'And I would like to see my son again . . . before I leave for Indonesia.'

Pause.

'I'm afraid that won't be possible.'

Nicole stiffened. The words were sharp and they cut a deep wound. She'd always assumed that she'd see Peter again, that they'd be together for a while before she finally went out.

'He's my son,' she said firmly. 'I demand to see him.'

The pause was longer on this occasion. 'I'm afraid it's no longer appropriate for you to see him.'

Nicole became rigid with anger. 'You can't do that! I refuse to carry out my instructions until you let me see my son again!'

The answer came back quickly this time. 'Then your contract will be void.' There was a slight click.

Nicole leaped up in fury, her chair tipping back across the floor. 'You can't treat me this way!' she shouted.

But now the room was filled only with the gentle hiss of static.

She seethed, gripping the table tightly, the muscles of her hands and arms like steel. *My God*, she thought, *how could I have been so naive?*

The lights brightened. A Secret Service man held the door open for her, watching, waiting.

Nicole stood for a long time, staring at the blank screen, her fists clenching and unclenching. Then she turned and stormed from the briefing room, pushing the Secret Service man to one side as she swept through the exit.

If this was what it took to secure her son's future, if an agent was what they wanted, then they could have one.

Then she'd leave this madness behind her – for ever.

Chapter Sixteen – December: Rahman's Palace, Bogor

The sultry night air hung heavily across the terrace. It clung thickly to the elegant rattan furniture and brought with it a damp smell of clove and nutmeg, as well as the steady rhythm of cicadas.

Thameena sat elegantly at one of the tables, gazing out into the darkness. Warm candlelight drifted across the smooth outline of her powdered cheeks, softened the hard made-up line of her mouth.

A blue-uniformed Palace official appeared and placed a tall glass at her elbow, a milky drink that glowed pink in the light of the candle flames. 'Major Lukman has arrived, madam,' he said discreetly. 'Will you see him here?'

Thameena nodded assent. She brought the cool glass to her lips, catching the sharp tang of lime before tasting the thick sweetness of the coconut milk.

The neat grey-suited figure of Major Lukman appeared out of the darkness and began to cross the broad expanse of the terrace. She saw the confidence in the manner of his walk, the self-assurance, and disliked him instantly. 'You wished to see me, ma'am?'

Thameena stared up with a cold penetrating gaze at the young man standing in front of her. She recognized the conceit lying upon that finely chiselled face, and thought she had the measure of him.

'Do sit down, Major Lukman.' She smiled sweetly, and indicated a chair opposite. The cane creaked gently as it received the weight of Lukman's trim body. 'Would you care for some refreshment?'

'No, thank you, ma'am.'

Thameena laughed to herself, noting the tiny beads of perspiration upon his forehead. She knew how uncomfortable he must feel, meeting her like this.

'My husband tells me that you can be a very useful man,' she said dryly.

Lukman's eyes slid carefully around the terrace, missing nothing. 'I am a loyal servant, ma'am. I serve my country.'

Thameena nodded gently. She raised her glass to her lips again, and studied Lukman over the rim. Her eyes narrowed. 'You have such loyalty, Major, that I hear it knows no bounds. It has even been said that you were instrumental in bringing my husband to power.'

'I'm a member of the *Kopassus*, ma'am. I do my duty.' His voice remained calm, cultured.

'Your duty, Major? But your duty that day in Jakarta might so easily have put your own life in jeopardy.' Then a hard note crept into her voice. 'If, of course, the truth were ever to be revealed.'

Lukman's expression flinched at this comment. His sharp eyes looked back at her – dark eyes, like those of a shrew. 'Ma'am?'

Thameena smiled thinly as she twisted the stem of her glass between her fingers. The refracted light from the candles spun a delicate wheel of fire across the white tablecloth. 'Major Lukman, what is about to pass between us must go no further.'

Lukman sat there, his black eyes shining.

Thameena felt her distaste deepening. He was like a leech, waiting to suck up bits of new information, waiting to hear titbits of tittle-tattle, always ingratiating himself with the higher strata of society, never giving anything of himself in return. She knew that you could buy Major Lukman, that you could enter into a deal with him, but that you should never turn your back on him.

'There are some who say that my husband has become, shall we say, a little over-ambitious; that he may be leading this country into crisis.'

Lukman's dark eyes continued to gaze intently across the softly lit table. Then he sat back in his chair, indicating the small wooden box standing on the table between them.

'May I?'

Thameena nodded.

Lukman opened the box and drew out a *kretek*. He lit the end with a gold lighter, snapping it shut and returning it to his pocket. He chose his words carefully. 'I *was* involved with the taking of the Utara oilfield. I had always thought that operation went smoothly.'

'There are some who would say the operation should never have happened, that it could have destabilized the whole South-East Asian region. That we risked a major confrontation.'

Lukman took a reflective drag on the *kretek*; the cloves glowed and crackled. He blew out a thin stream of smoke, which caught in the updraught from the candles and spun away into the night. 'I'm just a soldier, ma'am,' he replied quietly.

'Oh, come now – you're a soldier who moves in high places.'

He gazed at her through the curling smoke. 'I've been very fortunate with my friends.'

'Then you must get to hear things?'

Lukman flicked ash into the glass ashtray on the table. 'Sometimes.'

'Then perhaps you might become my eyes and ears ... if ever I need them?'

Lukman gazed at her through the soft candlelight. His eyes narrowed slightly, his lips thinned. Thameena saw the worm sniff at the trail – and waited patiently.

'A gift, perhaps?' she prompted.

Lukman leaned forwards, squashing the still-glowing stub of the cigarette into the ashtray. 'I've heard it said, ma'am, that you have ambitions of your own.'

The insolence of this remark stabbed at Thameena. She reacted angrily, rising quickly to her feet. 'How dare you say such a thing!' The table jerked forwards, making the shadows dance as the candles rattled in their holders.

Lukman looked straight at her, his expression as cold as ice. 'It was a suggestion, ma'am, that is all. But, as you said earlier, one that would put your position in jeopardy . . . if it were ever to be revealed.'

Thameena's arm swung instinctively, her open hand slapping him hard across the cheek. She glared down at him, her nostrils flaring. Who was he to see himself as her equal? To see fit to trap her with her own words? Anger coursed through her veins.

But Lukman didn't move, didn't even lift his hand to rub at the sting of her blow. He just sat there watching, waiting.

She forced herself to smile and sat down quietly behind the table once more.

Lukman was more certain of his position now. 'You have no loyalty to your husband,' he continued bluntly. 'That much is clear to everyone. Perhaps you intend to form a government of your own one day.'

'That is treason, Major Lukman,' hissed Thameena.

'Then perhaps we commit treason together, ma'am.'

The mesmeric rhythm of the cicadas in the surrounding Palace grounds played on the tension that lay taut across the terrace.

'You do not approve of my husband as head of state?'

'Let us just say that I can see the advantage of leaning towards the winning side.'

Thameena watched Lukman carefully. His confident manner, his careful calculation. She disliked him intensely, yet she needed him.

'I do not like my husband's use of Islam, Major Lukman, his callous disregard for my people. He is short-sighted, maybe even a fool. I believe that, one day soon, he will bring this country down.'

'Then if those are your thoughts, ma'am, let me assure you that you have friends in high places.'

'But do I have the friendship of my people?'

'Ma'am, the people will follow those who promise them what they desire.'

There was a pause in the conversation.

'Then shall we trade?' Thameena asked quietly.

Lukman sat back in his chair and crossed one leg over the other. 'I believe you are training a secret guerrilla army – backed by your father. I understand he's providing you with money and weapons ... which are, in turn, gifts from the CIA.'

A tremble ran through Thameena's body. 'You know too much, Major Lukman. Who else is aware of this?'

'No one. It was just conjecture.' He smiled broadly, and let the grin linger. 'So,' he continued. 'You see yourself as President one day? Ambitious enough to ally yourself to the Americans?'

'You speak unwisely, Major Lukman,' hissed Thameena. But curiosity still surged in her veins. 'Tell me, what else do you ... conjecture?'

'Your husband's minister for technology, Dr Jazid Hendra – I surmise that he's discovered uranium ... on the sea floor.'

Thameena was startled. Her body jerked upright. 'What,

uranium? A bomb? My husband is making a nuclear bomb?'

'Perhaps. Maybe more than one. Maybe a delivery system, too.' Lukman leaned forward. 'That car he brags about, the fuel-cell car – it's just a cover.'

Thameena's face paled and her features grew pinched. She gazed intently out into the dark. *My God!* Rahman's aspirations were worse than she'd imagined. Much worse. She turned to Lukman. 'He must be stopped!'

'I agree.'

'But how?'

'The President trusts me, ma'am, much more than he trusts you. I need only hint at the possibility of your personal ambition, and he'll have you exiled, as a trouble-maker. That will give you the space you need.'

'Exile? But I need access to my people, to com-munications.'

'If I put myself in charge of the operation, exile will give you all the freedom you could possibly want.'

Thameena watched his expression closely. Not even a flicker of fear crossed Lukman's smooth face. 'Can it be done – soon?'

'Of course! But not too soon. You must be patient. First we must distance ourselves from this little meeting.'

Thameena rose, gathering up the small wooden box and the ashtray. 'I want it done, Major Lukman. I want it organized. Now you must go, before your presence here is noted.'

Lukman stayed firmly at the table. 'But to be your eyes

and ears, ma'am, to do all of this . . . I shall be taking certain risks.' He looked at her pointedly. 'After all, it was you who asked me to trade.'

Thameena was getting agitated by his continued presence. 'Of course, your payment. Money?'

Lukman was startled for a moment, then laughed. 'No, not money!' His voice took on a harder edge. 'What I desire most is a position in your government, when you come to power.'

Thameena's eyes narrowed. 'That's a lot to ask, Major Lukman. I'm not sure such a thing would be possible . . .'

Lukman got up from the table. 'But I think the dice are loaded in my favour, don't you?' He looked at her carefully. 'I suggest that you give my suggestion your serious consideration.'

Then he turned and made his way confidently back across the terrace before disappearing into the night.

Thameena watched his retreating back and instinctively distrusted him. She guessed that he knew more than he was telling, that he was a dangerous man playing a dangerous game.

Well, she could turn the tables on him. Make use of him while she had to . . . then dispose of him.

Chapter Seventeen – early February: Arguni Island, forty miles off the north coast of Papua

Nicole leaned on the forward guard rail of the old and battered ferry as it rolled gently in the Pacific swell, observing the activity on the deck below. A warm breeze, sticky with salt, blew steadily across the bows. A tinny Indonesian voice rasped over the loudspeaker, announcing that they would dock in twenty minutes.

She gazed up at the flanks of the volcanic island materializing out of the blue-grey haze. She watched shreds of white cloud drifting gently through its rugged landscape, saw ravines plunging steeply down to the waterline and a dense mat of emerald rainforest covering everything. A huge brown scar slashed across the right flank of the island, marking the place where greed had torn into the mountain to get at the high-grade copper ore inside.

A tremor of excitement touched Nicole's soul. There was no longer anybody with her to direct or advise. She'd completed her training. She was now free to get on with the job, to fulfil her contract as quickly as possible.

Her stomach tightened. In the harbour, she could see

the unmistakable rakish lines of the *Ibn Battuta* gleaming brightly in the morning sunshine. She stared intently at the survey ship, dutifully checking its details against her memory of the photographs she'd been shown, looking for any significant changes made, any clues as to its real purpose. She studied the waterline, noted how the boat sat high in the water – emptied of whatever it was that she might previously have been carrying.

The ferry slipped past the *Ibn Battuta* and followed the deep-water channel through the reef before drifting into the calm water of the lagoon beyond. A flock of windsurfers scudded unexpectedly across the bows, their sails bright against the water. Passengers waved and shouted to them.

Nicole frowned – could it be that they were wrong about this place? The holiday atmosphere seemed so much at odds with the serious nature of her briefing.

Workers scurried around on the dockside as the ferry nosed up to the terminal. The loudspeaker blared instructions and the huge bows started to lift. Nicole picked up her two heavy holdalls, and squeezed down the narrow stairway onto the car deck below. It was empty save for two large container trucks and a grey box van. Dock handlers were busy, crouching by the wheels, snapping off the hold-down chains and rattling them out noisily through the axle housings. The engines were already running, filling the confined space with a hard diesel roar and an oily-blue haze.

Nicole walked down the ramp with the rest of the

passengers. The box van drove past her, its weight bouncing the metal plates beneath her feet and making them clank.

Security was tight: a cluster of red-bereted *Kopassus* stood at the end of the ramp, sub-machine guns slung loosely from their shoulders. They also had a small fleet of drab Suzuki jeeps drawn up on the quayside. She watched as one drove out ahead of the van, leading it off down the narrow tarmac road away from the terminal, its wheels splashing through the puddles of last night's rain.

As she stepped onto the quayside, a soldier came forward. He was a young officer, his Malay face smooth and well proportioned, camouflaged uniform neatly pressed. 'Miss Luard?'

Nicole slipped easily into her by now familiar identity. 'Yes?'

'Come this way, please.'

The young man took her bags and walked across to a jeep. He opened the passenger door for her and heaved the bags into the back.

The heavy-duty tyres whined noisily as they sped along the road. They began to run alongside a tall fence topped with razor wire, white insulators visible at every metal post. Behind the wire was a three-metre gap, and then another fence like the first. Behind that again was a large open area, scattered with felled logs and gridded by dirt roads pocked with water-filled potholes. Further back again were rows of newly built huts, sunlight flashing off their corrugated sheet-metal roofs.

The gulag! And the Indonesians had made no attempt to hide it. Was that a mark of their confidence – or of their arrogance? As the jeep swept past the entrance, there were guards on view, looking at documents, checking the box van, opening the tall wire gates between the watchtowers to let it through.

She turned to the young officer and shouted above the noise of his vehicle, 'What's the encampment for? Who lives in there?'

'*Transmigrasi* – peasants from Java.' He spat out of the open driver's window to emphasize his contempt. 'They work in the copper mine under government contract.' He laughed. 'A one-way ticket for some.'

He seemed to believe his own answer; perhaps he knew no different. She watched the rhythm of the wire rising and falling between the racing metal posts. 'So why the fences? Why all this security?'

He looked at her, eyebrows raised. 'It's a copper mine. We're not welcome here. We've got problems with the *Korowai*, the local tribesmen. They attack the machinery, kill the workers. They're a bloody nuisance.' He threw another glance at Nicole. 'That's our job here: security.'

The road began to rise up sharply towards a junction, and the young officer slowed the jeep. 'Some of them are OPM,' he continued.

'OPM?'

'*Organisasi Papua Merdeka*: the Free Papua Movement. You know, guerrillas! Communists!'

He gunned the engine and expertly changed down a

213

gear, swinging the jeep sharply onto a left-hand fork. 'Be careful while you're here. Don't go wandering around. There've been kidnappings, killings . . . rapes.' He grinned at her foolishly.

They were now running round behind the *transmigrasi* settlement, the road dropping down towards the spectacularly beautiful lagoon that filled the old volcanic crater. Nicole found herself struggling with the contrast: the breathtaking natural beauty all around, against the sinister gulag and its high security – like a hell sheltering inside a heaven. Despite the hot equatorial sun, a chill worked its way deep inside her. She felt uneasy, uncertain, knowing she might be on the track of something evil.

The road plunged down towards a small settlement strung along the shoreline: a scatter of tiny roundhouses with conical red roofs, set amongst clumps of palm trees. As they drew closer, she could see crazy-paved patios, colourful umbrellas, surfboard sails flapping brightly on a narrow sandy beach. It looked for all the world like a holiday village – except for the wire fence around the perimeter, and the guards at the barrier.

Their jeep was waved through and they pulled into the settlement proper. The place seemed very new; a tiny suburb of miniature homes winding along the shore, all linked up together by brick pathways. Banana trees and palms studded the lush lawns, and a gentle breeze rattled through the swaying foliage.

People wandered along the brick pathways, dressed in garish batik shirts and shorts. They were mostly male and mostly white. They looked at Nicole as if sizing up the new arrival. Some even waved a casual welcome.

The officer led Nicole up to one of the houses. 'This is where all our visiting scientific personnel stay. I think you'll find it very comfortable.' The key was already in the door, her name pencilled in capitals onto a scruffy label. He let her in and went back to fetch the bags from the jeep.

The interior of the house reminded Nicole of the tiny Javanese holiday lodges she'd stayed in as a child – small, friendly, but sparsely furnished. It had white walls, with geometrically patterned blinds over the windows and upholstered cane furniture standing on polished wooden floors.

The officer clattered in with her bags, then took his leave. Nicole heaved them through into the bedroom, brushing the mosquito net to one side so that she could dump them on the bed. Unzipping one of them, the first thing she pulled out was a small colour photograph of Peter. Damn! She knew straight away that she shouldn't have it here. He belonged to Nicole – not to Annabelle Luard.

She stared at the young face in the photograph, at the blaze of colour in the summer garden. However could she have made such a bad mistake? Just for a moment the picture brought back memories, put her back into Nicole's skin, and she felt the pain of her separation like a dagger.

She forced herself to be professional. Slowly she stepped into the bathroom and began to tear up the photograph carefully, slowly, piece by piece. And finally, like some sort of ritual expulsion, she flushed it away. Peter was now in good hands; she could do no more.

She looked at herself in the mirror. *You're not Nicole,* she told herself, *you're Annabelle, and you have a mission . . .*

The floor creaked loudly in the living room.

Nicole looked up with a start and listened hard, but heard nothing more.

She hesitated, then decided to investigate. She stepped carefully down the corridor . . . and came face to face with an astonishing apparition: a small, dark-skinned man with frizzy hair, his flattish nose spiked with slivers of bamboo. His well-muscled arms emerged from a scruffy red running vest, emblazoned with the Olympic logo. He had a Nike bag slung over his shoulder, and his badly stained grey slacks hung over bare feet shoved into tatty sandals.

The dark-skinned face broke into a wide smile. 'Hi!' he said, and held out a large rough hand.

Somewhat stunned, Nicole took his hand and shook it. His fingers were hard and rough, but the handshake was as gentle as a child's. His eyes sparkled intelligently.

'For you!' He held out what looked like a fragment of card.

Nicole looked down at what she'd been given. It was the bottom half of a torn postcard, showing the base of a huge monument. The caption read: *The National Monument, Merdeka Square, Jakarta.*

She flipped the card over.

On the back was scrawled a name: *Rykhlin.*

Chapter Eighteen – that afternoon: Arguni Base

The same young officer called again later in the day, to take Nicole to a preliminary briefing.

The jeep sped back along the access road, then turned left towards the copper mine. The road spiralled down inside a vast bowl of grey volcanic rock, cracked and fissured by blasting. The tyres squealed through a series of tight bends until a tunnel appeared ahead of them, its oval opening edged in smooth concrete. A sign fixed above the entrance read: *The Indonesian Islamic Government Centre for Deep-Ocean Studies.*

They plunged inside and pulled into a large underground car park. Getting out, the driver swiped his electronic pass through the reader on a substantial blast door. It opened with a whine of hydraulic rams and the clack of steel bolts. They walked down a long rubber-matted corridor. The air was cool and gave off a faint metallic smell. Other people trod the same route – some wore civilian clothes, some white laboratory coats with name labels. Everyone had security tags. They reached a pair of doors on the right of the corridor – *Submersible Pilot Briefing Facility* – and went in.

There were framed photographs on the walls: submersibles and submarines, some of the pictures signed by their crews. The officer pointed the way to a small lecture theatre beyond, then politely took his leave.

Three rows of grey fabric seats sloped up towards the back of the theatre. At the front was a small raised platform, with a lectern and a white screen. On a table to one side were two large ship models – one of the *Ibn Battuta*, the other of the *Gajah Mada*, the mining ship with its tall central derrick. Nicole sat down in the front row, and waited for something to happen.

Presently, the door swung open and a small Indonesian man wearing a dark suit and gold-framed glasses fussed into the room. He was accompanied by a young Asian man, wearing an open-necked shirt and slacks. He sat the young man down in the same row of seats as Nicole, then mounted the podium, shuffling his notes onto the lectern. He cleared his throat and peered over his glasses.

'Good afternoon. My name is Dr Hendra,' he began. 'I am Indonesia's Minister for Technology, and I'm directly responsible for this magnificent Centre for Deep-Ocean Studies, in which you now sit.' He smiled at them – a neat smile that switched on and off like a machine. His voice was as dry as silk.

'The fact that I welcome all our new scientific staff personally to this Centre reflects the high regard in which I hold you all. You have done well to pass our screening tests. As you know, they are very severe. Only the best receive the privilege of taking part in this venture.'

He pressed a button on the lectern, a large jewel flashing on one of his fingers as it caught the light from the projector beam. The lights dimmed. An image of the Earth from space came onto the screen, the vast expanse of the Pacific Ocean covering virtually one entire hemisphere. 'Our planet should be called Ocean, not Earth,' he said. 'The oceans cover seven-tenths of our world – we're actually a blue planet. Yet we know more about the surface of the moon then we do about the ocean floor. There are riches down there, a bonanza for anyone with the right technology.' He paused dramatically. 'And Indonesia now has that technology. We are the first country in the world to take ocean-floor mining of manganese nodules seriously.' A smile of self-satisfaction crossed his lips.

The lights brightened a little. He pulled a rock from a shelf hidden from view behind the lectern and held it up for them to see. It was about the size of a large potato, and shiny black, like a lump of smoothed coal. He passed it down to let them have a look. To Nicole it had a rough glassy texture and was surprisingly heavy.

'It's a manganese nodule. We're extracting them from the floor of the Pacific Ocean at a depth of about 12,000 feet.' He pressed the button on the lectern again. Another picture came onto the screen. 'The operation is simple enough. I can explain it, using this diagram. The mining ship moves slowly along the surface, connected to a machine like a giant vacuum cleaner that slides across the ocean floor. It sucks up the nodules and deposits them in a wire cage. The cage fills once every thirty minutes. We then winch the cage up to the surface, and empty it.' He looked up, a gleam of triumph in his small bright eyes.

Nicole interrupted with a question, wanting to test his reaction. 'These minerals, I assume they must be very valuable – to make this sort of huge investment worthwhile?'

'Very valuable,' crowed Hendra. It was obviously a suitable question. 'Cobalt's scarce on the open market at the moment, and its price is rising steeply. The same sort of thing could easily happen to nickel, or titanium. Our aim is to become self-sufficient in all the main strategic minerals over the next decade.'

But why? thought Nicole. *Why is it so important to a country like Indonesia to be self-sufficient in exotic minerals? Why the huge investment in all this deep-ocean mining? What are they building – some sort of launcher, for a nuclear bomb perhaps?*

Hendra went on at some length. He talked about the significance of the oceans, how all the world's continents would fit into the Pacific with room to spare; how half the planet was under 9,000 feet of water; how the new marine organisms found living around deep-ocean hydrothermal vents contained secrets for manufacturing new drugs and medicines. His talk was full of words like 'exploitation' and 'profit'.

Nicole listened carefully to this neat and fussy little man, detected the note of greed in everything that he said, and found the whole thing rather offensive. While the rest of the world's scientific community was focused on rescuing an ailing planet, desperately investigating the oceans in their urgent bid to unravel the chaos of global warming, Rahman's government was forcefully preventing some of that research from being undertaken, blocking data that was vital to the world's understanding of climate change. Just so that Hendra could plunder the ocean floor unhindered.

The young Asian interrupted Hendra with a question. 'Where do we come in, sir – the submersible pilots?'

Hendra smiled benevolently. 'Rest assured, you will have a very important role to play. The crushing pressures and cold temperatures of the deep ocean make our machines unreliable. It takes too long to haul them all the way back up to the surface. We prefer the flexibility of a human mind to robotic repairs. Your job is to shadow the mining operation and fix any problems as they occur. You will, of course, be given extensive simulator and real-time training before you will be allowed to operate a submersible on your own.' Hendra looked at them over the top of his glasses, their frames glinting in the dim light. 'I would also like to remind you that this is a security-sensitive operation. You must consider yourself privileged to be part of it, and it is not wise to ask too many questions.' He paused. 'You will, of course, be very well paid for your professional services.'

Then he grinned mysteriously. 'In a few weeks' time, we will be honoured by a visit from President Amir

Rahman himself, and then you will be able to catch a glimpse of Indonesia's exciting future.' He spoke in hushed tones. 'One of the projects we are developing here, in secret, is an advanced fuel-cell automobile. Just think for a moment. Half the world's population live in cities, most of which have been forced to impose zero-pollution policies within their boundaries. Our vehicle will provide a better answer to that problem than any car currently being developed in the West. It will convince the world of our newly developing technology – of our growing superiority.'

Nicole listened cynically to Hendra's garbage. She knew the whole project was almost certainly a front for something dark and sinister that lurked behind it. Something that had much more to do with power, wealth and personal prestige than saving the planet from its collapsing environment.

'Now, I do believe that I have talked to you for long enough,' suggested Hendra. 'You have much to do. Your training starts tomorrow. All the more reason for me to wish you well as we start out together on this new and exciting venture.'

He swept up his notes. The young officer at the door saluted Hendra as he went out, then held the door for them both as they filed into the corridor.

Nicole was intrigued. This place was like a set of Russian dolls. The copper mine was a transparent cover for the supposedly benign Ocean Studies Centre, but take that off, and beneath it you would find the Indonesians mining nodules off the ocean floor. And if she was right, nodule mining would in turn be a cover for the extraction of deep-ocean uranium, and—

'Hello, Nicole!'

She heard the name and spun round instinctively.

'I might have guessed you would be in on something like this.' A hand was held out towards her.

Her heart leaped. God! A face from the past.

She stalled for time. 'I'm sorry,' she stammered. 'Who did you say?'

He slowly dropped his hand, looking rather puzzled. 'Nicole? Nicole Tai-Chung?'

It was Glyn! The submersible pilot who'd almost killed her.

'No – I'm sorry, you're mistaken. I'm Annabelle. Annabelle Luard.'

Chapter Nineteen – two weeks later: Arguni Base

It had rained spasmodically all evening. Lightning flickered outside the windows of Nicole's lodge, and the crash of thunder rumbled and reverberated around the open bowl of the volcanic island. The air was hot and humid, making Nicole's bare feet stick to the wooden floor as she busied herself around the living room. Huge purple moths flittered in the corners and thumped around the light fitting.

A knock at the door rattled its flimsy structure. She crossed the room and opened it. Warm damp air wafted in, bringing with it the smell of wet earth and rank vegetation. A man stood under the shelter of the veranda as the rain rodded down behind him. He turned towards her, brown eyes smiling from beneath dark hair plastered down over his forehead, a folded golfing umbrella at his side. His craggy face was partially hidden by a poorly trimmed naval beard. He looked a little unkempt: his bright orange short-sleeved shirt was spotted by rain and his muscular legs were stuffed into well-worn sandals. A black sports bag swung from his shoulder. She remembered a slide from the briefing room – and guessed this was Rykhlin.

'Hi there!' He paused, and smiled pleasantly at her. 'Are you Miss Luard?' His soft accent was American – East Coast. He held something out to her. She took it – a torn postcard, showing the top half of some monument. She remembered being given the other half by Spike-Nose and reached back onto a little cane table to retrieve it. She fitted the two parts together. They jigsawed perfectly with each other. 'Come in,' she smiled.

'I've brought my Discman,' he said, and hauled a floppy plastic case out of his bag. As he passed it to her, she noticed a slip of paper hiding under his thumb. 'Say nothing!' it said.

Nicole nodded, showing him that she understood.

Rykhlin began to lay his things out on the table. He kept the small talk going. 'Say, how long have you been out here?'

Nicole was busy clanking coffee things in the kitchen. 'Just a couple of weeks.'

'How are you getting on?'

'Not bad. I've finished all my simulator training. Been booked in for my first trip on the *Gajah Madah* next week. And you?'

'Engineer. Do a lot of work on the submersibles. You damage them, I repair them.'

Nicole came back into the room with the coffee tray. Rykhlin was going around all the electrical fittings with a small black plastic device no bigger than a hand calculator, watching the read-out carefully, looking for any tell-tale feedback. He put the device back in his bag and smiled. 'It's clean!'

Nicole put the tray down onto the table and began to pour the coffee. Rykhlin busied himself with the Discman, carefully pointing the tiny speakers at the window. The heavy beat of Eric Clapton's 'Cocaine' pulsed into the room, its deep rhythm drowning out the sound of their conversation in case anyone was trying to listen in from outside.

Rykhlin sat down and produced a half-bottle of whisky. He showed Nicole the label, a questioning look on his face. 'Local stuff – illegal, of course. It's all you can get in this place. Warn you, though, it tastes like turpentine. Takes the roof off your mouth!'

She looked at the crudely printed label – 'Old Highland Stag Whisky'. She laughed. 'Go on! Why not! I'll see if I can find some glasses.'

While she was out, Rykhlin took a cigar from his top pocket. He clicked a gold lighter and leaned back in his chair, fingers tapping to the steady beat of the music.

'So – what d'you think?' he asked, as Nicole came back into the room. He blew a hazy plume of cigar smoke across the table.

'About what?'

'About this place.' Rykhlin began to pour two healthy slugs of whisky to go with their coffee.

'How much do you know already?' asked Nicole.

He took a long drag on his cigar, the tip glowing

brightly. 'Not much. I've only been out here a few weeks myself.'

Nicole took an experimental sip of the whisky – and coughed explosively. 'Good God! You're right. Whatever do they put in it?'

Rykhlin laughed. 'Turpentine? I warned you!' He raised his glass. 'The team!'

She nodded, and they chinked glasses. 'The team!'

The heavy beat of Clapton's music thudded around them. Nicole twisted the glass around in her hands, and returned to his question. 'Well, I know they're pulling manganese nodules off the ocean floor – but then, of course, they're not making any secret of that.'

Rykhlin chewed his cigar. 'Mickey Mouse operation.'

She looked up. 'I didn't think there was anything Mickey Mouse about their technology.'

'You haven't seen it yet. Believe me, those subs are old. Russian hand-me-downs. They spend more time out of the water than in it.' He drew heavily on his cigar, eyeing her through the smoke.

Nicole felt gently challenged. 'I think we should take this seriously.' She looked him straight in the eyes. 'Did you know they've found uranium?'

Rykhlin raised his eyebrows. 'Who told you that?'

'London.'

'Well, I'll be damned!'

Nicole nodded at him. 'So, we should ask ourselves: why are they so keen to mine these nodules – cobalt, titanium, nickel?'

The music changed – softer now. Rykhlin flicked a length of ash off his cigar. 'Because they need a delivery system – sounds like material for rocket motors to me.'

'That's what I thought.' Nicole fiddled with her glass again. 'I think this Ocean Studies Centre is deliberately transparent. They want people to discover that ocean-floor mining is going on here, to throw them off the scent. But I think this place is actually a cover for a nuclear weapons programme.'

Rykhlin dragged again at his cigar. 'So what about this fuel-cell car?'

'More smokescreening. It sounds good, presents a clean face to the world.'

'Possibly,' said Rykhlin.

'We need more information – that's my brief. How far have they got with weapons production? What type of bomb is it? Delivery method? Range? Target? That sort of thing.'

Rykhlin studied her. 'So where do you think all this is happening?'

'Beneath our feet. Copper mines go down a long way – sometimes for well over a mile. There's probably enough room to hide a whole mass of stuff down there.'

Rykhlin ground his cigar stub into the ashtray. 'You know, you could be right.'

Nicole was warming to Rykhlin as she began to feel included, part of a team. She was beginning to trust him. 'And I've got a contact – in the gulag,' she announced.

'Great!'

'Hi, Mr Rykhlin!' The chirpy interruption came from the doorway. Nicole looked up. 'Spike-Nose' was out there, standing on the veranda.

Rykhlin twisted round. 'Hey, Freddy! Come in, take a seat.' He turned to Nicole. 'You've met, of course.'

Nicole smiled thinly, irritated by the interruption.

Freddy came over and sat cross-legged on the floor by the side of the table. He placed a small battered leather case next to himself.

'Freddy's my friend,' explained Rykhlin. 'A tame *Korowai* who came down from the mountains looking for work. The Indonesians just let him go about his business around here. He works in the hospital – nobody pays him any attention.' He looked across at Freddy. 'Can you get us into the gulag, into the prison camp?'

Freddy considered the question. 'Very difficult. Big fence.'

Rykhlin looked back at Nicole. 'What's your contact's name?'

'Lim Tai-Chung. Dr Lim Tai-Chung.' Then she added: 'He might call himself Somchai Jornpaison.'

She carefully didn't mention this was her father; there was still a whiff of anger there – because of him, because of what he'd done.

'You think all those Chinese working in the gulag are involved in bomb production?'

Nicole realized Rykhlin was talking to her. 'Sorry ...

no, they're more likely to be used as slave labour, constructing the facility. My contact's an intellectual, an engineer.'

Rykhlin let out a low whistle. He passed the bottle of whisky to Freddy. 'Can you find out exactly where this man is, Freddy?'

Freddy tipped back the bottle. Then, 'Sure thing, Mr Rykhlin.' He looked at Nicole and giggled. 'I have girl business with soldiers. They not tell me this thing, then easy – I not get girl for them!'

Nicole tried to ignore him. 'So how do we get in?' she asked impatiently.

Rykhlin picked at his lower lip. 'We could get the *Korowai* to attack the generating station. Then cut through the electrified perimeter wire once the power's down.'

'How long would we have?'

'About forty seconds, until the standby kicks in.'

Nicole raised her eyebrows. 'That's cutting things fine.'

'Well, the lights would probably go off along with the current in the wire, so we'd be in darkness all the time. There *are* jeep patrols, but I'm sure we could dodge them if we timed it right.'

Nicole began to feel concerned. The whole thing seemed a rather desperate adventure – hinging just on Freddy and a bunch of locals. She didn't want them to fail, didn't want to get caught. She wanted to get this job done, get her father out and get back to Peter.

'Rykhlin,' she cautioned, 'is Freddy up to this?'

'Hell! You haven't seen the *Korowai* when they're all

fired up,' grinned Rykhlin. 'They've hated the Indonesians ever since Rahman pushed them off their own land for a resettlement scheme. Everybody's terrified of them: they're head-hunters – to a man.' He poked at Freddy's grubby clothes. 'And don't let these deceive you. When a *Korowai* warrior kills a man, he takes the head and spoons out the brains! Believe me,' he chuckled, 'you want them on your side.'

Freddy grinned at Nicole, showing off one of his front teeth that had been filed to a neat point. 'Don't worry, missy, I do this thing for you with great pleasure.'

Rykhlin grinned. 'No, Freddy, you do this thing for money. A fistful of US dollars and a big blow-out in Jayapura!'

Freddy fiddled with his leather case, and suddenly announced: 'Miss Luard, she been spotted.'

For a moment, Nicole's heart froze. How did Freddy know that?

Rykhlin looked at her. 'Is that right?'

She nodded. 'Yes, I'm afraid so.' She felt like she was a schoolgirl again, hauled up before the teacher. 'A man I dived with some time ago.'

Rykhlin picked a shred of tobacco leaf off his lower lip. 'Then we have to eliminate him,' he said simply. He picked up the old leather case next to Freddy, and put it on the table. 'What's his name?'

'Glyn,' she said quietly. 'I don't remember his other name. He's one of the submersible pilots.'

Rykhlin thought for a moment, toying with the leather

case. 'I think Rahman's got a visit pencilled in for the end of the week – to show off his new car. The *Gajah Madah* will be back in dock by then, so your man should be at the presentation. It'd be a good time to eliminate him. I'm sure London will agree, but I'll have to check with Washington.'

Rykhlin looked up and caught the look on Nicole's face. 'Hey, that really bugs you, eh?'

Nicole nodded. 'Yes.'

Rykhlin's expression softened. 'Well, it's what I'm here for, Annabelle. It's either you or him. And you're of no use to any of us if you're dead.'

Or to Peter, thought Nicole.

Rykhlin suddenly changed the mood. 'Now, here's the reason why we often meet together – Mah Jong!' With a flourish, he undid the chromium clasp on the leather case and took out a set of battered felt-lined trays. Tipping the ivory tiles onto the table top with a tremendous clatter, he began to mix them with his hands, the hard little blocks chirping and squeaking on the glass surface.

'I like this game,' he grinned. 'Picked it up on detachment in Sung Shan. It's Chinese. You know, that really gets to them! Now, we should have four hands – but what the hell, we'll play with three.' He gave Nicole a broad wink.

'But I warn you, Annabelle, the stakes are high!'

Chapter Twenty – two nights later:
Arguni Base

Narrow concrete drainage channels ran around the gulag, about one hundred feet back from the fence. Nicole lay wedged inside one, the lightweight Colt .45 with its stubby silencer awkward against her side. The warm night air rang with the high-pitched warbling of frogs. A spider crawled over her hand, tickling the skin with its long legs. She flicked it away. Further up the channel, Rykhlin shifted his aching limbs, rustling the dry grass that sprouted in clumps along the bottom of the storm drain.

A jeep patrol drove slowly past on the other side of the wire. Nicole could hear the changing pitch of the motor as the vehicle bounced over the potholes, its tyres crunching through the loose gravel on the dirt road. Slowly the noise faded. She thumbed the stopwatch button and checked the time that had elapsed since the last patrol. They were coming through at about five-minute intervals. That should give Rykhlin and her plenty of time to cut the wire.

She eased her head cautiously above the top of the culvert and observed the floodlit compound, the dark shapes of the wooden huts, fragments of light leaking past the shuttered windows. *What will it be like in there?* she wondered. *What am I about to see?*

Freddy had given them a sketch map showing the layout of the camp, and she'd memorized the details. She knew the intellectuals were housed towards the centre, isolated from the rest of the workers.

Nicole's legs began to feel cramped. She distracted herself, staring up at the canopy of stars overhead, trying to search out the familiar constellations of her childhood. What would she say to her father if she saw him?

Time passed slowly.

The silence was interrupted by a solid *thump* from the direction of the mine buildings. Then warlike shouts and howls drifted through the night air, along with the sharp crack of semi-automatic rifles.

Suddenly, the lights went out – everywhere. One moment harsh sodium illumination flooded the compound; then nothing, just velvet darkness. The *Korowai* had attacked.

Rykhlin's hands and feet scraped at the gravel in the bottom of the culvert as he rose to a half-crouch. 'OK, let's go!' he whispered.

Nicole checked the stopwatch. They only had forty seconds before the next jeep patrol.

Rykhlin was ahead of her, sprinting for the perimeter fence. She scrambled out after him, snagging her knuckles on the rough concrete edge, then followed his shadowy figure. Her feet pounded through some scrub, sprinted across a tarmac road, then hit the gravel by the fence.

Rykhlin was kneeling there. She skidded down beside him, full of adrenalin, wound tight like a spring. He was jabbing at the wire with the cutters. He snagged one strand and pressed the long handles together. The wire parted with a loud snap.

'Time?' he demanded.

Nicole checked the watch. 'Twenty-nine seconds.'

He jabbed at another wire, snagged it in the blades, and squeezed. *Snap!* Nicole could see the sweat gleaming on his face in the dim starlight. Shots were still being fired in the distance, and a red glow flickered among the quarry buildings. Somewhere, a siren began to wail.

Rykhlin finished. He bent the wires back to make a hole big enough for them to crawl through. Nicole went first, then, grabbing the cutters from Rykhlin's hands, ran on to the second fence. She glanced again at her stopwatch – sixteen seconds left. She targeted a wire and caught it. The cutters felt long and awkward in her hands. She squeezed hard – harder. *Snap!* She found a second wire. *Snap!* Then another. The stopwatch showed nine seconds to go. She could hear the roar of a motor in the distance. But still no lights.

Again Rykhlin quickly folded back the severed wires. Nicole squeezed through and ran across rough ground towards the huts, dodging scattered piles of timber that loomed out of the darkness. The intellectuals were housed in the fourth row of huts. She counted as she ran, leaping over debris, flying like the wind.

The security lights came on.

She reached the first hut and slammed against its side. Her breath came in gasps, her chest heaving, her body hot and sweaty inside the black tracksuit.

She looked around. Fifth hut along – she jogged down the row, counting off their dark looming shadows, found the wooden steps and stopped. She waited a moment to catch her breath, observing the slivers of light leaking round the shutters. She felt fully alive now, doing what she'd been trained to do.

Rykhlin came up behind her, boots pounding across the rough ground. He went straight to the door and found it locked. Nicole aimed a confident kick in just the right place, putting all her weight behind it. The door sprang open, slamming back against the wall. They were in.

For a moment the light flooding the interior of the hut blinded her. She squinted, focusing her eyes against the glare.

They were standing in a short corridor. Single doors to left and right. Disinfectant did a bad job of hiding the sharp stench from the latrines. The heat was stifling.

A man came out of a room on the right. Nicole swung automatically towards him and pulled out the Colt, two-hands on the butt. He was Indonesian, dressed in blue jeans and a T-shirt. His eyes grew round as he saw the gun. He backed off against the wall, hands held high, palms out.

Nicole's training in Belize worked well. She leaped forward aggressively, pressed the gun hard into his neck and shoved him further up against the wall. 'Stay there!' she hissed in Malay. 'Stay there, understand?' The man nodded vigorously, eyes still round with fear, hands held high.

She moved on, leaving him to Rykhlin. Now she had to find her father. He was in there somewhere, beyond the other door.

She pushed it open.

The fetid air hit her as though she'd run into a wall. They were caged, like animals, in rows of three-tiered bunks, imprisoned by heavy mesh around the sides. Nobody moved, nobody said anything. Eyes followed her in the silence as she inched forwards into the room. Faces stared at her from folds of dirty sacking – faces gaunt and hollow with starvation and illness. Skin hung loose from emaciated bodies. Where was he in all this misery? *Where was her father?*

She spun round and marched back into the corridor. She grabbed the whimpering Indonesian by the hair and dragged him into the room, shoving him up against the wall again. Slowly she eased the end of the silencer into his mouth. The man struggled to twist away.

'Which one is Dr Tai-Chung?'

He shook his head vigorously, not understanding.

'OK,' she said, more slowly. 'Which one of these is Somchai Jornpaison?'

He nodded in recognition of the name and started to move. Nicole let him go and followed him carefully, keeping her gun trained on him.

He stopped by one of the caged lower bunks. She saw an old man lying inside, the skin hanging in folds around his leathery face, a few wisps of white hair still fringing his skull. His hands shook involuntarily inside his blue cotton jacket. Nicole stared down at him.

A thin voice quavered out of the old man's mouth. 'Nicole?'

Was this really her father? This pathetic creature, now a mere shadow of the man she had recalled in her memories. Was this the man she had recently felt so much anger for, anger at the callous way he had dragged her into this mess? He cried silently before her, no visible tears, just a rhythmic qivering of the chest. Pity welled up inside Nicole, a sudden need to care for him, to hold him – to love him again.

She waved her gun at the Indonesian, then indicated the metal grille. 'Get this thing off!' she ordered.

'Yes, yes.' The man jangled through his keys and found the right one. Shaking hands undid the padlock and lifted the heavy wire grille to one side. Rykhlin grabbed the guard, spreadeagled him on the floor and kept his weapon trained on the back of the man's head.

Slowly, Nicole sat down on the bunk next to her father. She pulled him towards her, a frail shadow of a distant memory, brought his head down gently onto her chest. He was so thin, his body like a bag of sticks. She felt she might break his bones if she clung to him too tightly.

A tear coursed down one of her cheeks. 'My God! What have they done to you?' she whispered. 'Look, I'm here now. We're going to get you out.' She sat there for a moment, one arm around her father's skeletal shoulder, the other gripping his stick-like hand.

'They cage us like dogs.' His voice was a harsh whisper. Then rheumy eyes looked up at her. 'Jean?' he asked. 'Is he all right?'

Nicole hesitated. She gripped his hand tighter and looked away. 'No, he's . . . he's not here,' she said softly.

The old man was silent for a moment. She felt his body tense beside hers: 'He had information for you, important information.'

She squeezed his hand again, more gently. 'It's all right, he managed to get it out,' she reassured him softly. 'I passed it on and they've had it analysed. You were right, it was important. That's why I'm here.' All this time, she thought, and she'd never guessed at his secret double life. All those months and years away from his family, the bitterness, the recriminations. For what? To end like this?

'They made me work here. They said they'd captured you, they said they would kill you if I refused.' His voice was shaking with emotion. 'They lied to me?'

'Yes, they lied. I'm safe.'

Rykhlin was getting edgy. 'We need to go, Annabelle. We don't have long.'

The old man blinked up at her, confused. 'Annabelle?'

'He's CIA,' she explained.

His eyes widened. 'You too?'

'Like father, like daughter, eh?' She smiled. 'There's something I have to ask you. Something they want to know.'

He grabbed her arm, a surprisingly powerful grip for one so weak. 'Tell Washington, we're all technicians here . . . enriching uranium, centrifuges. Old Soviet technology.' His body shook with the exertion.

'Why?' asked Nicole. 'What are they centrifuging for?'

'A bomb . . . a simple one. Uranium, wrapped in cobalt. A dirty bomb.' The old man's eyes widened with desperation. 'They're mining it from the seabed. Tell them that.'

Rykhlin looked up from where he guarded the Indonesian on the floor. 'How long? How long before they have this bomb?'

The old man turned his head towards him. 'Not long – they're very close.'

Nicole studied the skeleton beside her, guessed he had radiation sickness. Just a few months, perhaps, at the very most. Maybe she was already too late.

'Launchers? We need to know how many launchers,' Rykhlin was demanding.

'No – from the seabed. They're launching from the sea floor.' The old man fell silent for a moment, breath rasping in his chest. Then he added: 'It's to protect this place. They're building something else here, something more important, but I don't know what.' His bloodshot eyes stared across at Rykhlin.

'What else? What else can you tell us?' asked Nicole.

'Underwater testing,' he rasped. 'They've been testing

something on the continental rise. Involving explosions.' He shook his head. 'That's all I know.' He sank back quietly into Nicole's embrace, trembling with the effort of it all.

'We need to go, Annabelle!' Rykhlin's voice was urgent.

Nicole embraced her father more tightly; she didn't want to leave him. 'Just a little longer.'

'No! Come on!' Rykhlin urged.

'Go,' her father said, and pushed her away gently. 'Get your information back to Washington. You risked your life for this. Don't waste it.'

He looked so small, so frail, so weak. Nicole's vision blurred. 'I love you,' she said.

'I know,' he said quietly. 'Now leave me. Go!'

'I'll be back, I promise.'

'Don't worry about me. Go!'

She stumbled across the room, following Rykhlin's retreating figure. Anger boiled inside her, anger for the evil of this place. She wanted to finish it, destroy it.

'*Kopassus! Kopassus!*'

Nicole spun round. Her father was off the bed, standing on shaking legs, peering through a split in one of the wooden shutters. The Indonesian guard had crossed the floor to silence him. He now hooked his arm around her father's neck and pulled him down. Her father sank to the floor, a terrible sound rising from his crushed windpipe. His hands fluttered around those of his attacker.

Without thinking Nicole drew the Colt, lined up the sights with the Indonesian's back, and fired.

Thud – the gun kicked.

The man jerked, his head rearing back. He bared his teeth, his eyes rolling back as the big .45 round splintered his backbone and ruptured a kidney.

Thud.

He was down, collapsed onto the floor. Dark red pooling out everywhere. Legs twitching.

Nicole stared at him. She'd just killed a man.

And she felt nothing.

Rykhlin was back with her father, lifting him up, swinging his legs into the cage. He rammed the grille back into place and snapped down the locking bolt. 'This way!' he shouted, running towards the rear of the wooden barrack block and through into the ablutions area.

Nicole followed.

The smell of human waste and disinfectant was overpowering. A large grey plastic pipe ran from the separate stalls down towards a trapdoor in the floor. Rykhlin was down on his hands and knees. A wooden stick had been propped up against the wall nearby. He grabbed it, levering the trapdoor up and letting the plywood square drop back with a clatter.

'Get out!' he shouted, pointing at it frantically. 'Go on! Go!'

The sound of shouting came from the front of the hut. Heavy boots clomping on the wooden floor. The soldiers were in, shouting for the hut's minder, shouting for the Indonesian guard.

Nicole dropped to her belly and squirmed through head

first. There was a fifteen-inch gap between the floor and the rubble below it. Her hands scrabbled at the stones underneath, then she was under the hut and worming away fast. A strong smell of damp wood, spicy with mildew, filled her nose. The sharp stones cut into her elbows. Then Rykhlin was down behind her, the trapdoor dropping shut with a bang. She heard stamping just above her head, shouted orders. They'd found the minder.

A few seconds and Rykhlin was beside her. 'You OK?' he whispered.

She caught her breath. 'Fine!'

He pointed to where the bottom edge of the hut made a dark silhouette against the light flooding in from the compound outside. 'OK, crawl! Fast!'

Above their heads, soldiers were shouting. They were slapping the Indonesian she'd shot, demanding why the door was broken, what was going on. She hadn't killed him! He started screaming in agony, screaming for help. There was a thud as he hit the floor again, then silence.

Nicole and Rykhlin reached the perimeter of the hut and peered out. Outside, an open-topped military jeep stood in the middle of the dirt road, heavy machine gun mounted on a pintle, lights on and engine running. A driver sat in the front seat; she could see the tiny red glow of his cigarette as he took a drag, could hear the sound of his radio – Indonesian voices, crisp military traffic.

Rykhlin gave her shoulder a nudge. 'Cover me!' he whispered.

Nicole drew out the Colt and levelled it carefully at the soldier's head.

There were more voices audible overhead. Someone in authority issuing orders, then a sound like a body being dragged across the floor, someone dropping heavily with a loud bang, bouncing on the floorboards.

Nicole waited.

After a while, a shadow moved up beside the jeep, then something was right behind the soldier, locking him in an arm grip. Another arm moved swiftly round the soldier's front, paused, and then carefully relaxed its grip.

No sound – the soldier simply slumped. The jeep's headlights were doused.

Rykhlin appeared close by, waving her forward. She crawled out from underneath the hut, and followed him down the darkened dirt road.

Suddenly the compound was plunged into darkness again. The *Korowai* were still performing their stuff. Nicole stumbled in the dark, and, somewhere ahead, heard Rykhlin swear.

The floodlights flickered, came on for a moment – then went off again. Rykhlin had reached the end of the row of huts. Nicole came up beside him and saw searchlights still on. Pools of blinding light were swinging across the broken ground, grotesque shadows pulsing and twisting as the beams probed mounds of earth and piles of timber.

Their way back to safety was a killing ground.

Rykhlin gave Nicole's arm an encouraging squeeze. 'Be

careful!' Then he was gone, leaping ahead from cover to cover.

Nicole waited for a moment, then followed him. She ran harder then she had ever run before, trying to stay in the shadows. The sound of the wind whistled in her ears, and her breath came in tight gasps. She reached a pile of scattered logs and dived down between them, cracking her knee badly, the pain numbed by adrenalin. She lay there, catching her breath, watching the pattern of the searchlights.

She ducked as they swept overhead.

Darkness again.

She counted the seconds, gauging when the time was right between the traversing beams. Then she was up, dashing for the fence, running hard . . .

Too late! She saw powerful headlights moving along the side of the fence. A jeep patrol.

Finding herself caught in the open, she dropped, covered her face desperately, willing herself not to be spotted – waiting for the glare of a searchlight to find her, the crack of a rifle, the thud of bullets.

She listened to the sound of the jeep's engine grinding slowly along the dirt road towards her. An age seemed to pass.

Then a searchlight's beam was upon her. Even through eyelids pinched tight with fear, the intense light blazed in. She could almost feel it enveloping her body.

But it swept on. They'd missed her. She heard the

sound of the jeep moving away. She twisted her head, saw its red tail lights disappearing into the darkness.

Now she'd lost track of the searchlights, lost their sweep pattern. There was only one option left: she got up and ran.

She recognized a pile of rubble they'd passed on the way in, changed direction, and pounded towards the fence.

Another searchlight! A pool of light racing swiftly over the ground.

She dropped, flattening herself. Chest heaving, body drenched in sweat.

The light passed over.

She was up again instantly, running, reckless. She neared the fence and panicked. The escape hole! Where was the hole?

'Annabelle!' a voice hissed.

Rykhlin? There! A dark figure waving frantically.

'They missed it!' he whispered excitedly. 'Did you see that? They drove straight past the damned hole, and missed it.'

Then they were through the first fence, and the next one, crossing the tarmac road and plunging into the scrub on the other side. They ran for some time before collapsing, safe for the moment. Now they lay together in the long grass, breathing hard, faces glistening with sweat.

The floodlights in the compound were back on. A pair of blue lights strobed in the darkness as an ambulance bounced along a dirt track in the distance.

Nicole twisted sideways to look at Rykhlin. He stared back at her, a grin spreading all over his face.

She was full of excitement. They'd made it – made it through hell together. Without thinking, she leaned across and kissed him. His beard felt soft and damp. Then, suddenly embarrassed by what she'd done, she pulled back quickly.

Rykhlin sensed her change of mood, and was quiet for a moment. 'Your father – I'm sorry, I had no idea . . .'

There was a pause before Nicole answered. 'He may not have long. He's very sick.' She lay back in the long grass for a moment, still recovering.

'We can get back at them,' Rykhlin suggested. 'Get the information out, then destroy this place.'

Nicole rolled her body towards him. 'We need to know where those missiles are going. That's what I'm here for. We need the target coordinates.'

'Then we'll have to find a way of getting into their computer system. But it'll be dangerous.'

Nicole's voice seemed very distant. 'Yes, I know.' She wiped the sweat from her face. 'You'll have to deal with Glyn soon. He's getting suspicious, keeps giving me funny looks. I can't avoid him for much longer. I think he might easily betray us.'

'I can't do anything over the next few days. Security will be too tight. I suggest that we lie low, at least until Rahman's visit. It'll give us time to sort things out, plan our next move. I'll deal with Glyn soon enough.'

'OK. But I also need to contact London, tell them about the missiles, let them know what we're planning to do.'

They lay there for another moment in the grass,

thinking quietly. Rykhlin broke the silence: 'Your father said there was something else. Something about the missiles only being there for defence, that there was another project. What did he mean by that?'

Nicole was anxious about Rykhlin's growing curiosity. She didn't want to be kept here any longer than was necessary; she had other priorities. 'Look, Rykhlin,' she said quietly, 'I just want to finish the job and get out as quickly as possible. Get home to my son.'

Rykhlin looked at her in amazement. 'You have a son?'

Nicole twisted her head and saw the concern in his soft brown eyes. 'It's a long story,' she said.

'But surely his father's with him?' Rykhlin persisted. 'He'll be fine.'

'He has no father,' Nicole responded. And even now, after all these years, it still hurt to say that.

Rykhlin went silent then, and Nicole sensed his disquiet. She didn't welcome this sudden intrusion into her private life. He had no business there.

By now pandemonium had broken out all over the camp. Lights were blazing, men were shouting, vehicles were driving around at speed. Nicole became increasingly concerned. 'Shouldn't we move on, get further away from this place?' she urged.

'Yeah, sure!' Rykhlin turned towards her, flicked her a smile. 'Good team?'

In the dark Nicole smiled. 'Yes, of course,' she said quietly. 'A very good team.'

Chapter Twenty-one – two weeks later: Arguni Base

Nicole made her way slowly up the steep forest track towards the northern rim of the island, her trudging feet kicking up little spurts of dry ash and crumbled lava. It was early morning, and already very hot. The air vibrated with the shrill screeching of insects and huge blue butterflies basked on the path in front of her.

From far away came the heavy beat of approaching helicopters. Nicole listened, then pushed her way into the dense foliage at one side of the track to crouch down within the bower formed by a large rhododendron. Large pink blossoms bobbed back into place.

The distant noise rose steadily to a heavy bass throb, then to a crescendo as three helicopters swept low overhead.

It was Rahman, making his Presidential visit to Arguni.

In the pilot's seat, Rahman skimmed low over the rim of Arguni's crater, then pulled his helicopter into a steep left-hand turn. As the ground tilted, he glanced left, centring the blurred disc of the spinning rotor blades onto a cluster of rusty sheet-metal quarry buildings by the ore terminal. He was showing off, enjoying himself.

In the cabin behind him sat Thameena, wearing an elegant veiled dress, her dark sunglasses staring impassively down at the unfolding scenery. She shifted her gaze and studied the back of her husband's head, watching him play with his toy, wondering whether Major Lukman had kept his promise – whether exile was about to become her path to freedom.

Rahman let the helicopter lose height until they were skimming through the forest canopy, the machine slipping in and out of wisps of early-morning mist. Then they were out over the lagoon. He straightened the machine and brought it steadily down towards the helipad, raising the nose to bleed off speed.

The powerful downdraught from the rotors kicked up some dust and swirled it over the welcoming party. Hands held on tight to hats and veils. The machine bounced lightly as the skids touched down. Rahman threw switches, going through the checklist with his co-pilot as the whirling blades slowly came to a halt.

A crewman in white overalls slid back the door, then stood smartly to one side. Rahman flipped off his harness and clambered back through the main cabin. He paused to check his uniform was straight, then descended the short flight of steps to the ground, strutting out along the brief stretch of red carpet, his gold braid and medal ribbons gleaming impressively in the intense sunlight. Thameena followed at a discreet distance, playing the role of the dutiful wife.

The band struck up the national anthem. Salutes were thrown, flags waved in the breeze. Rahman beamed. He was enjoying the show, bathing in the attention of the assembled international press.

He caught a glimpse of Lukman amongst the military and caught the man's eye, causing a memory to pass between them, a memory of a recent conversation – a conversation about Rahman's troublesome wife.

As the national anthem stopped, Dr Jazid Hendra, who'd been waiting for them, came forward like an excited child. He had to raise his voice above the continuing offerings of the band. 'Welcome to Arguni, sir. This is indeed an exciting day for all of us.' He gestured to where a low shape, draped in the red and white-crescented flag of the Islamic Republic of Indonesia, squatted mysteriously in front of the tented podium. 'And as you are about to see, sir, we have succeeded – beyond your wildest dreams.'

Nicole pushed on up the steep track, listening to the gonging and piping of exotic birds in the lush rainforest. She pulled a creased map from the waistband of her tracksuit. Sketched again by Freddy, it showed, with remarkable detail and accuracy, the twists and turns of the paths running up the side of the crater. She didn't have far to go, and as she walked she thought about Rykhlin. She found herself worrying about the risk he was taking in attending Rahman's visit; knowing how tight security had become since their raid on the gulag.

This was their last job. Then they could go home.

The band stopped playing and the crowd quietened. Hendra and Rahman stood in front of the flag-cloaked object. At a nod from Hendra, two white-coated technicians tugged hard, floating the flag away to expose what lay underneath.

Rahman was stunned. The machine sat low and purposeful on the tarmac – a sleek open two-seater, its bright yellow body sculpted into the flowing lines of an ultra-modern speedster. A glossy black aerodynamic wing mounted at the rear hinted at its high speed. The curved windscreen was steeply raked; fat tyres were enclosed in the vehicle's low, tight-fitting bodywork. A ripple of applause ran through the crowd, and a deep feeling of warmth suffused Rahman's body.

Hendra had done well – the car looked truly magnificent. Now the rest of the world would be forced to take notice.

The press gathered round. Cameras clicked, lights flashed. Hendra introduced the design team one by one, and Rahman shook their hands. 'This is a concept car,' explained Hendra, 'a show car.' He was obviously enjoying himself, doing his job so well for the press. He touched a side panel, which hissed open on a small gas strut, and waited for the cameras to zoom in. Rahman stared at the baffling technology: shiny metal boxes linked by neatly routed cables and metal tubing. 'These are the fuel cells, developed from the Mars Rover Project,' explained Hendra. The Russian members of the team smiled nervously. 'Hydrogen in here, steam and oxygen out there. No pollution, of course, and a remarkably long range between refuelling stops. At the moment we're making the hydrogen by electrolysing sea water, using a solar array on the cliffs. The gas is liquefied and pumped into a small tank, here.' He prodded at a flap on the rear of the vehicle, then bent down to point between the suspension arms. 'And down here, cobalt motors – one for each wheel. Very powerful, they give the car exceptional acceleration.' He straightened up. 'We use all our own metals, of course. Cobalt for the motors, platinum for the fuel cells, all from ocean-floor mining. Without our President's far-sighted support of this project, we wouldn't have been able to get so far so quickly.'

Rahman basked in this praise. Hendra's progress had indeed been remarkable. And later on that afternoon, when the press had left, Rahman would move on to inspect the uranium centrifuges and the missile-building facility. He guessed that progress there would be just as spectacular.

But, for all his brilliance, not even Dr Jazid Hendra would be allowed to know the true purpose of Rahman's visit. The truth was that even deeper within the bowels of this island, under conditions of utmost secrecy, a handful of people were developing a new weapon: a terror weapon. A weapon that would enable his influence to reach far beyond this corner of South-East Asia. Because Amir Rahman was an ambitious man, ambitious for his country – and, day by day, month by month, those ambitions were growing.

Hendra's insistent voice broke through Rahman's reverie. 'Now, sir,' he was saying. 'If you would like to climb on board, we'll go for a short test drive.'

And, beaming for the cameras, Rahman was only too keen to impress.

Behind the tented podium, out of sight of the crowd and the foreign press, a column of four jeeps pulled to a halt in a cloud of dust. Men in grey suits leaped out, wearing dark glasses against the harsh sun, weapons held high. They took up position by the small wooden stairway leading down from the curtained doorway, and waited patiently.

Nicole sighed with relief; the concrete ventilation tower stood just where Freddy had marked it. It was about twenty-five feet high and nine feet square. She looked up at the grilled opening high above her head, and saw the hooped metal footrests that were set, in a staggered formation, up the side. They had been thoughtfully provided for the maintenance engineers but started some fifteen feet from the ground, to discourage animals. She would need some way to get up there.

She searched around in the undergrowth and dragged out a dead branch. Propping it up against the tower, she climbed carefully, feet slipping on the damp wood, before gaining the security of the first footrest. She didn't stop climbing until she reached the opening.

The grille was held in place by large galvanized cross-head screws. She reached for her screwdriver and placed the tip of its blade in one of the slotted heads. It turned easily, and she continued with the rest. She let the grille fall to the ground where it thumped into the undergrowth, well concealed from anyone coming along the track.

Using Rahman's visit as cover, Nicole intended to navigate the complex of ventilation tunnels that riddled the island, find Hendra's office, and bug his computer.

She peered down inside the tower. A musty smell of damp concrete wafted out of black velvety darkness. She pulled herself up onto the eight-inch-wide sill and strad-dled it, the sounds of her scrabbling echoing back metalli-cally from inside the shaft. She eased off the small rucksack, took out a torch, and shone it down. The metal sides of a wide tube gleamed back at her. She switched off and tied the torch carefully to her wrist. Then she stuffed four balls of string into her pockets. Holding a fifth in her hand, she taped one end of the string to the shaft opening, careful to make it secure. Like Theseus's thread when he was about to descend into the labyrinth, this string would be her only guide to the way back out.

Nicole retrieved the large photocopied plan and folded it carefully to see the relevant section. It had come from Freddy, via one of Rykhlin's contacts among the maintenance engineers. It showed the twisting routes of the ventilation shafts as they wound deep into the underground complex. For security reasons not all of it was shown, only the first level – but that would do for today.

The first part was the short vertical drop through the tower itself, followed by a gently curving section – just like a child's 'death slide'. This curve would break her fall, sweeping her into the bowels of the old volcano. She shone her torch into the blackness again, and again the light glinted back off the polished metal sides.

She swung her legs over the side and got ready to drop. As she sat there, teetering on the edge, Nicole heard the sound of a heavy vehicle grinding its way up the track towards her. She shuffled forward, hesitated, and then plummeted into the darkness, the ball of string falling along with her.

Rahman mounted the podium, flushed and excited by his ride in the experimental car. He stood at the lectern as Thameena settled down behind him, sheltering from the sun under the gently flapping canopy. Above her head, little red and white national flags fluttered in the breeze.

Rahman looked at the teleprompter, and waited for the crowd to hush.

'My friends, this is indeed a proud day for Indonesia.

This wonderful vehicle that you see before you was designed and developed in great secrecy, right here at Arguni. And I believe it is destined to take the world by storm.' He looked down at the car parked enticingly in front of him, and for an instant caught sight of Lukman, saw him give the signal – the slight nod of the head, the sign that they were ready for Thameena.

His eyes swung back to the teleprompter. 'Here is a car that won't pollute our cities, or foul the air that we breathe. Here is a car that is friendly to our planet, that won't warm our atmosphere. But here also is a car with performance that people will find exciting to own and a joy to drive. It is a modern car for the modern city. A car of the future – here, now.' Polite applause rippled through the crowd. Rahman waited for it to die away before continuing in a more forceful tone. 'And most exciting of all, this car is Indonesian, and its technology is Islamic. It heralds a great technological awakening for our country. It is just one example of what we can do with our ocean-floor resources. The oceans are a new frontier for Indonesia; so blatantly ignored by the West that prefers to plunder the riches of other people's lands. Let the oceans be our way forward, not just for minerals, but for food, for medicines, for scientific understanding. Islamic science in search of peace. Our way forward to a more prosperous future.' More applause, stronger this time. 'Now we will step out and launch our new automobile onto the world stage. We will develop the technology for hydrogen production, take control of the infrastructure that will fuel these cars, and this will be the gateway to our economic future.'

Rykhlin stood at the rear of the assembled crowd, listening to Rahman's garbage. He eyeballed the car. Impressive, but Rykhlin knew it for what it really was – a distraction designed to hide the awful truth of this place.

He thought about Annabelle struggling up the side of the volcano, and worried about whether she was safe. Wondered what she'd discover once she'd bugged Hendra's office. Wondered what the hell she was doing here, when she had a kid back home.

How could she do that? Leave her kid behind for this awful place!

He guessed he knew about things like that, because he had a memory . . . of the innocent look of hope on two kids' faces as he left them to die. He lived again the dull pain of guilt that had sat like a toad in his stomach as he'd pulled the chopper away to safety above the neat red-roofed houses of Pristina.

He instantly erased the scene from his mind, just like he always did. He didn't want to look there. Coward-ice, that's what they'd said – but they were wrong. He hadn't given a shit then, thought that time would be the big healer. But Kosovo hadn't faded for him, and the guilt burned in deep, leaving a raw scar on the surface.

Which was why he was here, why he had chosen to live

in the shadow lands of the Service. Because it helped him to numb the pain.

The rhythmic clapping of the crowd brought him back to the present. He pulled himself together – he had a job to do.

He became aware of the people around him: technicians, designers, engineers, submersible pilots, all working under contract for Rahman, all seduced by big money. He focused his attention, narrowing his eyes in the sunlight, looking for just one man.

He pushed in among the crowd, clapping hands jogging his elbows. Rykhlin moved carefully, keeping his eyes on the nervous soldiers protecting Rahman from any potential *Korowai* attack, while grey-suited *Bakorstanas* eyed the crowd from the podium, looking for trouble.

He would be discreet.

Off to his right he found a small knot of submersible pilots. He edged his way over. There was more applause, the pilots notably less enthusiastic than the Indonesians around them. One man was smaller than the rest, with a head of brown curly hair. Rykhlin tapped him gently on the shoulder to draw his attention.

'Excuse me,' he asked politely, 'I'm looking for Bryn.' He used a false name, a carefully selected homonym.

The man turned. He fitted Annabelle's description exactly. It was him.

Rykhlin gave him a broad smile. 'Oh, I'm so sorry,' he said politely. 'Wrong man.' Glyn turned back to his circle of friends as the crowd jostled around them.

Rykhlin's eyes focused distantly on the podium. He casually slipped a cigar from his top pocket and put it to his lips. Taking the gold lighter from his pocket he thumbed the wheel, but too gently to spark a flame. He feigned a frown, raising the lighter to his eyes as if to examine the mechanism – carefully rotating the base as he did so.

The crowd were still roaring their approval of Rahman. Rykhlin's fingernail found the tiny chrome catch and clicked it down to prime the device. The crowd broke out again into enthusiastic clapping. Rykhlin's nail pulled once more on the tag of polished chrome and, with an imperceptible *phut* of compressed air, a tiny drop of VX, one of the world's most deadly nerve agents, shot from the base of the lighter. The crowd suddenly surged forwards, jolting Glyn sideways. Smaller than a pinhead, the tiny drop missed Glyn's neck and hit the collar of his shirt instead, soaking into the fabric.

But as the volatile liquid evaporated into the humid air, a whisper of gas passed across Glyn's skin.

His eyes dulled. His hands went up to his chest. He gasped for breath as his skin paled visibly, and then he slumped to the ground.

His friends looked down at the man who had fainted in the heat; some began to stagger themselves. They asked the crowd to draw back, to give them some air as they fussed around him.

Rykhlin melted quickly back into the crowd.

*

SLIDE

Nicole had long since lost track of time. Her knees ached from constantly crawling along the polished metal tubes. The torch's light pierced the darkness ahead, forming a bright halo around her. Hot, humid air poured over her, making sweat run from her temples and trickle from her armpits. Her clothes were soaked with it. There was nowhere to stretch, nowhere to reach out, no space to move in the tight metal tube. She hovered on the edge of claustrophobia and forced herself to halt, to stay calm. She pulled out the tatty photocopied plan, checking and double-checking her route. It couldn't be far now.

Rahman was winding up his speech. 'The future of Indonesia rests on you, the technicians – your unique skills, your determination, your imagination. But we must not forget the hundreds of ordinary people, the farmers and factory workers of Java, who have so willingly moved to Arguni to perform the difficult and often dangerous task of carving out workshops from the living rock of the volcano, processing the materials, operating the machinery.'

Behind the podium, Lukman was talking on his radio, checking out the *Bakorstanas*, confirming the final arrangements for Thameena's exit. For them, Rahman's speech was muffled by the quiet rumble of idling jeep engines.

*

Nicole turned off the main trunking and crawled for almost two hundred feet down a tiny square-section tunnel, twisting and pulling her body around the tight right-angle turns until at last she was right above Hendra's office. The long and difficult journey had sapped her energy. She lay still, panting, enjoying the flow of relatively cool air coming up through the ceiling grille.

Viewed from above, Hendra's office looked sparsely furnished. There was a large dark-wood desk, with an elaborately carved stationery stand and a green blotter. On it, angled across the velvety surface, its scalloped blade gleaming in the subdued lighting, was a *kris*: a warrior's blade, its handle heavily encrusted with jewels. It lay there as if breathing gently with an inner life of its own. Nicole's gaze slid curiously along the length of the blade, then carried on past its sharply curved steel tip to study the hard-edged box of Hendra's computer.

She'd found what she was looking for.

She rattled her rucksack across the grille, and carefully removed a small white polystyrene box. It felt warm and soft between her fingers, giving a little squeak as she twisted off the lid. Nestling inside was a tiny black plastic wafer, no more than an inch square, and very thin. Delicately, she removed the object – a digital video camera, courtesy of Rykhlin and the CIA. She placed it on the air-conditioning grille, checking that it fitted snugly between the cross-wires. She moved it to a corner where it would attract least attention, and then used her finger to angle the lens so that it focused directly down at Hendra's keyboard. Hands shaking with anxiety, she eased out the tiny microphone, no bigger than a button, and taped it carefully to the edge of the metal grille.

Nicole packed her stuff back into the rucksack and edged backwards down the narrow tunnel, pulling a wire-laying tool behind her, taping the wire secure as she went. Reaching the main tunnel once more, she travelled 'upstream' to find one of the booster fans. Using crocodile clips, she clamped the fine black wire to the negative terminal on the motor and the red wire to the positive. Now a trickle of power, carefully controlled by the intricate circuitry, would flow constantly to the camera and the microphone, and she could use the power cables to communicate with her 'bugs' at any time, simply by tapping into the Centre's electrical circuit anywhere she chose.

She began the long hot climb back out of the tunnel complex.

Rahman had reached the end of his speech. *Bakorstanas*, discreetly dispersed within the crowd, began to chant, punching their fists into the air – *Rah-man, Rah-man, Rah-man*. Others joined in, intoxicated both by the heat and the carefully choreographed excitement of the President's speech. Soon the whole crowd was swaying and chanting for the benefit of the world's press.

Rahman beamed down at them, waving benignly, absorbed in this orchestrated rapture. He'd told the crowd what they wanted to hear, and they loved him for it.

But his thoughts were focusing elsewhere, pivoting on Luckman's reported treachery of his wife. Now he longed to be rid of her, this thorn in his side. He'd never been in love with her. It had merely been a convenience – a political marriage, to give himself status and power – and had been barren from the start. He felt no remorse for his deceit. Why should he? He'd achieved what he wanted.

He could have got rid of her long ago, of course, when an accident would have been so much simpler. It was unfortunate that now it would have to be Lukman who would handle the situation for him.

The rat knew too much for his own good.

As her husband turned back from the lectern, Thameena saw him cast his gaze upon her, saw his expression darken with suppressed anger and disappointment, and then she knew. Knew that Lukman had kept his word. That they would be waiting for her.

Her heart began to beat heavily. She ignored Rahman's look, pretended she hadn't noticed. She rose calmly from her seat and turned to descend the steps at the rear of the podium. She saw the cluster of grey-suited *Bakorstanas*, stiff-faced behind dark glasses, weapons held at the ready. She saw Lukman, his face impassive, waiting for her, a radio in his hand.

They closed in as she came off the bottom step, seizing

her arms, and hustling her towards a waiting jeep. She made a show for Rahman, shouting to him for help. She tried to wrench her hands free, but felt her jewellery clatter impotently against the cold steel of the handcuffs being placed around her wrists.

The *Bakorstanas* bundled her into the jeep. Thameena stared defiantly out of the window, shouted for her husband – but saw his back turned firmly against her.

She felt no regret, no loss at their separation. She knew she had served his purpose, done his bidding. Now she was no longer of any consequence to him.

She was free.

It became difficult to hide her growing sense of elation, her sense of anticipation, her excitement. Her jaw tightened to stifle a smile. At last she would no longer have to play second fiddle.

From now on she would serve just one aim – her own.

Nicole had reached the final short vertical section of the tube – just ten feet to go. She'd jammed herself in, forcing her arms and legs hard against its slippery metal sides. Her chest heaved and her breath came in gasps, her limbs shaking with the physical exertion. Sweat was running everywhere, making her skin slippery. Tiny rivulets stung her eyes. Her throat was parched.

Slowly, she began to force herself upwards, pushing with her legs, sliding up the tube inches at a time, her back rubbing painfully against the metal, the rectangle of sunlight now so tantalizingly close.

The Suzuki jeep bumped and rattled at high speed along the road leading away from the presentation, while Thameena sat on one of the back seats. *Bakorstanas* guards sat stiffly at either side of her, not sure of the protocol, not sure how to deal with the President's errant wife.

The barbed-wire fencing of the gulag streamed past the window, while behind the wire, in the distance, row upon row of wooden huts flicked rapidly past. She turned in her seat to look for signs of life, but the place seemed deserted. The prisoners had all been hidden away for the day – to complete the lie for the foreign press.

Thameena studied the Secret Service agent opposite her, his face an impassive mask behind the sunglasses. She wondered what he was thinking, what he already knew.

Rahman was no different from the rest, of course. Sukarno had packed his enemies off to Ambon. Kartini had used the jungle and swamp-infested island of Buru. Now she too would be discreetly exiled on some tiny island far to the east. She wondered idly what little malaria-infested swamp Rahman had lined up for her.

Little did it matter. She was intelligent, she knew what she was doing, and Rahman was a fool. Exile would serve her purpose well. From now on her popularity would grow, not diminish. Already there was support for her among the disaffected and the ignored and, month by month, her secret army had quietly swelled its ranks. She had the backing of the United States. There were discreet arms caches, advisers, training camps hidden away in the forests. And she had the might of right on her side. After all, she was the true leader of the people.

And when the time was right, Thameena would return.

Chapter Twenty-two – the following evening: Arguni Base

At the end of her daily duties, Nicole paid a visit to the rest room in Submersible Pilot Briefing. There she stood on the toilet seat, unscrewed the air-conditioning grille from the ceiling, and crocodile-clipped a small electronic 'black box' into the wiring circuit feeding the fan motor. Plugging in her small palmtop computer, she then interrogated the devices already installed above Hendra's office and downloaded the information they provided.

Now she sat on the small settee in her bungalow, laptop on her knees, its lid flipped up, waiting for Rykhlin to arrive. She looked at her watch, saw it was getting late, and slowly tapped her fingers on the seat cushion. She was getting anxious. Where was he?

Outside, it was raining again. She could hear the depressing sound of water dripping heavily through thick banana leaves, the gutter splattering noisily onto the brick path that ran around the veranda. The familiar sound of thunder grumbled around the bowl of Arguni's crater.

Nicole sighed as a strong sense of foreboding seeped quietly into her soul.

Trying to ignore it, she booted up the machine and accessed the surveillance file, to watch the images recorded by the camera. They were sound-activated – and predictably disappointing. A cleaner vacuuming the floor, Hendra's secretary sorting papers onto his desk, then nothing, a blank – the camera simply triggered by the phone ringing.

Nicole fidgeted impatiently. She knew that she had to catch Hendra quickly, get his computer code while he was still here on the island. She got up from the table and made herself a coffee, checking out the window for Rykhlin.

She sat down and reactivated the machine. More mundane sequences, then . . . another image.

She watched the screen as the door squeaked open, then shut – and suddenly Hendra was there. He put his briefcase down and sat at his desk. There was the *kris* still lying on the table. He played with it for a moment, running his thumb along its wavy blade, watching the light catch the jewel-encrusted hilt.

Then came the sound of papers shuffling, and he was reading, signing something, writing a note at the bottom of a letter.

The door squeaked open and shut again – someone else arriving. Nicole leaned forward and peered hard at the screen. She thought she recognized the newcomer. She punched a key on the laptop to freeze the image, reversed, and played forward again to study the man just entering.

She knew him, she was sure. But it was difficult to tell from the camera angle.

'Good morning, Hari. Thank you for coming so promptly. Did you have a good flight?'

My God! It was Lukman!

The *Kopassus* officer. The one on the oil rig. The one who'd taken the disk from 'Sour-Face'.

Questions raced through Nicole's mind. What was he doing here? Why was he with Hendra?

Lukman flopped down into one of the easy chairs. 'I hear the President liked his new toy,' he said, his neat cultured voice sounding thin, distorted by the electronics.

'I let him drive it around for a bit,' replied Hendra dryly.

Lukman laughed. 'Did he visit the uranium centrifuges?'

'Yes, very impressed.' Hendra paused slightly. 'He's getting very ambitious, Hari. Sometimes I think he might be pushing things along too fast. We need to be careful.'

'I agree.'

There was a lull in the conversation as Hendra got up and walked across to Lukman, offering him a kretek from a large silver box. Lukman accepted. Hendra placed the box back onto the coffee table, and sat down again.

'Hari – we need to discuss the production figures for Indera,' he said.

Indera? thought Nicole. What's he taking about? Then suddenly she remembered what her father had said, that there was something else going on at Arguni. Was this *Indera*? Was this what had concerned him so much?

'. . . There's a serious shortfall. The labs are asking for more. They want to set up pilot production at Espiritu.'

Lukman lit his clove cigarette and pocketed the lighter. 'Can't they wait?'

'I don't think we can afford to delay any more. I'm worried about Rahman. Did you know that he put his wife under house arrest yesterday?'

Lukman took a long drag at his cigarette, and slowly blew out the smoke. 'Yes. I heard.'

'She's got a lot of support amongst the traditional Muslims, Hari. There was a big sympathy demonstration for her in Bandung last night. It ended in a full-scale riot. If we don't act quickly enough, that woman could topple Rahman before we're ready.'

My God! thought Nicole. What are they doing? What are they plotting?

Lukman shot Hendra an odd look, then contemplated the glowing end of his cigarette. 'You could be right. The value of the rupiah's plummeting – fell another four per cent yesterday. Things are going faster than we anticipated.'

Hendra picked up the dagger and played nervously with its blade, running his thumb dangerously along the serrated edge. The weapon flashed dully as he rotated it in his hands. 'I think the time has come for us to think about ourselves,' he said quietly.

He got up from his seat, and walked out of camera range. 'I'd like you to have a look at a new production site I've found.' A drawer slid open. There was the sound of a large sheet of paper being shaken out. He came back into camera view and smoothed a map onto his desk. It was a marine chart showing a mass of soundings and ocean-depth contours. Lukman got up and moved round the coffee table to take a closer look.

Hendra's fingers stabbed at the paper. 'Here, on the edge of the Marianas Trench.'

Lukman pulled the map towards him, kretek smoking gently between the fingers of his right hand. He chewed the tip of his thumb, studying the place that Hendra had indicated. 'Good God, Jazid! You're almost on top of Guam.'

'Yes, I know. But it's a very good site: large grains, up to five microns across. Density around twelve to twenty p.p.m. It's a good deposit Hari. Just what we need to start up production. But we've got to move fast – before it's too late.'

'No! It's too risky. Guam's a big American base. They'll have surveillance equipment, you'd be spotted in no time.'

'Oh, come on, Hari, the Americans can't stop us. We're in the high seas.'

'Like hell, Jazid! The Americans won't put up with you mucking about down there, and you know it. If you're discovered, they'll bring in the UN, and the International Seabed Authority – and then what? Rahman will squash you like a fly.'

'But we have to expand extraction somehow. We can't even get pilot production under way. This is our chance, Hari. Our chance to get rich, and get out.'

'Like rats from a sinking ship?' Lukman took the map and peered at it carefully. Then he took a ruler from Hendra's *desk, and measured a distance against the scale bar. 'This site's not in the high seas, Jazid. You're 180 miles off the coast. It's well inside the EEZ. You're in US territorial waters. What the hell are you suggesting?'*

Hendra started to roll up the map. 'We've already done some preliminary work.'

'Then you've been damn lucky to get away with it.'

There was a frosty pause before Lukman continued.

'So, tell me, how are you extracting it?'

'Leaching it. Chemicals keep the noise down.'

Lukman blew out through his lips. 'Those chemicals are toxic. If the Americans sniff out the pollution plume you're in big trouble.'

'Oh, come off it, Hari, we're very deep. The chemicals will mix with the abyssal water. There's no danger.'

There was a long silence before Lukman replied.

'I'm not prepared to agree to this. You're going too fast.'

Hendra sat back in his office chair, then moved the dagger to one side so that he could pull the computer keyboard towards him. 'Look, let me show you the recent extraction figures from Palau Ridge. Then you'll understand the situation we're in.'

Palau! Nicole's heart thumped as she caught that name. It was the name on the computer disk, the disk she'd passed to Simes.

Hendra was pushing the rolled-up map to one side, one hand reaching out to key the monitor free of its security window.

'Got you!' she breathed.

She paused the playback. Ran the sequence back a little, magnified the image, then let it play through again. She studied the screen, then repeated, watching carefully where Hendra's fingers fell on the keyboard.

0 – 4 – 0 – 4 – 9 – 3

She accessed one of her own secure files on the laptop, entered the code, then returned to the surveillance film.

Hendra leaned back from the monitor screen. 'There you are, Hari, look at the figures. See for yourself: extraction rates are right down. The site's almost worked out.' Hendra put his hands behind his head and gazed straight up into the surveillance camera.

His gaze seemed to linger there unnaturally.

Lukman was moving back from the monitor. 'Well, yes, I agree, the extraction rate has dropped. But that's no reason for you to go ahead and mine off Guam. It's a huge risk, Jazid. In fact, it's suicide! If the Americans find out, you'll blow the whole operation wide open.' He paused. 'In any case, it's a lot deeper than you've ever gone before. Look – the new subs aren't ready yet. You're too far ahead of yourself, Jazid. You're endangering everything.'

Hendra reached forward to pull a small white box across the desk towards him. He opened the lid and took out a round peppermint. 'I agree with you, Hari. It's a gamble, but . . .'

'A gamble! Jazid – are you mad?' Lukman exclaimed. 'Have all those little Papuan boys gone to your head?'

But Lukman had gone too far – he'd just overstepped the

margin of Hendra's sensitivity. In one fluid movement Hendra leaped to his feet, grabbed the deadly kris, *and lunged at Lukman. Lukman was too quick and caught his arm in a powerful grip. They stood there, locked together, eyes boring into each other, breathing heavily.*

'What did you just say about me?' hissed Hendra.

'That you disgust me,' snarled Lukman.

Hendra pushed against Lukman's restraining arm with his dagger hand. 'Just remember, Major Lukman, that without me you are nothing.'

They glared at each other, eyes blazing with hatred.

'You've still not recovered those disks, Jazid,' gritted Lukman. 'You would do well to remember that. If Rahman ever had access to that information . . .' And Lukman drew his other hand across his throat in a slicing action.

And you have that disk, thought Nicole. I saw you take it, and now I think I know why.

Hendra shook his hand free of Lukman and sank back into his seat. 'The disks are too well encrypted,' he said sulkily. 'The information's impossible to extract.' He stared up at the ceiling again, frowning.

They were both silent for a moment.

'I think the bait might have worked,' announced Lukman.

'I'm sorry?' queried Hendra, distracted from his upward gaze.

'The old man – Tai-Chung – someone came for him a few weeks ago. A well-organized operation by all accounts.'

275

'His daughter?'

Cold steel stabbed into Nicole's heart. 'Oh God, no!' she breathed.

'Could be. It's what we wanted. But if it was her, she must have had a lot of support.'

'CIA?'

'Maybe. But you need to be careful. If they are CIA, and they blow the cover off your Guam operation, I'm not with you.'

Hendra heeled his office chair back until it was directly underneath the ventilation grille. 'Can you spot anything odd about that grille, Hari?'

Fear slithered into Nicole's head. No! Not this as well! Please, God, not this!

Hendra got off his chair and placed a stool directly under the camera. His hands on the screen suddenly became distorted and bloated as he fiddled in close-up with the grille fixings. There came the sound of metal vibrating and scraping. 'There's something in here. Look – what's this?'

The grille came off with a bang and dangled from Hendra's free hand. The picture lurched as the camera dropped out, and then spun crazily as Hendra started to pull at it.

'Good God!' Lukman exclaimed. 'I don't know – a bug, I think. Don't pull it out, leave it where it is.'

The picture jerked. 'It won't come, anyhow. It's fixed by its wires. Get security in here, will you!'

The camera was left looking drunkenly at a wall.

Nicole stopped the playback.

The time of the recording blinked neatly in the corner of the screen. It said 15.38.

She'd been spotted! She'd been watching the overture to her own doom.

Her heart thumped painfully in her chest. They must be coming. They must be out there searching for her right now. They could already be in the village. If she was caught with the bugging equipment, who knew what they would do to her? Perhaps they'd already been watching her as she retrieved this data.

She stood up, fear stabbing pain into her belly. Where was Rykhlin?

Footsteps came running up the brick path. Nicole frantically tapped at the keyboard, shutting down her laptop. Feet were pounding on the wood planking of the veranda as she slammed down the lid. The flimsy door burst open. It was Freddy, red Olympic T-shirt and grey slacks soaked with rain, droplets beading his frizzy hair. His eyes were adrenalin-wide, his breath coming in gasps. 'Soldiers! *Kopassus*! They're looking for Mr Rykhlin. You must come now! Quickly!'

'Why? What've they found?'

'That man. The man you said knew you. He's in the hospital.'

'What? Glyn?'

'Yes. He just talked. He recognized Mr Rykhlin.'

'Go and warn him!'

'Already gone. Now they come for you. No time, please!' Freddy looked at Nicole, eyes full of fear.

'Wait a minute.' Nicole quickly prioritized what she needed. She ran into the bedroom and snatched up her small rucksack. Into it went her laptop, palmtop, battery chargers, the small antenna to communicate with London. She glanced around the room, guessed that was it.

Outside, the night was pitch black, the rain coming down like stair-rods. It pounded against her head and roared on the roof tiles. She was soaked instantly. Freddy shouted to her above the racket. 'Follow me, I show you where to go.'

His slim body darted away between the trees. Nicole followed, heaving the rucksack onto her back as she went. Her wet clothes stuck to her body, trousers flapping heavily around her legs, making it difficult to run.

They hit the beach by the lagoon and veered right, pounding along the wet sand, dodging round surfboards racked up for the night. From somewhere in the complex came the sound of engines roaring, doors banging, and shouted orders. Blue lights came strobing through the palms. Then a searchlight snapped on, its white beam piercing the rain-shot darkness. It began to play along the beach.

Nicole ran along the sand, covering ground as fast as she could. To her left small waves shushed into surf, the faint whiteness of the foam showing her the way. The searchlight flicked down onto the beach and caught Freddy. For a moment she saw his thin body running ahead; then the beam lost him and swung back, coming down on her with its blinding light. She lifted a hand as a shield against the glare and found it difficult to see, felt her shoes splashing in the shallows at the water's edge.

There were more shouts from the road. The searchlight was still fixed upon her, white and blinding; then came the sharp crack of a rifle. Freddy yelled anxiously from up ahead: 'Follow me, Missy!'

Nicole ran on for her life, her breath coming in gasps, her heart pounding, chest tightening. Still the searchlight followed. *Crack!* A fountain of water erupted in the waves. Where was Freddy? She couldn't see him. The rain battered on her head, seeped into her eyes. *Crack!* Another plume of water.

Then, looming out of the darkness ahead of her, the camp perimeter – a tall wire fence extending out into the sea. There was a small building on the causeway just above the beach. A soldier stepped out and levelled his rifle at her, shouting at her to stop.

Nicole faltered for a moment, then remembered her training: *Get inside the weapon. Get in close. Dare him.* She jumped up on the causeway and ran straight towards him. He shouted at her again. He was only young – the gun wavered slightly.

Suddenly a savage war cry pierced the rain-sodden night – it was Freddy, yelling up from the beach. For a moment the soldier was distracted. Then she collided with him, jerking his weapon up in the air with her hand. The rifle exploded, a deafening detonation. She brought up her knee, slamming it straight into his groin. The man doubled over, gasping. She grabbed his hair, yanking his head forward to expose the neck, then chopped down hard. Pain shot up through her wrist. They hit the ground together, rolling in the dirt, the rifle clattering away across the gravel.

Nicole crouched over the soldier's body, rain still pounding on her back. The young man lay motionless on the ground. She stared down at him, breathing hard, eyes wide. A laugh bubbled out of her, an obscene elation, hand-to-hand – so easy. Then Freddy was beside her, staring down at the body too.

The roar of engines broke their trance. Locked wheels slid through the gravel. Men were shouting orders.

Freddy grabbed her arm. 'Follow me!'

He waded out to sea to get around the perimeter fence. She followed him and felt the waves nudging up against her shaking thighs, forcing her to work hard against them. Then they were round the fence and heading back up the beach.

They plunged into the blackness of the forest.

Freddy slowed his pace to a walk, feeling his way along a forest path with practised hands. Nicole stumbled behind him, panting, one arm clinging to his shirt. Wet leaves slapped against her face and large drops of water pattered down from the forest canopy overhead. Then came a sudden explosion amid the foliage, and Nicole jumped as something crashed away through the undergrowth.

Freddy walked on, pace less frantic now, more certain. They marched on for over an hour, deeper and deeper into the rainforest, the damp air full of the smell of rotting vegetation and the normal night sounds of the jungle: the whirr of insects, the steady *zitt-zitt-zitt* of the frogs.

What now?

Nicole had no idea.

Chapter Twenty-three – the following morning: Arguni Island

Nicole followed Freddy all night, climbing along rough and narrow forest paths until they arrived high up on the northern rim of the island. Now cool early-morning mist drifted gently through the densely packed vegetation, and she felt utterly exhausted.

The sound of the awakening jungle echoed all around her – whoops and whistles, the incessant aviary chatter of thousands of birds. Her clothes were soaked by rain and by contact with wet leaves, and chafed heavily against her body. She was uncomfortable, itchy with dirt and sweat, nauseous with fatigue and hunger. Depression began to drag her spirits down. She had never felt more alone.

Her thoughts narrowed dangerously around her son. She began to see Peter in her imagination: him waiting for her to return, wondering why he'd been abandoned. In just a few short days her wretched mission had imploded, turned to vapour, run out through her fingers like mist in the forest.

My God! What had she done?

SLIDE

She kept hearing Hendra's words on that recording, over and over again – her father had been used as bait, for *her*! She'd been a fool. She should never have given in to Simes. Should never have got involved with his madcap scheme. She should have stayed at home and cared for Peter, the one person who really needed her.

Nicole found herself stumbling into a rough clearing hacked carelessly out of the forest. A nightmare jumble of branches and felled trunks littered the ground, a riot of secondary vegetation growing up through them. In the centre of the clearing stood a pair of isolated trees, tall and thin, with silvery bark. Tufts of leaves sprouted where branches had been hacked off. At the very top, at least fifty feet above the ground, a large rectangular tree house perched peculiarly, a giant's nest of sticks and leaves.

Freddy climbed on one of the fallen logs, and pointed, filed tooth flashing ivory in the weak morning sun, bamboo studding his nose. 'My house! See?' Nicole stared up at the rickety construction. Freddy smiled proudly. 'Up high, to keep out the sorcerers,' he informed her. 'To see the birds and the sea.' He began to thread his way expertly across the chaos of trunks and branches. Nicole followed slowly, often slipping awkwardly between the scattered branches, grazing her ankles and shins.

At the base of the tree a long pole swept up steeply through the scant foliage to the house far above. It had been crudely notched to make a kind of ladder. Freddy stood there, smiling, clearly expecting her to climb. Realizing she had no choice in the matter, she grabbed the pole with both hands and began the perilous ascent. The bark felt smooth beneath her fingers, polished by constant use, and it bounced alarmingly with every step. She dared not look down, so instead she stared fixedly at the texture of the wood as she inched her way upwards, her feet scrabbling wetly for purchase on the narrow notches, feeling leaves and branches brushing against her clothing.

At the top, she moved off the pole and crawled exhausted onto a narrow cane veranda that cracked alarmingly under her shifting weight. The sides of the tree house had been hung with parchment-like sheets of dried sago bark to keep out the rain. The only light entered through the rickety gable end – a rough cage-like structure made of sticks lashed together with fronds.

Fearful of the dizzying drop to the ground far below, Nicole crawled through the opening into the gloom of the house. A strong smell of charcoal and rendered fat filled her nostrils. She sat on the rough cane floor, letting her eyes get used to the dark. A tiny piglet squealed, and snuffled towards her, pushing at her with its snout, its tail wiggling furiously.

Nicole slowly became aware of other people in the hut, their eyes shining white in the darkness.

The hut trembled as Freddy swung himself confidently onto the veranda and walked in through the entrance. He spoke sharply to the others in their own language. They came forward slowly, dressed only in dirty shorts and torn T-shirts. Two of them were young men, bows held out threateningly before them, arrows drawn. Freddy spoke fast. The young men eyed Nicole and looked fierce. There was much argument and gesticulation. A female child clung to her mother's grass skirt and watched the drama impassively. Eventually, both the younger men went off down the 'ladder' in an exaggerated huff.

Freddy turned to her. 'They are frightened of you. They think you may be a sorcerer. They think you come to play a trick on them. I told them you need help. You can stay here. For short time.'

Freddy ushered Nicole to the back of the hut, to the women's hearth. Instantly all the women and children scuttled past her, and dropped off down the ladder to safety, to join their warrior men below.

As Nicole's eyes adjusted, objects began to materialize out of the gloom. Nets hung from the ceiling. In one of them was a pair of human skulls, eye sockets staring blankly. Nicole remembered Rykhlin's words – the *Korowai* were head-hunters, cannibals. She shuddered. Where was Rykhlin now? She felt very alone.

She crouched down awkwardly, and a great weariness began to seep through her body.

Soon she lay down on the hard ribs of the cane floor, her head pillowed on her rucksack. Pungent woodsmoke drifted gently into her nostrils. Vaguely, she wondered again about Rykhlin, whether he'd got away. Then she closed her eyes, listening to the sound of the awakening jungle far below, and finally she slept – the deep sleep of the truly exhausted.

*

She was in a canoe. They were going to fetch Peter at last. She was sat in the back of the canoe inside a grass hut. Brown-skinned men filled the hollow craft in front of her, their oars dipping strongly into the current, propelling the canoe at speed along a river. From somewhere came the sound of drums. A strong rhythm, its pace becoming faster and faster. The oarsmen were trying to keep the pace – they were becoming frantic. The hut around her began to split open, the framework snapping. She was falling . . .

Nicole awoke with a start, grabbing out at nothing.

It was hot and stifling in the tree house. She could hear the deep throb of an approaching helicopter, coming in fast. She scrambled to the rear of the hut and hid beneath a pile of dried sago bark, trying to make herself as small and inconspicuous as possible.

The hut seemed to swell with an explosion of sound – the rhythmical slapping of the revolving blades, the howl of the jet engine, the sharp buzz of the tail rotor. The hut quivered and shook in the downdraught and things began to flap around in the strong wind. The little piglet squealed in fright, running round and round in frantic circles. Something broke off and slapped against the wall behind her.

Slowly the sound changed pitch as the helicopter man-oeuvred. Nicole could sense it edging slowly around the hut like a malevolent insect. The structure shook and shuddered as the machine came in closer. She cowered at the back, her eyes tight shut. She imagined a crewman beyond the open doorway, his flight suit flapping violently in the slipstream, leaning out and peering into the hut. Looking for her. Searching for the spy who had evaporated into the night.

Then, as suddenly as it had begun, the sound dropped away. Finally it became just a hollow echo around the crater walls . . . and then, silence.

Nicole lay still, heart pounding against the hardness of the cane floor, waiting for the machine to return.

Instead, the sounds of the jungle slowly reinstated themselves: the steady *zizzizzizz* of the insects, the piping calls of exotic birds.

It was hot under the sheets of bark. They smelled musty, and dust peppered her face. She threw them back and they fell away like dried parchment.

For a while, she sat with her knees drawn up, forehead cradled in her hands. A headache throbbed painfully and there was a sick feeling in the pit of her stomach. Her tongue was dry and swollen, her lips cracked. She was hungry, and probably dehydrating in the fierce heat. She needed Rykhlin – where was he? She needed water and food.

She began to doze fitfully.

Freddy startled Nicole awake, the whole hut shaking as he came up over the side of the veranda. She looked up and saw that he was grinning mischievously, his hand mysteriously behind his back as he advanced into the hut. He squatted in front of her, and slowly revealed his secret – a palm leaf, carefully tied with grass. Like a small boy giving her a present he unlaced the frond and, peeling back the sides, held it out for Nicole to see. She looked inside. A wriggling mass of larvae, creamy yellow and each as big as a human thumb, undulated in the crowded space. She drew back in horror.

Freddy looked a little hurt, and retired to the men's fire. He stirred the charcoal with a stick and blew on it until it began to glow again. Smoke spiralled out of the clay-lined pit and collected in the roof space of the hut. With his bare hands he rummaged around at the edge of the hearth and found some flat stones. He began to lay out the larvae for roasting, biting off their heads to stop them from wriggling away. Nicole watched, her mouth badly parched. 'Do you have any water, Freddy?' she said at last.

'Sure thing, Missy.' He pointed up to one of the nets hanging from the ceiling where she could see an old polythene water carrier, streaked with grime. She got up and crossed over to the net, pulling it down to retrieve the container. The water sloshed as she unscrewed the top, revealing the dirt and stains that encrusted the screw threads.

'Is it safe?' she asked.

Freddy looked up. 'Sure!' he said, a look of surprise on his face. 'Water good!'

She took a careful draught. It was warm and beautifully sweet. She drank – long and deep.

Carefully wiping her mouth with the back of her hand, Nicole screwed the top back onto the water carrier. Then, as she reached up to return it to its rightful place, something shiny caught her eye, something stored in one of the other nets near the door. It was flat, white and smooth; some sort of blade manufactured by a technology quite alien to the tribal artefacts all around her.

The hut swayed gently as she walked over to the doorway. She reached up and pulled the net down so that she could fish out the object. As she turned it over in her hands, the light flashed on its glossy white surface. It was made of some light material – probably carbon fibre. Looking closely at its shape, she thought she recognized it as the guidance fin from some sort of missile. How the hell had Freddy got hold of such a thing?

Freddy sensed her puzzlement, and turned to look at her.

'Where did you get this?' she asked.

'From secret place – hole in the mountain.' He turned back to roasting his grubs.

Nicole's heart leaped. A hole in the ground. Had he found something? Another entrance to the underground complex? It had to be.

'Where is this hole, Freddy?' she asked, carefully replacing the fin.

He turned to her again, eyes wide with some memory. 'Big place, lots of noise . . .' He made a long screaming sound.

Jet engines?

'. . . And lots of doctors.'

'Doctors?'

'In white coats.'

For a moment, Nicole was baffled, then she realized what he was talking about. Of course – technicians, white-coated technicians. They *would* look like doctors to Freddy. He worked every day around the hospital on the base. 'Would you take me to this hole, Freddy? Show me where you got this?'

He nodded. 'But not go down.'

'No – I wouldn't ask you to go down.'

She went and sat by the hut's entrance, slowly drawing up her knees. She let her mind whirl through the opportunities opening up before her, feeling like the magician who'd just pulled the rabbit out of the hat. Could she, even at the last minute, make a success of this operation?

A flash of colour caught her eye as a pair of cockatoos darted across the roughly hewn clearing far below. She could see for miles across the emerald-green jungle canopy. In the far distance the sun sparkled off a narrow strip of jade sea.

Freddy brought over a handful of the roasted grubs, folded neatly inside a sago leaf. He prodded it at her encouragingly. Nicole took them, doubtfully. She was hungry, very hungry. But *this* hungry?

The piglet was keen. It rummaged and snorted around her, its tiny curled tail twitching, nosing into her food. She tried to push it away. 'When's Mr Rykhlin coming, Freddy?'

'Soon now. I go fetch him from other house.'

She looked at the roasted grubs again. Somehow, they

didn't look so bad as they sizzled like miniature pale sausages. She picked one up; it was hot between her fingers. She sniffed at it – odourless. She was surprised to find her mouth watering. If this was all there would be to eat now – she knew that she had to get used to it. She bit off a small piece, and tasted it experimentally. Crisp, light – rather like vanilla. If you forgot they were grubs, really not that bad at all. Perhaps she might acquire a taste?

And, cautiously, she began to eat.

Nicole must have been dozing. The shaking of the hut floor woke her.

It was Rykhlin, followed by Freddy.

'Hi!' Rykhlin smiled at her as he approached, eyes twinkling.

She suddenly felt safe, reassured by his presence. She got up and reached out to touch him. 'Thank God!' she said.

'Freddy been looking after you?' he asked.

Freddy called across from the far side of the hut. 'Sure thing, Mr Rykhlin. She come through the forest last night, and she not scared.'

'We had a helicopter nosing around here this morning,' added Nicole.

'Yeah, we had one too. Hate the damn things!' muttered Rykhlin, as he dumped his rucksack onto the floor.

Nicole sensed the venom in his voice. 'Why do you say that?' she asked.

'Hey,' piped up Freddy, 'you tell her, Mr Rykhlin. You tell her what those bastards did to you.'

Nicole glanced over at Rykhlin, saw that his eyes were sunk deep with exhaustion. Saw something hidden within them.

'Go on,' she prompted.

Rykhlin kicked reluctantly at his rucksack, then sighed. 'Know what a "Sandy" mission is?'

'They go out to pick up downed pilots,' she answered. 'Cheaper than training new ones.'

'Right! ... I was flying for the Air Force at the time, seconded from the Navy. Tried to pluck two little kids out of a firefight on the Pristina road – you know, in Kosovo, in the Balkans. J-STARs saw me on their radar, bawled me out. Told me that some hotshot's arse was worth a lot more than two little kids. Then we suddenly started taking incoming. There was hot metal spraying everywhere, and the PJ was squealing like a pig. So I had to haul us out of there.'

He started rummaging in his pack for something. 'The others got it wrong: called me a "kid-killer", like I was some sort of coward. Name stuck like shit, of course. Haven't flown a chopper since.'

Nicole envisaged the scene, the mayhem and violence, the chaos of battle, and recognized his guilt. She already knew he was no coward. 'You're not the only one who's left a kid behind,' she said quietly.

'Yeah, I know,' he said simply, and began to move his gear to the back of the hut.

'That why you're out here?' she called after him.

'Yep – volunteered for special duties.'

They were quiet then, lost in their own thoughts. Piping and whistling from the jungle echoed musically around them. A sudden welcome breeze drifted through the hut, ventilating the stifling oven heat.

Nicole finally broke their silence.

'Look, I want to show you something,' she said, and led Rykhlin over to the net hanging from the roof. She pulled out the missile fin, and passed it across. 'What do you think this is?'

He turned it over in his hands. Felt its weight. 'Carbon fibre?'

'Probably.'

He drew his finger along the fine edge, rubbing his thumb over the polished surface. 'Where the hell did you get this, Freddy?' he asked.

'I told Missy. In hole, under the ground.'

'I think he's found a way into the underground complex,' explained Nicole. 'But he won't go back in. Says he's too scared.'

Rykhlin looked at her. 'Well, I think it's part of some missile, don't you?'

'I agree.'

'Then I think we need to go in ourselves and take a look. It might answer all our questions.'

'I take you there tonight if you want,' interrupted Freddy. 'I got a boat we can use.'

'I think that's a good idea,' said Nicole.

Rykhlin threw her a glance.

'OK,' he said carefully. 'You go ahead and contact London. Tell them what we've found, and what we're going to do. I'll contact Washington, get them to stand by for evacuation early tomorrow morning.' The twinkle was back in his eye. 'Hey, you and I, we're still in business, right?'

Nicole smiled back at him. 'We're still in business.'

He clapped her lightly on the shoulder. 'OK, let's move this job along. Then we can both go home.'

Nicole retrieved her rucksack from the back of the hut, laid out the laptop computer, and popped up its small 'umbrella' aerial. She worried about the battery pack, knowing it had only enough power for a couple of hours' transmission.

She used the modem to log on to Blacknet – a parallel and top-secret version of the World Wide Web, it used highly sophisticated 'end-to-end' encryption techniques to avoid detection and code-breaking by even the fastest computers.

Her message was brief:

Hendra mining new type of mineral / code name *Indera* / off southern coast Guam / doubt Rahman any knowledge of this / intend penetrate underground complex tonight find out more / will evacuate 24 hours immediate

She reviewed the message, then pressed ENTER.
The message was encrypted, fragmented, then zipped

up into space towards one of the many communication satellites orbiting the Earth. From there, pieces found their separate ways via different satellites and landlines to GCHQ – an anonymous complex of dull office buildings in Cheltenham, England, that happened to be a highly secure intelligence listening post. From there, powerful computers automatically rerouted the separate bits of the message to London.

Simes's office was filled with the cold steady light of an early-April dawn as it reflected off the sullen grey waters of the River Thames at Vauxhall. Without a sound, the modem on Simes's desktop PC sprang to life. An electronic gate opened, and a short burst of Nicole's encoded data slammed onto the hard disk. Almost instantaneously, the modem shut the gate again, guarding against any virtual spies prowling the network.

And in this manner, bit by bit, Nicole's message came home.

Chapter Twenty-four – that evening: Arguni Island

Night comes quickly at the equator. The western sky was already ablaze with the violent reds and golds of a tropical sunset. The sun began to kiss the horizon, and a blazing path of light flickered and danced on the gentle swell of the ocean.

Nicole felt the warm gritty volcanic sand beneath her feet as she helped Freddy and Rykhlin prepare the outrigger canoe. Long and thin, it had been shaped from the trunk of a sago palm. The outer hull was beautifully smooth and polished, allowing it to slip through the water easily. The interior was roughly hewn.

Together they pushed the canoe down the beach towards the gentle surf. As they stumbled into the deliciously warm water, Nicole felt the waves slap against her body, as if trying to push her back onto the beach. For a moment, she wondered if they were trying to tell her something.

Nicole rolled herself into the canoe as Freddy and Rykhlin held it steady in the gentle swell. Then Rykhlin dropped his rucksack into the boat and climbed in himself, followed by Freddy.

Freddy lifted out the long-handled paddles with their leaf-shaped blades. They pulled strongly, driving the canoe clear of the gentle breakers near the shore.

Once out in deeper water, the canoe began to cut cleanly through the waves. They glided quietly around the island, heading west into the vivid blaze of the setting sun. Save for the gentle cut of the paddles, they travelled in silence.

Nicole felt alive, alert, like a hunting animal. She sat in the canoe, enjoying the simple rhythmic pleasure of the paddling. She was going into danger – she knew that. There were no plans, no contingencies; they would survive on their wits.

The sky darkened into night and a full moon spread its dim silvery light across the water. Slowly, the gently shelving beach gave way to a tall, cliffed headland, and Nicole could see a fringe of jungle silhouetted against the dense curtain of stars.

They paddled cautiously now, Freddy making them stop occasionally to check the shape of the coastline, using his natural night vision to bisect imaginary bearing lines. He suddenly became more confident, pulled the boat forward a little way, then turned and pointed.

'Deep hole, see? Under the "spirit bird".'

Nicole looked. The shape on the cliff top looked indeed just like a bird, its upstretched head and wide-open beak formed by a chance juxtaposition of silhouetted branches.

Freddy would go no further now. He refused to upset the spirit. The hole in the cliff clearly frightened him.

The canoe lifted gently in the ocean swell, and an occasional smaller wave slapped at its bows. Rykhlin made a final check of the small amount of equipment in his rucksack. He'd wrapped everything up tightly in plastic bags to keep out the water. He looked across at Nicole and gave her the thumbs-up. They both slipped quietly over the side and headed for the cliff.

Nicole swam lazily, conserving her energy. The water was warm and cleansing around her body. Rykhlin swam with her, the gentle splash of his strokes just off to her right. Steadily, the 'spirit bird' grew larger, until eventually it dominated the skyline above their heads, its shape now lost in a confusion of other detail.

Nicole could clearly see the open maw of Freddy's hole. It lay on the waterline, a squat, ragged half-oval, black against the pale grey of the moonlit cliff. She headed towards it and felt her feet touch bottom. The mouth of the cave was strewn with rounded black boulders, slippery with algae. She hauled herself out of the water, and sat for a moment on the worn rocks, looking out to sea. The place was magical: the sea glittered in the bright moonlight, and she listened to the rhythmic 'shoosh' of the waves as they broke against the boulder-strewn cliffline. She looked out across the water for the canoe, but the ocean was empty – Freddy had gone.

Rykhlin sat a short distance from her, wet hair plastered close to his head, beard dripping. He opened his rucksack and tossed a plastic bag towards her. She changed quickly into her black tracksuit and slipped on her trainers.

They moved off together in silence, Rykhlin leading the way. Nicole stepped quietly, feeling her way quickly but carefully over the stones like a cat, fluidly shifting her weight so as not to disturb them, muffling the sound of her approach.

Rykhlin shone his torch into the cave. Its sides were smooth and rippled, but the roof was jagged and sharp. Nicole guessed that they were in some sort of lava tube, a place where an ancient lava flow had cooled slowly from the outside, allowing the molten interior to drain away.

They pressed on up the winding tunnel, their feet crunching over deposits of sand and gravel strewn across the floor by regular flooding. Sometimes they had to double up beneath a lower section, the rough craggy texture of the roof snagging at Rykhlin's rucksack. In one place, the roof had sagged so much that they were forced to crawl. Their journey was slow and awkward.

Nicole spotted it first. A glint of chrome in the gravel bed. They scooped the sand back with their hands. A stainless-steel cover emerged from the flood debris, a heavy casting embedded in a concrete plinth with a thick rubber seal around its outer edge. In the centre was a chrome-spoked wheel about a foot across.

Rykhlin tried to spin the wheel. It refused to move. He tried harder, legs braced, grunting with the strain. This time the wheel groaned, moved an inch, then seized again. Rykhlin relaxed, rubbing his aching hands together. Then they strained together, both wincing with the effort. It began to turn, more and more freely, making a couple of full rotations before coming to a stop.

Rykhlin pulled upwards and the seal sucked gently. There was a hiss of air and a warm breeze drifted up into their faces, carrying with it the distinctive smell of hot metal and oily workshops. He shone his torch inside. Nicole saw a metal ladder descending vertically down a round concrete shaft.

There was indeed more to this island than was immediately apparent, much more. Something secret, deep below the mountain.

Rykhlin went first, the wavering torchlight causing gigantic shadows to jump and play around the roof and sides of the lava tube. Nicole stepped onto the ladder and began to make her way down behind him. She could hear his steps ringing faintly on the metal rungs below. She reached up and, in the pale dancing light of his torch, grabbed hold of the hatch and pulled it down behind her. It thumped solidly onto the rubber seal. She spun the inner chrome ring, locking it shut.

It took them at least two minutes to descend the full length of the ladder. Nicole estimated that they must be over a hundred feet below ground level. At the bottom they found a small room, its floor and walls lined with concrete. On one side was a large green sign printed with the universally recognized running-man symbol. They had come down an escape route – intended for use by whoever it was who worked beyond that grey-painted door in the opposite wall.

Rykhlin dropped his rucksack to the floor and tried the door lever. It was locked.

Nicole nudged him. 'Alarms?' she mouthed. Rykhlin shrugged. Nicole's heart was beating heavily.

Rykhlin fiddled around in the front pocket of his rucksack and produced a black plastic wallet. With Nicole holding the torch, he unrolled it onto the floor and revealed a small lock-picking kit – neat rows of probes, feelers, rakes and picks. He probed the lock gently with the tools, lifting the pins one by one. Then he tried the lever again. This time, it worked.

The door inched open a little, letting a sliver of light from the other side stream across the concrete floor. Rykhlin tidied up his kit and picked up the rucksack. Then Nicole doused the torch and carefully eased open the door. The hum of machinery became louder.

They were in a large well-lit room, resembling a locker room. It had bright yellow walls and racks of gas masks and rubber suits. Rykhlin nudged Nicole's elbow, and pointed. Beyond the suits she'd seen rows of steel lockers, each with a small radiation-hazard sign on the door. He went over and tried a handle, and the flimsy metal door swung open. Inside was a white overall with a name tag pinned neatly to the chest. A pair of pale green rubber boots stood on the locker's floor and placed neatly on the shelf above was a green hard hat.

Rykhlin tried a second locker – the same.

They quickly changed into this gear, shoving their tracksuits into one of the two lockers and pulling on the overalls. As Rykhlin dumped his rucksack, Nicole saw a gleam in his eyes, like a little boy on some late-night escapade. He walked over to the exit door and put a hand on the aluminium handle. Whatever they had come to see lay beyond that flimsy partition.

For a moment time buckled as they stood there rooted in its flow.

Then Nicole gave an imperceptible nod.

Rykhlin opened the door, letting in a flood of sound – and disappeared. Nicole followed him, head up and looking confident.

The scene smacked into her eyes. She was in a vast and brightly lit underground cavern, echoing to the sound of work. Her mind was full of questions. What was this place? What was going on here?

To her right lay a dock dominated by a huge black-hulled submarine. It looked vast in the confined space. Nicole estimated it as well over 200 feet long. She recognized it instantly from her training – Russian, Kilo class, the short, stubby hydroplanes jutting characteristically out of a slot just forward of the huge black sail. It was an attack submarine, capable of firing nuclear-tipped missiles from the forward torpedo tubes. But this vessel was unusual. Mounted aft of the sail was a large streamlined housing, its hatch propped open on hydraulic rams. And alongside on the dock stood a small yellow mobile crane, with two glossy white missiles sitting on a red tubular loading cradle. The sub was obviously a missile carrier – probably for the launch sites fanning out across the ocean floor. Her father's words spoke to her from the dark horror of the gulag: this was one of Rahman's secrets, utterly hidden from the rest of the world.

Rykhlin was already some way ahead of her, marching confidently along the dockside. Two technicians appeared round the far end of the missiles and began to walk towards him. They passed him without comment.

She stopped to study the missiles nestling on the cradle. They were large and imposing weapons, over twenty feet long. They had short stubby wings, with forward canards, and there was a red plastic intake cover beneath each pointed nose. That meant that they were air-breathing – probably cruise missiles. But aimed at whom? The Chinese? American Pacific bases?

Nicole looked closer, her mind cycling through end-less training films. The missiles seemed to be versions of the Russian AS-15. Long-range weapons, nuclear-tipped, designed to hit a target thousands of miles away. She reached up to finger the smooth leading edge of one of the stubby wings, pleased with her discovery.

'Hey! What are you doing?' Nicole jerked her hand down, and cursed her involuntary response. A soldier was coming towards her: red beret, combat clothing, weapon held at the ready – *Kopassus*!

'Your identification!'

Her mind froze for a moment.

The man eyed her quizzically, wondering at the slight delay. But she'd already aroused suspicion.

He jerked his rifle back, operating the bolt to slam a round into the chamber. 'You're under arrest!' he shouted.

Over his shoulder, Nicole could see a small knot of technicians watching them with interest. Then Rykhlin's broad American accent suddenly rang out in the cavern. 'Hey, that's my buddy! You can't arrest her.'

The soldier wavered for a moment, distracted by the shout behind him. Nicole sprang forward, grabbed the man's rifle, and threw him to the floor over her outstretched leg. He hit the ground hard, with a surprised grunt – then rolled away from her. He was good! But Rykhlin was good too – he was already there. He kicked the rifle out of the other man's reach, sent it clattering across the concrete, and then ran to pick it up. The soldier disappeared quickly into cover.

There was shouting from areas away from the dock. Nicole saw more soldiers running into firing positions behind nearby bits of equipment, aiming their weapons at the two of them. Rykhlin fired three rounds from the soldier's semi-automatic, to keep their heads down, the sounds echoing angrily around the cavern. Someone fired back, and a bullet cracked against the concrete and whined away. Then someone yelled out an order and there were no more shots.

'They're holding their fire because of the missiles. Here, cover me!' shouted Rykhlin.

He tossed the rifle towards her. She grabbed the weapon

out of the air and crouched down behind the missile loader, letting fly with another couple of rounds to keep the soldiers away. She saw them duck down.

More soldiers would be coming – they didn't have much time. They would soon be trapped. She looked desperately around for Rykhlin, wondering what he was doing.

He was running towards her, yanking a gas-welding trolley behind him, the canisters rattling and bouncing in their frame. He twisted the valves and lit the gas that began to hiss from the nozzle, adjusting the flame until it roared out at full strength. 'Keep covering me!' he yelled at Nicole.

She dodged up above the loader again. A couple of soldiers were trying to get in close. She levelled the weapon at them. *Crack! Crack!* A soldier went down, his scream reverberating around the cavern. The other dived to one side, and took up a new position behind some dockside equipment. A round came back at her, slamming into the side of the submarine.

Nicole turned to check on Rykhlin. He'd propped the nozzle of the welding torch inside the rear grille of the mobile crane. He saw Nicole glance at him. 'Butane!' he yelled back.

The welding torch was now roaring furiously into the engine compartment. Rykhlin pulled it out briefly to look inside. Nicole could see the hoses that fed butane to the engine glowing cherry red – almost melted through. He shoved it back in. 'OK, run!' he yelled. 'Get the fuck out of here!'

Nicole didn't think twice – once those hoses had burned through, the butane canister would ignite like a bomb. She ran, rubber boots pounding the dockside, ducking behind equipment for cover.

There was a dull thud. A blast of hot air slammed against the back of her head – followed by the raucous sound of an alarm. People were shouting. Nicole glanced behind. A sheet of flame had engulfed the crane, and was playing around the nose cone of one of the missiles. Another explosion. Fragments were flung into the air. Something arched overhead with a hollow roar, trailing smoke, and plunged sizzling into the dock.

Beyond the submarine, the dock ended abruptly against a wall of rock. She could see a sleek dark blue shape perched on a launching ramp, a streamlined nose pointing down into the water, an open canopy. A technician in the cockpit saw them coming and began to scramble out. Rykhlin jumped up onto the thick little wing. He planted his boot firmly on the man's chest, shoving him back into the cockpit.

Nicole climbed up onto the wing. She recognized the shape immediately: a submersible similar to the type she had trained on with the SEALS. It was a 'Deep Flight' design, a submersible that would perform like an aeroplane by 'flying' under water.

'Take it!' she shouted at Rykhlin. 'It'll get us out of here.'

As they clambered into the seats behind the pilot, he

craned his head back: 'I'm not going anywhere!' he shouted. 'You're under arrest!'

'Wrong, feller!' snarled Rykhlin as he reached down to the left of the pilot's leg and pulled at a large red handle. There was a solid thump from behind and the submersible slipped effortlessly off the ramp and dipped into the water. A bow wave surged up the nose of the craft and cascaded into the still-open cockpit.

Nicole jabbed sharply at the man's neck with her rifle. The man winced but took the hint, fumbling at the canopy to get it closed. It came down with a hiss, and she tugged at the locking lever, tightening the seal.

'Now, fly this fucker!' yelled Rykhlin.

The pilot's fingers began to punch slowly at the buttons. The computer came on-line and a command menu appeared on the screen. There was a sharp crack against the hull. 'They're shooting at us,' the man whimpered. 'If they pierce the hull we'll die.'

'Then fucking well dive!' Rykhlin yelled desperately.

With a whine of electric motors, the craft began to inch forward. But Nicole had been studying the controls. She'd used Earl's Deep Flight II during training, knew she could pilot this machine – knew it would be quicker if she did!

'Get him out of here!' she yelled, operating the lever on the cockpit sill. 'I can do this.'

The canopy hissed open again. They could hear the sound of shooting. A round smacked into the glazing and crazed it. With a strength born of desperation, Rykhlin grabbed the technician and heaved him overboard. Needing no encouragement, the man swam for his life.

Nicole clambered forward into the pilot's seat as the canopy hissed back down. She shoved the locking lever forward, pushed the throttle against the stop, and banged the side-stick hard forwards. There was a clunk and a roar as ballast tanks blew. The machine dipped sharply. They grabbed to keep themselves stable as the machine dived. Nicole yanked the side-stick back to pull the machine level again. 'It can't be that deep here, I don't want to hit bottom.' She fingered the buttons around the computer display and brought up some sort of sonar that drew a map of the dock area around them.

White shooting stars appeared outside the cockpit. Bullets were coming at them through the water. Nicole studied the sonar map carefully, located the exit from the dock, and immediately picked up speed.

The light from the surface dimmed quickly, then went black. They were now in the tunnel leading out to the ocean. The cockpit lighting gave off a dim red glow. Rykhlin fingered the crazing on the canopy, feeling for leaks. 'Will it hold?'

'Provided we don't go too deep.' She sounded more confident than she felt.

She shoved the throttle forward, then turned round to face Rykhlin, triumphant at this display of her ability.

'Hey – move over, Rykhlin.' Nicole grinned. 'It's my turn now. And don't you just like my style?'

Part Three: REACHING OUT

National Geographic
*Geo*graphica

April
WiF of heavy metal runs deep

Startling SeaWiF (**Sea**-viewing **Wi**de **F**ield-of-view) satellite images from the north-west Pacific Ocean have revealed a distinct pollution plume originating from a mysterious source just to the south of the US territorial island of Guam. Drawn northwards by the ninety-mile-a-day Kuroshio current, it can be seen plunging straight into the heart of the Japanese tuna-fishing grounds.

Michael Reid, a scientist working for OSC (Orbital Sciences Corporation) thinks the pollution – made up of toxic metals, including arsenic and mercury – may well explain the growing number of mysterious deaths from food poisoning that have recently terrified the Japanese population. Up until quite recently the Japanese government has been blaming the incident on toxic algae blooms triggered by climate change, or on Chinese industrial pollutants drifting out of the Yellow Sea; but now they have contacted the US Navy, who have agreed to use the USS *Deep-Search* (their latest Deep-Sea Rescue Vehicle) to investigate further. 'We know more about Mars than we do about the ocean floor,' explained Reid. 'The pollution may turn out to be of volcanic origin, but as yet we just don't know.'

Once the DSRV has located the source of the emission, it is likely that specialized deep-diving submersibles will be sent down to investigate. They will try and determine whether the pollution source can be neutralized.

Chapter Twenty-five – early morning: West Pacific Ocean

The Indonesian mining team sat in their dimly lit oper-ations room deep within the bowels of the *Ibn Battuta*. They were surrounded by an array of TV screens, banks of computer monitors and complex navigation displays. Three technicians watched the screens intently, gently nudging at joysticks mounted on the work surface in front of them. They were ROV (Remote Operating Vehicle) pilots, or robot operators, but they were on the payroll of Dr Jazid Hendra, not the Indonesian government, and their mission was top secret. They were here to mine something more precious than gold from the deep-ocean floor, a new mineral with unique and previously undiscovered proper-ties – a mineral code-named *Indera*.

One of the pilots was monitoring a fully loaded tub gliding steadily up to the surface. It was a routine oper-ation. The machine had been locked onto the *Ibn Battuta*'s homing signal and was coming up the guide slope under autopilot. While he waited, the pilot filled in data on a clipboard in front of him. Then something made him glance up at the screen – perhaps the glimpse of an unusual shape in his peripheral vision, or an unusual pattern of light. But now he saw nothing, just specks of marine 'snow' swirling past the TV lens.

The pilot returned to his clipboard, then looked up again to double-check and was startled by bright lights materializing out of the blackness: attached to a long, fat cigar shape with a clear perspex dome at the front. The pilot stared at the screen, eyes wide with surprise. He recognized the distinctive shape immediately: it was the USS *Deep-Search*, the American rescue sub. But what was it doing here?

He watched fascinated as his ROV passed straight through the beam of the American craft's powerful searchlights before plunging on into the darkness beyond. The stunned pilot turned to his controller. 'Sir!'

The controller came over and listened quietly to the pilot's report, then made his decision quickly. Dr Hendra had made it quite clear that secrecy must be maintained at all costs. They were mining in territorial waters, US territorial waters, and they were just off the island of Guam, one of the most heavily defended outposts of the American empire. Nothing must be discovered. Nothing must compromise the security of their operation. It was fear of terrible reprisals that drove the controller urgently forward. He spoke rapidly into his microphone, issuing a string of orders.

On the stern of the *Ibn Battuta*, covers were flung back from a small shape cradled on the operations deck. They revealed a sleek black submersible, her hull carefully lined with acoustic absorbing tiles. She was a beautiful machine with fine grooves etched across the gentle curves of her streamlined body to cut down on drag – like the skin of a porpoise. On each side were thick stubby wings, capable of pulling her quickly down to depth.

The submersible was pushed out onto its launcher. The pilot eased himself in through the hatch and lay prone in the nose, staring out through the streamlined acrylic canopy. The submersible launched and slipped quietly into the ocean.

The pilot dived fast. He switched on his highly sophisticated sonar. Software decoded the returns, projecting a picture onto his visor in the form of a virtual-reality landscape. He could 'see' the ocean bottom clearly, many miles below him: the vast canyon of the Marianas Trench off to the right, the colour-coded mining site, the tiny yellow dots of ROVs going about their business. And, in the ten o'clock low position, a red bar flashing brightly.

His target.

He thumbed a button on his side-stick and locked on, waiting ninety-two seconds for the target to come into range. A red circle bracketed the target symbol in his visor. He thumbed the trigger, felt a slight bump as the torpedo left its tube, heard the *whoosh* of compressed air, and watched as it tracked towards its target with unnerving accuracy.

*

The torpedo struck the USS *Deep-Search* amidships, puncturing first the outer hull, then the inner. Under the tremendous pressure of deep-ocean water, metal folded inwards as if it were made of paper. A huge bubble of air tried to rush out of the gap – and then the warhead exploded. The hull cracked and collapsed, the sides slamming together like the clapping of hands.

Death for the American crew was instantaneous.

Chapter Twenty-six – thirty minutes later: The White House, Washington, D.C.: seven p.m. local time

President Gilbert Byrd checked himself carefully in the wardrobe mirror and adjusted the hang of his tuxedo. He moved closer to examine his face. Not bad for fifty-five – a few wrinkles round the eyes, maybe, but his fair hair was still intact, and he'd retained a strong jawline. He spotted a speck of dust on his sleeve and tried to flick it away.

Somewhere outside the bedroom a telephone chimed discreetly. He heard his wife, Anne, answering it. She appeared at the bedroom door. 'Telephone for you, Gilbey. It's Walter.'

Walter Hickel, National Security Adviser, and a close personal friend of Byrd.

Byrd sighed and rolled his eyes. 'Tell him I've just gone.'

Anne smiled sweetly. 'Sorry, darling, I've already told him that you're still here.'

The President marched irritably out of the bedroom, his shoes thudding softly on the thick pile of carpet. He grabbed the receiver Anne had left resting on the delicately polished walnut table. 'Hi, Walter, can't it wait? We're just off!'

Walter Hickel's calm and steady voice came down the line. 'I'm sorry, Mr President. We've had a flash from the Pentagon.'

Whenever Walter called him 'Mr President', it was a bad sign. Anne saw her husband's shoulders droop. 'OK, Walter, go ahead. What is it?'

Anne came over and stood by his side.

'We've lost the *Deep-Search*!'

'*Deep-Search?*'

'A Deep-Sea Rescue Vehicle, Mr President. A submarine. She's down, with both hands, in about fifteen thousand feet of water, just off Guam.'

'Can't this wait until tomorrow?'

There was a moment's silence at the other end of the line, then Hickel continued: 'Mr President, they think she might have been torpedoed.'

Byrd stood there for a moment, letting the implications seep into his mind. 'Did you just say "torpedoed"?'

'Yes, Mr President.'

Anne put a hand on his shoulder.

Oh my God, could it be the Chinese? thought Byrd. *Please, God, not the Big One, not now.* 'OK, Walter,' he sighed. 'Meet me in the Oval Office – fifteen minutes.'

He replaced the receiver gently onto its cradle. His wife slipped her hand down to his waist, pulled him towards her. She looked up into his face and saw that it was pale and drawn.

'Trouble?'

'Yeah!' he said slowly. '*Big* trouble.'

Walter Hickel was already waiting for him, a big wad of papers under his arm. Standing next to him was a broad-faced and broad-shouldered man in a grey suit – Dan Carson, Secretary of State.

'Good evening, Walter, Dan.'

Hickel's voice was gruff, slightly gravelly. 'This thing broke about an hour ago, Mr President. I'm afraid it doesn't look very promising.'

Byrd motioned for them both to sit down at the mahogany dining table set in front of the white marble fireplace. From the mantelpiece a large china figure of a bald eagle glared down at them, its beady eyes alert for any slip-up, reminding them of their grave responsibilities here.

Byrd looked round at the tiny gathering. 'Shall we have some coffee?' No one answered, so he assumed assent. He motioned to his hovering private secretary, who busied herself out of the room.

Hickel unfolded a map of the West Pacific from one of his bulging manila folders. 'We lost contact with *Deep-Search* about here, Mr President, 150 miles due south of Guam.' His finger slid across the map and tapped at the precise spot. 'She's a rescue sub, but she wasn't on a rescue mission. They were using her to investigate that pollution plume – you know, the one that's playing havoc with the Japanese tuna catch.'

'Yeah.' Byrd stared at the map, stroking his chin.

'She's very deep,' Hickel added. 'About three miles down. I'm afraid there's no hope.'

Byrd nodded soberly. 'So what makes the Navy think she was torpedoed, Walter? That's one hell of an accusation.'

'Pattern of the explosions. The support ship picked up one explosion, then another less than a second after that – followed by a thud as the submarine imploded.'

'Well, couldn't it be just that? One explosion setting off another?'

'No, Mr President. The first was an impact, the second a small warhead going off. Both signatures are quite clear.'

Byrd bent over the map, running his hands through his hair, trying to make sense of this nonsense.

'It's all very typical of a torpedo strike, Mr President,' prompted Carson.

There was silence for a moment. Both men looked at Byrd, waiting for a reaction. Byrd's mind was working feverishly. He'd been in politics long enough to know the virtue of moving carefully. To be a tortoise, not a hare. Wait long enough and the problem often solved itself. 'Look! What if we're wrong? What if both explosions actually occurred on board the *Deep-Search* itself?' he persisted.

'The Navy say not,' grated Carson. 'They're pretty convinced it was a torpedo.'

'And they should know, Mr President,' added Hickel.

Byrd sucked at his bottom lip. He needed to tread

carefully here, very carefully: he was being pushed into making a decision. 'Well, a torpedo has to come from somewhere, Walter. Who do we think did it?' He paused. 'Not one of ours, surely!'

'No, Mr President, not one of ours – nothing like that,' answered Hickel. 'There were no submarines or surface warships within range at the time . . .'

'Well, hell, Walter! That's what I'm saying. So how could it have been a torpedo?'

'. . . Except for this one, Mr President.' Hickel rifled through his heap of files, looking for the right one. His eyes swivelled towards Byrd. 'The *Ibn Battuta*, an Indonesian research vessel. She was lying just fifty miles outside our territorial waters.'

He passed a glossy photograph across the table. Byrd picked it up, examined it, and then flicked it over to study the caption. He looked quizzically at Hickel. 'Walter, research ships don't carry torpedoes.'

'No, Mr President, but they do carry submersibles. I'd like you to have a look at this.' Hickel passed a second photograph across. Byrd peered at it carefully. It was an enlargement of the stern of the *Ibn Battuta*. He could see two objects on the rear deck, one sheeted over, the other uncovered. A cluster of orange-suited technicians were standing around something dark and squat, a streamlined object with short stubby wings.

'Hmm.' He handed the photograph back to Hickel. 'A nice piece of kit, Walter. You want me to buy one for the Navy?'

Hickel looked despairingly at Byrd. 'Please take this seriously, Mr President.'

'How the hell can I? You're trying to suggest that the *Deep-Search* was torpedoed by that tiny thing, off an Indonesian research ship, for Christ's sake!' Byrd looked first at Walter Hickel, and then at Dan Carson, an exasperated look on his face.

'There's more evidence. It's quite compelling,' insisted Hickel. 'That photograph was taken the day before yesterday, by a P3 flying out of Guam. But the Navy have been doing regular overflights ever since the *Ibn Battuta* first turned up, and they caught her again, by chance, just twenty-five minutes after *Deep-Search* went down. Look at this.'

Byrd peered at the next photograph. This time a gantry had been swung out from behind the stern of the *Ibn Battuta*, and from it dangled the tiny submersible. On the flanks of its streamlined nose, carefully arrowed by someone so that it was clear for all to see, was a small black oval aperture.

'J-2 have had a look at it,' continued Hickel. 'They say it's a torpedo tube.'

Byrd looked aghast. He shook his head in disbelief. 'Well, I'll be damned!'

Hickel looked Byrd straight in the eye. 'Mr President, Rahman's already forced China off the Utara oilfield, and he's put most of his Chinese population into concentration camps. Perhaps he thinks he can get away with anything now.'

'We think you should take this seriously, Mr President,' agreed Carson. 'Rahman's been tightening his grip on South-East Asia. We think he's deliberately threatening our interests in the Pacific. I would caution you, sir – I believe this could be a trick intended to pull us into a war.'

Byrd looked at them both, saw the fear in their eyes, and realized he had to take some sort of action.

He got up, strode purposefully across the ornately patterned carpet, and thumbed the intercom on his desk. The speaker crackled. 'Mr President?'

'Ellen – I want the Indonesian ambassador over here, right now! And get hold of the Director of Central Intelligence, will you? Tell him it's a matter of urgency.' He took his hand off the button, paused, and then pressed it again to add another request. 'Oh! And get me Sara Ackerman as well, the White House psychologist.'

Byrd looked across the room at Hickel and Carson. They stared back at him, their expressions deeply troubled. He could feel his own heart beating in his chest.

Events were shaping up badly and, as much as Byrd wanted to stop them in their tracks, this had all the signs of developing into a major crisis.

Ms Amira Pencastu, Indonesian ambassador to the United States, tapped the photos neatly together on the delicately inlaid coffee table and handed them carefully back to Hickel. She was smartly dressed, and discreetly veiled.

Byrd had gathered them all formally in the Red Room,

sitting on hard, upright Georgian chairs and settees. Sara Ackerman sat quietly to one side. There were no welcoming drinks.

Pencastu's voice was cultured American-Asian. 'I'm sorry, Mr Byrd, I know nothing about this. But I can assure you of one thing. The *Ibn Battuta* is a research ship, and that is all. Torpedo-carrying submersibles – well, it's so silly. Submersibles are so tiny, how can they? I'm sure there will be some completely innocent explanation. Naturally we are very sad at your loss, and I can understand your anguish at this time – but really, this is a most unfortunate accusation.'

Dan Carson's gravelly voice interjected. 'Ms Pencastu, what exactly is the *Ibn Battuta* investigating at the moment?'

Pencastu looked at him coldly. 'Hydrothermal vents, Mr Carson. Our boat is equipped solely to further the progress of science. We are studying the unique ecology found at a number of deep-ocean vent sites in the Pacific, and trying to understand the processes that lead to the deposition of hydrothermal minerals.'

Hickel eyed her suspiciously. 'Ms Pencastu,' he said carefully, 'I don't understand. Why would your country want to know about such things?'

Pencastu's eyebrows shot up in surprise. 'Mr Hickel! The Muslim world was already highly advanced in matters of science way back in your ninth century, when Europe was still struggling through its Dark Ages, and what would become your America was populated by savages. It is a pity that you later chose to crush our achievements – in the name of Christianity.'

Byrd frowned, not understanding.

Pencastu sighed, a little despairingly. 'I'm referring to the Crusades, Mr President. Please don't try to patronize me. Many of the new species we've found at these hydrothermal sites could significantly advance our understanding of medicine and drugs.'

Byrd stared coolly back at the woman. 'I assure you, Ms Pencastu, I do not mean to be patronizing. But we are puzzled about this sudden desire of your country to increase its scientific knowledge.'

Pencastu gave a loud tut of disapproval. 'Mr Byrd! President Rahman is keen for Indonesia to become one of the most technologically advanced of the Islamic countries. How else can we achieve this goal except through research? Surely you are not trying to hold us back solely in defence of your own interests?' She paused, then added softly: 'The world is changing, Mr Byrd.'

'She doesn't know anything about it, I'm pretty sure of that,' said Sara Ackerman.

'Who doesn't?' demanded Hickel.

'Pencastu.'

'Doesn't know anything about what?' demanded Byrd.

'Perhaps there's nothing to know.'

Sara sighed. Dan Carson shifted in his chair; he was getting frustrated with Byrd's constant stalling. 'Mr

President, you saw the pictures. Walter told you what the Navy thinks.'

'Look – the Navy has a vested interest in bogeymen, Dan,' answered Byrd. 'You know that. They need somebody to shoot at to justify their existence. This sub may simply have gone down because something malfunctioned on board.'

There was a knock at the door. The President's private secretary entered. 'The DCI is here, Mr President.'

Byrd looked up at the new arrival. 'Greg! Good of you to come over at this ungodly hour. Can you put any flesh on this submarine thing?'

Greg Noble was a tall, rectangular-faced man who wore thick black-rimmed glasses. 'I'm afraid I can, Mr President.'

His words jarred instantly. This wasn't quite the phrase Byrd had been expecting. He looked up from behind his desk, waiting for some elaboration. But none came.

'Well?'

Noble settled himself down into a chair. 'I think we already know quite a lot, Mr President.'

Byrd's heart sank at Noble's reticence and he began to fear the worst. The CIA had been caught out badly by the September 2001 attack on New York, and the Chinese had been infiltrating nuclear weapons research at Los Alamos for years before they'd finally been discovered. Was this going to be another spectacular foul-up? 'Greg, we haven't got all night. If it's bad, I need to know.'

'Well ... there's been a rumour floating around for some time that may be connected with this incident.'

'Go on!' demanded Byrd impatiently.

Noble straightened himself visibly, acting like a wayward pupil hauled up before the headmaster. 'It's our belief, Mr President, that the Indonesians have developed a cruise missile, probably using an especially stretched version of the Soviet AS-X-15.'

There was a stunned silence. Everybody sat staring at Noble.

Then Dan Carson sucked in his breath noisily. 'That's damn good technology, Greg. That thing's got a range of over 1,800 miles.'

Noble warmed a little to his theme. 'Yes, a few appeared on the black market when the Soviet empire collapsed – we wondered where they'd gone.' He paused, an anguished look coming over his face. Then he dropped his second bombshell. 'Mr President . . . we also believe that they may be developing a nuclear warhead.'

Byrd jolted visibly in his seat. Indonesia a nuclear power? In the heart of South-East Asia? And he didn't know about this?

He flushed with anger and tried to calm himself by listening to the precise ticking of the large gold carriage clock on the mantelpiece. It began to chime midnight, a beautiful silvery sound quite out of keeping with the gravity of the situation unfolding in front of him.

Then he exploded. 'For God's sake, Greg, you're supposed to *tell* me these things! Why is it that the CIA never tells anybody about anything?'

'Because they're a secret service,' muttered Dan Carson.

Noble fidgeted. 'Mr President, we only found out ourselves a few days ago.'

'*How* did you find out?' demanded Byrd. 'Can you verify this information?'

'Yes, we have two agents out there ... or, rather, we have one agent. The other's British. Our information comes via London – hence the delay.'

Byrd groaned, and put his face into his hands. 'It gets worse. Go on, tell me: why are the British involved?'

'Because they picked it up first, Mr President,' explained Noble, 'from one of their sleepers. It's a joint operation, part of the Penkovsky Protocol. They asked for a minder, and agreed to share the intelligence.'

Byrd removed his head from his hands. 'This is the first I've heard of our having any involvement in Indonesia, Greg. Did this go through the Senate Select Committee?'

'All our operations in Indonesia were authorized by the previous President, sir.'

'Yes, but did he know exactly what he was authorizing?'

Noble remained silent.

'OK: what sort of bomb are they developing, what type of warhead?'

'We think it might be simple – uranium, with a cobalt jacket.'

'That's not good, sir,' interrupted Walter Hickel. 'That's a dirty bomb, it's designed to kill people.'

'They're *all* designed to kill people, Walter,' grated Carson.

Hickel ignored him. 'It's a radiation bomb,' he explained. 'It's offensive, not defensive.'

Byrd swung round in his chair and studied the large floor-mounted globe at the side of his desk. He spun it round to reveal Indonesia, spacing his fingers to measure out the distance. '1,800 miles,' he mused.

'Far enough to hit almost anywhere in South-East Asia,' prompted Noble. 'And most of the big cities in eastern China.'

'But not us?' queried Hickel.

'No, not mainland America.'

'But they could easily go for Guam, surely,' called out Sara Ackerman.

The President swung back in his seat and played with the point of his pencil, tapping it on his desk. Then he pointed it at Ackerman. 'You're right. But why would they want to do that?'

'They probably don't,' she replied. 'But it's our nearest interest.'

'You know what I think, Mr President?' said Carson slowly. 'I think this is about Islamic expansion. Rahman's taking advantage of the world-climate issue – we're all preoccupied with it at the moment. He's going to push the Chinese back and put himself in power over much of South-East Asia, probably as some sort of sultan. And Sara's right – we'd side with the Chinese in any such conflict, so Guam's got to be a prime target.'

Byrd thought about all the recent trade deals with China

that had helped to keep his country afloat – he knew where his loyalties lay. They wouldn't be caught out this time, they would act quickly: nip this thing in the bud. He stood up from behind his desk. 'Well, hell, I don't see any problem here. Why don't we send in some cruise missiles and take out his missile facility? Chan Hung would support us, so would the Japanese, and most of ASEAN for that matter. Nobody wants Rahman calling the shots down there. I say we should remove his nuclear capability – surgically – overnight. Castrate the bastard.' Byrd grinned at them, a confident boyish grin, the grin of a man with some of the most sophisticated weaponry in the world at his fingertips.

But Greg Noble looked most unhappy at this proposal. He stared at the President through his thick black-rimmed glasses. 'Ah ... Mr President, I don't think that option's really feasible.'

Byrd looked askance. 'Why not?'

'Because he's building the missiles in an old copper mine, and the galleries go down a long way. I don't think we could take it out even if we wanted to.'

Byrd shook his head in disbelief.

'The production facility's on an island off the coast of Papua,' continued Noble.

'Where?' demanded Byrd.

'Papua New Guinea, Mr President. Just to the north of Australia.'

Byrd looked again at the globe beside his desk. 'We could attack his launch sites.'

Noble looked awkward. He was a trapped man. 'That would be fine, sir – if we knew where they were.'

'For Christ's sakes, Greg!' roared Byrd. 'We've got satellites, haven't we?'

'Steady, Gilbey,' Sara warned quietly.

'It's not that simple, Mr President,' answered Noble. He coughed. 'We think they're under the sea.'

'Hell, that's illegal,' muttered Carson. '1971 Seabed Treaty.'

'What?' snapped Byrd.

Noble shrugged his shoulders.

Byrd began to doodle on a pad with his pencil, his chin resting on his other hand. 'We need more information,' he muttered.

'We've already got two spooks on the island. Surely they can locate his command and control,' suggested Carson. 'We could stop him that way.'

Noble hesitated. 'I'm afraid that's another problem. The operation to penetrate the missile facility – it failed last night. They've blown their cover. They're asking for immediate evacuation.'

'Out of the question, Greg. We need them out there,' snapped Byrd.

'But their lives are in danger, Mr President.'

Byrd said nothing and continued doodling on his pad. 'OK, let's try another direction. Who's supplying the uranium? For the warheads?'

'Nobody – he's mining it himself,' explained Noble.

'Holy shit!' exploded Byrd.

'From geothermal deposits, Mr President, around deep-ocean hydrothermal vent sites – you know, "black smokers".'

The meeting erupted into separate conversations:

'So that's what they're up to,' intoned Sara Ackerman.

'And maybe that's what he's doing off Guam,' exclaimed Dan Carson.

'The hell he is!' answered Hickel. 'Can he do that?'

'No, it's illegal,' exclaimed Sara Ackerman.

'You're right,' said Hickel. 'He must be operating inside our 200-mile zone. It's against international law. Christ! He's taking the bloody uranium off the sea floor – from right under our noses. *Our* uranium.'

'Can you get uranium on the sea floor?' asked Carson.

Greg Noble held up his hands to stop the babble.

'No – I mean, yes. Look!' He paused for a moment. 'It may be possible to find a form of uranium ore being deposited around a hydrothermal vent; but no, it's not uranium – not off Guam, anyway.'

They stared at him, waiting for him to continue.

'He's extracting something else. It's code-named *Indera* and we've no idea what it is.'

'*Indera*,' mused Sara Ackerman, 'I know that word. It comes from Pacific mythology. Indera's an Indonesian god. He wields a lightning weapon called *vajira*. It's his job to resolve any conflict, whether in heaven or on earth.'

Byrd looked at her, horrified. 'Jesus, what's that bastard found down there?'

'I suggest we maintain the highest security classification

on this,' demanded Hickel. 'If any of this leaks out, the Chinese won't stand for it. An Islamic nuclear power right on their doorstep – they'll go to war.'

'Yeah, Chan Hung won't hang back,' Carson said, his voice tight. 'He'll go nuclear, and so will Rahman. We're sitting on a time bomb here.'

Byrd drummed his hands on his desk. Rahman couldn't be allowed to get away with this. The man was dangerous: they had to act, it was their responsibility. 'Sara – what do you make of Rahman? Would he risk a nuclear conflict, or would he back down?'

Sara sat quietly in her chair and thought for a moment. 'He's very assertive. He believes strongly in the superiority of Indonesia. He's a crusader and a visionary who wants to be head of a Pan-Islamic South-East Asia. If pushed, he'll feel under threat and he'll try and fight his way out. He'll be convinced that he can win.' She paused. 'Yes, I think he *would* fire his weapons – if someone forced his hand.'

There was silence in the room as they all absorbed Sara's statement.

'So how do we deal with him?' asked Byrd soberly.

'With difficulty,' said Walter Hickel. He counted off the points on his fingers. 'One: you can't attack his missile-production facility, it's too well protected. Two: we don't know where the launch sites are and they may even be hidden under the sea. Three: if you try and do something he doesn't like, some sort of direct action, he'll threaten our biggest Pacific base with a nuclear holocaust. Four: he's happy to play brinkmanship with the Chinese. The man's a menace. I really don't know what to suggest at the present time. We'll have to go to the UN, and try and keep the lid on the Chinese—'

'Wait a minute,' interrupted Byrd. 'He could just have a weak spot. Let's go back to command and control. Where does he fire his weapons from, Greg?'

Greg Noble looked at him dolefully. 'We don't know yet, Mr President.'

'Then damn well find out! And we need to know what this *Indera* is. We've got to know what we are dealing with here.'

'What about our people on Papua, Mr President? They're obviously in danger. They need to be taken off.'

'No, Greg! You tell them from me, direct orders: one more mission, then they can come home.'

'But one of them's not even CIA. She's MI6, and London won't like it.'

'Penkovsky Protocol, Greg. They've got no choice.'

'That's stretching things very fine, sir.'

But Byrd was already collecting up his papers, indicating that the meeting had come to an end. He looked across at Carson. 'Dan, step up the propaganda a bit, will you? Leak a photograph of the submersible; let Rahman know that we're onto him. In the meantime, I'm going to the UN over this ocean-floor mining. We need to slap a Resolution on that before it gets out of hand. We'll try and do most of this legally, but, whatever happens, don't let Chan know about the nuclear thing. We'll have to find some way of stopping Rahman that keeps China well out of the loop.'

Chapter Twenty-seven – the following morning: Rahman's Palace, Bogor – thirty miles south of Jakarta

President Amir Rahman thumped a rubber hand-stamp onto the document he was reading, scribbled a signature, and swept it into his out-tray. He glanced at the ostentatious face of his gold Rolex and frowned, drumming his fingers. Behind him, a set of full-length curtains whispered and rolled in the gentle early-morning breeze that sighed in through the half-open window. Morning was a better time now; it lacked the extreme heat of recent days, the smog of Jakarta, and the smoke from the torched forests that often came billowing up the sides of the mountain.

He threw a glance at Lukman sitting confidently in his easy chair, and a scowl soured his face. This young man had once been his hired assassin, had once been a useful ally. Now he was a strutting Head of the *Kopassus*, a peacock who'd overreached himself. A feeling of contempt gripped Rahman as he considered the man's shifty eyes and arrogant voice. Lukman was not to be trusted any more.

Rahman picked up the copy of the *Washington Post* the young officer had brought with him, studied the headline picture, and slowly shook his head. He still couldn't believe what he saw there.

He got up from behind his desk and went over to stand in front of a large painting; a rather intense and gruesome early-twentieth-century picture of Islamic fighters fiercely resisting Dutch control. He stared at the rifles spitting fire, the dismembered bodies – but he did not see them. As always, he struck a powerful pose, but his mind was elsewhere, troubled by the newspaper's revelation.

The door to his study opened with a discreet click. Rahman turned, an expectant look on his face. A blue-uniformed Palace official was standing respectfully in the doorway.

'Dr Jazid Hendra has arrived, sir.'

'Good! Ask him to wait outside for me, will you, at the front of the Palace. And have one of the golf carts brought round.'

Rahman set off towards the side door that led directly into his private quarters, snatching the newspaper from the desk as he went. 'Would you wait for me here, Major Lukman,' he said, as he reached for the door handle. 'My private secretary will look after you until I return.'

Rahman dressed himself casually in an open-necked shirt and grey slacks, then emerged onto the imposing front steps of the Palace. He paused briefly to pull on a pair of immaculate golfing gloves, observing how the heat of the day was already beginning to make itself felt, how small cumulus clouds were beginning to show through the smoggy haze covering the distant mountain peaks.

Rahman could see Hendra waiting by the white electric golf cart, stiff and formal in an immaculate grey suit; and he noticed how the jewelled ring had gone from the scientist's finger. It was the sign of a man in trouble, the sign of someone who wished to disguise his wealth.

Rahman jogged down the steps in bullish mood. 'Good morning, Jazid. Splendid day, don't you think?' And he stood deliberately in front of Hendra to shake his hand, his large frame dominating the smaller scientist. 'I thought we'd take the opportunity for a little golf – before it gets too hot. What do you say?'

'Of course, sir, a splendid idea.' Hendra was putting on a brave face, but fear showed in the man's eyes – and Rahman knew it. He could see it, smell it, and he was glad of that. He had a lot of questions for this Dr Jazid Hendra, and the more uncomfortable the treacherous worm could be made to feel, the better. He tucked the newspaper carefully into the pocket of the golf cart and swung himself on board.

'Come on, Jazid, let's get out onto the fairway. We can have a little chat in private. I haven't heard much from you since my last visit to Arguni. Tell me, how are things? How close are we to completing the centrifuging?'

Without waiting for an answer, Rahman floored the pedal and gunned the electric golf cart away from the steps.

Hendra staggered back in his seat, and the sun canopy shook as the cart rattled over the gravel before jolting onto the golf course proper.

Rahman couldn't resist a backward glance. He was proud of his Presidential Palace. It shone brilliant white against the pale morning sky. A row of columns flanked the grand flight of steps at the front, and two wings spread out gloriously to either side, rectangular windows beautifully proportioned by their eighteenth-century architects. Rahman had to pitch his voice high above the whine and vibration of the golf cart. 'Magnificent house, Jazid, don't you think? Built by the Dutch in the last days of their East India Company. Our spices certainly made Cohen a rich and powerful man.'

Rahman glanced across at Hendra and saw him clinging to the bodywork as the cart jolted over the rough turf. He grinned; he was enjoying this little game. He sparred, teasing Hendra with another subtle hint. 'Of course, you know what brought Cohen down, don't you? Power struggles, from within. Greed and corruption, eating away at the Company.'

Still Hendra said nothing. Rahman let his point take effect for a moment, then he struck again. 'Of course, now that you've found all this wealth beneath our seas, it's such an opportunity – to make our country great again.' Now he looked at Hendra fixedly. 'That's the whole point of the operation, isn't it? Working together, on ocean-floor mining, for the good of the nation. A team effort, eh, Jazid?'

'Of course, sir.' Hendra's voice wobbled slightly with

the jolting of the golf cart. 'You have said that before, many times.'

Yes, and many times you have failed to listen, Dr Jazid Hendra, thought Rahman. *But you will listen today. With all your wealth, and that damned jewel you usually sport on your finger, and your little boys – you disgust me!*

Rahman skidded the golf cart to a halt at the first tee. In front of them they could see the fairway winding its way around the vast open area of parkland. It had rained the night before, and an iron smell of damp earth drifted in the air. A clump of tall *rasamala* trees swayed gently in the breeze, and a flock of grey Java sparrows squabbled in the nearby bushes, flashes of white around their heads.

Rahman teed off first. His heavy wood sliced through the air and, with a resounding *thwack*, he drove the ball far down the fairway. Hendra bent to position his own ball. Rahman watched as Hendra eyed the course, waited until he had his arm held high in a back swing, then struck: 'Have you seen the *Washington Post* this morning, Jazid?' He flapped the newspaper from out of the side pocket of the golf cart. 'Interesting photograph on the front page.'

Hendra glanced at the newspaper picture, and let his swing come down automatically. He missed the ball and tottered slightly on his heels. 'Sir, I think we need to talk.'

'That's why you're here, Jazid – to talk. But do go on – take the ball, I insist.' Hendra was going to say something else, but thought better of it. His wood cracked against the ball. It arced inaccurately off into the distance. 'Oh, bad luck!' tutted Rahman. 'You're out of practice.'

They both mounted the golf cart to drive further down the fairway. As he drove, Rahman passed the newspaper into Hendra's hands. 'Tell me, Jazid, what *are* you doing, mining so close to Guam? Aren't you perhaps being a little bold?'

Hendra took the paper, giving Rahman an odd look. 'We're prospecting for minerals, sir.' He scanned the article. 'We certainly do seem to have worried the Americans.'

'You certainly have. They called in our ambassador – very embarrassing.'

When Hendra said nothing, Rahman stopped the cart. He reached across and took the newspaper, pointing again at the photograph. 'So, what's all this about a submersible?'

Hendra looked puzzled. 'A submersible, sir?'

Rahman examined his face – saw the anxiety manifest there. He was on the bastard's tail, all right. He smiled sweetly. 'I've never seen one of that type before, I didn't realize that we possessed anything so sophisticated. Tell me, what do you use it for?'

Hendra's answer came easily. 'To bring up mineral samples.'

'But you haven't been anywhere near the vent site mentioned by this American reporter, have you?'

'Well . . . yes, we have. We've been investigating deposits all along the Marianas Trench.'

This candid answer surprised Rahman. He raised his eyebrows and nodded. 'Is that so? Interesting!'

He clambered off the golf cart and reached for an iron. 'But you had nothing to do with the sinking of the

340

American submarine, of course. I mean, you wouldn't do anything so stupid, would you? After all, we've nothing to hide, have we?'

'No, of course not, sir!'

Rahman studied Hendra again. There was something there, something in the set of the man's expression. It was revealing more than his tongue did. The man was lying.

It was then that Rahman decided that he couldn't be bothered to stalk Hendra any further. He would go in for the kill, as soon as the time was right. He grunted as he swung his iron with an obvious skill born of assiduous practice. The ball arced away towards the first hole, and they headed off towards Hendra's ball, a small white dot on the well-kept turf. They walked beside each other, the warm wind wafting a strong scent of cloves and nutmeg across the fairway.

'Tell me, what is *Indera*, Jazid?' asked Rahman quietly.

Hendra's expression froze. He halted and paled visibly, staring at Rahman. 'How did you know about that?' he responded, his voice quavering.

Rahman gazed straight into his victim's eyes, a little grin beginning to tease the corners of his lips. 'Major Lukman passed me a computer disk this morning. Apparently it comes from the *Ibn Battuta*. I had it analysed . . . it was rather interesting.'

Rahman watched carefully as the sky fell in upon Jazid Hendra. He watched as the very spirit of the man drained into the soil beneath his feet.

Hendra finally found his voice. Suddenly it had become dry and cracked: 'It's just a new mineral, sir, one we discovered quite recently. Possibly an important one.' He gave Rahman a haunted look. 'One that could help us win our victory against the West.'

Rahman nodded, laughing inwardly at Hendra's allusion to loyalty, at the surprising naivety of the man. It wasn't victory against the West that he wanted. It was power, power for Indonesia – to make her great again. 'Really?' he continued. 'That important, Jazid?'

'Very important. I'm sorry you had to find out this way, sir. Major Lukman had no authority to pass on this information. *Indera* is still at a very early stage of investigation, and we'd hoped to surprise you with our findings – on Independence Day.'

Rahman glared disdainfully at Hendra, and his voice took on a hard edge. 'But you've known about this mineral for a long time, Dr Hendra. That disk was one of the two stolen from the *Ibn Battuta*. You've been mining it in small quantities for months, processing it in laboratory facilities at Arguni.' Rahman's voice hardened with anger. 'Facilities that I paid for, Dr Hendra ... to process uranium, not *Indera*. So why did you withhold this information from me?'

Hendra looked at the ground. He was a trapped man. There was no answer, no answer that he had not already given. He said nothing.

Rahman continued to stare at him, breathing hard.

'You were mining *Indera* when you were caught by the Americans?'

Hendra looked up. 'Yes. But our discovery will be of great value to this country, Mr President. It's my own belief that *Indera* is a previously unknown isotope of gold – one that superconducts at room temperature.' He waited for Rahman's reaction.

Rahman looked puzzled. 'Superconducts? I don't understand.'

'A room-temperature superconductor, sir, is something that would revolutionize our technology. It would make us a world leader in electronics almost overnight. Think of computers, sir, computers immensely more powerful than any we have today – because of their fantastic speed. Think of the global market for such a thing. Or think of super-powerful electric motors, because their wiring offers no resistance to the current . . .'

'Ah – the car I tested! Is *that* why it performed so well?'

'Partly, although our understanding of the material was then still at an early stage . . .'

'So what's going on at *Espiritu*, Dr Hendra?'

Hendra blinked.

'*Espiritu*, Dr Hendra?' Rahman repeated. 'What do you do there?'

Hendra's voice was strangled. 'The missile-control centre, sir. You asked Major Lukman to make it secure, so . . .'

'. . . We placed it on Palau, yes, I know. But why wasn't I told about your additional facility?'

'But . . .'

'You fool, Dr Hendra. *Espiritu*'s the place where you planned to manufacture *Indera*, isn't it? Hidden away alongside the missile-control centre.'

Hendra didn't answer.

'Out of sight – from me. For your own benefit. To line your own greedy little pockets.'

Hendra remained silent.

Rahman went quiet, too, for a minute. Then, in a chilling voice, he added: 'I no longer have any need of you, Dr Hendra.'

Hendra pleaded quickly, 'You do need me, sir. Without me you cannot develop this new material.'

Rahman's eyes were shining like two hard, brightly polished pebbles. 'I beg to differ, Jazid. I think your work is over. Your technicians will develop this material for me now. You plotted against me, you concealed information from me, you over-extended yourself – you can no longer be trusted. You are a traitor,' he hissed, 'to me, to your people, to your country – and to your God.' He paused. 'And you will pay the price.'

He could see that Hendra was petrified, only just in control of his emotions. Rahman could smell the other man's fear, and he enjoyed it. It confirmed his own superiority, his strength. This, of course, was why he was President – and Hendra was not.

Rahman stepped up into the golf cart and left Hendra standing there. 'My position does not allow me to tolerate any weakness, Dr Hendra,' he called back. 'I will not flinch from my duty.' He pushed hard on the pedal. The back wheels spun briefly in the soft turf before the cart jerked away through the spacious parkland and began to climb the gentle slope back towards the Palace.

Rahman calmly reached down onto the seat of the jolting vehicle for his mobile phone and issued a simple pre-arranged order. As the cart lurched onto the gravel by the Palace steps, a jeep full of red-bereted soldiers sped round one corner of the Palace and bounced away onto the golf course. Rahman caught a glimpse of dark sunglasses, smooth brown faces, rifles held at the ready. *Kopassus* – his loyal Special Forces Regiment. At least he knew that *they* would carry out their duty – without question.

He parked the golf cart and stood on the steps of the Palace, waiting.

The sharp *crack* of a rifle shot rang out through the stillness of the park. A flock of birds broke cover, crashing out of the trees, sending tiny shreds of vegetation spinning to the ground.

And Rahman smiled – an ugly, twisted smile.

Rahman strolled back into his study. Major Lukman was still there, waiting patiently in a chair by the window. He stood up confidently as Rahman entered, full of expectancy.

The President sat down behind his large antique desk. 'Major Lukman, I'm going to promote you to colonel – a field promotion in recognition of your loyalty. I would like you to return to Arguni. You will take charge of security

345

there. Put the base on full alert – I think we may soon have a visit from the Americans. I also want you to root out and destroy that little nest of spies we seem to have acquired on the island. Is that clear?'

'Yes, sir.'

Rahman rotated a pencil between his fingers; his shiny eyes stared at Lukman. 'Colonel Lukman, these spies, did they penetrate the nuclear facility?'

'Yes, sir.'

'How far did they get?'

'Only to the loading bay, sir.'

Rahman nodded. 'Good. Then maybe this picture in the Western press is just a ploy.' He slammed the newspaper into a waste bin. 'A threat, to try and undermine my resolve.'

Lukman looked down at the floor.

Rahman sat back in his chair and rubbed at his chin. 'Well, we can play games too, of course.' He reached across his desk and scribbled on a memo pad, tore off the sheet, and thrust it at Lukman. 'Have this message sent to Washington by fax, direct to President Byrd.'

Lukman glanced down at the memo: 'THE TIGER HAS CLAWS'. He gave Rahman a questioning look.

The President laughed a deep, arrogant laugh. 'Literature, Colonel Lukman. It comes from a poem, an ancient Sumatran writing about the *Korinchi*.'

Lukman looked puzzled. 'Sir?'

'*Korinchi*, man – were-tigers! Men who turn into tigers!' He recited the poem:

> *'Rolling dice*
> *and tiger's roar.*
> *Reaching out*
> *the tiger's claw.*
> *Fear the tigers' strike*
> *when Korinchi stalk the night!'*

Rahman grinned confidently at Lukman. 'Have you never seen the *Bakorstanas* tiger head? That silver medallion they wear around their necks?' He chuckled. 'The Tiger has claws, Colonel Lukman. You should learn to fear the Tiger's strike!'

Rahman stared fixedly at Lukman for a moment.

'But you see,' he added quietly, 'I myself have no fear, Colonel Lukman.'

Chapter Twenty-eight – the following day: Arguni Island, Papua

Nicole snapped the lid of her laptop computer down and glanced at Rykhlin as he sprawled, exhausted and unkempt, across the dirty floor of Freddy's tree house. She watched him as he lay there stretched out, his hair tousled and matted. He'd been very good to her, had cared for her. He was strong, intelligent, and capable – yet, like her, he was caught up in his own tragedy.

As if he could feel her stare, he stirred slightly before waking from his doze. She looked away quickly.

'Batteries are going fast,' she said, stuffing the laptop into her rucksack. 'We're going to have to be careful how often we use this from now on.'

Rykhlin propped himself up on one elbow and rubbed sleep from his eyes with grubby fingers. 'So what did London say? How long before they come and pick us up?'

Nicole began to dismantle the satellite aerial slowly, folding it up with tired and deliberate movements. 'They're not!'

An incredulous look spread across Rykhlin's face. 'They expect us to get out of here on our own?'

Nicole slid the rest of the electronic equipment back into her rucksack and pulled the drawstring tight. 'It seems Washington are putting London under pressure. They want us to go back in.'

Rykhlin shook his head with disbelief. 'That can't be right. I warned them that we'd fouled up. Christ, the island will be crawling with *Kopassus* soon. They'll search everywhere. We won't be able to move.'

'They want more information. They want to know about *Indera*. And they want the missile launch sites and targets.'

Rykhlin laughed cynically. 'Great!'

Nicole buried her rucksack under one of the piles of dusty sago bark, then sat down with her back against the flimsy wall of the tree house. The air was thick with heat, and the humidity made her clothes stick uncomfortably to her body. She stared out of the 'bird cage' front of the tree house and watched the afternoon's crop of dark cumulus clouds building steadily over the far side of the island. The floor of the hut swayed gently as Rykhlin got up and came over to sit with her. She felt his presence close to her.

'What are you thinking?' he asked gently.

'That we haven't got any choice.'

Lightning flickered above the far horizon, and a loud rumble shook the fragile structure around them.

'We could always pack it in,' he said. 'Demand to be taken off tomorrow night.'

'No! I don't want that.' Nicole was surprised at the depth of her conviction.

Rykhlin glanced across at her. 'Are you sure?'

She nodded.

'This got something to do with your son?'

The words made Nicole go cold. Suddenly she wanted to tell him. Tell him everything. Pour it all out, the whole tragic story. The weeks of bottling it up, holding it back – now she wanted him to know.

'It's cancer.' Her throat was dry, and the words came out sounding tight and anxious.

Rykhlin stared at her. 'They promised him a cure?'

She picked up a broken shard of bamboo and tossed it out through the door. It dropped out of sight. 'They also promised to get my father out of here, as part of the payment.'

'Jesus!' Rykhlin swore under his breath.

Thunder ripped through the air, as if splitting the atmosphere in half, the echo rattling around the clearing before bouncing off the nearby hills. Fat blobs of rain began to splatter on the palm roof.

'Which means I've got to finish the job, Rykhlin. There's nothing else I can do.' Her fingers found another piece of bamboo and began to play with it. She felt the smoothness of its skin; and the razor-sharp edges where it had snapped.

'Have you got any children?' she asked.

'Hell no!' He laughed. 'It's been bloody lonely since Kosovo. Imagine: "What did you do in the war, Daddy?"

What would I tell them? That I left a couple of kids in the shit? No way I can tell them that!' He shook his head. 'No way.'

'I told you before,' she said quietly. 'You weren't being a coward.'

'Wasn't I?' he demanded.

She rounded on him. 'Look, you let this go on eating you, Rykhlin, and you'll die – slowly, from the inside. Believe me, I know.'

Rykhlin gave her a funny look, then held out his hand, palm upwards, a mischievous twinkle in his eyes. 'Partners, right?'

She caught his meaning, smiled, smacked her palm down on his.

But he clasped her hand impetuously instead of letting it go. Suddenly the cracked roughness of his palm was against hers, and she didn't mind. 'We'll get you out of this,' he said. 'We have to. You're a valuable asset now.'

Then he withdrew his hand, and his eyes narrowed, focusing on the horizon. 'OK, so they want more information. Where do you suggest we go from here?'

Nicole gazed out at the storm, watching as it edged slowly towards them. Fresh rain began to deluge the far side of the island, drifting out of the cloud in great ugly swathes of grey. 'Perhaps it's time to have a go at breaking into their computer net,' she mused.

'Can you do that?'

'Using DEMON, yes. It's a computer hacking program.'

Rykhlin whistled appreciatively. 'What do you need?'

'A computer terminal. Any terminal, as long as it has access to their main network.'

He watched the gathering storm thoughtfully. 'I think the guards have terminals in their huts.'

'Yes, but that's not a good idea. We'd be trapped too easily. I've already seen them: the guard posts are well defended and monitored by surveillance cameras.'

Rykhlin stroked his dishevelled beard. 'There's one guard post that doesn't have a camera. The one at the entrance to the solar-cell array, on the cliff top near the mine. I've been up there on maintenance duty.'

'But it's a long way from here. It's right over on the other side of the island.'

Rykhlin turned to her, his brown eyes shining in the gloom. 'I think we could do it, if we pushed ourselves hard enough.' Rain began beating heavily on the roof of the tree house. 'We can't stay in this place for too long. They'll have helicopters out looking for us.'

A grey murk descended over the jungle clearing as the rain started to come down in sheets, miniature waterfalls splattering off the thatched roof. 'Not in this they won't!' laughed Nicole.

She thought for a moment.

She didn't want to let Rykhlin down, not after they'd come so far together. If they could get this job done quickly, it would be their surest way off the island. She looked up. 'Would Freddy guide us up there?' she asked.

Rykhlin laughed. 'Sure – for dollars!'

Nicole kicked at the dirt on the floor. 'No problem, then. We could go tonight.'

Lightning flashed, illuminating the interior of the tree house, making grotesque shadows flicker on the walls. Nicole absent-mindedly counted the seconds, marking the miles to the centre of the storm like she had as a child. Thunder crashed, then grumbled noisily around the rim of the crater.

'What do you think?' she asked.

Rykhlin got up slowly and rummaged around at the back of the hut. He produced the semi-automatic rifle he'd taken during their raid on the missile facility. Removing the magazine, he checked the number of rounds left, then pushed it back in. He gave her a direct look. 'Do you want this – or the Colt?'

Nicole stared at the rifle – and thought it was too long, heavy and awkward for her to carry. 'The Colt,' she replied. 'I'll find it easier.'

Dawn slowly lit up the far horizon, painting a thin streak of brightness across the black canvas of the previous night. Nicole lay in the cover of dense scrub above a gravel track that threaded its way around the southern cliff. A warm breeze drifted in from the sea, stirring the tall grass around her. She was close to exhaustion, her eyes sore with fatigue. She had to fight to keep them open; all she wanted to do was sleep. Her clothes were soaked from lying in the vegetation, and hunger gnawed at her belly.

A loud rustle in the undergrowth broke into her doze. She automatically reached for the Colt and rolled onto her stomach. But it was only Rykhlin returning. 'They've just changed the guard,' he whispered. 'We'll give it another half-hour, then we go in. OK?'

Nicole nodded. She knew what she had to do. Two soldiers – both hers, while Rykhlin covered the approach. Rykhlin gave her a broad wink and disappeared.

She lay back, the need to finish this job fuelling her determination. She wanted to see her son again, to find out whether his treatment was working. She was doing this whole thing for him; and for her father lying in his cage. She felt their presence, their *pressure*. They were both waiting, wondering why she hadn't come back.

She lay quietly in the long grass, watching the cold light of dawn slowly make sense of her surroundings. Listened to the forest waking up around her, the rising crescendo of birdsong, the gentle rush of surf breaking on the cliffs far below.

From off to Nicole's left came Rykhlin's urgent muffled command. 'Go!'

Her heart leaped – this was it! Adrenalin surged through her. She belly-crawled quickly through the scrub, tall grasses parting in front of her face, and wormed her way carefully to the top of the slope. She looked down onto the scene ten feet below and assessed the situation.

A gravel track. Two soldiers with black berets – thank

God they weren't *Kopassus*. A small wooden hut with a red and white barrier pole. A military jeep parked to one side, with a pintle-mounted machine gun. Off to her left, the vast glassy expanse of solar cells waiting blankly to catch the morning sun.

One of the soldiers slouched in front of the barrier, smoking. The other busied himself inside the hut.

She waited . . . and watched. An insect whined past her ear.

Then Freddy came up the road.

Nicole kept her gaze focused tightly on him. He hailed the soldier outside the hut in his tribal language. The soldier stubbed out his cigarette and moved forward, keeping his rifle slung over his shoulder. The other man came out of the hut and stood in the doorway, watching in amusement. The first soldier challenged Freddy, who put up his hand and waved in a convincing friendly gesture. He jabbered away at the soldier, as if trying to make himself understood. He held their full attention now. They began to laugh, poking fun at him. They had their backs to her. She had her job to do.

She stood up carefully and, stretching both hands out in front of her, took careful aim with the Colt. Picking out the soldier with the rifle first, she breathed in slowly, and brought the fat barrel of the silencer down until it lined up with his body, finding the spot where his heart should be.

She squeezed the trigger gently, felt it take up the slack . . .

Thud!

The pistol kicked. The soldier went down, screaming, and lay there, eyes rolling. She swung the pistol round towards the wooden hut. The other soldier had vanished! He'd taken cover.

Be aggressive! Get in close!

She ran, half stumbling, down the steep earth bank onto the track, trainers skidding on the loose gravel. She crouched down behind the jeep, arms stretched out with the pistol held steady. A rattle came from the throat of the man on the ground.

Rykhlin shouted from somewhere. 'In the cabin!'

Nicole looked over and saw a hand through the window, saw it coming from low down to grasp the telephone. She fired again. The pistol kicked, glass shattered. The hand disappeared.

She ran over to the hut and slammed open the door. The second soldier was sitting on the floor, hands across his face, whimpering, pleading, legs scrabbling with fear. She hesitated, feeling pity. Then she saw an image of her father, eyes staring out blankly from behind the grille, saw the rows of other caged and emaciated bodies, saw the evil of this place. She brought up both hands, shut her eyes, and fired.

When she opened them, the soldier was slumped forward – a big chunk missing from his skull.

'Jesus!' Rykhlin and Freddy were standing by her side. She let the gun drop, feeling nothing but the barrel warm against her thigh and in her mouth the chemical taste of spent ammunition.

Rykhlin shoved the rucksack at her. 'OK, it's all yours. How long?'

She stared at him, not comprehending his question.

'Hacking into the computer,' he said. 'How long do you think it'll take?'

She had no idea. 'Ten minutes?' she suggested.

Rykhlin was anxious. 'OK – no longer. We go in ten.'

He and Freddy dragged the body from the hut, then went off to tidy things up.

She went in, put the rucksack on the little table, and pulled out her laptop – she didn't look at the wet redness sprayed all over the wall. She focused on the PC instead, checking it out, twisting it round, finding the correct port to plug in her own machine. She booted the laptop on the batteries, accessed the file called DEMON, and waited for it to load.

DEMON – Device for Electronic Management of a Network – a superfast program for hacking into somebody else's computer. State-of-the-art, highly classified – not to fall into enemy hands.

Nicole thought about what she had to do, what they'd taught her back in Belize. Machines like the PC in the guard post would be networked into a main server some-where, which in all probability talked to an even more secure network. But there'd be a firewall between them, one that would require a sophisticated electronic key to get through. DEMON had to find that key: the key that would breach the firewall and then go on a rampage through the secret realm of Arguni's computer network, hunting down Hendra's files . . .

The program had loaded. Using the tracker pad, Nicole clicked INTERROGATE NETWORK, and then START. The program began to barrage all the computers on the first-level network with questions. It analysed their responses, calculating with its cold logic which was the server, which were the slaves. She rigged the satellite aerial while she waited, keeping it low down and out of sight inside the hut.

One minute.

Long chains of commands and computer addresses still scrolled jerkily up the screen.

Two minutes.

She went outside and leaned up against the side of the hut, expelling some pent-up energy. She looked down the track, almost expecting to see someone approaching, but nothing moved. Rykhlin and Freddy had gone to ground, lying in ambush to prevent anyone coming their way. She was alone.

Three minutes.

The laptop computer beeped. Nicole turned back to the machine. LEVEL ONE SERVER LOCATED. She clicked OPEN GATE. Now the programme fired thousands of spurious requests for information at the server, analysed the replies, looking for clues to the algorithm that would break down the electronic wall.

Four minutes.

Rykhlin reappeared outside the hut. He was getting edgy. He kicked at the gravel on the track, little puffs of dust erupting around his boots. Nicole ignored him, drumming her fingers on the tabletop, watching the cursor blinking on the screen, willing the machine forward.

Five minutes.

Rykhlin put his head round the door, a questioning look on his face. Nicole looked back at him, just shrugged. He bounced the rifle into his other hand and withdrew.

Six minutes.

The printer suddenly burst into life, making her jump. A sheet began to roll out into the tray. She picked it up and read it – a roster of guards for the next shift. She screwed it up and threw it on the floor.

Seven minutes.

A bleep. GATE OPEN. Yes! She'd done it! She gave a little squeal of joy.

Keep calm, one last task. She clicked CREATE SERVER X.

In the main security block, the morning shift was just coming in, all very calm and professional, soldiers dressed in smart camouflage uniforms, red berets tucked under epaulettes. A line of PCs stretched all around the darkened security room, and banks of TV screens showed different camera views of the complex, both above and below ground. The screens flicked slowly between one camera and the next. On the wall was a sign in red-illuminated letters: ALERT LEVEL ALPHA. The soldiers exchanged places with their night-shift colleagues.

A young sergeant sat down at station seven and began checking in to the patrols and gates under his command. He received replies, logged in each answer. He keyed in GATE 26. The cursor blinked but nothing happened. He tried again; still the cursor blinked – no response. For a moment, he wondered whether to ignore it – this was not the first time the machine had failed. But then he looked up, saw the alert level, and noticed that the colonel had come in this morning. He swung round in his seat.

'Sir?'

Colonel Lukman came across, and the sergeant explained the problem. Lukman tried himself, punching the number onto the keyboard – but he too got nothing. 'Have you checked the camera view?' he asked.

'No camera at Gate 26, sir. Too far out.'

Something worked in Lukman's mind. He frowned: intruders? No, not the solar cells, surely – not important enough. So what could it be? The computer? Someone trying to break into the network? *Of course.* They would have to block the log-in port to get access.

The sergeant sensed his commanding officer's growing concern. 'Shall I get a jeep up there, sir?'

No, Lukman thought, *play it cool. Catch them red-handed, and hopefully alive.* 'Just keep trying,' he said quietly.

The sergeant shrugged. Lukman walked calmly back to

the control desk and spoke to the young lieutenant on duty. 'I think we might have intruders at Gate 26. Be careful – I don't want them frightened off.'

Then the telephone on the lieutenant's desk buzzed. The lieutenant picked it up, listened, and acknowledged the call. He looked at Lukman, his face blank. 'Sir, the computer alarm's just blown. "Sniffer" reports an intruder on the network.'

Lukman's heart leaped. 'Right, that's it! Shut it down.'

'We can't do that, sir. Not without Dr Hendra's authority – not without his access code.'

But Hendra's dead, thought Lukman, *and I don't know the numbers*. 'Who else has the code?' he demanded.

'No one, sir. Dr Hendra insisted on the highest level of security.'

Damn him! Damn Hendra's efficiency! Lukman stared at the soldier. The computer firewall was very sophisticated, so it should hold out for some time yet.

'Ready the helicopter for immediate take-off,' he ordered. 'And get Alpha Company to stand by.'

Chapter Twenty-nine – Gate 26

Eight minutes and DEMON had done its stuff. It had breached the firewall into the second level and conned the network into thinking it was the server. Now Nicole had two-way communication with every workstation on the base's second-level network.

There was one last procedure. She clicked FIND PASS-WORD, whereupon DEMON scrolled through the vast root directory, looking for patterns in the words and numbers.

Hendra had been a careful and logical man. He'd changed his password regularly, but his tidy mind had made a classic security mistake, just like thousands before him. He always used a number with the same root function: his birthday.

Nine minutes – and DEMON found it. She was in. Nicole wiped the sweat from the palms of her hands and, using the tracker pad, opened Hendra's first directory. She began to rifle through the files.

*

SLIDE

Outside the security block, Alpha Company ran towards the edge of the helipad, the sound of their feet drowned by the rising whine of two big turboshaft engines spooling up to speed. Anti-collision lights flashed bright red against the boxy olive-drab fuselage of the big Puma helicopter. Its blades began to rotate, slowly at first, then faster and faster, whipping dust into the eyes of the fifteen soldiers kneeling at the side of the pad, waiting for the order to mount up.

Ten minutes.

Hacking away at the keys on her laptop computer, Nicole thought she could hear the characteristic chopping sound of helicopter rotors far off in the distance. She'd been in the hut a long time now and she was getting nervous. She stopped what she was doing and glanced briefly out of the door but saw nothing.

Eleven minutes.

Rykhlin appeared. 'I can hear a chopper somewhere. I think we should go.'

Nicole was scrolling through one of Hendra's files. 'Wait! I'm in! I've just got to find the right files. Give me five more minutes.'

'I think we ought to go now.'

Nicole turned towards Rykhlin. 'No! This is what we came for.'

Rykhlin stood there, stiff with anxiety. He turned and looked out through the door, scanning the sky, concern etched into every sinew. 'How long?'

'Two minutes.' She lied.

He disappeared. She continued checking Hendra's files, her fingers flying over the keys in frantic desperation.

Thirteen minutes.

Then she found it: what they were looking for. Hendra's knack for organization had been his downfall again – she couldn't believe it, but most of the relevant files seemed to be in the same directory.

First a report on *Indera*. Something about the novel crystallization of gold due to the extremes of temperature and pressure at a deep-ocean vent. Electrons bonding with the crystal lattice as they moved through it – no resistance. They thought they'd found a superconducting material that would work at ordinary room temperature – a high-temperature superconductor. No wonder Hendra had kept it so secret: he stood to make a vast fortune.

Another report. She scanned it, found references to 'Cooper pairs', the shape of the crystal lattice. All the theory. More files – long lists of production figures and schedules. Then a laboratory report, with lots of data . . .

Nicole scanned the remaining reports as fast as she could. They were mining in minute quantities, processing the mineral chemically, forming a powdered oxide blended with copper to turn it into a ceramic. There were reports of trying to mould it, cast it, even draw it into a fine wire. She wondered how successful that had been.

Fourteen minutes.

'For Christ's sake, Annabelle!' Rykhlin's anxious face appeared at the door.

'Have you seen anybody yet?' she snapped.

'No, but we—'

'Then let me finish!'

She used the tracker pad to open another file and scanned its contents. Maps and diagrams showing the location and nature of the deposit. There was masses of it, a complete dossier. She copied the whole directory onto the hard disk and began to transmit through the modem onto the Blacknet.

Fifteen minutes.

The fruits of Hendra's work, thousands and thousands of hours of careful research, were encrypted by the software, fragmented, fired up to an orbiting satellite, and then almost instantaneously downloaded piece by piece onto a secure file on Simes's desktop PC in London.

Lukman was the last to clamber into the waiting Puma. He felt the machine rock slightly, then rise quickly as he buckled up his harness, M16 clasped securely between his knees. He hooked up his intercom and instructed the pilot to fly round the northern end of the island in order to approach Gate 26 from the east. He told him to come in low and land on the beach, using the cliff to mask the sound of their approach.

Seventeen minutes.

Nicole concentrated hard on her work. She heard the

sound of boots outside. Rykhlin again. 'Jesus, Annabelle, come on!' he pleaded.

'I've done it! I've sent a lot of files already. I'm almost there. I just need to find the missile system. Hendra's very thorough – he's making it easy.'

Rykhlin turned. He thought he could hear something, the muffled beat of helicopter rotors. He listened intently. He wasn't sure – just getting jumpy, perhaps.

But they'd been here too long already – much too long. He stood outside the hut, rifle at the ready.

Eighteen minutes.

The pilot brought the Puma in low and hovered over the beach. Lukman's troops leaped the last few feet to the ground and ran into cover among the palms. The helicopter made a careful turn and accelerated away, nose pitched down, keeping low. The sound of its rotors quickly died away.

Lukman briefed the young lieutenant, using the sand to draw a map. He explained what he wanted his men to do. They'd trained here and knew the terrain well. They split into sections and headed off towards Gate 26.

Twenty minutes.

Nicole found the directory dealing with the missile system. There were files on the weapon itself, the delivery method, missile sites, command and control. Masses of it, far more than she'd thought. More than she could read. She simply loaded the whole directory onto the hard disk and began to send it.

She went to the cabin door and looked out. Rykhlin had gone to ground again. She could hear the *chirr* of insects in the forest, the piping calls of jungle birds, the gentle *swoosh* of waves breaking against the cliffs. Beyond the guard post, bright sunlight flashed off the huge flat panels of the solar cells.

It was very hot.

She wiped the sweat and tension from her forehead and turned to look back down the track towards the base. She knew Rykhlin and Freddy were still out there somewhere – waiting for her.

Twenty-two minutes.

Lukman swung his binoculars carefully, to avoid any tell-tale lens flash from the sun. He could see a female standing in the doorway of the sentry post. There must be others. Where were they? Probably somewhere down the track, lying in ambush. The woman went back inside the guard hut.

It had to be the computer. Yes, there she was, tapping away at the keyboard. He grinned and turned gently, trying not to disturb the foliage. He signalled to the lieutenant – one intruder.

Silently, the sections spread out.

He would wait a few minutes until they were in position. Then they'd go in – for the kill.

Twenty-six minutes.

Nicole had found yet another file – *Espiritu.* There was simply too much stuff! She scanned the material: maps and plans about some sort of secret base on Palau Island, concealed as part of a flood-defence scheme. It looked like their missile command and control centre. Why would they put it there? Were the Pacific Islands involved in this as well?

Nicole realized the significance of what she'd found and knew she had to mine it for all it was worth. She began to load the file into the laptop and got ready to send that too. She was getting agitated. The danger was mounting with every moment she stayed.

She watched the computer send yet another string of data. But there was still one thing missing: the missile targets . . .

BANG! – a blinding flash of white. From out of nowhere, something solid had slugged her painfully across the back of her head.

Then . . .

Blackness . . .

*

The soldier watched the woman slump to the ground. His gaze darted nervously around the guard post. He was young and this was his first taste of combat. He was fully charged-up. He saw a laptop computer and guessed that it shouldn't be there. A funny-looking aerial pointed up at the sky. He looked at the leads coming out of the machine but didn't understand them. They must be sending information; in fact, they could be sending it now. He'd stop it. He lifted his rifle and brought the butt down sharply onto the aerial, smashing it into a crumpled heap. He yanked at the leads. They wouldn't come loose, so he drew his combat knife and severed them. Then he turned to the small computer, knocked it off the worktop, and smashed that too, watching in fascination as the little plastic keys jumped out of their sockets and spread all over the floor.

A smile of satisfaction spread across his face. Bitch hadn't stood a chance.

Lukman stood in the doorway of the guard post and ran his eyes over the mayhem inside. The woman lay unconscious on the ground. He kicked at the electronic debris with his booted foot and bent down to examine some of the pieces. A laptop, lid off, keyboard smashed. Some sort of dish that looked like a satellite aerial. Spies! He'd caught them. Rahman would be pleased.

He checked the screen on the main computer. It still showed the last message the guard post had received that morning. He guessed they hadn't penetrated far into the system and certainly hadn't broken into the main network.

He kneeled down beside the woman. His fingers explored her neck, felt her pulse – slow, but strong. He moved her head to one side and let it flop back. A small trickle of clear fluid smeared with blood seeped from her ear. He looked again, and thought he'd seen this woman before. He lifted her face and stared at it, but couldn't quite remember where . . .

Then he remembered. Of course, the oil rig.

This was Tai-Chung!

So, the bitch had come back for her daddy after all.

Lukman smiled sadistically.

He clumped across the wooden floor in his heavy boots and went outside. His men were dragging another body up the dusty track towards the hut. He reached for his combat radio and spoke into the microphone tagged to his jacket. He ordered the helicopter back in and asked for a doctor to stand by in the cells.

If the woman lived, he'd find out how much she'd learned from that disk and see if she'd found out anything he didn't already know about Hendra's secret little operation. In fact, he'd do his utmost to extract from her anything useful she'd learned from Hendra's computer files that he could use for his own purposes.

Then he'd kill her.

Part Four: THE TIGER'S CLAW

The State Department, Washington, D.C.

09.00, 26 April

As David Austen, State Department spokesperson, mounted the podium in the Press Room, an expectant hush fell across the gathered correspondents. A wild rumour was circulating that the officially 'leaked' picture of the Indonesian submersible was linked in some way to the sinking of the *Deep-Search*, and they were all here to see if it was true. Austen gazed intently across his lectern at the assembled press corps.

AUSTEN: 'As you know, three days ago, on the morning of 23 April, the USS *Deep-Search*, a Deep-Sea Rescue Vessel, was lost with both hands 150 miles south of Guam. The submarine was engaged on a humanitarian mission on behalf of the Japanese government. The President has asked me to issue the following statement: "Since the sinking of the USS *Deep-Search*, investigators have been working hard to establish the exact cause of the accident. The United

$States government wishes the world to know that careful examination of the available evidence points conclusively to an explosion, almost certainly caused by the impact of a torpedo fired from an unknown vessel."' A murmur of excited voices rolled around the room. Austen turned over a sheet of paper. 'I have a second statement: "United States intelligence sources have recently established that the Islamic Republic of Indonesia is using submersibles and other specialized deep-ocean mining equipment to covertly extract an exotic mineral from the floor of the Pacific Ocean at a site close to the vicinity of the *Deep-Search* incident. This activity directly contravenes the 1994 Convention on the Law of the Sea."' Austen paused, waiting for the excited chatter to die down. 'Are there any questions?'

QUESTION: Are you saying that the Indonesians torpedoed the *Deep-Search*?
AUSTEN: No.
QUESTION: Is there any evidence that they might have done so?
AUSTEN: No.
QUESTION: So what *are* you saying, David?
AUSTEN: That the most likely cause of the incident was a torpedo – fired from an unknown vessel.
QUESTION: But the Indonesians were the only ones in the area at the time?
AUSTEN: As far as we know, yes.

QUESTION: Can you tell us any more about this mineral?

AUSTEN: Sorry, no. We don't know ourselves, and the Indonesian government has declined to comment. The ocean floor is over three miles down at this point, and not immediately accessible. It's our intention to send one of our own submersibles down at the earliest opportunity.

QUESTION: You said the incident occurred 150 miles south of Guam. Surely that's well within our own 200-mile Exclusive Economic Zone.

AUSTEN: Yes, it is. As I said, Indonesia is seriously in breach of the 1994 Convention on the Law of the Sea, which places a moratorium on ocean-floor mining, and agrees to sovereign rights of mineral ownership within the 200-mile EEZ.

QUESTION: So Indonesia's committing theft?

AUSTEN: Yes.

QUESTION: What is the United States government intending to do about that?

AUSTEN: Talks are already under way at the United Nations, the International Seabed Authority has been informed, and the Tribunal for the Law of the Sea has agreed to hold an emergency session in New York later today.

QUESTION: But you're letting Rahman flout the Law of the Sea just like he flouts human rights in his own country. Is America prepared to take matters into her own hands?

AUSTEN: I can assure you that the President intends

to deal with this matter urgently – but in a peaceful manner, and strictly in accordance with international law.

QUESTION: If it turns out that the Indonesians did torpedo the sub, is that also going to be a matter for international law, or are you about to send in the cruise missiles?

A ripple of laughter passed through the assembled press.

AUSTEN: No comment.

Chapter Thirty – the same morning: National Military Command Centre, Washington, D.C.

President Gilbert Byrd hurried down a thickly carpeted corridor deep inside the Pentagon building. He hated the place. Something about the air-conditioning – the actual smell of the air – it always gave him a headache. He found the subdued lighting and bright yellow walls depressing, and the canned soft music, designed to obstruct eavesdropping, irritating.

In his hand he held a red wallet file. Inside was just one piece of paper. A fax. A message from Rahman. Who the hell did he think he was? Sending the US President a fax. Threat or theatre – who knew? He would wait until he'd heard all the latest intelligence reports before he dropped *this* little bombshell.

Harry Wedemeyer, the Vice-President, a slightly rotund figure with grey hair, struggled to keep up with Byrd's irritated athletic stride.

'You OK, Harry?' Byrd called over his shoulder.

'Sure, Gilbert, I'm still with you.' There were little beads of perspiration at Wedemeyer's temples.

They reached Room C353. A marine in dress blues came smartly to attention, a white-gloved hand snapping down from his forehead. Byrd acknowledged his salute and entered.

The large room was a common venue for the National Security Council. It was not unlike a company boardroom, with a neatly executed false ceiling and hidden fluorescent lighting to give a feeling of spaciousness. But there were no windows.

Five people sat round a large mock elmwood table, each flicking through a thick stapled report or a clutch of papers contained in a blue-covered folder. A map of the West Pacific had been taped up on an easel. They all looked up expectantly as Byrd entered. Byrd dropped his own red wallet file onto the table and sat down. Wedemeyer sank into the vacant seat to his left.

Byrd looked around the assembled Council and felt clear about his position. He held the responsibility here; it was their job to come up with the answers.

'Good morning, gentlemen, Sara,' he said briskly. 'OK, let's get to work.' He scanned the room, singled out the Head of the CIA. 'Greg, are we any closer to knowing the missile targets yet?'

Greg peered along the table through his thick black-framed glasses. 'Well, Mr President, London have had another long data-transmission from Arguni. It seems our people managed to hack their way into the main computer net.'

Byrd nodded impatiently.

'A vast amount of material came through,' Noble continued, 'so we've paraphrased it into summary sheets. You'll find them in the stapled report, along with appendices in the—'

'Greg!' Byrd interrupted. 'Just cut the crap, we haven't got the time. Do we know the missile targets yet?'

'No, Mr President, but—'

Byrd's sharp blue eyes fixed on Greg Noble. 'Hell, Greg, that's our number one concern!'

'Yes, I know, Mr President, but that particular piece of information never came through. Our agents are working under extreme conditions out there. If you remember, they'd already asked to be evacuated.' He paused. 'I'm afraid their transmission ceased abruptly last night. It's our belief that they've either been captured or killed.'

There was a moment's silence.

Yeah, well, that's what they get paid for, thought Byrd.

He flicked through the sheets of paper in the report, ignoring the hostile glances around the table. There was too much to assimilate here: why the hell couldn't Greg keep it nice and simple? He cleared his throat. 'OK, so we don't know the targets. Do we at least know where the missiles are located?'

'Yes, Mr President, we do. If you would have a look at Document B, Map C, it shows the locations of all five sites.'

Papers shuffled again. Byrd fumbled through the report, trying to find the right sheet. Wedemeyer helpfully passed his own across, neatly folded at the right page. Byrd saw a black and white map of the Pacific Ocean floor, with little black squares extending in an arc to the north of Papua – the missile sites. There were lines connecting them all and leading off to a tiny island called Palau.

'Well, I'll be damned!' rumbled Walter Hickel, the National Security Adviser. 'Noble was right. They're on the ocean floor, on top of the seamounts.'

Byrd swivelled towards Dan Carson, his Secretary of State, eyebrows arched questioningly. 'What do you think, Dan?'

Carson drummed his fingers thoughtfully on the table. 'Mr President, this is seriously in breach of the 1971 Seabed Treaty. I quote, and I think I'm correct: "To prevent placement on the seabed and the ocean floor of nuclear weapons, or any other weapon of mass destruction."'

Byrd fingered the red wallet file, thinking of the cryptic message from Rahman. He glanced back towards his DCI: 'All this stuff still classified, Greg?'

'Yes, Mr President.'

'And Chan still doesn't suspect what Rahman's up to?'

'Not as far as we know.'

Byrd stroked his chin carefully. 'The UN are really dragging their feet over the mining issue – we're going to have to be real careful how we deal with this one. A lot of people would like to see us go down.'

'You mean that little shit could get one over on us?'

'We don't have many allies in the UN right now, Walter. Islamic influence is growing – Rahman's got some influential friends out there.'

'But those missiles are a serious threat to our national

interests, Mr President,' said Carson soberly. 'We can't just ignore them.'

Byrd doodled with his pencil on the map of the missile sites: tiny drawings of rockets, with exhausts blasting out of their nozzles. He glanced across the table at James Cordrey, his Secretary of Defence: 'Can the Navy take out the missile launchers, James? Some sort of covert response?'

'No, sir, they're too far down. We could develop some sort of mine to drop on them, but it'll take time to devise that. In any case, if you read Greg's report, Rahman juggles his missiles between the sites. You never know which ones are armed and ready to go, and which are empty. We'd have to go for all five at once.'

'I advise against any sort of covert action,' intoned the gravelly voice of Hickel. 'America tramping around on the floor of the Pacific Ocean – it'll do untold damage to our international relations.'

Byrd thought for a moment about China, about trade agreements and his fragile economy. 'All right, let's go down another route. What about his command and control – have we got anything new on that?'

Greg Noble peered nervously up the table. 'Well, it's very puzzling, Mr President. They seem to have located their missile command centre on the island of Palau – south of Guam. Code name's *Espiritu*.'

Good God! Now a Pacific island had become part of the act. Byrd felt a cold hand clutch at the pit of his stomach. This thing was getting big, sliding out of control. It was beginning to smell like an international conspiracy. Why were they all turning on the United States? What had his country done to deserve this?

'We're going to program one of the Lacrosse satellites to take a look,' continued Noble, 'but in the meantime you can see the place quite clearly in Image D.'

More rummaging through the blue file. Wedemeyer stared over his half-spectacles at the image: 'I can't see anything, Greg. What are we looking for?'

'It's the large building, on the waterfront.'

They all peered closely at their copies of the photo.

'But it's just a warehouse!'

'Does the Palau government know about this?' demanded Byrd.

The long face of Greg Noble stared at him down the length of the table. 'We've been asking ourselves a different question, Mr President: does Rahman himself know about this?'

'Hand of Hendra!' muttered Sara Ackerman.

Heads swivelled in her direction. 'What do you mean, Sara?' asked Byrd. 'Hand of Hendra? I don't understand.'

'Dr Jazid Hendra,' she explained with some exasperation. 'Rahman's Minister for Technology. If you read Greg's paper carefully, you'll find that *he*'s the author of much of this work, not Rahman. He's known to be a secretive and fastidious man, so he may well have created much of this set-up without Rahman even knowing.'

Byrd looked puzzled. 'Why the hell would he do that?'

'Greed, most likely! He'll be following his own agenda.'

'Sara may well be right,' said Noble. 'All this stuff came

out of Hendra's personal computer files . . . and we've also found out what they're taking from the mining site near Guam.'

Byrd sat back in his chair, rolling his pencil between his fingers. 'Go on, tell me.'

'A highly exotic type of gold, Mr President, precipitated out of hot geothermal water at a hydrothermal vent. Hendra thinks it might be capable of superconduction – at room temperature.'

Byrd gazed down the table, eyes far away. 'Well, I'll be damned!'

'Superconduction – that's an extremely valuable asset!' said Carson excitedly. 'We've have been trying to develop something like that for years. It would put Indonesia centre-stage in the world economy. Advanced electronics, power generation, electric motor production—'

'But that stuff's ours!' exclaimed Byrd. 'It's within our own jurisdiction. It's just what we need for our own industry.'

Silence descended upon the Security Council. Paper shuffled noisily as the reality of the situation came into sharp focus.

'You know, in one way, this seems very simple to me, Mr President,' growled Hickel. 'He's found a cherry tree in our backyard, and he's leaning over the wall and stealing all the cherries for himself. Dammit, we've got to stop him!' He glared at the stony faces around the table.

Byrd thought of the fax he'd received from Rahman. He pulled the red wallet file from underneath the paperwork spread out before him and thumbed open the lid, extracting a single sheet of paper. 'Before we go any further, I think you should hear this.' He fingered the edge of the flimsy message. 'I received it this morning, via the Indonesian Embassy. It's from Rahman himself.' He looked round the room to make sure he had their attention. 'It reads: "The Tiger has claws."'

There was a shocked silence.

'In all my years in Washington, I've never heard anything like that,' growled Hickel at last. 'Is that some sort of threat?'

'And what the hell does it mean?' demanded Carson.

Byrd looked across the table. 'What do you think, Sara?'

She laughed. 'What do I think? Well, it's obviously a warning – telling us to keep away. It's a threat.'

'We've got a fight on our hands, then, Mr President,' growled Hickel.

Byrd stiffened his shoulders. 'Well, if he wants one, he's got it!' He looked at Cordrey. 'What's his weakest link, James? We'll go for that.'

'His command and control centre, on Palau. But hold on, if we goof it, he'll hit the nuke button and it'll be "Goodbye, Guam" or, worse still, some Chinese city. What do we do then?'

'After a full-scale nuclear exchange – not a lot!' rumbled Hickel.

'That's certainly his threat,' agreed Sara Ackerman.

Byrd flushed with anger. He hit the tabletop with the flat of his palm. 'Look, for Christ's sake, we can't just walk away from this! Dammit, he's holding us to ransom. I thought we were meant to be the most powerful nation on earth. We've got a responsibility here. There must be something we can do, there's got to be.'

'Well, I don't think we have many options right at this moment,' answered Hickel, 'unless you can think of an invisible weapon to hit him with. Something the Chinese won't even know about.'

There was silence for a moment.

'Sir!' Greg Noble was staring along the table. 'Sir!'

'What is it, Greg?'

'Walter's invisible weapon. Well . . . there may be such a thing. Have you ever heard of Dr Kuls, sir?'

Chapter Thirty-one – two days later: Los Alamos National Laboratories, New Mexico

As Greg Noble jolted the hired blue Mercury compact along the rough rubble track, the wheels whipped up stones that cracked noisily against the underside of the car. He peered through the windscreen, watching the headlights bleach out the pockets of pine trees amid the mountain scrub. He struggled continually with the unfamiliar manual shift, trying to keep the engine revving as the vehicle laboured up the steeper gradients.

The headlights finally swung dramatically across the neat whitewashed walls of a large single-storey house: an imposing building built in the Spanish tradition, with rounded arches and a red-tiled roof. Noble stopped the car in the driveway and doused the lights. The door groaned as he swung it open.

The Santa Clara mountain air was cool and slightly damp. A feast of stars shone brilliantly overhead, casting a hard silver half-light across the chaparral landscape.

Noble hunched down into his jacket and crunched his way to the front door. No bell, just a set of chimes hanging from a stunted pine nearby. He tugged at the braided rope, and a wonderful tinkling peal sang out into the night air.

A handsome middle-aged woman came to the door. She was clad in a thick jumper, her tight leggings showing off the full curve of her thighs.

'Good evening. I've come to speak with Dr Kuls.' He took a leather pass-wallet out of his inside jacket pocket, and showed her his card. 'Greg Noble. I telephoned earlier.'

The woman looked at the card. Not a flicker of emotion passed across her face. 'You'd better come in.' She closed the door, and led the way into a beautiful open-plan house – pine ceiling over rough white-plastered walls. 'My husband's not here at the moment – he's still working at the labs.'

They moved towards the tastefully furnished living area.

'You're not bothered by my turning up like this?'

'Mr Noble, I married my husband when he worked for the CIA. You learn to expect anything – at any time.' She smiled formally. 'Would you like some coffee?'

She went off towards the kitchen, and called back: 'I'll have to phone Cyrus, tell him you're here. I can't guarantee he'll come straight away; he sometimes stays at the labs all night.'

Noble sat down in one of the wing chairs. His eyes ran around his surroundings, noted the opulence – the antiques, the musical instruments, a wood fire that spat and blazed in a large stone fireplace. Mathematics in the service of the government obviously paid far more than the CIA ever would.

The coffee arrived and Mrs Kuls poured carefully from the cafetière. 'Shall I tell him what it's about? He gets very involved with his work. He'll need something special to lure him away.'

Noble looked at her, a slight smile on his lips. 'Just say "Stormfury". That'll get him interested.'

Dr Cyrus Kuls was a mild-mannered and quietly spoken man. He had a slight speech impediment that made him sound as if he was talking through a wad of cotton wool stuffed into his mouth. He glided into the room in a motorized wheelchair, the sleeves of his blue denim shirt rolled up, black leather gloves protecting his hands. His hair was white and close-cropped, his intelligent eyes piercing in a mature, fine-featured face.

'Noble!' he barked. 'I don't always come running just because someone else has decided to see me – but you sounded interesting. Are you CIA or private?'

Noble fiddled in his inside pocket, brought out a crisp manila envelope with the Presidential seal. 'Let's just say government.'

He passed the envelope to Kuls, who tore it open with the end of a pen and began to read.

A log slipped in the fireplace, sending a blaze of sparks up the chimney.

'Hmm, interesting!' Kuls put the envelope on his lap, clasped his hands under his chin. ' "Stormfury" was a long time ago, Mr Noble. I was just a young postgraduate then.'

'You're still the best authority on seeding hurricanes there is, Dr Kuls.'

Kuls's eyes narrowed. 'Hurricanes! How very interesting.' Then he frowned, his blue eyes focusing directly on Noble. 'You've read my paper, of course: *The use of hurricanes as a weapon of war.*'

'Not exactly, Dr Kuls, but I was aware of it. That's why I'm here.'

Kuls shook his head with incredulity. 'So long, so long before someone finally comes to realize what can be done. I was just too far ahead of my time!'

'Project Stormfury,' Noble prompted, 'did you think it was a success?'

'Oh, yes, it was!' Kuls enthused. 'We learned how to modify the entire energy structure.'

'So why did it all come to an end? Why did you stop?'

'Too dangerous: difficult to predict precisely what would happen. Then, in the mid-1970s, Mexico and Cuba put pressure on the government. Claimed we were steering the hurricanes over them.'

'Were you?'

Kuls looked at Noble, smiled, shrugged his shoulders.

'Why did you get out of the CIA, Dr Kuls?'

'Money – and Vietnam.'

'I'm sorry, I don't follow you.'

'I was seeding clouds over the Ho Chi Minh trail, using silver iodide. They wanted me to change the climate, increase the monsoon rains. Make floods, destroy roads, collapse bridges, sweep away villages – that sort of thing.

Deny the enemy their supplies. They thought it would bring the war to an end. Stupid idea, of course. The VC just built another road, took their trucks round by a different route. I told them, wrong way to use the weather weapon! They didn't listen. We had an argument. I left.'

Mrs Kuls came back in, refilled their cups from the cafetière, and sat down with them.

Noble must have looked anxious. 'You mustn't worry about Madeleine,' said Kuls. 'Everything I know, she knows.' He sat back and slipped his gloved hands down between his knees. 'These hurricanes, typhoons in your case – the power they unleash! Something like the explosion of 500,000 Nagasaki bombs. Every day! Terrifying, isn't it?' He leaned forward. 'I can control that power for you, Noble. Intensify it, steer it . . .' He shook his head. 'It's not something I would want to confront: 200 m.p.h. winds, over thirty feet of water sucked up and driven onshore, torrential rain. I can give you a great swathe of destruction over thirty miles across. It's a terrible weapon, a destroyer of cities!'

Kuls leaned forward in his wheelchair, like a cat waiting to pounce. 'But it's also a humane weapon, Noble. Hurricane Andrew, hit Florida in '92. Cost us over twenty-five billion dollars to put the damage right. For three days anarchy threatened the region. Ripped out the infrastructure for weeks. Over a hundred thousand people homeless, whole neighbourhoods in ruin. Even the might of the United States economy staggered under that blow . . . but fewer than sixty-five people lost their lives! Because of the warning, you see.' Kuls leaned forward again. 'That's a hell of a bomb, Noble. Hits where it hurts – the places, not the people.'

There was something chilling in Kuls's logic, a sort of neat madness in his damage-to-death ratio.

Kuls clapped his gloved hands together in the praying position. 'So, tell me, Noble, how can I help?'

'Am I right in thinking, Dr Kuls, that the major problem in Stormfury was unreliability – the problem of predicting turbulent airflow?'

'Absolutely! How clever! Plus the fact that in those days we had no way of knowing exactly how successful our seeding attacks had been.'

Noble guessed that Kuls was going to prove an easy recruit. An intellectual challenge, a little flattery, a noble cause, the chance to prove his point – all this was irresistible to a man like Kuls. Noble began to reach out to the man. 'Well, as I understand it, Dr Kuls, your recent work for NASA, on the dynamics of turbulent flow – it's actually got you very close, hasn't it, to being the first person able to predict the outcome of any outside random disturbance?'

Kuls's eyes were now shining like bright stars in the light of the log fire. 'Why, that's right, Noble. I am indeed very close.' He steepled his gloved fingers together once more. 'I see your thinking. With better flow-modelling I could work out how much material to seed, and where, for any given effect. This is most interesting, Noble, a real challenge.'

He suddenly pushed on the control stick of his wheel-chair, and whined out of the room.

Noble sipped the rest of his coffee, placing the mug back onto the low table in front of him. Meanwhile, Mrs Kuls made conversation. 'My husband, when he gets his teeth into something, he never stops until it's solved.'

'Do you understand everything of Dr Kuls's work?'

She laughed a round, confident laugh. 'No, not every-thing. He sometimes gets that glazed look in his eyes, then I know he's far away inside his head.' She shrugged. 'Sometimes I can't talk to him for days.'

Kuls fussed back into the room, clutching pad and pencil. He parked the wheelchair next to Noble, leaning across to draw on the pad so that he could see. 'The principle's quite simple. I'll show you.' He sketched what looked like a doughnut, then pointed to the hole in the middle. 'This is the eye of the typhoon, the calm centre where the air is gently falling.' He drew in some descending arrows to confirm the point. 'No clouds in the eye, com-pletely clear.' Then he swirled his pencil anticlockwise round and round the doughnut, close to the central hole. 'This is the airflow round the eye. It has huge power. A category five storm generates winds of over 150 miles an hour.' He looked up at Noble. 'I can make it more than that. Have you ever tried to stand up in a 250-mile-an-hour wind?' He paused for effect. 'Difficult to imagine, isn't it? Did you know that the force exerted on your body would be 160 pounds per square foot. That means that even if you held on to a street lamp, you would be blown out like a flag. Probably bend the lamp over, too. Fascinating, isn't it? Is that what you want? A typhoon like that? Turn it into a weapon?' He looked at Noble, demanding an answer.

Noble nodded.

Kuls laughed, a sort of excited giggle. 'OK, well, the heart of the typhoon is here.' He jabbed his pencil at one side of the doughnut hole. 'The eye wall. This is where huge amounts of water are being evaporated from the ocean below. Like the invisible vapour rising off a hot bath. As the moist air rises, it cools, and the vapour is squeezed out into millions of tiny little water droplets – clouds! On this scale, of course, it produces hundreds of enormous thunderheads, like this.' He scribbled furiously, adding towering cloud columns in a tight band around the doughnut's central hole. Then he rubbed his gloved hands together.

'Now – the typhoon as a weapon. The secret of it lies in every one of those little droplets of water. As each one is formed, a tiny bit of heat is given off. Not much from each one, but there are billions and billions of these droplets, so in the end you get a huge amount of heat. A vast amount, in fact – more than that given off by a hydrogen bomb. Big typhoons release energy equivalent to over 500 megatons – *every hour*, Noble! The heated air blasts up into the sky, cooler air rushes in below to fill the gap, and this of course causes yet more evaporation. Now there's so much water vapour condensing into droplets that prodigious amounts of energy are being released. The whole thing starts to run faster and faster, the winds accelerating, getting out of control...' He swirled his pencil vigorously round the doughnut, obliterating what he'd drawn earlier. 'And there you have it – a killer typhoon.'

He gulped at the remains of his coffee and wiped his lips with the back of his gloved hand. He tore off the sheet of paper and started a new one. 'Now, you want me to control that a little bit? We can't use brute force, of course – wouldn't work, much too big. The secret is to go with nature, create a small change that will upset the natural balance of the storm, make it spiral out of control even faster.

'So, what we must do is place a carefully measured amount of hygroscopic nuclei, a powder, shall we say something like calcium chloride, at roughly cloud-base height – *here*' – he jabbed at the sketch – 'right inside the eye wall. Each speck of powder will cause a microscopic droplet of water to form. That means faster condensation, and more cloud development and, as the eye shrinks in size, the winds will spin faster and faster – like an ice-skater pulling in her arms – up to 200 miles an hour easily.' He paused. '*And* – we get a bonus. With very low air pressure inside the eye, the ocean will be sucked up into a major flood surge.'

Noble was about to say something, but Kuls was in full flow, swept along by his own enthusiasm. He put up a gloved hand to stop him. 'We learned something else from Hurricane Andrew. In the eye wall there were tornadoes with wind speeds of over 300 miles an hour. Real killers: blasted whole buildings away, lifted trucks right up into the air. Now, if I could find a way of predicting where those would form . . .' His piercing blue eyes turned expectantly to Noble, black-leather-gloved hands poised over the fresh paper.

Noble shifted uneasily in his seat. This guy knew what he was doing, all right. And he was enthusiastic, committed. If anybody could control a typhoon it would be Dr Kuls – but there was something demonic about him, a touch of Dr Strangelove.

'Dr Kuls,' he began, 'could you write a paper for me, telling me exactly where you would seed a Pacific typhoon, and what quantities of hygroscopic salts you would need?'

'Yes – in theory. But I'd need to build a generic computer model first, to investigate what would happen as a result of seeding. You must remember that every typhoon is different, Noble. We need a math model of the target storm before we know exactly what to do. This is not an exact science – you need a feel for the beast as well.'

Noble thought for a moment. 'OK, can you get this generic model operating within the next two weeks? Then I'll be in touch again.'

'That's a tight schedule, but . . . yes, I already have a base model, and I know a lot of the parameters. It could be done.'

'Good!' Noble got up to leave. Madeleine stood up with him and began to show him to the door.

'Noble!' called Kuls from his chair. 'How are you intending to deliver the seeding agent?'

Noble turned back to him. 'By plane.'

'I hope it's a good one. Have you ever flown through an eye wall?'

Noble shook his head. 'I'm not a pilot, Dr Kuls.'

'Nor I, Noble. But I once went through the eye wall in an old B-29, which weighed over fifty tons. She was bounced around like she was made of tinfoil. You'll need a strong plane, Noble, especially in *my* storms. Have you got one?'

'We have a plane, Dr Kuls.' He noticed Madeleine was smiling politely from the hallway, waiting for him to leave. 'Good night!' he called back. There was no answer, so he turned and headed off along the hallway.

'Hey, Noble! Who's the enemy?'

Noble stopped for a second time and called back. 'Sorry, Dr Kuls – "need to know".'

'Ha!'

As Madeleine held the door open for him, cold damp mountain air flowed into the warm house. Stars still spread gloriously across the blackness of the night sky.

'You have a magnificent place here, Mrs Kuls.'

'*Doctor* Kuls – I'm a physicist as well as his wife.' She smiled disarmingly. 'Goodnight, Mr Noble.'

He crunched across the rubble to the hired compact, and something began to bother him – something that wormed away at his soul. He'd been around weapons for a long time, 'honest' weapons – explosives, lasers, that sort of thing. Technology. Man-made. But using a storm, turning the planet itself against your own kind; that was evil, frightening. What was he starting here?

A comment from Kuls replayed in his ears as he creaked open the door of the battered Mercury and sank into the driver's seat. *That's one hell of a bomb, Noble. Hits where it hurts – the places, not the people.* He was right, of course, a typhoon would terrify them – but they would have ample warning to get clear. Hit a city with the force of a nuclear bomb, rip out the infrastructure, tear down the buildings, flood the rubble that remained: a sort of biblical Armageddon – but not necessarily too many dead. A benign weapon – what a sick contradiction in terms!

Noble started the engine and crunched into first gear, swearing at the manual shift. Then he was too fast on the clutch, and the wheels spun momentarily on the stones.

But this thing could certainly stop Rahman in his tracks and give them the breathing space they needed. It would disable his command and control long enough to get Special Forces into the missile facility *and* give them a chance to seize back the source of that mineral for themselves.

And, of course, no one else need ever know.

After all, a typhoon was an Act of God. Control it – and you had the ultimate secret weapon.

Chapter Thirty-two – the same evening: Arguni Base, Irian Jaya

From far away came the sound of someone screaming, the squeal of dry metal hinges, the repetitive banging of a heavy metal door. A loud buzzing, the sound echoing inside her head.

Then voices, demanding voices: 'Tai-Chung!'

Who was this Tai-Chung? She didn't know. She felt confused, let her mind drift for a while, found that peaceful.

Slowly she became aware of an intense headache – like an iron band tightening around her head. She moved her hand up to try to relieve the pain, but metal rattled over wood and tugged her hand back down. Her mind began to swim. She felt a wave of nausea. She tried to move her legs in order to turn over, but found them chained, held fast, immobile. She groaned with the agony of it all. Felt so ill, more ill than she'd ever felt before. She couldn't find any relief from the discomfort, couldn't shift her body against the chains holding her down. Her face felt hot and flushed.

She began to open her eyes cautiously, but painful light

burst into her brain, made her wince. She caught a glimpse of a dazzling white ceiling, paint cracked and peeling; then she clamped her eyes tight shut again, till she felt the pain receding.

Gentle now, drifting.

Soft darkness . . .

Someone was there, holding her hand. Was it Rykhlin? She couldn't tell.

A scream, from far away.

Nothing to do with her.

Sleep, she must sleep.

Very tired.

Chapter Thirty-three – the following morning: Lockheed-Martin Skunk Works, Palmdale, California

Byrd unbuckled and tried to stand up, finding it difficult to keep his tall frame within the confining four-foot-eleven of the CIA's private Lear jet. He was tired and stiff after the long haul across the States. He'd dozed only fitfully, despite the leather-upholstered reclining seats. His legs felt heavy and ached with fatigue.

Walter Hickel remained seated. 'If you would stay on board for a moment, Mr President,' he grunted, 'Noble should have arranged transport for us.'

Byrd nodded and bent down to stare out of one of the windows. Hot sun blazed down onto the concrete apron outside, shining brightly against a huge beige-coloured hangar door where a solitary man was walking, his tiny figure emphasizing the vastness of Lockheed-Martin's secret assembly building.

He turned to Hickel. 'Get any sleep, Walter?'

'Like hell!' came the disgruntled reply.

A long white Cadillac with black windows cruised round the corner of the hangar and began to make stately progress towards their anonymous business jet. It parked close-up to the side. They made their way forward, one of the bodyguards popping open the airstairs at the last minute. Hot air blasted into the air-conditioned comfort of the Lear jet.

'Hey – who opened the oven door?' joked Byrd.

Greg Noble, suit crumpled, was down on the concrete, waiting for them. He didn't look like he'd slept much either. 'Good morning, Mr President. I hope you had a comfortable flight.'

It was pleasantly cool inside the functional office corridor. To the left stretched a long row of offices – mostly devoted to design and engineering. To the right was a wall lined with photographs of past exotic aircraft.

A small tubby man in a white short-sleeved shirt stood uneasily at the end of the corridor, a large security tag clipped to his chest pocket. He watched with obvious agitation as the Presidential posse advanced towards him. Greg Noble introduced him. 'I'd like you to meet Dr Hans Fricke, Mr President – Project Manager and Chief Designer of the Wraith.'

Byrd shook his hand – found it wet and rather limp.

'Mr President, I'm so pleased to meet you,' Fricke said. 'I'm sorry, but nothing is really ready for you. I wasn't given any notice of your arrival until just half an hour ago.'

'That's OK, Dr Fricke,' said Byrd, trying to calm the man's nerves. 'This is not an inspection.'

'If we could just show the President current progress on the Wraith, Dr Fricke,' said Noble.

'Yes! Yes, of course!' Fricke was obviously surprised. 'Well . . . this way then.'

He led them to a small door a short distance along the corridor. The company guard eyed the President and his small entourage. 'It's OK, Ray, I think we can let the President through,' said Fricke. The guard keyed a number and held the door open against the spring for them to enter.

The air inside the hangar smelt of hydraulic oil and fresh rubber. The Wraith sat alone in the middle of a huge echoing empty space: A squat black delta, its wings cranked up gently from the fuselage and then sloped down again to make a shape which, from the front, looked like a flattened letter M. There was no fin, no vertical surface of any sort. To Byrd, it looked for all the world like a large bat squatting there.

Fricke chattered animatedly as they walked across the polished concrete. 'This is one of two Wraith prototypes that we're currently flying, Mr President. It's one of the most advanced stealth combat aircraft we've ever built.'

They reached the plane. Byrd stood by the downward crank of the port wing-tip and looked around for the cockpit. He was puzzled. 'Dr Fricke, where does the pilot sit?'

Fricke stared at Byrd, a disappointed look on his face. 'Mr President, that's the whole point of the Wraith. We got rid of the pilot's canopy – it produces such a strong radar return.'

'So how does he see out, then?'

'Virtual reality – he flies wearing a VR helmet. That way he can see what's in the sky all round the aircraft – no blind spots. The computer highlights any targets and threats for him.'

Byrd nodded wisely. 'Is she strong?'

'You bet! Because the pilot's lying down, we can regularly pull real tight turns – up to 12G, no problem. She's stressed to 20G, strong as an ox!'

'And the payload? How much will she carry?'

'Eight thousand pounds.' Fricke got down on his haunches and pointed under the belly. 'In there – in the weapons bay.'

'What about long-wavelength weather radar?' prompted Noble. 'Would she be spotted on that?'

'Weather radar?' Fricke smiled curiously. 'No, sir, not this baby! She's got virtually no radar return at all.'

'And infra-red satellite imagery?' asked Noble.

Fricke looked startled. 'Satellite imagery? These things are cloaked against heat-seeking missiles – she won't be picked up by any satellite!' He looked puzzled. 'Just what the hell have you fellers got in mind?'

Noble turned to Dr Fricke. 'Perhaps we could use your office, just for half an hour, Fricke?'

Fricke's office was a disaster. Three PCs hummed away with no concession to security, each one abandoned at the screen Fricke had last used. His desk was heaped with papers, documents, and open textbooks. A styrofoam cup, half filled with cold coffee, had been placed on one end of a large technical drawing to stop it from slipping to the floor. The waste bin was overflowing with balls of screwed-up paper. Shelves were littered with books and files shoved in at odd angles. A discarded pair of dirty running shoes stank quietly in the corner.

Byrd sat behind Fricke's desk, carefully removed the coffee cup, and folded up the plan. Greg Noble and Walter Hickel moved some files and sat down opposite. 'OK, Greg, you have the floor,' said Byrd. 'Tell Walter what we've found out.'

'Do you know anything about Project Stormfury, Walter?' asked Noble.

'In a word, no!' grated Hickel.

'Dr Kuls was part of it. The project ran from 1960 to 1974. We were flying aircraft into hurricanes, seeding them with silver iodide, trying to make the storms either change direction or grow weaker. Weather modification, in other words – aimed at controlling the impact of hurricanes on the east coast.'

Hickel cottoned on quickly. He looked aghast. 'You're suggesting that we do this in the Pacific? Try and hit Palau with a typhoon?'

Noble paused for a moment. 'Yes, I think it can be done – but using hygroscopic salts. They're more effective.'

'Now wait a minute!' said Hickel. 'You're talking about messing with the weather here. What if it goes wrong? You'll end up killing thousands of innocent people.'

'Not with a typhoon, Walter. Rahman's built a Warning Centre on the island, part of his flood defences. They'd evacuate the population before the storm hit.'

'You're crazy, Greg! Who is this Kuls, some kind of nut?'

Noble ignored the comment and pressed on. 'It's the storm surge that would do the most damage. The missile command centre's built on the edge of a bay with a shallow floor, so it's got no protection. The bay would really build up the surge and that makes it an ideal location for this sort of an attack. We blow the centre down with a typhoon – then flood it. Nobody would be any the wiser. It would look just like a natural disaster. Then, with his missile control centre out of action, and the nukes disabled, we go into Arguni with Special Forces and take out Rahman's nuclear manufacturing facility. Stop him dead. Nip the whole thing in the bud before the Chinese know anything. And, of course, the mineral will then be ours.'

Byrd was doodling on a piece of paper, saying nothing.

'You're asking the President to break International Law, Greg,' rumbled Hickel.

'What law?' asked Noble.

'The Environmental Modification Treaty, signed back in '77 – when nobody thought anyone would ever be stupid enough to use nature as a weapon!'

'OK!' interrupted Byrd. 'Devil's advocate, Walter! What happens if we don't do this?'

'Then that's bad,' Noble pointed out. 'Rahman will

continue to take *our* superconducting mineral out of *our* ocean, and laugh all the way to the bank. We end up handing it to him on a plate.'

'And Rahman gets away with threatening the United States!' exclaimed Byrd. 'Hell, I thought we were the most powerful democracy on earth, fighting for freedom and justice! I'm not cowering before any jumped-up little shit who decides to have a go at us. We didn't go down that route the last time, and I'm sure as hell not going down it now. Dammit, that stuff's ours – by law!'

'But you can't break the law in the name of justice, Mr President,' protested Hickel. 'That's double standards.'

'And I won't stand by and have the law pissed on,' retorted Byrd.

'Then keep on working through the UN,' retorted Hickel. 'Keep it legal. Stop Rahman that way.'

'Hell, Walter! The UN aren't going to do anything right now, and you damn well know it! The Muslims are a powerful lobby, they think that stuff's his by right – he found it. They've got us in an armlock, and they're loving every minute of it. They'll wait until Rahman abandons the mining site before they let go, and then he'll just have his knuckles rapped – by which time it'll be too damned late for us.'

Hickel turned to Noble. 'I suppose you want the President to authorize the use of the Wraith for this thing?'

'He already has, Walter. You heard Fricke, they can't be picked up by weather-radar or satellite, and they're tough enough to fly into the eye wall.'

'But they're top secret aircraft,' exclaimed Hickel. 'We can't afford to risk either of them.'

'We haven't any choice, Walter!' snapped Byrd. 'I don't like this any more than you do, but what's the alternative? Let this jerk hold us to ransom?'

'Mr President,' rasped Hickel, 'I have to formally advise you against this course of action. You're starting a new type of war here – and hell, I'm scared . . .'

'What course of action, Walter?' Byrd glanced over at Noble. 'Greg, did I agree to anything?'

'No, Mr President.'

'Christ, Gilbey, don't be so stupid,' urged Hickel. 'There's no one out there who'll support you. People are getting really concerned about the climate right now. They're fighting storms, droughts, tornadoes, rising sea levels, and God knows what else. People are dying every day in natural disasters, Gilbey, because we messed up the climate. And now you propose to use a typhoon as a weapon? You're getting yourself into some seriously deep shit here.'

'The UN talks are bogged down, Walter. I'm under pressure from Congress to get this thing resolved. I want that mineral back. It's *ours*.' Byrd turned to Noble. 'Can you deal directly with Kuls and Fricke?'

'Yes, Mr President.'

'When the missile system goes down, we'll need to get our Special Forces into Arguni quickly. We need to update our ground knowledge. Find out where your two people are being held by the Indonesians. Find out if they're still alive, then get them out of there as soon as possible.'

'Yes, sir.'

'And while you're at it, contact that Thameena woman as well.'

'Sorry?'

'Rahman's wife. She's on Bandaneira, in exile. She's an important source of information.'

'Mr President,' growled Hickel. 'I'm warning you again, formally: Thameena Rahman – you're treading a dangerous path through some thorny Asian politics here.'

Byrd looked at him, openly hostile. 'Oh, come on, Walter! Thameena's defection is very important to us. You know that Rahman's regime is tottering. It only needs a gentle shove to push it over. She could provide it.'

'You haven't consulted with the Select Committee on this issue, sir!'

Byrd rose from his chair and began to walk to the door. 'Sorry, Walter, I don't know what you're talking about.'

'You haven't got my support on this one,' warned Hickel.

Byrd glared at him, then stomped out of Fricke's office. He found Fricke a little way down the corridor, hovering in the doorway of a colleague's office.

Fricke came forward to meet Byrd. 'Can I do anything for you, Mr President? It must have been a long flight from Washington.'

'Yeah!' called out Byrd as he swept by. 'Get your damned office tidied up.'

Chapter Thirty-four – the following day: Arguni Base, Irian Jaya

Sounds dissolved slowly into Nicole's consciousness. Odd sounds that she recognized. The scrape of a metal bucket, the sharp clanging of a gate, and loud voices issuing commands. She felt confused and disorientated, and became aware of an intense headache – sore eyes, a sort of dizziness like suffering a bout of flu. Her body ached from where she had been lying on the cold floor.

Then came the sounds of a truck pulling up outside, its brakes squealing, cab door opening. More shouts.

She opened her eyes and found it difficult to see at first; she couldn't focus. At eye level: a concrete floor stretching away like a great stony desert, tiny specks of grit scattered like stones, then a white wall soaring up on the horizon. She lay there, staring at this scene, not moving.

Finally she shifted one of her legs and found the chains gone, found it easy to slide her leg across the concrete.

The truck door slammed shut. The diesel engine restarted and rattled at idle before being accelerated into action. The truck drove away, causing a faint shadow to pass across the dimly lit room.

Nicole tried to sit up, but her head swam. She managed to prop her back against a wall and sat there for a moment, eyes closed, recovering from the exertion. Carefully, she opened her eyes again and looked around. White walls, blue door ... and a memory about something that had gone wrong, something she couldn't remember.

Her gaze roamed the room. It was tiny, just enough space for her body to stretch out. There was an incongruous pink chemical toilet in the corner, and a plastic bottle of water by the door. Bright sunlight poured through a narrow slit in the wall, which served as a window, throwing a golden bar of light across the floor.

There was nothing else.

Where was she? She drew up her knees, placed the soreness that was her head onto her folded arms, felt the hardness of the concrete floor through her buttocks. She watched the sunlight reflect a cool iridescent blue light-pattern off the plastic water-container. She was too weak even to quench her thirst.

Something had gone wrong. Something she couldn't remember.

Slowly Nicole's eyes closed, and she slept.

A fitful sleep filled with distant screams.

Chapter Thirty-five – the following morning: Lockheed-Martin Skunk Works

Fricke came fussing round from behind his desk and removed a great wad of sheets so that Noble could sit down. Body odour wafted up as he flapped around. Noble curled his lip as he caught the sour smell under his nose.

'You want some coffee?' asked Fricke.

Noble couldn't think of anything better. He was getting tired of all this shuttling around. He needed to get this thing organized.

Fricke barged out of the office and returned carrying a couple of styrofoam cups of brown stuff. It had slopped during its journey from the machine and now dripped onto Noble's clean trousers. He wiped it away irritably and searched for somewhere on the desk to place his cup.

Fricke sat down heavily in his chair. 'So, do I get to know what all this is about?'

Noble sipped at the coffee. Hot, watery, very bitter – it would have to do. He slotted the cup carefully back into the clear space on the edge of Fricke's desk. 'That was no ordinary visit the other day, Dr Fricke.'

'Noble, when the President arrives out of an early-morning sky with the DCI, I know it's no ordinary visit.'

Noble grinned and decided he would play it straight. No point in messing around. 'Dr Fricke, I want you to fly the two Wraith prototypes into a Pacific typhoon.'

Fricke jerked his cup back onto the table, spilling some of the hot fluid across his hand. 'A typhoon? She's a strike plane, Noble, not a weather plane. If it's reconnaissance you want, there's plenty of aircraft out there you'd be better off with.'

Noble rubbed his eyes with his free hand, trying to push away the tiredness. 'No, it's the Wraith I want. This is your big chance, Fricke, to show us what these things can do.'

Fricke looked at Noble. 'Why the hell do you want to fly two of the most secret and most expensive aircraft in the world into a typhoon?'

'To seed the eye wall with hygroscopic salts – without anyone knowing.'

Fricke stared at him, eyes popping out of his head. 'Well, I'll be damned! You want them to go cloud seeding?'

'On the nail!' Noble took another sip of the styrofoam coffee. The stuff was foul, he decided and winced.

Fricke reached across his chest to scratch at an itchy spot near his armpit and gave an almighty shrug. 'Well, hell, if that's what you want.' He pulled his chair over to one of the PCs and brought up a green computer drawing: a 3D rendition of the aircraft. He pressed the keys, retracting the undercarriage, turning the drawing upside down, opening the two weapons-bay doors on the belly. He tapped at the screen with his ball-pen. 'She carries an 8,000-pound payload in the weapons bay. Two aircraft – that's over seven tons of the stuff. Is that enough?'

Noble didn't answer – he didn't know. It all depended on Kuls. It might need more than one sortie in any case. He hadn't got it all together yet: not enough time. He changed tack. 'Dr Fricke, could you design some sort of system to distribute a full load of, say, calcium chloride into the clouds, just inside the eye wall?'

Fricke finished scratching at his armpit, then put his hands behind his head. 'Are you certain the President is willing to risk these aircraft?'

Noble caught the whiff of body odour again. 'Would you like me to write it down for you, Fricke, on White House notepaper?'

But Fricke was right. Noble had no official sanction for what he was doing. He had to maintain the President's 'plausible deniability'; it was part of his job. A President could never say 'Yes' to this sort of thing. He could only give a nod, or look the other way. It was the only way a President could keep his arse in the White House chair.

'These machines, they're third-generation stealth technology – you realize that?' said Fricke.

'That's why we want them.'

Fricke's arms came down. 'Well – of course it can be done. Anything can be done.' Fricke thought for a moment. 'You might spray the stuff, I suppose, out of some sort of pressure tank. Or release tiny canisters that spring open at a pre-set altitude. No – better if they're flares; pyrotechnics will spread the powder more efficiently. How precise do you want to be?'

Noble shrugged.

'You've got somebody else working on that?'

'Of course.'

'Can I speak with him?'

Noble shook his head. 'Programme's top secret.' Damn right it was! They were going to fight a war on a sick planet, using the weather. If any of this ever leaked out, if ever the media got hold of this, it was more than his own head on the block. He eyed the mess in the office. 'And that means top secret here as well, Dr Fricke.'

'How long have we got?'

'Two weeks, maximum.'

'Two weeks? It'll be tight.'

'Two weeks. By then we're well into May and the start of the typhoon season. We want to catch the first one, if we can.' Noble dumped his empty coffee cup into Fricke's waste bin, where it perched on a pile of other debris. He picked up his coat and made for the door. 'I'll see myself out, Dr Fricke. Just remember, this has the highest security rating.' He pointed at the PCs. 'And for fuck's sake, keep those screens turned off!'

Fricke swung from side to side in his chair, watching him go. 'What are we doing this for, Noble? Are we at war?'

Noble was stepping into the corridor outside. He put his head back round the door. 'Trials, Fricke – just trials.'

Chapter Thirty-six – first week in May: Arguni Base, Irian Jaya

Nicole sat with her back propped up against the wall of the cell: knees drawn up, arms folded across her knees, chin resting on her arms. She'd been sitting like that for a long time, watching the bright bar of light from the tiny window edge its snail-like way across the concrete floor, waiting for it to shine on a special part that was the trigger to mark the passage of yet another day.

It made contact.

She got up and her vision swam for a minute, grey mist pushing in from the periphery. She steadied herself, waited for her sight to clear, then took two steps to the chemical toilet in the corner. She worked at the hinge on the loo seat, prising loose a rivet, and then reached up to carve another tally into the breeze-block wall.

She counted the marks – eleven days.

Well, they wouldn't get her. Solitude, isolation, loss of sleep: the classic first steps to try to break her down. Knowledge was her weapon. Establish a routine, mark the days, exercise, think positively – fight back.

Nicole replaced the rivet, pushed the toilet into the middle of the cell, and started her routine in the corner. Deep breath. Walk. One, two, three, four. Stop. Turn left. One, two three. Stop. Turn left. One, two, three, four. Stop. Turn left. One, two, three. About turn. Back the other way. Ten times each way. As fast as possible. She measured out the sides of her cell the same way every day. Routine focused her energy, got the adrenalin running.

But if her body was weak, her mind was strong. She was determined to get out, as quickly as possible.

Peter was safe in California – she was sure of that. She would speak to him as she paced her cell, tell him that she was fine, that she would soon be home.

She knew a chance to escape would come. It had to.

She would never give in to them – never!

She pushed the toilet back into the corner and sat down in the middle of the floor. Clasping her hands behind her head, she began the first of ten slow sit-ups – all she could manage with her weakened body. A small tear of frustration beaded out of the corner of one eye as she finished the last one. She stopped, wiped it away with the back of her sleeve, and rolled onto her front. Then she did twenty press-ups.

I'm surviving, Rykhlin. I know all their tricks. Are you still out there?

She shuffled back against the wall, chest heaving with the exertion. It was hot in the tiny cell. The sweet-sour smell of her unwashed body funnelled past her nose. She reached for the plastic bottle of water, unscrewed the blue cap, and took a mouthful, rationing it carefully, swilling it around her mouth and moistening her lips. She replaced the bottle on the floor.

The exercise, the heat of the day, the weakening condition of her body – it quickly made her tired.

Nicole laid her head down onto her folded arms and began to doze.

A loud metallic bang. The hatch on the steel door lifted and a hand came through, dropping a red plastic bowl of rice onto the floor. The hatch banged shut again. Nicole scuttled forward on her knees, grabbed the bowl and returned to her position. She wiped her hands on her overalls and began to scoop out the rice. She ate fast; meals could come at any time, sometimes they didn't come at all. She shovelled the rice down as quickly as she could, knowing she must keep her strength up. She worried about her diet; she lacked a lot of what she needed.

As she finished the rice, she picked the last bits out of the bowl with her finger, then lay back, feeling drowsy again.

Keys rattled and scraped in the metal door. It swung open, letting cool air waft in from the dark corridor outside. A guard stood there, in neatly pressed combat clothing. There was another guard behind, who kept his rifle trained on Nicole all the time. They said nothing, just waited.

She knew the routine. Picking up the chemical toilet,

she took it outside and walked along the corridor to the end, past two other steel doors. Unlatching the lid, she emptied the toilet down the large metal drain set into the concrete floor. A powerful sewer-stench came up through the grid. She replaced the chemicals from a box of plastic bottles standing nearby, then latched down the toilet's lid.

Suddenly, there was a commotion behind her. She started to turn round, but the guard barked at her and told her to keep looking to the front.

She turned on a tap and hosed off the grid. She could still hear voices and a commotion. She picked up the chemical toilet and turned to go back up the corridor.

The middle cell door was open. There were people standing in the entrance, one of them in a white coat. As she passed the cell, she stole a look inside.

Rykhlin! Lying on the floor. Unmoving. Dressed in shabby olive-green coveralls.

A small pool of blood spread out from beneath his body. His beard was dark against an alabaster face that was blotched with yellow and purple from a heavy beating.

In a rush of fear, Nicole moved forward instinctively, her whole body reaching out for him.

'*Tidak!*' The guard's guttural command rang out along the empty corridor. A rough hand grabbed at the collar of her overalls and yanked her back painfully.

Anger welled up inside her. 'You bastards!' she yelled. 'What have you done to him?'

But the hard barrel of a rifle slammed into her back

and propelled her along the corridor. She was bundled quickly into her cell.

The door slammed shut.

She stood, listening, trying to find out more, but could only detect a murmur of voices from far away. Carefully, she replaced the chemical toilet in its normal position, then slowly slumped down against one of the walls of her prison.

What had happened? What was going on?

She stared ahead blankly. Thought of Rykhlin's pain. Thought of his tortured body lying so close to her, yet so out of reach. She should have tried harder to help him.

A dark tide of guilt began to well up inside her. It was all her fault: her fault for remaining so long at the guard post. Her fault that he was dead. Now she was trapped — and alone.

And slowly the dark walls of Nicole's cell began to close in around her.

Keys rattled in the lock. Nicole stood up, her pulse quickening. Was it her turn now?

A tall, smartly dressed soldier entered the cell, boots shining in the patch of sunlight. He had perfect creases in his camouflage uniform, a red beret — a colonel of the *Kopassus* . . .

It was Lukman.

A broad grin temporarily creased his smooth Malay face, showing off the line of perfect teeth. 'Good afternoon, Miss Tai-Chung.' His voice was soft and cultured.

A soldier followed him in, carrying a fold-up table and two folding chairs. He set them up in the middle of the room, then left. The cell door stayed open but, somewhere outside, an outer door clanged shut and keys rattled against metal bars.

Lukman scraped back the chair nearest the door and offered it to her. 'Please, do sit down, Miss Tai-Chung,' he said smoothly.

'My name is Annabelle Luard,' she said listlessly.

'Please, do sit down!' he repeated kindly.

Slowly, she did as she was told.

'Good. That's better.'

Lukman took off his beret and put it down carefully on the table between them. He pulled a packet of *kreteks* from his top pocket, took one out and placed it between his lips. Flicking a gold lighter, he drew heavily on the cigarette. Cloves crackled in the silence of the cell. He blew the smoke steadily up towards the ceiling. 'You know,' he began, 'you really shouldn't be in here, Nicole. It's quite possible that we might have made a mistake.'

His eyes shone as he spoke. He looked sleek and arrogant. 'I expect you were led into all this foolishness by the man called Rykhlin. He's confessed to everything. So perhaps we could just have a little chat, you and I, and then I might consider letting you go.' Lukman took another long drag on the *kretek* and the cell began to fill with its spicy smell. 'You have a boy, haven't you? Tell me about him. Tell me what I want to know, and I can have you back with your family in just a couple of days.'

Alarm bells rang in Nicole's head. *Don't be fooled!* 'My name is Annabelle Luard,' she repeated firmly. 'I have no family.'

Lukman ignored her statement. 'I'm very concerned about the way in which you've been treated.' He looked at her and tutted. 'Those dirty clothes – that should never have been allowed. I really am very sorry. We'll have those changed at once.' He snapped his fingers. A soldier came in with a fresh pair of overalls, neatly folded. Lukman took another drag at his *kretek*. 'Please – put them on.'

Nicole looked at the fresh overalls. They were very inviting: fresh, crisp and clean. She wanted to put them on. Whatever happened, she *wanted* those overalls.

Lukman could see that, too. He stood up. 'Please, put your old overalls by the door. I'll have them taken away,' he said – and he politely left the room.

Nicole moved fast. She ripped through the buttons of the clothes she was wearing, dragging the grubby overalls down over her shoulders before pulling them right off. She grabbed the new set, shook them out, and stepped into them. The feel of fresh clothing on her body was an immediate relief – it made her feel happier, more confident, better altogether. She threw the old overalls on the floor by the door and sat down again.

Lukman came back. 'Good!' He nodded approvingly. 'You look a lot better already. I expect you'd like a bath, too.'

His stare slid over her thin body.

She didn't like that, and her guard slipped. 'Yes.'

Lukman laughed. 'Good! And how about some real food? It's usually only rice and water in these places.'

Nicole wanted the food. Whatever this charade was about, she wanted the nourishment it would give her. 'Yes,' she said again.

Lukman smiled. 'We'll do that straight away.' He shouted something in Indonesian to one of the guards outside.

Lukman continued to smile agreeably. 'So, how did you get on with Freddy? That *was* his name, wasn't it?'

Freddy! What had they done to him? Had they killed him, maybe like they'd killed Rykhlin? She wanted to know, but she didn't answer.

'Would you like some food now?' Lukman waited for an answer.

Yes! Oh God, yes! Of course she would.

'Yes,' she said.

Lukman flicked his fingers. A soldier brought in a wooden tray and placed it in front of her. There was a beautifully patterned plate, neatly laid out with fried slices of Javanese chicken covered in a pale brown sauce. It gave off a rich tangy smell of lemon, ginger and coriander. Nicole's mouth watered instantly. Her stomach ached for it. She seized the wooden chopsticks and ate fast, alternating slices of tender chicken with dips into the accompanying bowl of rice. She ate rapidly, before they could snatch it away again.

Lukman watched with amusement.

She finished quickly, before using the finger bowl and a paper towel.

'There, you see, I don't lie.' He smiled graciously. 'You know, you really did do well, hacking into our computer network like that. I was surprised you managed to get as close as you did to Dr Hendra's files. I thought they were so well protected.'

Suddenly she remembered how she'd been caught. The thud on the back of the head. The sharp pain. The blackness.

'I suppose we've lost all that data now,' Lukman continued. 'Sent back to Rykhlin's masters in America – over the satellite link.' He looked carefully at Nicole.

Don't tell him. Don't tell him how much you sent. He doesn't know. He's only bluffing.

But Lukman noticed the shadow that passed across her face.

Nicole blanked her mind and tried to concentrate on the gorgeous feeling of warmth surging in her stomach.

'I hope you were impressed by the security of our network. Tell me, how did you discover Hendra's key code?' He finished his *kretek* and ground it out on Nicole's finished plate.

Keep your face a mask, she thought. *Give nothing away. He's probing. Wants to know what information you have.* 'My name is Annabelle Luard,' she said.

Lukman's smile froze. 'Miss Tai-Chung, you still have another disk – the one you were given on the oil rig. Who did you pass it to?'

She stared straight past him, studying the pattern of the bricks on the wall beyond his shoulder.

His voice became hard-edged. 'Hendra's key code – you must have discovered it. What was it?'

So he wanted access to Hendra's computer. Why would he want that? Was the worm working for himself? She said nothing.

'Tell me.'

His eyes were glassy and unblinking. 'The computer code, Miss Tai-Chung? Come on, you must know it.'

Only silence.

Lukman got up from the table. 'Oh dear, you do make this so terribly difficult.'

He left the room. Nicole reached forward to run her finger round the plate, gathering up the remaining sauce and licking it off her finger. Perhaps Lukman would let her go. Perhaps she would soon see her son again after all.

Strong brown arms reached around her body. They seized the wooden tray, picked it up, and slammed it against the cell wall with a crash. Bits of broken china ricocheted from the impact. Then one of the arms locked around her neck and pulled her up out of the seat. A foot kicked the chair away. The ceiling swayed above her eyes as she heard the table being knocked to one side. There was an almighty blow straight to her stomach, and a dull pain shot through her body. She doubled over, gasping for air. But nothing would come, her lungs wouldn't open. It was like sucking against a plastic bag. She wanted to retch.

Wanted to breathe. Tried to do both. But couldn't. It hurt. Tears flowed down her cheeks.

She vomited suddenly, the undigested food splattering down over the man's bare arms, fouling her own overalls, pooling on the floor.

'Fucking bitch!'

The arm let her go and she dropped to the floor. She was on her hands and knees, gasping, trying to pull some air back into her lungs. Then a boot kicked her savagely in the thigh. She gasped, choking on the vomit still in her mouth.

A grey mist narrowed her vision and started to close in. She was looking at the concrete floor through a grey tunnel. She could hear someone shouting, felt other hands under her armpits.

Then . . .

Blackness.

'Wake up, bitch!'

A stinging hand across her cheek. Nicole opened her eyes; the lids felt sore and swollen. She was on a chair now, in front of the table, hands tied behind its back. She must have passed out. A man sat opposite her: yellow T-shirt, loose black trousers, black boots, black beret with a silver tiger's head.

Bakorstanas, in full regalia.

She saw vomit dribbling over the man's forearm. He was wiping it away with a paper towel.

He stood up, thrusting his face into hers, his breath smelling strongly of stale spice and tobacco. She twisted her head away. He put his hand in her hair, twisted it back to face him. His young Malay face was contorted and a thin moustache darkened his upper lip. He spat. She jerked away; wetness glistened as it began to slide down her cheek. 'Watch the TV, bitch!'

They'd put a TV in the corner of the cell. She saw the white hands of the countdown clock jerking towards zero.

A flicker of light.

She watched the screen and saw a picture. A surveillance picture taken in secret: blurred edges, brickwork glowing in warm morning sunshine, cypress trees swaying gently in the breeze. Windows? A house? Her own house! A boy in school uniform came out of the front door and kicked carelessly at the gravel. A young boy with slightly Asian features, fresh-faced and open. He smiled straight into the camera . . . smiled at her.

Peter!

The screen went blank.

Someone screamed inside her head.

Simes! The bastard! Peter shouldn't have been there. He shouldn't have still been in her house. He should have been in California – at that clinic. Why had Simes brought him home? She didn't understand. Did they think she was dead?

Nicole's body jerked as the *Bakorstanas*'s fist went through the TV screen, which exploded with a loud bang. Glass showered onto the floor. Then he was there again with his foul breath, his ugly grinning face shoved right up against hers. Beads of perspiration gathered around the fuzz on his upper lip. He spoke in a thick Asian-American accent. 'OK, we know about your kid. We know what he does, we know when he goes out to California, and we know when he comes back. Now we get some answers to Mr Lukman's questions, OK?'

She was confused. What did he mean, 'comes back'? He shouldn't be coming back. He should still be out there.

Say nothing. Look straight ahead.

'Do you fucking understand?' he shouted.

What have they done to him?

'Nicole Tai-Chung – is that your name?' he screamed.

Don't make it worse for Peter. Say nothing. Look at the wall. Don't incriminate him.

He drew out a heavy rubber cosh. Slammed it down on the table. Nicole jumped.

'Tai-Chung? Your fucking name, right or wrong?'

Her body began to shake with reaction. She mustn't tell them. Mustn't link herself with Peter. They'd hurt him, kill him. A slippery bead of sweat trickled from her right armpit and ran down the side of her body. She stared at the bricks in the wall, studied the patterns in the cement.

The cosh slammed onto the table again. 'Is – that – your – name?' he shouted.

Her jaw chattered momentarily. She clamped it tight, said nothing.

Large hands grasped Nicole's wrists, released the cords that bound them, wrenched them away from the chair and thumped them onto the table. She saw the blur of the cosh out of the corner of her eye. White pain exploded in her hand, lanced up her arm. She screamed, jerking back in the chair. He leaned right over her, looking down into her face, and smiled. His rough hand, scratching at her skin, began to knead the back of her neck. 'Dr Hendra's computer files. The key code, OK? For Mr Lukman.'

Her arm trembled violently from the vicious assault. The pain from her smashed fingers ran all the way through her body. A vile feeling of nausea sat leaden in her stomach. She looked up and recognized her interrogator's slobbery perversion, saw the enjoyment in the set of his scabbed lips, and she despised him.

He leered down at her. The cosh became a blur in the air again ... another blow, a solid crack to the upper arm, another deep pain, a sudden involuntary gasp that took all the breath out of her. She tried to grip the sides of the chair but couldn't move the fingers on her right hand. Looking down, she saw the pulped flesh, saw clear fluid running through the thicker blood.

Another blow, sharp and stinging, on her left calf. A scream that might have been hers.

The rubber cosh crashed back down onto the table.

'The computer code!' he screamed. 'Come on, the fucking numbers, you bitch!'

Nicole wondered how much more she could stand. She waited for the next blow.

It came. A blur. Pain lanced through her body again. Greyness began to cloud the edge of her vision, her head swam, and the picture slipped to one side. Someone was groaning, far away, distant.

Now his face was right up against hers, the walls swaying behind him, his hand running through her hair. 'And you've got another disk at home, haven't you, my lovely?'

What's that? What is he saying? She shut her eyes. Tried to shut him out. Felt the room sway beneath her.

'Fucking hell!' The rubber cosh slammed against the back of her neck.

Dull pain stabbed hard into her forehead. Nausea, vomit splattering. Sounds buzzing and echoing inside her head.

'Leave it! You'll lose her.' A commanding voice.

Heavy breathing. Her own breathing – wet in her throat.

A new voice, a calm voice: 'The key code. Come on, Nicole, you can tell me. Just the computer code, that's all I want.' A hand fondled her neck, and she looked up . . .

Lukman!

Their gazes locked for a moment. She saw the tip of his tongue slide across his lips, felt his neatly manicured finger begin to trace the outline of her mouth . . .

She bit hard into the rubbery flesh. There was a loud yelp – and his skin tore as he jerked his hand back. She tasted the metallic saltiness of his blood.

The *Bakorstanas* yanked her back, thumped the cosh hard up against her neck, and then forced it into her mouth and down her throat until she was choking.

'You fucking bitch . . .!'

Then it was Lukman again, his breath hissing through his nostrils. She saw his hard balled-up fist coming fast, punching the air out of her . . .

Lukman let Nicole go, let her slide off the chair. He gave her body a kick. 'She'll talk now!'

The two men began to wheel the broken TV and the video recorder out of the cell. As they went past, one leaned down and whispered hoarsely in her ear. 'So, now it's your fucking son, OK?'

Then the door slammed shut behind them. Keys scraped in the lock, and there was a distant yowl of triumph as they made their way out of the cell block.

Nicole lay on the floor, her overalls badly stained with vomit. Pain burned through her whole body. She lay there for a long time, drifting in and out of consciousness . . .

Nicole's eyes opened. She looked at the mess that was once her right hand, and saw the fingers split, puffy and bloated like cooked sausages.

The image of Rykhlin hovered before her; curled up on the floor of his cell, white face over red blood.

She saw again the blurred video: Peter walking out of the house – their house. No point in going on – not any more. She'd become a danger to her own son. To save him, she must die.

She rolled over and shakily picked up a shard of broken china that had landed on the floor. She played with it in her fingers, remembering what they'd said. How they'd use Peter, abuse him to get at her.

Nicole studied the sharpness of the broken ceramic, drew her thumb slowly across it, and watched with fascinated detachment as a fine line of blood beaded out from her skin like sap from a wounded stem.

Chapter Thirty-seven – second week in May: Andersen Air Force Base, Guam

22.00 hours Pacific West time

Colonel Jack Taylor watched the tiny white numerals in his helmet display count off the final moments to the start of the mission. With just seconds to go, he reached out, grasped the thick moulding of the throttle levers, and fingered the transmit button to speak to the control tower.

'Buckshot 1, take-off,' he said tersely.

The controller responded with a single click through the earphones.

Taylor lay well back inside the body of the Wraith, inclined like a racing driver to withstand the body-crushing combat turns. He saw the outside world not through a canopy but via computer-generated images displayed inside his insect-like helmet.

Taylor glanced left, and the synthetic view of the runway panned with him. He checked the dark shape of the F-15 on his flank and saw its red anti-collision light strobing brightly in the darkness. It would sit on his wing throughout the take-off, masking the sound of his own engines from anyone with an excessive interest in air movements around Andersen.

A shadowy figure in the F-15 raised a thumb above the cockpit sill and Taylor eased the throttles forward. The subdued whine of the General Electric turbofans gave way to a hushed roar. Brakes off, and he felt a strong push from behind as the Wraith accelerated rapidly down the runway.

Almost immediately the same terse request for take-off came from his wing man, Buckshot 2.

07.05 hours Washington time

Greg Noble hurried down the corridor towards the Pentagon Special Operations Room. The two marine guards on the armour-plated double doors came smartly to attention. He swept past with barely a nod and punched the code of the day into the keypad. The big steel doors ran back smoothly on their nylon bearings, giving Noble immediate access to the blue-carpeted balcony that ran across the back of the darkened room.

A giant video map of the West Pacific dominated the opposite wall. A whirling blue star symbol rotated to the north-east of New Guinea, marking the present location of Typhoon Anna. Red lines showed aircraft missions between the big air base at Guam and the storm, code numbers being used to differentiate the various types. Across the top of the screen were two digital clocks displaying both Washington and Pacific West time.

Noble walked down the stairs and onto the floor. He strode between the two banks of computers that were using satellite imagery to track every aspect of Anna – black and white displays for real time, infra-red for clouds, psychedelically coloured and computer-enhanced to show wind speeds, cloud-top temperatures, sea-surface height and so on. In front of the computers were large plotting desks covered with meteorological charts, and a bank of telephones and printers that connected the Operations Room to the outside world.

The duty controller was sitting at his desk, tapping away at a laptop. He looked up as Noble entered. 'Buckshot 1 and 2 outbound from Guam, right on time.'

Noble smiled and searched for Dr Helen Carver in the screen-lit gloom. He located her, a large, rather bony figure in her mid-thirties, leaning over one of the monitors. She was a senior scientist at the National Centre for Atmospheric Research and Kuls had insisted that she should be present during the trials; she was one of the few people he was prepared to work with. Noble had to rely on her forecasting if he was to make any sensible decisions – and he hated having to rely on anybody.

'How are we looking at the moment, Helen?'

Carver looked up from her screen, the light accentuating her heavy features. 'Quite good. Anna's still gathering strength.'

'How severe is she?' asked Noble.

'Category two – that means 100 m.p.h. winds. But she's deepening all the time.'

A mild thrill ran through Noble. He thought for a moment. This was really meant to be a dummy run, a sort of proof-of-concept exercise. But Special Forces were ready to go, and if this typhoon really was any good . . .

'Dr Kuls?'

Kuls pulled his wheelchair out from a workstation and came across.

'What are your predictions if we seed Anna now?'

Kuls turned to the PC and clicked away with the mouse. 'These predicted paths are based on my new fluid dynamics model.' Noble stared intently at the screen. 'As you can see from her present track, shown in red, she should cross latitude 10 degrees north in about three days' time, probably making landfall over Luzon – that's part of the Philippines. But with seeding – see these green lines? – we could delay the moment when she starts to veer north and give you an 85% probability that she'll stay on this track' – he jabbed with his finger, looking up at Noble – 'and cross right over Palau.'

Right on target! And this thing was awesome. It had the power to rip across the island and tear down its infrastructure. The sea would flood over the dykes and pour into Rahman's missile control centre.

Carver had brought over one of the meteorological charts while Noble had been studying the screen. It was large, flapping awkwardly in her hands as she tried to show it to him. He looked at the mass of neatly plotted weather-station symbols and the wavy lines of pressure contours.

'The steering currents in the upper atmosphere aren't

very strong at the moment,' she said. 'The subtropical jet stream's very weak, so it's likely that Anna will be reluctant to swing north. It should be quite easy to keep her on a more southerly track.'

Carver and Kuls both stared at Noble, waiting for his decision. He looked back into their blank faces, wondering how they could be so detached from the whole thing, so clinical in their approach. This was a weapon they were discussing, a weapon as potentially devastating as any nuclear strike. A secret weapon, cloaked as a storm, it had the power to spread panic, to destroy cities, to wreak havoc wherever it went.

Noble stalled for time, turning to the man at the operations desk. 'When will our aircraft first make contact with Anna?'

'Just after midnight, local time – that's in a little over two hours.'

Noble chewed at his thumb, staring at Kuls's green computer prediction line: 85% probability. Get this wrong, and he would be in serious trouble. He was risking two highly advanced prototype aircraft, two expensive test pilots, perhaps even the President's position and the international reputation of the United States – certainly his own career. And if he went for broke now, he would be going with a more than one in ten chance of failure.

Carver was sitting on the edge of the table, the rolled-up met chart dangling from her hand. 'You won't get any better than this for some time,' she prompted him.

But get this right and the United States would be off

the hook. Arguni would be seized, the UN neatly side-stepped, and the exotic mineral back in US hands.

Noble drew a deep breath.

'OK, let's do it!'

23.50 hours Pacific West time

Ten miles high, Colonel Taylor disengaged from the refuelling boom of the huge KC-10 tanker aircraft. A spurt of wasted fuel flashed into white as it vaporized instantly on the smooth rounded upper surface of the Wraith. Taylor banked the delta-shaped aircraft gently away, its strange wing batlike against the starlit sky.

The air was smooth, like glass. Moonlight bathed the quilted spiralling cloud banks far below. Ahead of him towered the huge anvil peaks marking the eye wall of Typhoon Anna.

07.52 hours Washington time

The controller turned in his seat. 'We've just had an Alpha, sir.'

Noble nodded. This was the sign that both aircraft had been successfully refuelled. He stood up and put down his plastic cup of machine coffee, its skin now thickened and wrinkled. He went over to Helen Carver. 'What are conditions like inside the eye wall?' he asked quietly.

Carver turned from the monitor, pushing back a lock of unruly hair. 'The last report from the WC-130 was an hour ago. The eye's about nine miles across, wind speeds 120 miles per hour at 10,000 feet, convective cells topping out at 49,000 feet.'

A cold lump sat like a toad in Noble's stomach. Figures? Numbers? What he really wanted to know was what it was going to be like flying into that damn thing. The great towering cliffs of cumulus – a bedlam of updraughts, downdraughts, and vicious wind shear. He looked around the Operations Room, with its glowing electronic displays and hushed tones of confident organization. They were about to meddle with one of the most potent forces of nature and send it hurtling towards a Pacific island, destroying people's homes – their lives, hopes and ambitions all crushed. For God's sake, where was their sanity? What were they doing?

He began to feel more than just a little afraid.

00.30 hours Pacific West time

Taylor was in position. Below the aircraft, the smooth white cloud-tops had suddenly dropped away to reveal a vast black hole, a hole that plunged right down through the storm to the Pacific Ocean heaving almost ten miles below. This was the calm central eye of Typhoon Anna.

He sent his single-word message. 'Bravo.'

Then his gloved left hand slowly throttled back the power, and the nose of the Wraith dropped gently into a descent. Now great cliffs of moonlit cloud soared all around him in his helmet display. He was descending into the centre of a great rotating whirlpool of cloud. Nothing in all his thirteen years of flying had prepared him for this.

As 6,000 feet came up on the HUD, the Head-Up Display, he levelled out the Wraith and began to curve in towards the eye wall. Turbulence jiggled the aircraft slightly. He brought the speed back to the recommended 180 knots for seeding and thumbed the button on the control stick, hearing the whine and thump of the weapons-bay doors opening.

Taylor really had to concentrate now: keeping his air speed down in the low-pressure air of the eye meant that the aircraft was getting close to stalling speed. And there was no computer-aided guidance system for cloud seeding, just old-fashioned judgement.

Violent turbulence suddenly hammered at the aircraft. A strong updraught threatened to throw the plane on its side. He corrected, then a downdraught slammed his stomach up into his throat. *Too close!* He eased back out of the worst of it, and thumbed the weapon-release button on the stick.

The first of two pods, especially designed and tested by Fricke, began to release a stream of twelve-by-three-inch aluminium cylinders, each one filled with fine hygroscopic powder. Canister after canister flicked out into the saturated air. As they tumbled, the tops snapped off, the pyrotechnics ignited, and microscopic crystals streamed out in a broad swathe.

The effects were immediate. In the supersaturated air at the inside edge of the eye wall, water vapour began to gather on the microscopic nuclei. Clouds formed, and a new eye wall began to grow at the very heart of Anna, tightening the vortex, a tightening that would soon make her scream in furious anger.

00.35 hours Pacific West time

Eight hundred miles due west of Palau, in the city of Davao on the southernmost Philippine island of Mindanao, Dr Gaudencio Tobias was still going about his business despite it being the early hours of the morning. He pushed a key into the door of his battered Toyota saloon and twisted the lock open. He slipped in behind the wheel and put the paper bag of medicines onto the seat beside him. His hands went up to his face as he rubbed his fingers against his eyes, trying to push away the sleep his body craved for.

He started the engine and swung out onto the dirt road that bounced down between the cramped rows of shacks on either side. This was the shanty town of San Nicolas. Over 30,000 Filipino Muslims lived here, squatting together in cramped conditions on marshy land near the coast, threatened by the ever-rising level of the sea. They were the

Moro, victims of a huge land theft that had happened when logging companies had callously ripped the forest cover from their islands – while the Philippine government sat back and did nothing. Now insurrection simmered behind the corrugated-iron walls of this huge waterfront slum. An insurrection whose angry proponents were encouraged by the growing might of an Islamic Indonesia to the south.

00.40 hours Pacific West time

A warning bell chimed in Taylor's helmet, followed by a strict digitized female voice: 'Fire in the weapons bay! Fire in the weapons bay!'

Taylor instantly guessed what had happened. Turbulence affecting a new and untried system. One of the flares had probably hung up in the pod and ignited the others. The heat would be building up rapidly. He reacted professionally and thumbed the button on the throttle lever to jettison the pod. But he heard no reassuring clunk, saw no reassuring message in his helmet display. He pressed the extinguisher button, jabbing it hard with his thumb. Still nothing.

The persistent female voice spoke again: 'Check ice! Check ice!'

What?

His fingers automatically felt for the correct position of the switch, confirmed that the intake heaters were on. He realized the fire was taking hold fast, that it must be chewing away at the kilometres of cable that threaded the airframe – that it must have taken out the de-icing system.

Icing was critical on the Wraith – the air intakes sat on top of the rounded fuselage. They were covered with a fine-mesh wire grille to stop radar reflections, but the grilles iced up badly – and far too easily.

Taylor knew this. He pulled the aircraft away from the eye wall, intending to search out warmer air lower down. A second warning chime sounded: 'Left engine stall! Left engine stall!' Another red warning light glowed in his helmet display. The engine was being starved of air now – its intake must be icing up fast. He throttled the engine back to idle, went through the start-up procedures and pressed the relight button.

Nothing.

Then came a great hammer blow on the aircraft. The whole machine shuddered, and Taylor felt as if he was being pushed upwards by a giant hand. He looked at the data in his helmet display and couldn't believe the speed of ascent now being shown.

He pressed the relight button again. But the G-force suddenly slammed him upwards into his harness, his helmet straining at its chinstrap as the aircraft now plummeted violently in a gigantic downdraught.

Taylor was becoming disorientated. He had to think fast or lose the aircraft. He had to trust his instruments.

The aircraft stopped descending and seemed to quiver beneath his feet. It felt as if it was hovering. He looked at his helmet display. *Jesus Christ!* She was pitched nose down, diving! He yanked the side-stick back, fought against what his senses were telling him, tried to recover from the dive. But his airspeed dropped rapidly off the clock. Now he'd stalled! *Nightmare!* He couldn't believe what was happening to him. He pushed the stick hard forward and shoved the throttle on the good engine against the stop. Heard the reassuring roar of the jet. But he was going backwards. All his senses said he was going backwards. Believe the instruments. Airspeed – 250 knots? How could it be? Only a moment ago it had been zero.

Taylor was becoming totally confused. His senses were doing one thing, his aircraft another. He was losing control – he was locked inside a demented fairground ride. His helmet display showed brilliant lightning strobing outside the cockpit. Explosions of sound reverberated against the outer skin of the aircraft.

Another warning chime, and again that commanding female voice: 'Right engine stall! . . . Right engine stall! . . .' *Jesus!* Relight button. *Quick!* But he got no response. His heart was thumping now. Both engines running down meant electrics out, hydraulics out. No power to control the aircraft. Warning lights were flashing everywhere inside his helmet. The Wraith couldn't be flown without the computer: it would become unstable, would break up in the air.

Disorientated, confused, dazed by the incomprehensible signals entering his brain, Taylor suddenly found himself in real danger. He instinctively reached down with both hands for the black and yellow corded loop between his legs, grabbed it and pulled up hard against the tension.

For a moment, nothing happened.

Then, with an almighty bang, his canopy was blown away, his ears popped. There was a huge kick underneath his seat – and he was out, tumbling and spinning.

The seat was heavy and dragged him quickly down through the storm. The barometric device sensed the height as he fell, and loosened the straps at the right moment to jettison his seat. Taylor jerked in his harness as the big orange parachute ballooned out above him.

Thank God!

01.05 hours Pacific West time

The visit to his patient over, Dr Tobias walked back across the rough track to where he'd parked his car. A street light was on next to the ramshackle mosque deep inside the heart of the shanty town. A small group of youths were still playing football under its soft light, bare feet sliding around in the rough dirt. To one side, a palm tree swayed gently in the gathering breeze.

Tobias slumped into the front seat of the Toyota and slammed the door. He started the engine, switched on the radio and rolled off down the narrow potholed track. The local radio station was issuing the first storm warning of the season. High wind and heavy rain were expected as Typhoon Anna drifted past well to the north. Tobias watched the rubbish-strewn track pass beneath his head-lights, thought about the heavy rain that would follow and worried about possible outbreaks of typhoid if the sewers backed up against the rising sea level.

09.05 hours Washington time

Noble stared at the operations desk, waiting for one of the screens to come alive. 'Still nothing?'

'They've been in the eye for about forty minutes. Seeding should just about have finished, probably on their way back.'

'When do we next hear from them?'

'We get a Charlie call when they've hooked up to the tanker.'

Noble breathed out forcefully and began to pace the floor again.

He had a feeling about this.

No reason – just a feeling.

01.06 hours Pacific West time

Almost as soon as the canopy had opened, the next violent updraught snapped straight into Taylor's chute. The acceleration was terrific: the harness strained at his groin, hoisting him aloft at an alarming rate. He squeezed his eyes tight shut against the pain, wishing it would stop. Cold icy air slammed into his body – air that was full of water. It worked its way beneath his oxygen mask and made it difficult for him to breathe. He swung violently up towards the top of the storm, his belly distending with the severe decompression. He screamed out in pain. Lightning flared, and in its brief quivering light he saw the roiling mass of cloud around him. There was a terrific explosion, a loud crack in the chute, and Taylor's body accelerated violently. His head whiplashed. His neck stretched then dislocated, and his spinal cord snapped.

His body lolled uselessly like a rag doll.

Now Anna snatched at the corpse in her savage fury, whirling it away in a macabre and triumphant ride around the maelstrom of the eye wall.

She had just claimed her first victim.

09.35 Washington time

Noble looked up, white-faced, from the sheet of paper that he'd just lifted out of the printer tray. He stared disbelievingly at the huge video map of the West Pacific.

'We've lost an aircraft!'

He stood there, hypnotized by the whirling blue symbol of Anna, and watched as the alphanumeric code for Taylor's aircraft flickered – and then disappeared from the screen altogether.

'The eye wall's contracting!' Helen Carver's excited

voice cut through the surrounding tension. Noble rubbed at the back of his neck and walked slowly across the floor to where she was studying the latest satellite image scrolling slowly down the screen of her PC. Dr Kuls's chair came up beside them.

'Measure it, Helen,' he commanded. 'Find out what the difference is.'

I've lost one of the aircraft, thought Noble. *A top secret prototype.* In his mind's eye he saw its debris scattered all over the West Pacific.

Carver reached onto the desk behind her to retrieve a plastic ruler and a previously printed satellite image. First she measured the image on the screen, tapping at the keys on the keyboard. Then she assessed the printed copy by hand, using the ruler. She did a simple calculation. 'It's contracted by about three or four miles. We're building a new eye wall.' She was elated by this success, either forgetting or simply not caring about the loss of the aircraft.

Noble stood there, holding his ground. 'Dr Kuls, would you please calculate a new predicted track for Anna.'

Kuls's black-gloved hands went down and quickly propelled his wheelchair back across the floor to the PC that he'd been working on earlier. He keyed in the new parameters and waited for the programme to run. A new set of green lines plotted across his monitor.

I've lost one of the aircraft, thought Noble. *How am I going to tell the President?*

Kuls looked at the result for some time, then shook his

head. 'That can't be right,' he muttered. He started to key in more numbers, trying to work out what had gone wrong.

'What's the new prediction for Anna, Dr Kuls?' Noble called across the room.

Kuls looked up. 'I don't understand. Maybe there's a glitch in the program, something I've overlooked . . .'

Noble shook his head. 'No, Dr Kuls, I'm sure your program's right. We've lost an aircraft, remember? Anna's not seeded properly. Your predictions won't be valid. She's taking a different course.'

Kuls looked at Noble. 'Yes . . . so simple!'

'So where's she heading for now, Dr Kuls?' demanded Noble.

Kuls looked back at the screen in front of him. 'Davao,' he muttered quietly.

'Where?'

'Davao – it's the southernmost city in the Philippines,' said Carver. 'About the size of Anchorage in Alaska.'

Noble sat down.

They were about to miss the command and control centre on Palau – and devastate an innocent city instead, home for over half a million people. This whole thing was out of control. He felt as if a juggernaut, a monster, was bearing down on him. Something that would bring down the Presidency, destroy his own life.

'Call it off!' he called out.

Kuls shook his head quietly. 'We can't call it off, Greg. You know that. There's no way we can stop this thing now.'

Chapter Thirty-eight – three days later: The Philippines

Tuesday morning

After several previous typhoons had slammed across the island of Luzon, leaving in their wake over half a million corpses and a tottering economy, the Philippine government had learned to fear the political impact of a natural disaster.

Global warming was triggering ever more powerful typhoons – storms that threatened to tear whole cities apart, storms that were coming earlier and earlier each year. A rising sea level was making the waves surge further and further inland. Civil unrest had already erupted after the government had failed to deal adequately with the last catastrophe. They knew they had to be better prepared for the next one.

But to Dr Tony Yeh, in command of the new Typhoon Warning Centre in Manila, it looked like the next one had already come. Standing before a huge wall map of the Pacific Ocean, he tried to look confident for the cameras.

YEH: We've had two developments today, neither of which look good. Forecasting a typhoon track is difficult at the best of times, but Anna's been a real tease. Two days ago it looked like she would pass over Luzon as a Category Two storm, but she's stayed stubbornly to the south, and now it looks like she's heading for Mindanao Island.

ANCHOR GIRL: How strong do you expect this storm to be?

YEH: Well, that's the other big surprise. Three days ago, the eye shrunk considerably, and Anna went from Category Two to Category Four overnight. She's still intensifying. This could be a real superstorm, and it may go to Category Five. We're predicting wind speeds of at least 150 m.p.h., and a major storm surge, producing extensive flooding in low-lying coastal areas.

ANCHOR GIRL: So are you calling for an evacuation?

YEH: Not yet. But if Anna stays on course, we'll want as many people off the island as possible. Believe me, this storm's a real killer.

Tuesday afternoon

A warm wind blew up from the Gulf and started to toss the fronds of the two moth-eaten palms that struggled to survive amongst the muck and rubbish at one side of Dr Tobias's health centre. Litter scudded across the road and added itself to the sizeable drift that was accumulating under a battered and abandoned car on the pavement.

Dr Tobias held up a box of nails for the tall thin man who was hammering big sheets of protective plywood onto the window frame. 'You should try and get your family out of here once you've finished, Tondo.'

Tondo looked down, mouth grim beneath his straw hat. 'Go where, Dr Tobias? This is my home. If I leave my home, when I come back' – he waved a hand to emphasize the point – 'perhaps all stolen.'

'When this storm comes, the sea will rise. It will wash your house away,' explained Tobias.

Tondo banged away solidly at the plywood, a nail held between his lips. 'My daughter, she's not well this morning. It's very difficult.' He took the last nail and held it ready for the hammer. 'We've survived before, we can do it again.'

Tuesday night

Tony Yeh had been on duty for over twenty-four hours now. His back ached, and his head was muzzy with fatigue poisons. He looked over his colleague's shoulder at the PC monitor, a glass of water in one hand, paracetamol tablets in the other, and indicated the foot of the screen. 'That the latest infra-red?'

'Yep.'

'Still contracting?'

His colleague clicked with the mouse, then typed on the keyboard to bring up a time sequence of images. The computer rescanned Anna and made her into a huge multicoloured swirl – purple for the rain bands, green and yellow for cloud-top temperatures. In the centre of this swirling mass was a hole, painted blue by the computer. It contracted visibly with each frame in the sequence. 'Down to about six miles across now. Never known a system so ferocious.'

Yeh expelled his pent-up breath forcefully. 'It's only May, we have the first one of the season – and it's a big one! Things are getting serious.' He gulped back one of the paracetamol. 'Wind speed and pressure data?'

'The last US weather sortie didn't fly – conditions were too dangerous. Radar shows wind speeds in the eye wall averaging 160 m.p.h., but gusting to over 200 in some of the bigger convective cells.'

'Well, that makes her Category Five. What's the predicted track?'

'Sticking stubbornly in the lower latitudes. Should pass over Davao about midday tomorrow.'

'OK, issue a Level One typhoon alert. Get the people off Mindanao. Make sure they're clear about the strength of this thing.'

Wednesday morning

Dr Tobias had decided not to leave. He had no relatives, and no family to shelter. He felt his place was on Mindanao among the Muslim minority, the landless and jobless of the shanty towns, people with nowhere to go and no money to buy their way off the island.

He unlocked the door of the health centre and let the wind slam it shut behind him. He could taste salt on his lips. He switched on the lights to brighten the gloom of the boarded-up consulting room and then turned on the radio – evacuation instructions, messages about roads being blocked by traffic. An overloaded ferry had capsized in heavy seas during the crossing to Leyte.

Tobias began to check his medical supplies. He opened the cupboards, listing each of the items he had on a clipboard. As he worked, a violent gust battered at the boarded-up front window. Tobias looked up, then went back to his task.

It began to rain heavily. He could hear great torrents of the stuff lashing against the protective boarding. He went into the little kitchen at the back, hooked a jar of coffee out of the wall cupboard and spooned some into a mug. The kettle began to boil.

There was a crash and rumble of thunder outside. The lights dipped, then came on again. Tobias poured the coffee, sat down at the table, and flicked through the pages of his inventory.

Lunchtime

The lights had gone out. The wind now roared steadily round the walls of the health centre. There was a sudden hammering at the door. Tobias groped his way through the darkened corridor. Bits of dirt and dust were being driven through the narrow gap below the door and came skating across the floor tiles towards him. He felt for the key in his back pocket and inserted it into the lock. He found that he had to push really hard against the pressure of the wind to make the door open. Tondo stood there, rain lashing at his drenched clothing.

Tobias stared past him at the scene outside. The world had become a swirling grey twilight. Great sweeps of torrential rain hosepiped past the clinic. A shallow river surged along the road, pushing along small dams of refuse and broken palm fronds. The wind hissed through the cables strung across the street, flinging them around in wildly bucking loops. Thick clouds rolled low overhead.

Tobias guessed why Tondo had come. 'Your daughter?' he shouted.

Tondo nodded wildly, eyes round with apprehension.

Tobias turned and went back into the clinic. He fetched his doctor's briefcase, pocketed the key, and slammed the door shut behind him.

Outside, the rain drummed violently against his body, cold water soaking into his clothes and running down his neck. The wind had real power, pushing violently at Tobias and Tondo, making them stagger backwards as they set off across the flooded road.

They headed down the track that ran between the flimsy corrugated shacks of the shanty. Metal sheeting groaned and shrieked, straining against its inadequate fastenings. A large plastic bag flew towards them and struck Tobias in the chest before flapping frantically away.

'Dr Tobias?' Tondo shouted. 'Will the wind get stronger?'

Tobias shrugged as he drove himself forward against the wind. 'I don't know, Tondo. I've never lived through a real typhoon. Been on the edge of one, yes – but nothing like this.'

Tobias began to feel anxious. He thought there was something sinister about the wind. It didn't come in gusts – it just held a steady strength, as if confident of its power.

Tondo led him down a side alley towards his shack. A large sheet of corrugated iron on the neighbour's roof was flapping and banging, wrenching at flimsy nails, threatening to break away at any moment. Tondo took the doctor inside, where his wife and four children were cowering in a corner, eyes round and white in the gloom. 'It's all right,' said Tondo. 'Dr Tobias is here. I told you he wouldn't leave us.'

Tondo's wife looked despairingly up at him, hopeless in her ignorance, struck dumb by her fear. Tobias knelt down in his sodden clothing beside the little bed containing the sick child. Tondo brought the gaslight over. It hissed and popped near his face as the wind roared outside.

The girl couldn't have been more than six years old. She lay beneath a pink ribbed blanket, the tiny delicate features of her face pale and drawn in the dancing shadows thrown by the lantern. Shining brown eyes stared up at him as an angelic smile spread across her lips.

Tobias took her hand and gave it a squeeze. 'Hello, Nagira.' Her skin felt hot and dry. He gently let go, and opened his case. He took out a thermometer and put it under her tongue, then held her wrist to feel the pulse.

The whole shack shuddered with a mighty buffet from the wind. The metal sheet next door banged even more violently against the roof. Then, suddenly, the sound ceased – there was a loud crash as the corrugated metal slammed into something on the other side of the street. A flicker of blue-white light came through the chinks in the wall. Thunder growled and rumbled above the sound of the wind screeching through the vibrating metal wall. Torrential rain hosed across the shack's corrugated roof, the din assaulting their eardrums. Tondo's wife whimpered and drew her other children close around her.

Tobias withdrew the thermometer and twisted it round to see it in the light of the lamp; it read 103 degrees. He looked at Tondo. 'She ought to come up to the clinic. You'd better bring your whole family.'

The roar of the wind rose another octave. Tondo nodded, wide-eyed. The whole shack began to shake and shudder, a fine mist of rain spraying in through some of the widening cracks. 'You'd better come now!' yelled Tobias. 'All of you!' Tondo reached for the door and opened it. The wind caught at its flat surface and whipped it out of his hands. With a loud bang it was gone, flung off down the street. Belongings were sucked out after it – sheets of paper, bits of clothing. Tondo's wife howled in fear, the children shrieked in terror.

Tobias scooped up the little girl from the bed and held her close to his chest. She weighed so little, and her tiny body seemed to disappear inside the blanket draped around her. Her hot little hands clung trustingly to his neck. 'Follow me!' he shouted.

Once outside, Tobias found it difficult to stand up straight. The wind swirled round the neighbouring shacks, slapping him this way and that. He fought against it, legs wide apart, shoving hard against the blast. Now Tobias began to feel real fear, knowing how weak and puny he was against the powerful demons shrieking around him. At the end of the street, a savage gust blew his legs out from under him and knocked him over. As he fell, he rolled over on his back to protect the tiny fragment of life in his arms. It was then that he caught a glimpse of the sky: clouds rolling and boiling above his head, scudding across the city with unbelievable speed. Lightning flickered and flashed, illuminating this skyscape from behind with shimmering electric blues and whites. Tobias rolled back over onto his knees, trying to keep the child clear of the pools of dirty water and mud.

The wind was roaring like a jet. It had become impossible to stand up against its fury. It punched and pummelled them as he clung on to the little girl. A shack on the corner of the street suddenly exploded, sheets of metal swinging wildly through the air and cannoning off other houses and battered cars parked at the side of the dirt road. Fear clutched savagely at Tobias's heart, clamping it in a vice.

He crawled along the ground, one hand supporting himself in the wet mud of the track, the other holding up the child. He saw an old rusted Nissan Patrol parked no more than twenty feet away. He turned and tried to yell at the pitiful group groping their away along behind him. 'The jeep, OK?' but the force of the wind sucked the words from his mouth.

Then he became aware of another sound. A sound embedded deep within the jet-roar of the typhoon. He glanced further down the track and saw large waves sweeping up towards them, debris thrashing around in the foaming white, shacks collapsing as the torrent rammed its way through the fragile township.

The storm surge! Death was near.

Tobias managed to pick himself up, clamped the child close to his chest, and ran like he'd never run before. The wind pushed him forwards, and even buoyed him up – his feet hardly seemed to touch the ground. A large sheet of plywood scythed overhead, crashing into the wall of one of the buildings nearby.

He slammed into the side of the Nissan and yanked frantically at its door. His breath was coming in gasps, sheer terror clutching at his throat. The door opened and crashed back against its stop. He tumbled in, and something hard fell on top of him, crawled over him. *Tondo!* Tondo squirmed round in the seat and reached out towards his wife, who was already holding up one of their children. A tiny face peered up through the open door of the Patrol, little eyes round with terror. Tondo's fingers reached for the delicate hand . . .

The first wave hit. The jeep lifted, lurched forward, and grounded again. The water streamed back, gathering for

the next wave – slamming the door shut. 'Laila!' shrieked
Tondo. He was clawing at the window, trying to open the
door against the force of the water now raging past outside.
Tears streamed down his desperate, muddied face. Tobias
looked at him, and knew it was hopeless. Knew there was
worse to come. He dumped Nagira on the centre seat,
yanked the plastic cover from the base of the steering
column and found the bundle of wires. But which one?
Which one to start the jeep? He yanked at the wires,
desperately touching different pairs together. He had no
idea.

'Tondo!' he yelled.

Tondo stared back at him, face set in a terrible mask of
anguish and torment. 'Tondo!' Tobias pointed at Nagira.
'Do this, or she dies too!' Tondo's hands were suddenly
there – strong hands shaking with fear. They twisted the
correct wires together, touched the ends. A crackling blue
spark, the engine turned over – and stopped. They touched
again: the engine lurched – died. Tondo began to pray,
muttering under his breath. 'God is Most Great. God is
Most Great. God is . . .' Again he touched the leads – the
engine finally caught.

Tobias floored the throttle, the engine screaming in
protest. He pushed the sick child onto Tondo's lap and
slammed the vehicle into gear. The jeep leaped away as
Tondo wailed in fear and grief, clasping the quiet child on
his knees. 'In the name of Allah, the Merciful . . .'

Tobias looked in the rear-view mirror. Saw the white
foam of the next wave coming in fast.

'Praise be to Allah, Lord of the Worlds . . .'

The wave ran under the speeding vehicle. Water sprayed out to either side like the wake of a boat, roaring in the wheel arches.

'Thee alone we worship . . .'

Debris banged and thumped against the bodywork. Then they were out of the water, heading for the clinic.

'Thee alone we ask for help . . .'

On their approach to the clinic, they could see that cables hung down over the road, snaking about in the storm, gouts of molten metal spitting out as they shorted against each other. Both palm trees were down, snapped off – just sharp splintered stumps remaining.

'Show us the straight path . . .'

The wind tore at the Pepsi-Cola sign on the corner, hanging from one last strand. The wire parted: the sign whirled away, hit the ground and bounced. It disappeared behind the clinic.

Somehow Tobias found himself inside. They heaved the door of the clinic shut against the wind. 'Upstairs,' yelled Tobias, 'or we'll drown.'

The surge hit as both men scrambled up the stairs, Tondo clinging desperately to his tiny daughter. Powerful waves pounded the walls. The house shuddered under the hammer blows. Tondo was shouting his prayer now. 'Not the path of those who earn Thine anger, nor of those who go astray.' There was an indescribable sound as the wind rocketed over the clinic; it sucked and yanked at the roof.

Their ears popped with the sudden change of air pressure. Bolts and nails broke loose with a bang ... the front eaves lifted ... then the wind roared in under the gap, the pressure inside rose violently, and with a mighty crash the roof peeled back and was flung away.

For a moment Tobias felt himself lifted up with it as he clung desperately to a heavy metal filing cabinet. Something large slammed into the outside wall. The whole structure of the building quivered, the floor tilted, and he was sliding, sliding. He grabbed for something to hold on to. Found nothing. Couldn't stop himself. Hit the rising water. The filing cabinet crashed down on top of him, pinned him against some debris. Pain sliced into his arm, unbelievable pain. He opened his mouth, cried out to God in his terror. Water flooded his lungs. He tried to breathe but, his chest heavy, he couldn't fight against the volume of water inside him. Didn't see the massive concrete lintel plunge down to smash against his head – and bring to a merciful end this nightmare at the end of his life.

The young Filipino soldier slouched amongst the debris piled up on the San Nicolas foreshore. He wore a white mask across his mouth to ward off the stench and disease from the bloated bodies, and carried a bundle of red marker flags under his arm.

He looked back, fascinated by the devastation. A vast area of low-lying land had been scraped clean as if by a giant hand. He'd been told that over ten thousand Muslim squatters had once lived here. Now nothing at all was left but drifted mud and sand – and bodies.

Behind him, the city of Davao looked unharmed, but he'd flown over it in the helicopter that morning and seen thousands of suburban houses, rich men's houses – gutted and roofless. In the city many tower blocks had toppled, filling the streets with rubble. The city was no more.

A shapeless mound rocking in the surf caught his attention. He wandered down to the water's edge and heaved his boot against another body, tipping it over. The head lolled ridiculously, the face white and puffy from exposure to the water.

It was a military pilot, dressed in an olive-green flying suit. His black life-preserver bulged around his head and across his chest. An oxygen mask, with its ribbed tubing, dangled to one side.

The soldier looked for some sort of identification, a name-tape or a shoulder flash. But there was nothing – just blank patches of Velcro. Then something shiny distracted him. Bending down, he found a gold pen clipped into a shoulder pocket. He plucked it out and stood up to look at it. There was a name engraved on its side in flowing script – *Jack Taylor*. He pocketed the pen, extracted one of the cane markers with its red flag, and shoved it in the sand to mark the body.

As he trudged off to find his superior officer, one of his dragging feet kicked at a small metal cylinder and sent it scudding and rolling across the sand. He bent down, and rolled it between his fingers. Stencilling flashed in the morning sun: 6210–01–657–04939. He poked inside and found a white, almost silvery residue in the bottom. He looked at it, smelled it, and wiped it off against the sharp edge of the cylinder.

There seemed to be quite a few cylinders lying about in the sand.

So he pocketed one of those, too.

Part Five:
FEAR THE TIGERS' STRIKE

CNN Television
Transcript of News Broadcast

Thursday, May 16

Last night the typhoon-ravaged streets of Davao on the southernmost tip of the Philippines were the setting for one of the most macabre spectacles I have ever witnessed. Survivors from the San Nicolas squatter settlement impaled what they believed to be the body of a United States Air Force pilot on a tall wooden stake and paraded it through the rubble-strewn streets of their shattered city. As in some morbid medieval spectacle, passers-by hurled abuse, or pounded the drooping corpse with stones and rubbish.

The discovery of the body, along with numerous small aluminium canisters, has fuelled fierce speculation among the Muslim minority on Mindanao that United States trickery lies behind the catastrophe of Typhoon Anna, in which 200-mile-an-hour winds claimed the lives of at least 6,000 people, and left over two million homeless. Highest casualties were among the impoverished Muslim community.

Rumours abound here that the United States has been carrying out secret weapons-testing to modify typhoons in the West Pacific. They say that the white powder found inside the aluminium tubes contains calcium chloride – a typical agent used for cloud-seeding operations. I have taken a close look at some of the canisters and a stencilled code on their casings can clearly be seen. It points to the manufacturer as being the Lockheed-Martin missile plant in Florida.

President Rahman of Indonesia is using the incident to further inflame anti-US feelings. At a rally in Jakarta this morning, he declared himself outraged that the United States was prepared to use the environment as a weapon to wage a secret and satanic war against povety-stricken Muslims in South-East Asia. It was an attempt, he announced, to destabilize regional econ-omies in order to take control of an important mineral that Indonesia itself had discovered on the ocean floor. Agitators supported his speech by whipping up the crowd into a frenzy of anti-United States chanting. There were shouts of 'Kill the *kufra*!', and hysterical demands for a *jihad* – a holy war. Rahman did nothing to calm this situation, rather he supported their demands. Referring somewhat chillingly to a new 'super-weapon', he promised them revenge.

A White House spokesperson has dismissed Rah-man's claims as 'absolute rubbish', suggesting that this was yet another attempt to stave off mounting criticism of his own government, and pointing out that Rah-man's seabed mining operation was tantamount to theft of a United States resource.

Whatever the truth, the remarkable events of last

night certainly indicate a dramatic up-shift in the growing hostility between America and Indonesia. But if the CIA has been involved in a 'dirty tricks' campaign with the weather, then this government is courting future political disaster. With the world sliding towards increasing climatic chaos as a result of global warming, no one is in the mood for such a remarkably callous act. The US President has so far denied all knowledge of the incident.

This is William Wiesner for CNN – Mindanao, Southern Philippines.

Chapter Thirty-nine – the same day: eight miles above West Virginia

The huge Boeing E-4B Airborne Command Post cruised high above the Appalachians, trailing its faint shadow across the gently ribbed layer of thin stratocumulus far below. One of a small fleet of converted 747s, it acted as a mobile nerve centre for the American government – and a useful tool of command in the event of a major natural disaster.

Inside, President Byrd sat alone at the head of a long wood-effect conference table, watching the CNN news broadcast from the Philippines. Bright sunlight streamed in through the row of windows to his left, sunlight that cruelly accentuated the lines that were beginning to erode his famous boyish looks, sunlight that belied the chaos that had marched across a million square miles of the Great Plains the previous night.

Byrd switched off the TV and thumbed through the National Weather Service briefing document laid out in front of him. He sighed. He'd read all that he wanted to. Yesterday, a huge tongue of unusually hot, moist air had surged up the Mississippi from the Gulf of Mexico, and then collided head on with a block of cold, dry air sitting 200 miles to the south of the Great Lakes. Thunderstorms had boiled savagely along the meteorological battle front. Squall lines had swept across state boundaries. A scattering of over 200 tornadoes in less than fifteen hours had smashed across Middle America, making it the worst tornado outbreak ever.

The statistics hammered at Byrd's mind. Over 500 dead, 20,000 families made homeless. The figures gave him a growing sense of unease. As the planet warmed, nature was becoming ever more violent.

The storm couldn't have come at a worse time.

CNN had somehow got hold of the typhoon story from the Philippines, and were worrying at it like a dog with a bone. Suspicion hung in the air and, now that America had a climate disaster of her own, they were pointing the finger of blame at the President and baying for his blood. His ratings were plummeting.

Byrd jabbed at the communications panel in front of him, calling up a secure link through to CIA Headquarters at Langley. He sat quietly in his chair and waited, using the hands-free transceiver so that he could flick through the tornado report at the same time.

'Mr President?' The voice came back clearly and without distortion.

'Good morning, Greg.' Byrd put the document down, and sat back. He linked his hands behind his head. 'Have you seen the news this morning?'

There was a slight hesitation at the other end. 'Do you mean the CNN report, Mr President?'

Byrd unhooked his hands and leaned aggressively towards the speaker. 'Of course I mean the CNN report!' he said angrily. 'Look, I'm on my way to Louisville right now – I've got to say something about these tornadoes. I'm going to meet the people, run a press conference. What do I tell them, Greg? What do I say if they ask about the typhoon? Do we have a cover story yet?'

'This is not good, Mr President.'

'Hell, I know that, Greg! That's why I'm talking to you! CNN claim they've found some seeding canisters. Is that true?'

There was a distinct pause.

'They might be ours, sir.'

'Dammit! Are they ours or not? *You* should know. They had a code on the side – that's pretty conclusive, isn't it?'

There was a dry cough from Noble. 'Yes, Mr President.'

Byrd loosened his tie. *Damn the CIA! Damn their bloody incompetence!* 'I've got to deny it, Greg. I don't know anything about this, OK?'

'Yes, I know, Mr President.'

'Look, what the hell else do you expect me to do?' demanded Byrd. 'How do I tell people who've lost their homes, their family, and their livelihood that, yes, we've been messing about with the damn weather in the Philippines! Look, it was your idea to go for Kuls, Noble – not mine.'

'Yes, sir,' said Noble dryly.

There was a pause while tension crackled across the airwaves like frost.

'They're trying to blame me for the tornadoes, too, Noble. You know that? If they find out what we did in the Philippines, I'll be the fall guy for every damn natural disaster that happens forever after.'

'Yes, Mr President.'

Byrd put his elbows on the desk and rubbed his eyes. He hadn't slept well, and the strain of his job was beginning to tell. 'OK, Noble, relax. Do we know anything certain yet?'

'I'm sorry, Mr President?'

'Do we know anything yet?' snapped Byrd. 'About the loss of one of the Wraiths?'

'We think it probably broke up in the storm, Mr President. Kuls may well have underestimated the recent growth of typhoon wind speeds . . .'

'Like hell he did.'

'It was a very powerful typhoon, sir,' Noble said defensively. 'The wind shear, the predictions were all wrong for the airframe.'

My God they were! He'd seen the pictures from the Philippines – the tops of buildings ripped off, rubble filling the streets. 'The damage that thing did, Greg – I had no idea.'

'The violence of nature, Mr President, yes, very impressive . . .'

'Impressive? Goddamned terrifying! We can't take responsibility for that.'

'But that was the whole point, Mr President. You wanted a powerful weapon that could be used without detection . . .'

'Well, it's hardly undetected *now!*' shouted Byrd.

He calmed himself.

'OK, we need to think carefully about our position here. There'll be questions in Congress. You'll have to come up with something – and make it convincing.'

'That's not going to be easy, Mr President. The evidence is strewn all over the beach.'

'I know it's strewn all over the beach. I've just seen it!'

Byrd made a visible effort to relax again. 'Look, we'll tell them it was an experimental aircraft – that's not a lie. And something went wrong: it got caught in the storm, came down in the Pacific, blame it on pilot error. The canisters are flares of some type – I don't know, you think of something, that's what you're there for. But the typhoon was just coincidence, OK? We did *not* cause the typhoon. Deny it!'

'Yes, Mr President.'

Byrd picked up a pencil and began to doodle on the pad laid out in front of him. He swirled his pencil round and round, tightening the spirals. 'This new "super weapon" of Rahman's, Greg – the one he's boasting about on CNN. Is he talking about a nuclear weapon?'

'I don't see what else it could be, Mr President.'

'Do you think he intends to use it?'

'No, he's just whipping up the crowds, taking the pressure off his own problems back home.'

'Sara thinks we should take him seriously. Look, we still need to take out the command and control centre for those missiles, Greg. And I want this *Indera* stuff back. It's too valuable to be left to the likes of Rahman.'

'Well, we've been giving Rahman's wife a helping hand for a long time, Mr President. She's keen to take over in Indonesia and she'd be more than happy to destabilize Rahman for us.'

'No, Greg! That's too slow. I want results *now*. What about those two agents of yours? Have you got them out yet?'

'No, but we've located them. We can move in quickly if we have to.'

'Then do it! I want them back – to find out what they know. We need to get Special Forces onto Arguni as soon as possible, and terminate Rahman's weapons production before it's too late.' Byrd flicked the end of his pencil thoughtfully against his lips. 'So what's Rahman going to do, Greg? What's your assessment of the situation?'

'We don't think he's fully nuclear-capable, despite all the hardware he's putting onto those seamounts.'

'Then we must strike now, Greg, while we've still got the chance, and before we lose the advantage. We need a result that'll keep Chan happy. Then we can stop Rahman at the UN. I want *Indera*, Greg. It's ours, dammit!'

Chapter Forty – third week in May: Arguni Base

Nicole lay on the floor in the suffocating heat of her cell, watching the bar of light from the tiny window slide snail-like across the concrete. She shifted her position on the slab of dirty yellow foam that served as a mattress, and felt its roughness against her face, felt it tear at the scabs crusting her sores. She felt the stomach pain of fifteen days of self-inflicted starvation – now slowly giving way to an intense dull headache, her mouth thick and gritty, her hearing becoming difficult. Without a proper tool, starvation had now become the only way. Pray God it would end things quickly enough.

Sweat stung at the mess of her wrists. She no longer bothered to exercise, just lay there in a timeless void, feeling the burden of her guilt, waiting for her death.

The hatch in the cell door dropped with a bang. A plastic bowl of rice was thrust through onto the floor, and the hatch banged shut again. Once her body had craved sustenance, but now she no longer harboured any interest in food at all.

She stared blankly at the rice bowl, watching the steam curl smoke-like into the humid air. Then she became aware of a grey cardboard tube peeping out from behind the bowl, a flash of white inside its shadow. Nicole fixed her eyes on it and wondered what it was, wondered whether it mattered.

She rolled clumsily onto her knees, wincing at the raw pain from her wounds. Holding her damaged right hand close to her chest, she shuffled over to investigate. She found an old toilet-roll interior with a sheet of paper folded inside. Dragging herself back to her mattress, she flopped down. Keeping her back to the door so as to conceal her actions, she eased the paper out with her thumb. It was a sheet torn from a spiral-bound notebook, pencil writing neatly executed in a childlike hand:

> Your father died last night.
> Keep strong!

She stared at the slip of paper, her thoughts confused. For a moment the news of her father's death failed to register. Instead she wondered about this unexpected friend. Who was it? Freddy?

Dreamily she folded the paper carefully into four, then again, and again, until it was just a tiny block. She pushed it with grubby hands into a crevice in the wall, then lay staring at the thin streak of white. It blemished the blankness of the surrounding wall, and she smeared it with dust to camouflage her handiwork.

Slowly, through the fog of her muddled thinking, this

news of her father began to sink in. She felt a welcome release from the torture of worrying about him. Release from that distressing vision of his cage. In death, he would no longer feel the pain of his forced labour, or his sickness. And in death, she too would be released and Peter would go free . . .

She shook her head, aware that her mind was drifting.

She forced herself to think.

If Rykhlin was dead, it must be Freddy. There was no one else who would write her such a note.

'*Keep strong!*'

Why would Freddy write that?

Then it was as if a window had cracked open. A tiny speck of hope wafted in and took root in her mind. Of course: '*Keep strong*' – two words that meant so much.

Code words.

From a memory of a distant briefing room.

They were coming to get her out.

Her cell door swung open and crashed heavily against the wall, jerking Nicole out of her sleep. A soldier dragged in a hose, removed the bucket, shouted at her to get up. Too weak to stand, she slumped with her back against the wall, shivering with the effort. He dragged out the filthy foam mattress and turned on a tap. As water ran out of the hose, he put his finger over the end of the tube and let the water spray out in a strong fan as he hosed down the cell. Then he brushed out the resulting mess with a large broom and sprayed the cell with disinfectant. Replacing the bucket with a new chemical toilet, he dragged in a couple of plastic stacking chairs, threw a clean pair of overalls onto one of the seats, and ordered her to get changed.

Slowly, shakily, Nicole struggled to put the new overalls on. Then she sat on one of the chairs, head drooping, confused, wondering what was about to happen.

The soldier checked over the cell, grunted approval, and banged the cell door shut behind him.

Nicole waited.

The cell door swung wide again, rousing Nicole from her doze. She looked up. The soldier shouted at her, ordered her to her feet, then stood to attention by the door.

She rose carefully, holding on to the chair for support against her giddiness. For some time nothing else happened. Voices muttered outside, then the sound of leather shoes clicked down the corridor.

A tall figure appeared in the doorway: an athletic middle-aged Malay, well groomed, impressively dressed in the full uniform of a colonel-in-chief. He had four rows of medal ribbons, and heavy gold braid that looped across his chest. He studied Nicole strangely, a twinkle within the sinister depths of his eyes.

She knew that face. She'd seen it a thousand times before.

It was Rahman.

His powerful presence dominated the doorway, strong

in the narrow confines of her cell. A sweet smell of polished leather wafted from him, contrasting with the raw sharpness of the disinfectant that the soldier had sprayed.

'You know who I am?' He had a deeply resonant voice, and he beamed at her from the doorway, curiosity written into the lines of his face. 'Of course you do. Well, I thought we might have a little chat, you and I. Alone.'

Rahman advanced into the cell and, drawing the other chair away from the wall, indicated to the soldier that he should leave them. He swung the chair across the floor and sat down on it backwards, straddling the seat with his arms folded along the backrest. He eyed Nicole as she shivered by the side of her own chair, his eyes roving across her body. She felt uncomfortable and drew her new overalls tight to her shaking and emaciated frame.

'Please, Nicole,' Rahman said, 'do sit down.'

She did as she was told, glad to be off her feet. Rahman maintained his stare until Nicole found his gaze intrusive and looked down at the floor. 'I think you made a big mistake coming here,' he boomed. 'I think you underestimated me.'

He paused, waiting for her reaction.

She said nothing.

He leaned forward. 'What did you think? That I was some sort of madman?' He laughed slowly, a confident laugh.

Nicole stared at him.

He frowned back at her. 'Tell me, what makes a woman leave her sick child?'

The question stabbed hard into Nicole's guilt. It unsettled her, drove her towards anger. She hadn't left Peter; she was giving him life. She gritted her teeth, refusing to react to Rahman's taunt.

Rahman got up from the chair and walked over to the tiny window, his hands now thrust deep into his pockets. For a moment he just stood there, gazing upwards. Then he spoke. 'The Americans have attacked my brothers and sisters in the Philippines,' he said quietly. 'Thousands of innocent Muslims lie dead.' He looked at her over his shoulder. 'Why do you think they did that, Nicole?'

She stared straight ahead, confused by Rahman's question. What was he talking about? What had the Americans done? Were they at war?

'Was it something to do with the information you sent back to them?' he demanded.

What was she being blamed for?

'Why do you think they wanted to cause so much suffering?' he persisted. He turned back to the window and lowered his voice. 'There's something I don't know, isn't there? Something I don't understand?' He stared out of the window. 'And I think *you* have the missing piece to this intriguing puzzle.'

Nicole stared at the wall, still wondering what the Americans had done, wondering why they had angered Rahman so much.

'Perhaps they're frightened of me,' he said, then he slapped the wall with an empty hand as if laughing at the absurdity of the idea. 'Or maybe they're just frightened of

Islam!' He paused. 'No, I'm sure it has something to do with what you found in Dr Hendra's computer files.'

He spun round to face her.

'I need to know,' he growled. 'I need to know what it is. Byrd's not the only one who may think he has power over nature. He'll regret what he's started.'

Rahman came and stood close behind her, putting his hands on her thin shoulders.

She didn't like that. Didn't like his touch. Wanted to squirm away.

'Why did you come here?' he asked.

Nicole felt his hands still on her body, wanted to get away from him.

'Were you spying for the United States?'

She just wanted him to go away. 'No!' she said.

'You're not wanted here, Nicole. Not you, nor your kind.'

'I didn't want to come here,' she spat out defiantly. 'I came only to save my son.'

Rahman laughed. 'Well, you can't save him now, Nicole -- because *I* have your son, in the palm of my hand.' His open hand appeared before her eyes. The cold light of the cell glinted off a gold ring on his finger. Then, very slowly, his hand squeezed shut. 'I can squash him' – his voice became dark and menacing – 'like a butterfly.'

Nicole stared at the clenched fist.

'What have you done with him?' she demanded.

Rahman ignored her. 'If you want to see your son alive again, talk to me. Tell me what it is the Americans want.

Tell me about their plans. Tell me why they chose to attack the Philippines.' He put his cheek down close beside hers. 'Tell me about their next cowardly plan.' She could feel the roughness of his stubble, the faint whiff of perfume. 'You know, don't you . . .?'

'I don't know anything!' she said defiantly.

He straightened up. 'You lie! You're a spy. You know what's going on.' Rahman's face came back closer to hers. 'If you want your son to live, you must tell me what you know.'

In the quietness that followed, a metal chain rattled through an iron loop, and somewhere beyond the cell door a human voice whimpered.

Nicole's mind was in turmoil. If she knew, she *would* tell him – anything to save Peter. But she didn't know, and she didn't understand.

'Your silence won't protect you, Nicole. I've already decided your future. You are to be executed. Now, save your son – and talk!'

Nicole was desperate. What could she say?

'Have you ever heard of Krakatau, Nicole?' boomed Rahman. 'Two minutes past ten on the twenty-seventh of August 1883. It was the biggest volcanic explosion of all time.' His hands pressed down on her shoulders, his voice becoming excited. 'All the cities around the Sunda Strait were obliterated – 36,000 people killed in an instant.'

He began to run his fingers gently along the side of her jaw. Nicole felt the rising heat of anger starting to erupt inside her.

'Surely you read about that in Hendra's files. Krakatau, such power! Such power in my hands.' He laughed and began to stroke the upper part of her arm beneath the coarse fabric of her overall. She clenched her jaw and felt the muscles tighten. 'Such anger! But then, you've seen our technology, haven't you? The Americans are fools to think they can mess with me. Come on, tell me what you know. What did you discover that terrifies them so much?'

His hand drifted down onto her breast, began to squeeze it gently . . .

Nicole sprang from her chair and it clattered to the floor behind her. She pressed up against the cell door, facing him, breathing deeply, eyes wide and alert. 'Leave me alone, you bastard!'

Rahman glared back at her. 'You meddle with things you don't understand, Tai-Chung.' He advanced towards her.

She dodged round to another wall, trying to avoid him.

His voice was rising. 'Don't you understand? With *Krakatau* I can destroy any city I choose.' He was excited by the violence of the idea.

She twisted away, dodging further along the wall.

'See the power I have. The power for revenge.' He stared into the future. 'An eye for an eye, a tooth for a tooth – evil for evil.' She was forgotten for the moment as his eyes focused on the enemy far away. 'And the heathen shall be visited by the very plague they set upon us . . .' He muttered the words, almost in reverence.

Then he stopped and looked at her. 'They sent a storm against the Muslim innocents of Davao. How could they do that? How could they slaughter so many in cold blood? Don't they know me? Don't they know that I have my answer ready? *Krakatau* – a tsunami, Nicole. A terrible wave that will punish the *kufra*. It will come from nowhere. It will be the judgement of God.'

Nicole watched Rahman's steady eyes, the ruthless expression moulded onto his face, and the flesh crawled on her body.

His voice lowered to a hiss: 'If you don't tell me about the Americans' plans I shall unleash this terrible weapon upon them, Nicole. Your son will die – and you alone will bear the blame.'

He rapped with his knuckles on the cell door. A soldier entered, bearing a tray of steaming food. 'Eat, Nicole!' Rahman's voice boomed out as he eyed her up and down. 'You need to be strong – for your execution tomorrow.'

Nicole stared into his eyes and recognized his coldness, his callous disregard for life. She looked down at the food, the way it slopped on its plate, and felt nauseated by it. Anger fused her body and gave her a strength she should not have had. She picked up the tray, fumbled for a moment as pain sliced through her damaged hand, then hurled it at him with all the force she could muster. It crashed against one side of the cell; bits of china spraying across the floor like shrapnel.

For a moment there was silence, punctuated by the gentle splatter of food dripping down the wall.

She stared at him, panting from the exertion. 'Go back to your pigsty, Rahman!'

He looked at her, hatred boiling in his eyes. 'I haven't finished with you yet, Tai-Chung,' he hissed. 'I will be back, Chinese bitch!' Then he spun on his heel and marched out of the cell. The soldier banged the door shut behind him. The key scrabbled in the lock.

Nicole slid down the wall, her back against it, and slumped onto her haunches. Anger had given her courage. Lifted her out of her weakness. However could she have allowed herself to lie like this, day after day, in a morass of self-pity – with this dictator on the loose?

She looked across the cell and saw the tiny piece of white paper wedged into the wall. Then she looked across to where the food lay in a splattered heap on the ground.

She shuffled over, kneeled down, and began to scoop the food frantically into her mouth.

Rescue would come tonight.

She would get out of this place and find her son – before it was too late for either of them.

Chapter Forty-one – that same night:
Arguni Base

The streamlined Marauder assault craft were line abreast, hurtling through the night towards the Irian Jaya coast. Three *ekranoplans*, surface skimmers, storming in undetected just above the waves at 380 knots. Inside the command vehicle was Lieutenant Meyer, United States Special Forces. Strapped into his green webbing seat, he relaxed in the exhilaration of the smooth floating ride as he listened on his headset to the crew's chatter. He checked out his team, who were cramped together around him in the dim red-lit interior. Seven men – all hand-picked, all men he trusted. Meyer grinned to himself. They were SEALS, members of the US Navy's elite, a highly trained combat force. And they were the business. Those Indonesian bastards had no idea what was going to hit them.

'Ten miles!' The pitch of the engines changed abruptly as they slowed for the enemy coast. Meyer ran through his GPS navigation system, and checked in with the AWACS command post cruising five miles overhead. His men stirred and began to sort out their kit. The light by the forward ramp turned from red to warning orange. Meyer stood up against the weight of his equipment, felt the adrenalin rush as he rapped out the familiar order.

'Stand by to disembark!'

Nicole lay on her foam mattress, drifting in and out of a half-sleep, waiting. A pale bar of moonlight eased in through the window-slit, illuminating the cell with the barest hint of detail. She became aware of a truck pulling up outside, and watched its headlights sweep a strip of light across the ceiling. She heard doors banging, loud raucous conversation, laughter dying away. Then silence.

She turned over on her mattress. Sleep drifted back to cloud her mind. She was in Belize, charging through the assault course . . .

A burst of machine-gun fire split the night apart. She was awake instantly, bolt upright, heart racing. Had she imagined it? No – another burst of gunfire, single shots in reply. Shouting and yelling. Had they come already? It seemed very close.

A brilliant white flash strobed under the door. *CRAMM!* The sound rang in her ears, deafening her briefly. Another flash. *CRAMM!* Her ears sang. She could hear the guards coughing and retching outside. White gas came creeping in and caught at the back of her throat, making her windpipe close up. Nicole found it difficult to breathe; she was coughing and choking. She forced her mouth hard against the sleeve of her overall to try to filter the stuff out. Her eyes stung with tears and she couldn't see. She staggered weakly to her feet.

An amplified voice rang loudly out across the cell block. 'Americans, get away from the outside wall! Lie down!' She staggered back to the middle of the cell, coughing against her sleeve. 'Lie down!' the voice repeated. 'Get away from the outer wall!' She did as she was told, dragging her mattress up against the cell's steel door and crouching down behind it.

There was a brilliant yellow-white flash, a sharp detonation, and a shock wave slapped against her body, sending a shower of debris stinging against her face. Suddenly the cell was full of swirling dust. A gloved hand came out of the gloom and grabbed Nicole firmly by her damaged wrist, pulling her upright. She cried out in pain, then saw light flooding into her dust-filled cell through a jagged hole in the outer wall. Saw a soldier silhouetted before her, his face covered with a gas mask, a sub-machine gun hanging from his right hand.

His voice was muffled: 'Luard?' he grunted.

She nodded.

'Welcome to freedom.'

He pushed her unceremoniously towards the gaping hole. She stumbled out through the jagged rubble to see white smoke drifting around a line of Suzuki jeeps. Indonesian soldiers lay awkwardly on the ground, blood seeping from their wounds. There were black-clad troops scattered among the vehicles, their weapons at the ready, protecting her as she came.

The soldier propelled her at a half-run between the jeeps and out of the prison compound, then up the road leading past the gulag. Nicole saw the wire fence, the watchtower – its searchlight still blazing into the camp, a soldier hanging lifeless from the upper platform.

A steady, powerful roar began to fill the air. Then she saw two aircraft squatting on the rough ground beyond the road, their engines tilted upwards at the end of stubby wings, huge propellers spinning horizontally like helicopter blades – CV22 Ospreys, tilt-rotors. She was hustled towards the nearest machine, but her legs felt weak. She stumbled and had to be almost carried in the soldier's strong arms. She caught the powerful downdraught from the blades as she rounded the back of the aircraft and smelled the sweet smell of jet fumes as she pounded up the loading ramp.

It was dark inside the fuselage. Nicole was pushed down onto a flimsy seat and felt the lap strap being yanked tight around her waist. Someone else had been taken in with her and was being lowered onto the seat opposite.

Another soldier came pounding up the ramp. 'Where's Rykhlin?' he shouted to her.

'He's dead!' she replied weakly, too exhausted, too drained of emotion to think any more. For the time being, she set aside the pain of his loss. The soldier stared at her for a moment, then turned and disappeared into the night.

I'm alone, she thought.

A whine of hydraulics and the ramp began to lift. The engine note deepened and she could feel the floor of the aircraft start to quiver. Nicole watched the lights of the gulag tilt and swing outside the tiny window, then drop away steadily as the Osprey became airborne. She saw Peter in her mind. She was on her way to get him.

A sudden loud clatter came from further up the fuselage – the door gunner putting down suppressing fire, bright flashes erupting from his machine gun, a stream of empty cartridge cases cascading into the collecting bag. The ramp sealed shut with a solid thump.

Nicole glanced at the person sitting opposite, just a shapeless shadow in the dark.

CRACK! A blinding flash. Dust shaken up from the floor.

The sound of the engines changed abruptly. *Oh God!* she thought, *no, not now, not so close to freedom.* The sharp, acrid smell of cordite filled the cabin. There was a loud mechanical graunching, then a steady vibration that began to rattle the fuselage. She gripped the flimsy aluminium tubing of her seat. She had to survive this. She'd already come through so much. She had to keep going.

A crewman stumbled back with a torch, its beam piercing the dust-filled cabin. He pointed it down at the floor to reveal a jagged hole, the torn metal around it folded back like the petals of a flower. He swung the beam upwards and found a sheet of green-quilted fabric hanging down, the edges still smouldering. He tore it away and exposed two large girders running across the roof – the main spars, designed to hang the weight of the aircraft from the wings. There was a large jagged exit hole immediately behind them. An aluminium casing shone in the torchlight, with thick shafts spinning out to the wings. Whatever had gone through had cracked the metal, and now it wept golden oil, laced with black. The crewman put his hand up, felt the casing and jumped back as he caught the heat.

The torch beam came back down to Nicole. The crewman put his head close to her ear so that he could shout above the noise. 'We may have to ditch, OK?'

She nodded. Her body trembled with shock, reaction and fatigue, and she felt sick with weakness. The crewman reached up above her and took down a life preserver like a waistcoat. The thick covering felt comforting against her body. She saw the shadowy figure opposite undoing the belt and getting up to come over. She saw frizzy hair shining like wool in the crewman's torchlight. There was a moment of recognition. Surely not . . .

'Freddy?'

A filed tooth shone back at her.

Things were suddenly slotting into place. 'You CIA?' she shouted.

'No, Missy,' he grinned. 'Free Indonesia – "buffalo" man!'

'Buffalo man?'

'OPM!'

Nicole had underestimated him – should have guessed.

Freddy turned towards the crewman. 'I know small island, with airfield,' he shouted. 'Kep Ruang – about fifty mile from here. I know someone with plane there.'

The crewman spoke into his throat mike and had a

conversation with the pilot. He shouted back at Freddy. 'OK, we'll try that. Sit down and strap up.' Then he bent down to speak in her ear again. 'We'll get you out – trust us?'

Nicole looked up and nodded. The crewman grinned back. She knew that she had no choice anyway.

Freddy grabbed Nicole's arm as soon as the Osprey set down on the tiny grass strip at Kep Ruang. 'Come!' he yelled.

They trotted across the grass towards the dark shape of a wooden house that stood at the edge of the forest. She felt strangely light-headed and was surprised at her continuing reserves of strength. Lights flicked on inside the building, the occupants disturbed by their noisy arrival. A white-haired Papuan staggered bleary-eyed onto the veranda.

'Hey, Lester!' yelled Freddy.

The Papuan blinked disbelievingly. 'Freddy? What the hell are you doing here? What's that thing on my airstrip?'

'Need your plane, Lester!'

'But I got a trip tomorrow—'

'We need you to get us out of here – fast!'

Lester eyed them suspiciously. 'No way! I got a living to earn.'

'Maybe good money, Lester,' said Freddy encouragingly.

There was a bright yellow flash and a sudden detonation.

Everybody ducked instinctively. Nicole felt the warmth of the flash against the back of her neck. 'What the fuck was that?' yelled Lester.

'Machine's broken,' said Freddy.

Light from the Osprey flickered against the side of Lester's hut. Small secondary explosions began to rock the aircraft as it burned fiercely from the demolition charges set by the crew.

'You can't leave that wreck here.'

'No choice,' said Nicole.

'Look,' Lester pleaded, 'I got a plane load of tourists tomorrow . . .'

Freddy pulled a gun from somewhere and shoved it hard into Lester's belly. Lester looked down in surprise. 'Hey! Go easy, man!'

The pilot of the Osprey pushed between them, eyes glowing in the light from the burning wreck. He was a big man. He looked first at Lester, then over at the shape of another aircraft standing in the shadows at the edge of the airstrip. He pointed. 'That your plane?'

Lester looked at him, eyes wide. 'Yeah! Why?'

The pilot pulled his pistol and pointed it at Lester's head. 'We want to borrow it, OK?'

Lester stood there, weighing up the situation, looking first at the pilot, then at Freddy. 'There's a charge. Cash. A hundred thousand dollars.'

Freddy spat heavily in disgust.

Lester studied the pilot, saw his steely mouth and tight jaw, and reviewed his request. 'Fifty?'

The pilot prodded his pistol against Lester's head. 'Cut the crap! It's either the plane, or I spray your brains out all over the grass and take it anyway.'

'OK! OK, you got the plane. Where to?'

'Teleformin,' said the pilot.

Lester's eyes widened. 'That's over the border! I haven't got the papers for that!'

Freddy was tucking his gun away. 'Hey, he run guns for the OPM, mister. He don't need any papers. He never use them.'

The pilot suddenly shifted his pistol and fired a round into the dirt at Lester's feet. The sharp detonation rang around the jungle clearing, making the animals shriek and squawk. Lester leaped back, the sweat on his brow like little beads of moonlight. 'OK! OK!' shouted Lester. 'I've got to think about this. How many of you?'

'Five – plus you.'

'Any kit?'

'No.'

Lester chewed at his bottom lip. 'It'll be tight. We'll have to burn off some gas to get over the mountains – won't leave us much in reserve.'

The pilot pointed to the flaming wreck of the Osprey. 'Listen to me, Ace! That thing's burning like a torch, and it's going to attract some real unhealthy attention. If you don't get us out of here in the next few minutes, you won't *have* a fucking aeroplane, OK?'

*

Nicole sat hunched on one of the thin bench seats that ran across the fuselage of the ancient Islander. The co-pilot from the Osprey sat in the seat just in front of her, then came the crewman, seated next to Freddy. The pilot sat right up in front, his big frame dominating the tubby figure of Lester.

Nicole was struggling to grasp what had happened. It had all been so quick. She was out of jail, out of Rahman's clutches, on her way home. She looked down at her grubby overalls, at the puffy purple and yellow bruising on her hand, and was amazed that her body could have kept going for so long.

Lester ran through his checks, started the engines and taxied the aircraft noisily onto the short grass strip that gleamed dull silver in the moonlight. He pushed the throttles up against the stops. The Lycoming piston engines coughed, then roared, making the whole cabin vibrate. Slowly the still-burning wreck of the Osprey slipped by to their left as they gathered speed, bumping and jolting over the ruts. The jolting stopped as the machine finally became airborne and began to climb noisily and slowly out over the ocean. The flaps came up with a harsh whine of servomotors. The blare of the exhaust and the rasping buzz of the two spinning propellers made shouting the only way to communicate.

The Osprey pilot pulled on a headset, and Nicole could see him punching numbers into the radio. He turned round, saw her gazing at him. 'I'm getting in touch with the AWACS,' he yelled. He began to speak into the microphone, in clipped sentences. Then he pulled the mike back from his mouth and twisted round in his seat. 'OK, listen up! We've got two aircraft outbound from Biak. One heading our way. Probably a MiG-29.'

The co-pilot shot him a look. 'Can't the F-14s deal with it?'

The pilot shook his head. 'Political!'

'This pile of rivets versus a MiG-29? We're canned meat!'

The pilot motioned him to be quiet and talked some more to the AWACS, his expression contorted as he strained to hear against the roar and vibration of the Islander while it struggled for altitude. He shifted in his seat and shouted across to Lester. 'Bandit! Thirty miles, eight o'clock high – you understand that?'

Lester turned, his eyes bulging. 'Hey! This wasn't part of the deal. I'm not doing this. I'm not losing my plane for anybody.'

'Get this thing on the deck, fast. I tell you what to do, you just do it! OK?'

Reluctantly, Lester pulled back on the throttles. Nicole felt her stomach lurch as the floor seemed to drop away beneath her. Soon she could see the twin wheels of the undercarriage skimming low over the ocean, the flash of the moon's reflection on the waves. Then a beach slipped by, followed by the dull gleam of moonlight on the metal roofs of a fishing village and the silvery pillows of forest canopy as they headed inland.

'Hey – what about flares?' yelled the crewman. 'We

probably got flares in here.' He twisted round in his seat and pointed past Nicole. 'Look behind you, check out that box.' She squirmed round in her seat and saw the green box fixed to the bulkhead. She dropped down its cover, found what the crewman wanted and passed across the heavy flare pistol, along with a plastic pouch of signal flares. The pilot saw what they were doing, rummaged around at the front and passed another pistol back from the cockpit. The crewman began to load a flare into each of the pistols.

'Never know,' he shouted at Nicole. 'Might work. See if you can get that door off. Knock the pins out. Use the axe in the escape kit.'

Nicole did as she was told. She pushed down on the handle and managed to shove the door open a tiny crack against the 150 m.p.h. blast outside. But the door was large, with a lot of windage, and she was weak. She had to put all her weight behind it to push it open just an inch. The slipstream roared past outside, sucking through the gap she'd just made.

The adrenalin was flowing through her now, masking the pain from her smashed hand. She started to bash away with the axe at the metal pins in the hinges. The door loosened, then suddenly the slipstream tugged it out of her hands and whirled it savagely away. She heard it crack against the tail fin. Lester spun round, his face full of anxiety, wondering what they were doing to his plane.

Now the steady roar of the engines bellowed in through the hole in the fuselage. Opposite her, the co-pilot had done the same thing to the door on the other side of the fuselage. He signalled to her to fasten her lap strap tighter to stop her from falling out when they manoeuvred.

The pilot was still listening intently to messages from the AWACS. 'Fox One!' he yelled.

'Missile coming in,' shouted the co-pilot to Nicole. 'Lean out and look for it!'

Do what? They wanted her to do what? She bent down as far as the seat belt would allow, doubling over to stare up into the night sky. Good God, he was right! She could see it! As clear as anything, like a white flare – a brilliant dot in the sky, growing by the second. 'I see it! I see it!' she yelled.

The co-pilot was out of his belt in an instant, staring out of the window. He quickly passed one of the loaded flare pistols to Nicole. 'When we turn, put a flare across its nose.'

She stared out at the onrushing glare, the aircraft's slipstream tugging violently at her hair and overalls. No time to think. 'Break now!' someone screamed. 'Hard left!' The Islander lurched over, almost standing on its wing tip, the engines roaring as they turned in towards the missile. Nicole grabbed at the doorway, felt the grip of the belt tighten around her waist. Christ, she'd lost the missile! Couldn't see it any more. She pointed the pistol out the door anyway, shut her eyes, and fired. The gun jerked back with the recoil. A flare smoked away into the night, then burst into a brilliant shiny red against the forest canopy. Something streaked past their tail and impacted below them with a violent yellow-orange explosion. Flames billowed out among the trees. The Islander bucked in the shock wave.

'Yoh! We did it!' yelled the co-pilot. 'We fucking did it! Scratch one missile!'

The Osprey pilot stayed calm, still listening intently to his headset. 'Bandit inbound.' He leaned over towards Lester and shouted. 'I want you down in the weeds, feller.' His finger jabbed towards the ground. 'As far as you dare.'

Lester strained forwards, working hard at the controls, jinking the Islander from side to side, throttles pushed hard up against the stops. Nicole grabbed at the seat back, jammed her other hand up against the doorway to stop herself sliding about and felt the pain from her injury shoot up her arm. There was no time to be frightened, no time to think. Sudden rapid hammer blows rang through the Islander, sparks zipping away in the slipstream as rounds slammed into the wing. Red tracer flashed past Nicole's open door. She heard the roar of the jet, caught a glimpse of its twin tail fins as it banked steeply away to the left, afterburner flames stabbing out into the darkness.

'Hold on!' yelled Lester from the front. 'Real tight!'

He racked the machine into a tight turn and swung sharply into a deep, narrow valley. Now silvery forest canopy flashed past the windows. He banked the Islander hard from side to side, keeping up with every twist and turn of the gorge. Hut roofs flashed by just below the wheels, a patch of paddy fields, then yet more forest. Nicole saw a pale grey cloud streaming back from the wing. 'We're losing fuel!' she shouted.

But the Osprey co-pilot was leaning out of his door on the other side, buffeted by the slipstream, and caught sight of a shadow against the moon. 'Bandit six o'clock!' he yelled.

'OK, do it!' the pilot screamed at Lester.

Lester heaved on the control column and stamped hard on the rudder pedal, slewing the Islander into a violent airborne skid. The slipstream drummed on the fuselage as the aircraft slowed violently. Nicole had to slam both hands hard up against the doorway to stop herself from being catapulted out, her waist straining painfully against the belt. She found herself looking down at the jungle rushing past below. The MiG flashed by. Lester straightened the plane.

'Jesus Christ!' muttered the co-pilot, face and knuckles white as he gripped the seats to either side. The MiG pulled up into a steep climb. The afterburners kicked in, twin jets of incandescent gas thrusting out the back.

Perhaps it was insufficient flying hours, or lack of training, or disorientation in the dark and unfamiliar valley – whatever, the pilot had no chance.

'Where's that fucker going?' yelled the crewman.

'Heaven!' yelled the pilot.

They watched the machine trying to claw its way slowly up the steep shadowy side wall of the valley. Watched the bright orange-blue flames of the afterburners lighting up the forest canopy. Watched them getting closer and closer to the ground ... A brilliant flash lit up the whole valley, and a dull orange-red fireball rolled briefly through the night sky.

'Scratch one MiG!' yelled Lester from the front, thumping the cockpit side with excitement. War-whoops filled the Islander. The Osprey pilot turned round, wide-eyed, then released his breath forcefully through pursed lips.

'So which way home, Ace?' asked the co-pilot.

Lester twisted in his seat. 'Over the border, so we can patch her up. Then – if the money's good – Cairns, in Queensland, my friend.'

And he laughed loudly, the laugh of a man who had just been scared out of his wits.

Chapter Forty-two –
the following morning:
Arguni Base

President Amir Rahman padded along the thick red carpet on the floor of the corridor, and felt sudden pain in his right calf muscle. A hot stabbing pain where a knot of tissue pressed hard against the sural nerve, it made him hobble slightly. A sign of age – a sign of stress, too, the doctors had said.

He worried about his health, and he felt alone. The United States was trying to steal his minerals, Hendra had betrayed him, his wife had betrayed him, and there was rioting daily in the streets of the capital. They were all against him. He must not lose his grip, not when so much had been achieved.

He reached the end of the corridor and pushed open the heavy wooden doors leading into his office. There were no windows there. There were no windows anywhere in the Presidential suite at Arguni; not six hundred feet below ground in a military command centre.

A steward quietly brought him coffee and poured it from a silver pot. Rahman watched the dark liquid swirling slowly around in the china cup, but found little in its spiralling patterns to inspire enthusiasm. He rubbed at his face, feeling the loose skin of his cheeks fold softly beneath his hands. Then he stared across the bare polished expanse of his desk at the monotony of the cream-coloured walls. Action was required – swift and decisive action to show who was on top.

He heard the quiet knock at the door. A young uniformed lieutenant came in and stood deferentially in front of him. 'Colonel Lukman to see you, sir.'

Rahman looked up, wondering why the man was still there. 'Well, go on!' he barked. 'Send him in!'

Rahman studied Lukman's face as he approached and noticed his eyes looking straight ahead when they normally slid around like a snake's. *My God, the fool wears his guilt like a cloak. Doesn't he realize that he can be read like a book?*

'Colonel Lukman,' he began steadily. 'I was very disappointed in your performance yesterday.'

Lukman's face remained a mask. 'Sir?'

'Explain to me, how did we come to lose the prisoners so easily?'

Lukman avoided his gaze. 'The Americans came in force, sir. They took us by surprise.'

'By surprise?' Rahman paused. He'd expected better than that. 'But I had such faith in you, Colonel Lukman. I gave you sole responsibility for the defence of this facility.'

Sweat began to bead on Lukman's forehead. 'But, sir,

with respect, we had no idea of the importance the Americans attached to these people – especially Tai-Chung.'

'You had no idea . . .?' Rahman was incredulous. 'But, Colonel Lukman, that wretched woman broke into our computer network. She even worked here; she had a detailed knowledge of so many parts of this complex. Of *course* she's important to the Americans.' He felt his chest tightening and paused, trying to calm himself. Then suddenly he snapped. 'This disaster should never have happened!' he shouted. 'You're incompetent, do you hear – utterly incompetent!'

He needed to stand. He got up from behind his desk and began to pace up and down, feeling the anger surge uncontrollably through his veins. 'My God, I'm forever held back, surrounded by halfwits. For God's sake, do I have to tell you everything? Do I have to do your thinking for you? Is there no one here with any brains?' His eyes bulged, bloodshot from lack of sleep. He leaned forward over the desk, looking straight into the other man's face. 'I think you deliberately let the Americans in, Colonel Lukman. I think you're in league with someone else . . .' Rahman stared directly into Lukman's eyes. 'My wife, perhaps?'

Lukman flinched slightly. His eyes flickered across to Rahman's and looked into them for a moment.

'No,' muttered Rahman, 'maybe you wouldn't have the guts for such treachery.'

'No, sir,' Lukman agreed, stumbling slightly over the words.

Rahman smiled thinly. 'But, then again, maybe you're just too frightened to tell me.'

Lukman's gaze was fixed on the wall again. 'Sir?'

'Now ... why would they want Tai-Chung?' muttered Rahman.

Silence filled the room. A telephone rang in the outer office.

'I think the Americans are planning to return, don't you?' he continued.

He stared at Lukman for a long time, looking for signs of submission. Not a muscle moved on the officer's face, not an eye twitched. And that was when Rahman decided what Lukman was. An opportunist. A worm wriggling his way up. Always in the right place at the right time – he'd even volunteered to be his personal assassin. Pieces were falling into place. He'd kept the disk; he'd plotted against Hendra. He'd masterminded Thameena's exile, had even suggested the thing in the first place.

My God, the man is dangerous.

Rahman let his hand drift down to a drawer hidden below the level of the desktop. He found its small brass handle and gently slid it open, feeling the wooden runners slide smoothly. 'Let me tell you about one of my new ideas, Hari,' said Rahman gently. 'It's my secret weapon, to keep the Americans at bay.'

He saw Lukman's eyes shift down to the desk.

Now! he thought. *Before the bastard guesses.*

His hand closed comfortably on the pistol grip, felt the weapon's weight, and lifted it.

'The price of failure, Colonel Lukman.' He drew out the pistol swiftly and levelled the long silenced barrel at Lukman's chest.

Lukman began to back away, trying to dodge out of the line of fire.

Rahman fired – a dull thud, the shock of the recoil punching up through his wrist. He fired again as Lukman's body began to fall.

Hatred seethed through Rahman. Years of frustration at the incompetence and disloyalty of the people around him came to the boil.

He fired again.

And again.

And again – until the squeezing of the trigger brought only an impotent click from the falling hammer.

Dimly, he realized that he'd emptied the clip – there were no more bullets. His ears rang and acrid fumes drifted around his office. He slowly lowered the pistol, placed it back in the drawer and slid the drawer gently shut. He slumped back in his chair, the dull sounds of the silenced shots still sounding in his ears.

Rahman watched as Lukman pulled himself up from the floor to stare at the cluster of little white craters that had been hammered into the wall. Watched as the colonel brushed off the flecks of paint and plaster dust that peppered his uniform. He could see the fear now stamped onto Lukman's face. Could see his trembling, the dark stain at his groin – and he laughed, cruelly. Laughed at the incongruous nature of this man now cowering before him, at how the power of a gun had reduced this self-important upstart to a shaking wreck. He laughed at the absurdity of it all – at the people around him, their scheming, their whispering.

Then he stopped laughing. He glared at Lukman instead and when he spoke his voice was thick with hate. 'I wipe shit like you off my shoes every day, Colonel Lukman.'

He reached down to press a buzzer beneath his desk, then began to pack his papers into his briefcase. 'Death is too good for you,' he muttered.

Then Rahman stood up and swung out of the room.

He had no intention of ever returning.

The sign on the big grey doors, which had wire-reinforced windows, read 'Maritime Engineering'. The guard saluted, and turned to punch in a security code. He held the door open to let Rahman through.

Through the door was a vast open space dominated by a huge pale grey water tank the height of a man's waist. A girder ran across the tank, supported by a track on either side. It could run at high speed along the full 300-foot length, and was used to tow scale models of boats to test their dynamics. Rahman felt secure here. This was where he'd once enjoyed scrutinizing, with Hendra, the test results for the *Ibn Battuta* and had had fun looking at the designs of high-performance submersibles.

He set off along the side of the tank towards a knot of white-coated technicians gathered at the far end. His leather shoes clicked on the concrete floor, and the men eyed him nervously as he approached.

A portly figure with thin black-rimmed glasses detached himself from the expectant huddle and came forward. 'Mr President, how kind of you to show such an interest. You're just in time to witness one of our tests.'

Rahman nodded to Dr Akimas. He didn't like this man, didn't like his patronizing attitude. He stood by the side of the tank and waited. Akimas fidgeted nervously, uncertain what to do next. 'Commence!' ordered Rahman.

Akimas walked over to his control station and pulled the microphone towards him. 'Stand by for test,' he said nervously. 'Test commencing in thirty seconds. All personnel to stand clear.' A raucous alarm started. Orange beacons in the ceiling flashed.

Rahman glanced towards the far end of the tank, where a great slab of material sloped down to a miniature cliff modelled across its full thirty-foot width. Numbered white contour lines had been painted on the surface. 'Firing in ten seconds – 10 . . . 9 . . . 8 . . .' Rahman took a pace back from the edge. '. . . 3 . . . 2 . . . 1!' There was a sharp bang. A shock jolted up through his feet and a column of water shot into the air, before collapsing back into the tank. Water sprayed onto the floor.

For a moment, nothing happened. Then a huge mass detached itself from the slope and slid smoothly into the water, pushing a great bow wave before it.

'Test over. Cameras off. Data recorders off. Pumps to standby.'

Rahman was disappointed. He'd expected something more spectacular.

Akimas came across, the harsh fluorescent lighting casting a sheen on the smooth skin of his podgy face. 'A number of tests have already been successful, sir. If you would like to come to my office . . .' He flapped his hands ineffectually.

Akimas's office was bare, functional, and unimaginative. Just a line of textbooks, journals and scientific papers shelved on one wall, a TV in the corner, the man's desk and a couple of chairs. As they sat down, the scientist picked up the telephone and punched two numbers. 'Would you run the test video, please?' He replaced the receiver and waited for a moment, staring nervously at Rahman. Then he thumbed the remote to activate the TV screen, but nothing had come through yet.

Akimas tried to fill in the silence. 'The small charge simulates an explosion at a depth of about 500 feet, sir. At the far end of the tank we've modelled an exact copy of a coastline, using a clay slope. The wave propagates . . . ah!' The TV screen had come to life. A white countdown clock clicked off the seconds. 'As you saw just now, sir, the shock wave lifts the material along a shear plane, which allows it to slide. It has to be big enough to displace a large amount of water, and, well . . . you will see for yourself, sir.'

The TV showed an overhead view of the model coastline at the other end of the tank. It included a miniature city: tiny yachts tied up in the marina, restaurants along the waterfront – complete with umbrellas – office blocks and luxury housing further inland.

At first the water was calm, glasslike. Then a wave arrived, a small one, washing gently up to the waterfront, making the yachts bob up and down. After a pause, a second wave, bigger than the first, flooding right in among the waterfront buildings before washing back down into the tank. Then the third wave, huge, breaking all along its crest in a welter of foam. It surged right across the model city and slammed against the end of the tank. Water cascaded everywhere. When the water eventually calmed, Rahman could see that most of the model buildings had either collapsed or been completely washed away. Some of the tiny yachts had sunk. Others had capsized, or were floating around in a bobbing sea of smashed material.

Akimas thumbed the remote and turned back to Rahman. 'Mr President, I see no reason why we can't initiate a successful strike with this weapon.'

Rahman nodded; he could see what Akimas meant. A vast wave running onshore at such high speed. Terrifying – quite unstoppable.

'How much power do these waves have?' he asked.

'Difficult to be certain. You see, only ten per cent of the energy from the shock wave is transferred. Real waves can't be modelled exactly in a tank because of the Reynolds number . . .'

'Power?' Rahman shouted. 'I just want to know how much power I have in my control.'

Akimas reached for his hand calculator. 'Ah, I see. Well,

a simple equation is wave energy proportional to the product of wavelength and wave height squared.' He glanced up at Rahman, saw the blank eyes staring back, and went quiet. He held the calculator in his left hand, pressing the number keys with his thumb, scribbling figures onto a notepad with his other hand. He raised his eyebrows. 'Hmm, approaching 40,000 times more energy than a ten-foot storm wave. It will probably run right into any low-lying coastal city . . .'

Rahman beamed and stood up. 'I want it ready in two weeks.'

'But we need more time. We haven't finished looking at all the parameters yet.'

'Stop the testing, get the team together. Time is no longer on our side.'

'But, sir, you wanted to keep this weapon secret, create a major slide off the continental slope . . . a surprise attack.'

'I've changed my mind. I'm not cowering before the United States any longer. They attacked first with a typhoon. Now I want them to know just what *we* can do. I want them to see the power of this country. Find somewhere, Akimas, somewhere to make a big landslide. I want them to see it; I want them to know what's coming. I want revenge!'

'There is a problem, sir . . .'

'I'm not here to discuss problems, just solutions.' Rahman began to make for the door.

'Sir, the wave will propagate right around the Pacific . . .'

'Akimas! This is war.'

'But,' faltered Akimas, 'tsunamis travel out in all directions . . .'

Rahman was already out through the door of Akimas's office, striding back along the side of the tank. His booming voice echoed around the cavernous room. 'Those who raise the sword shall die by the sword, Akimas. It is the will of Allah.'

Chapter Forty-three – the same day: Washington, D.C.

Nicole lay quietly in bed. She watched the warm sunlight pooling on the rich fabric of the carpet and gazed absent-mindedly at the tiny specks of dust spinning lazily in a column of light, each one a bright star against the sombre oatmeal colour of the far wall. A distant roar of traffic seeped in through the closed windows while, outside, a skein of white cloud edged slowly across a bright early-summer sky.

She shifted her position and felt the stiffness of the hospital bedclothes rub irritatingly against her skin.

She struggled with her orientation. Her gaze roved around the room, taking in the squareness of its dimensions, the iron bed in which she lay, the lack of personal effects and comforts.

High in one corner a dark glassy eye stared balefully down from a grey steel box.

She was under surveillance.

Nicole lay back and sighed. She flung one arm across her forehead to try to relieve the dull pain that now sat heavily across her brow. She lay like that for some time, eyes closed, letting herself sink into the silence of the room.

The door opened, the harsh squeak of its hinges chasing away fragments of a gathering dream. Nicole listened from behind deliberately closed lids and heard the soft sound of precise footsteps coming across the carpeted floor.

'Hello, Nicole.' It was a soft English voice, a familiar voice.

She looked up and registered how tall the man blocking out the light from the window was. His head was crowned with snow-white wavy hair, his face lined but well preserved; his mouth tight and thin-lipped. Stony eyes stared down at her, their expression one of superiority.

It was Simes.

She struggled to sit up.

'Oh, please!' he said, his voice calm, the vowels Oxford-round. 'Don't get up. Do tell me, how are you?'

A memory pushed itself forward urgently – a memory that involved Simes. The nightmare from a television screen. The film of a house, her house – her son. And then the pain . . . the excruciating pain . . .

'You betrayed me!' Her voice was sluggish, thick from sleep.

Simes arched his eyebrows. 'Betrayed you, Nicole?' he asked.

'My son, Simes,' she shot back. 'What have you done with him? Where is he?'

He paused for a moment, considering the question, his expression puzzled. 'Your son's safe, Nicole. I haven't betrayed you. He's in California – and doing very well, I believe.'

Nicole struggled to grasp the inconsistency of his words against the evidence.

'But the *Bakorstanas*, they showed me a film – of Peter, my house. They must have him. They must have my son . . .'

'No, Nicole!' Simes interrupted. 'Not at all. Believe me, he's safe, and always has been. He's not left that Institute once since you went away, I promise.'

Simes sounded genuine. Nicole allowed herself to feel cautiously relieved.

'I want to see him,' she demanded.

'You will, Nicole. You will, soon.'

A heavy jet thundered slowly overhead. The noise made the window glass buzz gently in its frame. Nicole waited for its roar to recede, still uncertain.

Simes picked up a chair and brought it across to her bedside. He sat down and crossed his legs, placing his hands neatly in his lap. He watched her carefully, as if studying some sort of interesting specimen.

'Where am I?' she demanded.

'In a military hospital,' he answered carefully.

'In America?'

'Washington. You were close to exhaustion.'

She pointed up at the metal box. 'Why am I under surveillance?'

'For your own protection.'

Nicole glanced down at her body. Saw the thinness of

her limbs, the bandages that swathed her hands tightly. She felt a soreness and stiffness in her fingers. After what she'd been through, surely she deserved better than this.

'Why hasn't anybody been to see me? Why haven't I been debriefed yet?'

'Because your contract's finished.' A gentle smile crossed his lips. 'You did a wonderful job, Nicole. You can go home now . . . back to your son.'

She wanted that. She wanted it very badly. But before she could go back to her earlier life there was something she had to tell Simes: something Rahman had said to her in the jail. She debated the necessity, worried that it might delay her return. But the nagging doubts about Rahman wouldn't go away.

'I've something to tell you. Something else you ought to know.'

She'd caught his full attention. His gaze was questioning. 'The Americans,' she queried, 'did they attack Indonesia while I was away?'

Simes gave her an odd look. 'What do you know about this?' he demanded.

'Rahman came to see me, in prison. He kept asking the same question, over and over again. Why did the Americans attack him? Why did they, Simes? I need to know, it could be important.'

Simes shifted uneasily in his chair. 'Rahman's accused the Americans of manipulating a typhoon, using it as a weapon and steering it across the Philippines. It's absolute nonsense, of course,' he said carefully.

Nicole stared into Simes's eyes – and registered something there. Was it concern? If so, was it for her? Or for what had happened?

'I think you know something more,' she responded.

Simes was tight-lipped, avoiding her gaze. 'I'd like to know what Rahman said to you.'

She hesitated. In the clinical atmosphere of a Washington hospital, her fears seemed ludicrous.

'He plans to retaliate. He's threatening to use something, something almost biblical – you know, an eye for an eye, a tooth for a tooth, that sort of thing.'

'Go on,' said Simes quietly.

'He calls it *Krakatau* . . .'

'A volcano!' Simes seemed faintly amused.

Nicole felt irritated.

'No, not a volcano – a tsunami wave.'

Simes looked at her, his face full of disbelief. He laughed. 'But that's preposterous. How could he ever manage such a thing?'

She sat up in bed. 'Like the Americans used a typhoon against him! Look, you hired me because of my expertise, my ability to pilot a submersible, because I was an oceanographer. You've seen my CV, you know about my PhD. I've done research into long-run-out landslides. They can generate huge tsunamis in the Pacific.' Simes was staring at her incredulously. 'He's going to do it, Simes. He's got some sort of weapon, and he's going to use it. I believe this country will be threatened by a tsunami attack.'

She paused, waiting for him to react.

Simes got up slowly from his chair and walked towards the window. Silhouetted against the May sky, his hands thrust deep into his pockets, his appearance mirrored an earlier meeting – a meeting in a prison cell.

'But how, Nicole?' he asked. 'How could he do such a thing?'

'A massive explosion on the continental slope,' she explained patiently, 'where the shallow floor of the continental shelf plunges down into the ocean proper. The whole slope's covered by a thick layer of sediment, a great slab of unstable mud. Some of it's just ready to slip three miles to the ocean floor. Such a huge slide would displace a vast amount of water, create a huge tsunami wave.' She detected his disbelief in the set of his body. 'It's quite possible, Simes. I know because I've studied the phenomenon. It's happened in the past – and it could happen again. The consequences would be terrifying.'

Simes was quiet for a moment. 'But how could such a thing threaten the United States?'

Nicole felt exasperated. 'You obviously don't appreciate the scale of this.' She was sitting bolt upright now, eager to get his attention. 'Take one of the small trench systems off the American West Coast. A huge slide there would trigger a tsunami capable of laying waste the neighbouring coastline without warning. It would be a vast wave, big enough to devastate whole cities: Los Angeles, San Francisco . . .' She paused suddenly, mention of the last city having pierced her with alarm, like a thrust from a dagger. She paled visibly. 'Oh my God! ... Peter, I want him out of there.'

Simes was stunned by her reaction. 'I'm sorry, Nicole . . .?'

'My son! For God's sake! The Institute, it's on the coast, isn't it?

'Gazos Creek? Yes, lovely place, right on the cliff top.'

'Then I want him out of there. He's in great danger.'

Simes looked at her oddly. 'You believe Rahman? You really think he will do this?'

'I don't *think*, Simes, I *know*! He's got the technology. And, with a big enough bomb, he could create a massive slide, causing a huge wave.'

Simes was clearly grappling with this concept. He'd come here to debrief Nicole, to look at satellite photographs, identify targets. Now he found himself talking about tsunami weapons and some sort of mad environmental war. 'Just a minute,' he stumbled. 'Let me try to understand this. You're telling me that you think Rahman is preparing to strike at the United States – with a tsunami?'

'Yes!' Nicole sounded close to the end of her tether. 'Look, the West Coast is in enormous danger. We've got to warn them, get the population out of there.'

Simes looked at her, uncertain of his position. 'Well, I suppose if you really think we should take this possibility seriously . . .'

But Nicole had swung her legs over the edge of the bed, energized by the urgency of the situation and by Simes's scepticism. 'This sort of madness is right up Rahman's street, and I'm not taking any chances. I want my son out of there, right now!' She felt giddy and had to grab at the bedside cupboard to support herself.

Simes came across from the window to take her arm, as if concerned for her safety. 'Hey, now steady on . . .'

'You've got to take me to the CIA,' she said. 'They'll know about this typhoon attack – they'll take me seriously. But we need to be quick, we've probably got less time than we think.' She was scrabbling for her clothes, yanking them down over her hospital shirt.

Simes towered over Nicole's slight figure. 'Just a minute, Nicole. We need more proof of this . . . this allegation.'

'Proof? We don't need proof, Simes. The proof is in my head. I understand the science, and I know what this man can do. I know what he's capable of. I was with him – remember?'

'Then let Rykhlin deal with this.'

Rykhlin!

It was as though electricity had shot through Nicole's body, jolting her memory. Suddenly she saw his face again, in vivid technicolour, alabaster against a spreading pool of dark vermilion . . .

'But Rykhlin's dead!' she blurted out.

Simes looked at her. 'Dead?' he queried. 'Of course he's not dead. He's very much alive. He came out behind you, on the second plane.'

This was too much. She didn't believe Simes, not after what she'd seen.

'But I told them he was dead. I told the loadmaster.'

Simes sighed. 'Well, he *is* alive, Nicole. Trust me.'

She wasn't ready for this. A turbulent surge of emotion cascaded over her, a confusion of thoughts tugged at her mind. *Rykhlin . . . alive?*

'I want to see him!'

'No, it's better if you stay here. Let *me* see Rykhlin. I'll tell the CIA about all this, explain the situation to them.'

'Why?' she demanded. 'Why should I stay behind?'

Simes looked at her, his eyes cold and grey.

'Because of this information that you have, about the Americans. It's extremely sensitive, and I think you should stay here . . . for your own safety.'

Nicole stared back at Simes, her expression hardening. 'No way, Simes. I know the situation better than anyone. This is my area of expertise. I go with you, OK?'

Chapter Forty-four – later that same day: CIA Headquarters, Langley

Nicole stepped briskly into the interview room. It was generously carpeted in a soft charcoal hue. One wall had been lined with leather-bound books in glass-fronted shelves, carefully separated by displays of corporate emblems and mementoes. The adjacent wall was simply white, punctuated by a rather plain round clock. There was a rectangular window at the far end of the room, metallically screened against electronic eavesdropping. It made the view of the pleasant wooded parkland outside take on a dark and sinister coppery tint.

Two flags had been draped either side of the window: the stars and stripes of the United States, and the eagle and shield of the Central Intelligence Agency.

A modern pale-oak conference table dominated the centre of the room. Simes sat down on one side of it.

Simes's hands fiddled incessantly, prodding at a red cardboard file, fidgeting with its corners, straightening it to make it lie parallel with the edge of the table.

Eventually a young woman appeared at the doorway,

smart in her grey jacket and skirt, a large plastic identity tag pinned to her lapel. 'Mr Rykhlin's here, sir. Would you like me to show him in?'

Simes's hands stopped flicking at a corner of the red file. He placed the dossier neatly in front of him him, then nodded.

The door swung open, and Rykhlin was standing there. Better groomed now, his beard neatly trimmed, eyes shining bright, and very much alive.

'Hi!'

Nicole stared at him, uncertain, then stood, hesitating to go forward. 'Rykhlin?'

'Sure is!' he said encouragingly, grinning broadly.

'But I saw you . . . in the prison. I thought you were . . .'

'Dead?' He chuckled. 'Yeah, damn nearly was.'

My God, she thought, *am I ready for this?*

'But why didn't you come to see me?' she asked. 'When I was in the hospital.'

Rykhlin shrugged. 'They thought it better that way.'

'Who did?'

'The CIA. Hell, you know the score. Clean break, no ties – that sort of thing.'

Rykhlin crossed the carpet to the conference table, looking smart in his city suit. 'Look, Nicole,' he said, 'there's something I need to tell you. This information you've brought back, it's raised the stakes. They want me to go out again, NOC. They want me to deal with Rahman.'

Nicole stared at him, this man who'd just come back from the dead, his brown eyes sparkling with intelligence.

She was confused, uncertain of her position. 'NOC?' she quavered.

'Non-Official Cover,' he explained as he sat down. 'Means I'm on my own, no diplomatic protection. You can guess the rest.'

Nicole was working hard, trying to keep up with him.

'I'd like you to come out with me,' he added.

'What?'

'I'd like you to come out with me,' he repeated. 'To Jakarta.'

'I can't!' she blurted out. 'I have to get back to my son . . .'

'But I asked specially for you,' interrupted Rykhlin. 'I'd hoped you'd say yes.'

'Look, I've done my job, Rykhlin. It's finished. I'm through with the Secret Service now.'

Rykhlin slowly shook his head. 'You're never through with the Service; it just doesn't happen that way.' He looked at her carefully, studying her eyes. 'They think you know something. Something about a typhoon, right?'

Nicole glanced across at Simes, wondering how far she could go. The older man nodded encouragement. She turned back to Rykhlin. 'Go on.'

'I don't think you stand a chance.' He sounded quite emphatic. 'You've got to come back with me.'

Nicole was startled. 'Why?' she demanded.

Rykhlin's deep-set eyes looked directly into hers, checking her out. 'Because if you don't, there's a possibility that you may never see your son again.'

An iron fist gripped Nicole's heart. 'What did you say?'

'This knowledge you have, it could bring down the administration. These people won't let that happen. They're dedicated to their jobs, they're ruthless.' Then he added quietly: 'You wouldn't even make it as far as California.'

A steel shaft slid into Nicole's guts.

God, she'd been such a fool. She hadn't thought about this. Hadn't even considered the implications of what she'd been blurting out to Simes.

'Is he safe?'

'Your son? For the moment, yes. Because he doesn't know anything. But if you go out and see him, Nicole, you'll contaminate him. You've got to leave him alone, give him a chance. Let him be evacuated like all the rest. Buy yourself some time by coming back to Indonesia.'

She sought guidance from Simes, but his face was turned away.

She turned back to Rykhlin. 'No, this isn't right!' she declared angrily. 'I didn't ask for any of this.'

'None of us asked for this,' Rykhlin said softly.

She hesitated. 'I don't know . . .'

'It's a deal, right?' he insisted. 'They want to get rid of you, but this way there's a chance you might get rid of yourself. It'll make it easier for them – just the way they like it, no mess. They'll buy it.'

Trapped! Snared! By a snake, a snake in a deadly game with no ladders.

Again she looked across at Simes, saw him sitting there,

quiet anxiety set into the lines of his face. She didn't know which way to turn. A moment ago she'd thought this whole nightmare was coming to an end, that Peter was only a breath away. Now suddenly they were telling her that she had to keep away from him. Worse, that she'd become a danger to him.

Simes glanced down at his watch. 'The DCI will be here in a minute,' he warned.

Rykhlin got up. 'Promise me that you'll do the right thing and come out to Jakarta – for your own sake.'

Nicole was confused, uncertain of what to do, her mind reeling from the flood of emotions boiling inside. Desperate to see Peter, yet desperate to keep him safe. 'I don't know,' she faltered. 'I just don't know what I'll do.'

The Director of Central Intelligence swept into the room. He was wearing a dark suit, an expensive striped silk tie and heavy-framed glasses. He eyed Rykhlin suspiciously and acknowledged Simes with a nod.

With him were two grey-suited figures, faceless men from deep within the organization. Large identification tags swung from their breast pockets.

They sat down at the pale-oak conference table, positioning themselves in a line opposite Simes and Nicole. Rykhlin sat quietly at the end. Greg Noble introduced his colleagues with a wave of his hand. 'This is Conrad Bolden, Deputy Director of Intelligence; and Leon Curtiss, from the Office of South-East Asian Analysis.'

Both men stared curiously at Nicole. It was as if she was the first real agent they'd ever seen.

Noble looked across the table at Nicole. 'We've been briefed, of course, Ms Tai-Chung, but we'd like some more detail. We're trying to see just what we're up against here.'

The room went quiet for a moment. Heads turned expectantly towards her. She hesitated for a moment, deciding on the best tactic, wondering how to find out just what the Americans knew.

'I was imprisoned by the Indonesians,' she began. 'Held at a place called Arguni for four weeks.'

She paused for a moment, trying to think it through carefully before she continued.

'While I was there, I was visited by President Rahman. I think it must have been just after Typhoon Anna struck the Philippines.' She said it pointedly, baiting them, waiting for their reaction.

But none came. Not even a flicker.

Noble's face remained as if cast in stone.

She pushed the point further. 'Rahman seemed to think that the United States controlled the storm and used it as a weapon.' Still nothing. 'He got very angry and excited about it. Some of the things he said referred to plans for his revenge.'

'What exactly did he say?' asked Noble quietly.

'He talked about something called *Krakatau*. I think it may be a code word, possibly for a military operation, or maybe a weapon.'

'An atomic bomb?' interrupted Bolden. 'Are you suggesting that his weapons programme is far more advanced than you first reported?'

'No, I don't think it's a bomb . . .' She paused, suddenly reluctant to pursue the point. In the coppery light of the tidy and well-organized interview room, the idea of a tsunami weapon now seemed rather absurd. 'I think Rahman may have something else up his sleeve,' she muttered.

'Go on,' prompted Noble.

'You have to understand the way that Rahman thinks. He's got it into his head that the United States used a geophysical weapon against the Philippines.' She looked around the room, holding their attention. 'I think that he'll try to retaliate in the same way, to prove that he can do it. The key word is "Krakatau". It's a volcano lying between the islands of Java and Sumatra. It last exploded in the nineteenth century, causing a huge loss of life. But the volcanic explosion wasn't the real killer – that was the huge tsunamis which followed.'

She paused again to let the idea sink in, listening to the ponderous tick of the clock on the wall as its mechanism measured out their silent heartbeats.

Noble shifted uneasily in his seat. 'So, the Tiger really does have claws,' he muttered quietly.

Nicole caught the words, and a deep chill ran through her body. So she *was* right. The Americans *had* done something with the typhoon.

'What are you suggesting?' demanded Bolden suddenly. 'That he's going to trigger some sort of tidal wave – against us?'

Nicole looked across the expanse of the table, straight into Bolden's eyes, and saw they were hard and glassy with incomprehension. 'Yes,' she said. 'That's precisely what I'm suggesting.'

Bolden leaned back, a smirk creasing his face.

Noble ignored him and glanced down the line of officials towards Curtiss. 'You're the regional analyst, Leon. What do you think? Is he really capable of this?'

Nicole looked curiously at Curtiss, wondering what his response would be. 'I've no idea what he's capable of, Greg,' said Curtiss, his jowls wobbling as he spoke. He paused, staring at Nicole through piggy eyes. 'Actually, Ms Tai-Chung, we think he's probably nuts!'

'Well, if he's nuts, Leon, that's a good enough recommendation for me,' retorted Noble.

Curtiss shifted heavily. 'Well, I really can't comment on the technology, Greg, but yeah, Rahman likes to boast about his science, and Tai-Chung was clearly a captive audience. He might have told her something about his plans – he probably didn't expect her to live long enough to tell the tale.'

'I was due to be shot the following day,' agreed Nicole quietly.

Bolden coughed. He seemed to be finding it all a bit melodramatic.

Noble turned to Nicole and Rykhlin. 'You two have been out to Arguni, you've seen his technology. Come on, convince me! Tell me that we aren't talking science fiction here. How do you think he could do this?'

'Because he has a limited nuclear capability,' answered Nicole, 'and his submersible technology is more advanced than anything I've ever seen.'

Bolden sniggered. 'Yeah! But that doesn't explain how he can trigger a tsunami.'

'It's not as difficult as you might think, Bolden!' answered Nicole irritably. 'All he needs is a big enough landslide into the Pacific.'

She saw the look of incredulity on Bolden's face. 'Look – I explained all this to Simes. I know what I'm talking about. I did my PhD on this – in Hawaii, on Big Island. A sudden displacement of a huge amount of water can create an enormous tidal wave – a tsunami. It's happened before. It's well documented.'

She looked at Simes for confirmation, but his face remained an impenetrable mask.

There was silence for a moment. The glow from the embers of the setting sun filtered in through the window, bathing the room in a dark and sinister twilight.

'Let's get this right,' said Noble. 'You're suggesting some sort of natural weapon, to decimate – what? Our West Coast cities – San Francisco, Los Angeles?'

Nicole flinched. The names hurt badly. 'Those cities are especially at risk,' she agreed.

'Christ! This is ridiculous!' interrupted Bolden. He was leaning back in his seat, jacket open, paunch ballooning above his trousers. 'Come on! Explain it to me. Explain how Rahman can do this – set off a landslide, I mean – in detail.'

'It's easier than you think,' insisted Nicole. She spoke

urgently now, anxious to minimize any delay. 'He would use a small fleet of submersibles, maybe with a submarine carrier, moving round the edge of the Pacific. If it were me, I would take the subs deep down into the ocean trenches, follow them right around the Pacific Ring, then work my way along the American West Coast. It would be very easy to escape detection. I'd drill holes in the seabed at the appropriate point and plant enough explosives – probably nuclear – to provide a big enough shock wave. Then I'd let nature do the rest.'

'But where do you suggest this would happen?' asked Noble. 'Where would you actually go to create such a big landslide?'

'On the continental rise,' said Nicole confidently. 'It's the point where the shallow waters of the continental shelf plunge down to the deep-ocean floor. The slope's covered in a thick layer of soft sediment. The stuff slides very easily. Often does just that after a major earthquake.'

'Yes, but exactly where would this happen?' persisted Noble. 'Geographically, I mean.'

'Just off the Californian coast,' said Nicole. 'It's ideal. It's got the right geology, with lots of sediment, and the tsunami would hit San Francisco and Los Angeles without warning. Look, you wouldn't even know that you were under attack. You'd put it down to a natural disaster, some sort of seismic activity along the fault lines.' She was fighting a vision – a vision of a vast wave, dark and flecked with foam, powerful, unstoppable.

There was silence in the room.

'And just how big do you reckon this wave would be?' asked Bolden, leaning forward.

'Not one wave, a number of them,' corrected Nicole. 'If the slide's big enough, the largest wave might easily reach – what? Something well over 120 feet when it hits the coast. You've got to get the size of this thing into your heads. It's a wall of water about the size of a ten-storey building, travelling at roughly 100 m.p.h.!'

'Jesus!' muttered Bolden.

'OK, let's get this straight,' insisted Noble. 'You're suggesting that Rahman has a geophysical weapon called *Krakatau*, and that he plans to hit the West Coast with it, at any time, without warning.'

'Yes, maybe.'

She had a picture in her mind. Her son being flung against the rocks like a rag doll, limbs broken. It was a picture that wouldn't go away.

Noble sat back in his chair. He suddenly seemed much older than his middle years. 'You know what's happening, don't you?' he said, looking around the room. 'We're commandeering the planet to fight our wars for us. Hell, we're inventing new science here.'

'And turning the cradle into a grave,' muttered Simes darkly.

Nicole watched the thin rays of the early-evening sun as they crept in through the copper-tinted window of the interview room. Simes's phrase echoed strangely in her head. It transported her back in time, stirring up something from the pool of her memory.

'OK, we're convinced!'

Nicole looked up to where Noble had been talking to Bolden and Curtiss. The DCI glanced across the conference table at Simes. 'Malcolm, what do you think?'

Simes looked up from where he sat next to Nicole. 'I was convinced all along. Tai-Chung and Rykhlin are both good operatives. You should listen to them.'

'Yeah.' Noble pondered the point. 'Well, they sure made a good team. Maybe they can handle it again.' He looked at Nicole. 'Rykhlin wants you on board for a go at Rahman. God knows why – you nearly got him killed last time. Still, you've got the right expertise; and you know this lunatic, and his country. We'd be glad to have you. You got any problems with that?'

She thought about what Rykhlin had said, about her son. About the chill wind of danger that now whispered around both of them. She'd been here before, with Simes in that private hospital ward. She swallowed the lump in her throat.

Noble had already turned to Bolden. 'Have the Navy monitor the ocean floor around Papua, will you? You never know, we just might spot those submersibles heading our way.'

Nicole spoke up. 'I want to see my son first!'

Noble looked stunned for a moment. 'I'm afraid that's out of the question.'

'It's the only way I'll do this.'

'There can be no contact between you and your son, Tai-Chung,' said Noble sharply. 'Not until all this is over. It would put your mission in jeopardy and both your lives at risk. You clear about that?'

Suddenly all the pent-up emotion and frustration of the last few weeks erupted inside Nicole. Rage exploded from her. 'Who do you think you are, deciding whether I can see my son or not!' she shouted.

Noble stared at her; he was granite-faced and mean-mouthed. 'You volunteered for this, Tai-Chung. You'll take orders like everybody else. Just remember, if it weren't for our payments, your son wouldn't even be here now ... getting teatment in an American clinic!'

Nicole leaped to her feet. 'Don't blackmail me, you bastard! You deliberately kept me separated from my family, knowing perfectly well that I had no choice. But I damn well have one now, and I'm sure as hell going to exercise it. You're not taking my son away from me this time. I'm going out to Jakarta when I choose, and only after I've seen him.'

Noble's face was livid with rage. 'You do that, Tai-Chung, you so much as leave this room without my permission, and I'll have your fucking ass! Is that clear?'

Nicole stared at him incredulously. 'What the hell's wrong with you, Noble? What's eating you? What makes you so frightened ... of a little boy?'

'Oh, grow up, Tai-Chung. You're way out of your league.'

Tension froze the room into silence. Nicole was gripping the table edge tight, glaring straight at Noble. Noble was quivering with rage, his face florid.

Rykhlin spoke quietly through the appalling silence: 'I don't think the DCI is frightened of your son, Nicole. I think he's just frightened of what you know.'

It was a reminder, and he said no more, just held his counsel.

Nicole listened to his calm voice, remembering their earlier conversation – and the icy hand that had gripped her body. She'd seen the fear in his eyes. It was the same fear that drove Noble's anger now. They were grappling with something beyond their comprehension, but she was only a bit player. If she didn't toe the line, Peter and herself would cease to exist, snuffed out like flies. She had to back down now, for both their sakes.

She slowly slipped back into her seat and said nothing more. Just glared at Noble with undisguised loathing.

Tapping his ball-pen against his pursed, thin lips, Noble stared back. He weighed up the situation with steely eyes, recognized Nicole's capitulation, nodded his long head just once and relaxed a little. 'OK, that's better. Leon, do we have somewhere safe to put these two until we need them? What about Steen's Barn? That's out in the wilderness.'

'Well, it's not in use at the present time,' answered Curtiss.

'Right, start making all the necessary arrangements. Get Tai-Chung and Rykhlin organized for some training.

There's already enough weaponry in Jakarta to stock an arsenal, so that's not going to be a problem.'

He paused.

'Just remember, Tai-Chung, this is a termination. There's no rescue mission.'

'God help you if you fail,' muttered Simes.

Nicole looked up sharply. 'No! God help my son if *we* fail.'

Chapter Forty-five – three weeks later: the Pacific Ocean

The USS *Cincinnati* hung motionless in the black depths of the Pacific Ocean, five miles above the bottom of the Marianas Trench. She was a Los Angeles-class nuclear attack submarine – a huge 360-foot-long fat metal cigar. Six thousand tons of killing machine – just sitting there, watching, waiting.

To either side of her, strung out in a cordon over a thousand miles long, lay other hunter-killers.

In the sonar room, six men listened to the sounds of the deep ocean, watching an image like luminous grains of sand drifting down their computer screens, each grain a blip of sound detected in the water.

Lieutenant Troutman stood among the operators, wondering how the hell he was supposed to spot a tiny submersible way down in the clutter of the trench. A brawny forearm with a unicorn tattoo suddenly moved forward to push a button on the console. 'Sonar contact, sir!'

Troutman eased out of his position and stood behind

the crewman. He looked over his shoulder at the display and saw the little blip of light, no bigger than a pinhead. It teased him, coming and going like a ghost, lacking the strength for a good contact. He doubted any good response from this piece of kit, knowing it was struggling to pick up anything sensible from such a depth. 'Probably just another squid,' he grumbled.

'No, sir,' replied the crewman. He screwed up his eyes, listening hard through his earphones. 'I think it's cavitation, sir.'

Cavitation – the sound a spinning propeller makes as the microscopic bubbles it generates implode in the water.

Troutman disconnected his own headset and plugged it into the operator's console. He listened hard, hearing the faint rustling echo from the far depths. Maybe it was familiar after all. Faster than usual, and very indistinct, but . . .

Just for a fleeting moment, the screen clarified.

Five strong blips, in loose line-astern, edging slowly through the trench. Then they were gone.

'Mark!' he ordered.

The crewman tapped at his keyboard. They waited while the computer analysed the pattern of sound. It came back with cavitation, but at a very low level of probability – and it couldn't identify the vessel.

'You going to inform the captain, sir?'

Troutman chewed at his fingernail and thought how to interpret his orders. A fleet of small vehicles, working their way along the trench. *Well*, he supposed, *that could be them*. He plugged his headset back into the comms channel.

'Captain? ... Sonar! ... We might have a possible contact.'

But he seriously doubted the accuracy of what he'd just seen.

Chapter Forty-six – Steens Mountain, Oregon

Nicole sat on the wooden bench, watching the rising sun paint the long granite wall of Steens Mountain a delicate shade of pink. The log cabin cast a long shadow in front of her, darkening the flat desolate wasteland of bunch grass and sagebrush. Her breath steamed vigorously into the chill morning air. In the distance, she could hear an approaching helicopter as its rotors beat a steady throb that reverberated against the mountain ridge. Looking hard, she could just make out a black dot crawling along the granite face. She watched as it swung in towards her.

Nicole sighed. Three weeks of tranquillity and happy isolation with Rykhlin were about to be shattered.

Rykhlin came to the door, his hands thrust into the pockets of his jeans. He glanced up at the approaching helicopter, then came over slowly and sat beside her.

'You OK?' he asked.

She nodded: 'Yeah.'

The sleek Bell 222 moved steadily in towards the cabin. It settled on a patch of bare earth with a clatter of noise, a hurricane of dust swirling out from beneath the spinning blades. Nicole got up and gripped the collar of her jacket, pulling it tight around her.

Blades still turning, the door of the helicopter opened. A tall man stepped out. He was dressed in a smart black overcoat, and held a city briefcase. His heavy glasses flashed briefly as they reflected the sunlight.

Noble.

He began to walk towards them. 'Good morning!' He beamed cheerfully. 'How's the R-and-R?'

'Coming to an end, I think,' replied Nicole stiffly.

'Funny! Thought you'd be tired of counting grass stems. Can we go inside? It's goddamned cold and noisy out here.'

It was dark in the front parlour of the cabin, and musty with damp. A gaslight hung from the ceiling, doing its best to lighten the gloom. A butane stove hissed gently in the corner. Noble warmed himself against the cherry red of the flames.

Rykhlin sat at the table, puffing hard to light one of his cigars. 'OK, Noble,' he said, 'we've already guessed this isn't a social call.'

The smoke from Rykhlin's cigar spun away in the thermal rising from the stove. Noble held his glasses in front of him, wiping condensation away with his handkerchief. 'You're right, I haven't come here for a chat. I've got news for you – Rahman's made his move.'

'What, *Krakatau!*' exclaimed Nicole.

'Maybe. We've had a possible on five subs – but the Navy can't say for certain. Anyway, *something* went through the Marianas Trench yesterday, heading north, and we're not taking the risk of ignoring it. We're assuming it's them.'

Nicole let a hiss of air escape through her pursed lips. 'So, this is it.'

'Maybe. I don't think we should take any chances, do you? Are you ready to go?'

'Looks like we'll have to be.'

'How long have we got?' asked Rykhlin, the cigar now shoved into a corner of his mouth.

'Providing they maintain their present speed and course, and stay skulking in the trenches – nine days.'

Nicole's heart lifted. That was good news; it gave them time to plan.

'So I want you in Jakarta within the next forty-eight hours.'

'What!' exclaimed Nicole. 'That doesn't give us any time for preparation.'

Noble put his briefcase on the table. 'Look, just forget everything you ever learned in Belize, will you. This isn't *The Day of the Jackal*. We just want you to squeeze the trigger – crude, fast and effective.'

Noble clicked open the briefcase and drew out a blue folder. 'Here's your brief, for what it's worth – and don't forget to destroy it before you go. Rahman's got a submarine launch coming up in a few days, a big occasion, in Kali Baru harbour. Your Papuan – what's he called? Freddy – OPM, isn't he? He's in Jakarta right now, and he's agreed to divert the motorcade. He's shipped in some weapons for you already. He's got the safe house all set up – here's the address.'

He passed over a folded sheet of paper and a street map.

'Remember, you're on your own. The United States has no knowledge of either you or your intentions. We get you to the airport, that's all. We've booked you both on a Garuda flight to Jakarta, separate seats. Jakarta's pretty chaotic right now, so you shouldn't have any trouble sorting yourselves out when you get there.'

He paused, the dull red light from the butane heater highlighting the creviced features of his long face. 'Any questions?'

Nicole looked at Rykhlin, then shook her head.

'Right, well, it's all pretty straightforward. Chopper comes in at 06.30 tomorrow morning. Be ready.'

Noble clicked his briefcase shut and made for the door. Then he turned, his hand resting on the latch. 'Oh, and don't forget: leave the key under the mat.'

He gave them both a sickly grin, and left.

Nicole found it difficult to sleep that night. Her room was cold, and dampness wafted against her face every time the wind pushed at the ill-fitting panes. There were no curtains, and a bright moon cast its silent black velvet shadows across the walls and ceiling.

She wanted to be with Rykhlin.

Returning to Jakarta worried her, brought back too many recent memories. She felt fragile and vulnerable.

SLIDE

She slipped gently out of bed, the moonlight silhouetting the soft curves of her body as she slid into her shirt, buttoning up the front. She wrapped the thin duvet around her against the chill and crept from the room.

When she pushed open Rykhlin's door, she could hear his steady breathing. She padded across the timber floor and eased herself in beside him. His skin was smooth, his muscles firm and well formed.

As he turned over, his eyes were open, deep and black in the soft moonlit room.

The warmth of his body was exciting.

Afterwards Rykhlin snuggled up behind Nicole, his body fitting close to hers, one arm wrapped around her. She felt the pain and the tension of the last few weeks sloughing away and a peace she hadn't known for a long time descending like drifting snow.

They talked long into the night, sharing their pasts, talking cautiously about the future, their fear of the nightmare to come that was Jakarta. And Nicole's desperate need to bring her son safely home again.

Part Six:
WHEN KORINCHI
STALK THE NIGHT!

Catching Cold in Aceh

Time magazine: June 24

Banda Aceh lies at the northernmost tip of Sumatra, over a thousand miles from the heaving mass of Jakarta. It is here that Arab traders first introduced Islam into the region, and it is here that Islam is most enthusiastically practised in Indonesia.

President Sultan Amir Asad Rahman II of the Great Islamic Republic of Indonesia was also born here – in a shack, part of the squalid slums that once surrounded the Great Mosque. When he first came to power, the town proudly marked the spot with a statue and a brass plaque. But when I visited the place today, the statue had been daubed with paint, and the plaque graffitied with political slogans.

The feeling in Banda Aceh, especially amongst strict Muslims, is that Rahman has failed them. The talk in the mosques and on the streets is of growing economic and political chaos. The 'disappearance' of vast numbers of Chinese has led to the near-collapse of the Indonesian banking system. Industry is forced to struggle on in a climate of inflation and corruption. Unemployment is spiralling out of control. Essential services such as schools and hospitals are near to breaking point. Smog blankets the big cities, rising sea levels have flooded many low-lying areas, and droughts ravage the eastern islands. Food has become scarce and expensive, almost beyond the reach of the poor.

Yet, with the country on the verge of environmental and economic bankruptcy, spending on defence has risen to new and idiotic heights. Why? Rahman appears aloof to the plight of his people. He holds spectacular political rallies. He talks of a golden future for Indonesia, promises his people a New Age of Islamic Technology. But right now, for most of the population, such promises are seen for what they really are – hollow. Having once thought of him as a saviour, Rahman's people are beginning to turn on him.

Attention has increasingly focused on his wife, Thameena. For many ordinary Indonesians, Thameena has become something of a folk hero, and a rallying point for opposition. Mysteriously plucked from exile by the OPM a few weeks ago, possibly with help from the Americans, the bush telegraph is alive with talk of her imminent return. Dissident Islamic groups are preparing for the time when Rahman will be overthrown, and many would like to see Thameena in his place. They are looking for stability and unity in a country struggling under the chaos induced first by Kartini and then by Rahman, and they believe that Thameena's brand of religious honesty and true Islamic values might provide it.

Chapter Forty-seven –
Tuesday, 25 June

6.00 a.m., Jakarta

Nicole watched the bloated red disc of the sun struggling to lift itself above the jumbled roofs of the *kampung*. A thin veil of smog stained the sky, bathing the crowded slum in a thick and ominous light. In the distance, the chanting wail of a muezzin rose and fell, calling the faithful to prayer.

She turned back from the dirt-streaked window and felt lack of sleep sandpapering her eyes. The room behind was dark, lit only by the feeble coppery glow of morning. Large boxes of illegal American imports were piled high to the ceiling. Some had been torn open, the bubble-wrap frothing out to display their contents. A filthy mattress had been pushed up against one wall. A putrid smell from the stagnant canal opposite hung ripening in the morning air.

Nicole looked across at Rykhlin as he lay propped among some boxes, eyes closed wearily against the early dawn. They were a team now, an item, drawing strength from each other.

'Freddy should have got here by now,' she fretted.

Rykhlin's eyes remained closed. 'Give him time,' he grunted.

She turned back to stare out of the window.

Through streaks of grime, she observed the street running arrow-like beside the canal, watching an old and weary *becak* driver thread his way along the same road, legs pumping slowly at the pedals of his three-wheeled pedicab.

She waited, chewing nervously at her lower lip, listening to the distant background roar of traffic as it surged into central Jakarta.

6.10 a.m.

President Rahman lifted himself to his feet, gathered up his prayer mat and beads, and stared moodily through the gently swaying net curtains of the Palace window. The flesh on his face had sagged badly, and now hung in soft folds from his cheeks. His eyes were bloodshot and sore from lack of sleep.

He stared angrily at the red globe of the rising sun. There was a growing weakness in his government, their steps were faltering. Fools! – they couldn't stop now, not when so much had already been achieved.

There came the familiar squeak of the study door as it opened behind him. 'Your car will be ready within the half-hour, sir.'

He turned, and saw standing there a blue-turbaned

Palace official, old and wrinkled. Rahman struggled to bring his thoughts into perspective.

'You said you were having breakfast at the Defence Ministry, sir?' ventured the official.

'Yes, yes, of course,' snapped Rahman.

He gazed back out of the window and felt anticipation lift the stony weight that had settled in his gut. He was meant to be looking forward to today: the day chosen to launch his new 'Weapon of Justice' and reveal it to the world for the first time.

'Weapon of Justice' – such an appropriate name. It made his chest swell with pride.

This was power.

Real power.

The power that Rahman had always wanted for his beloved country.

But what would the weak fools who hung around him know of that?

6.20 a.m.

Nicole saw the little red *bajaj* careering down the narrow street towards the safe house, a blue smoke-haze following its progress. The frantically driven three-wheeled scooter-cab lurched to a halt below her vantage point, and the acrid smell of its two-stroke put-put engine came drifting in through the window.

The door banged below and footsteps hurried up the bare wooden staircase. Her heart began to beat strongly and she looked across at Rykhlin. He too was sitting upright now, eyes alert, waiting.

The door opened. She saw the familiar face: frizzy hair, bamboo-studded nose, a broad grin, one filed tooth shining in the gloom. 'Hi! Big day, Missy, eh?'

He dumped his tatty sports bag heavily on the floor and looked around the room. 'Hey, Mr Rykhlin!' Freddy reached into the back pocket of his scruffy jeans and brought out a tightly folded scrap of paper, and handed it to him. 'Department of Defence, Room 061.'

Nicole watched as Rykhlin unfolded the sheet. It was another one of Freddy's meticulously drawn plans, showing the layout of a building.

One room had been clearly marked 'Operations'.

'What's that, Freddy?' she asked, pointing to it.

'Control *Krakatau* from there,' answered Freddy. 'It's Ministry of Defence building – Merdeka Square, near RRI building.'

He reached down into his bag and slid out an impressive sub-machine gun: a Heckler and Koch MP5A1. It gleamed in the half-light, dull black and precision engineered. He pulled out the stock, locked it in position, pushed in a magazine until it clicked home and checked the safety. Then he grinned at them again, before crossing to the window and peering out through the grime.

Nicole watched him standing there, gun in hand, silhouetted against the orange glow of the polluted sky. This was a different Freddy, no longer the semi-literate warrior from the rainforest; this was Freddy the Freedom Fighter – confident and in control. She should have guessed, of course, back at Arguni, and on their escape plane. Should also have realized, when she found that missile fin in his hut, that he was a capable warrior – and clever, in a cunning sort of way.

'We need to be briefed, Freddy,' warned Rykhlin, refolding the piece of paper. 'We need to know what you've got planned for us.'

Freddy turned back towards them, put down his weapon and squatted on the floor in order to spread a dog-eared street map across the dirt.

Rykhlin and Nicole gathered round to see.

'Rahman will attend submarine launch at eleven this morning,' Freddy explained. He checked his watch. 'In four hours, right?' He held up four fingers. 'Convoy will drive down from Palace to Ministry of Defence. They'll come up the toll motorway from the south, along the Subroto, then straight into Merdeka Square.' His fingers stabbed at the key points. 'While he's in the building, convoy gets armoured up, OK?' He looked at them both, checking for comprehension.

Rykhlin nodded, stroking his beard thoughtfully as he stared at the map.

'Now, his route to submarine launch, look!' Freddy's finger stabbed again. 'First big road junction, at the Post Office – blocked. Collapsed sewer.'

'So what's his alternative route?' asked Nicole.

Freddy looked at her, frowning. 'No, Missy, he doesn't know about this block. We do it – will happen this morning. That means he has to come through here.' His arm swung expansively towards the window. 'Narrow road, canal, *kampung*, all squashed in – easy target. No chance!' He grinned broadly.

'Yeah! That's good, Freddy,' said Rykhlin.

Nicole could see it too. Freddy had chosen his killing ground well.

'Motorcade heavily armoured,' said Freddy. 'Armoured car in front, then armoured limousine, two cars of *Bakorstanas*, and a troop carrier.'

'That's a lot of stuff. Are you sure we can handle it?' asked Nicole.

'Chopper, too,' said Freddy enthusiastically. 'Gunship flying overhead.' Freddy ran the palm of his hand across the floor, made the right sounds like a little boy. Nicole caught the look on Rykhlin's face, and guessed what he was thinking.

'Don't worry,' said Freddy. 'We got lots of stuff, too – you see.'

He folded up the map and held it out to Rykhlin. 'You getaway driver, OK? You been trained. When we finish, you get us to Merdeka Square. Black Toyota, big four-by-four, parked on the road.' He groped around in his back pocket and tossed something over to him. 'Keys! You need handgun, too.'

Freddy rummaged around in his bag and produced a neat Glock-17 and a box of ammunition. 'This one good, easy to use, very fast.' He demonstrated, making the right noises again.

'I'll need an MP5, too,' said Rykhlin, pointing at Freddy's gun. 'Things'll get pretty hot around here.'

'Sure, no problem.'

Nicole watched as Rykhlin took the pistol, weighed it expertly in his hands and bent down to pull a plastic ammunition tray out of the box, inspecting the neat rows of 9mm ACP rounds. He seemed impressed. Then he thumbed the empty magazine out of the butt and started to load it, round by round – carefully and methodically.

7.00 a.m.

Rahman hunched down inside the luxury of his big air-conditioned limousine as it swept through the gentle curves leading out of the mountains. He gazed at the black ribbon of motorway unwinding beneath the long white bonnet, the national flag fluttering wildly in the slipstream; and at the police outriders, white helmets gleaming in the morning sunshine, their wailing sirens cutting through the dense traffic.

He reached down to the richly carpeted floor and hooked a black leather briefcase up onto his knees. He operated the robust combination and sprang the locks. Opening the lid, he drew out a fat maroon-bound file. His fingers caressed the heavily embossed gold title: *Krakatau*.

He slowly opened the cover and read the first page:

'One of the most innovative military strikes the world has ever seen.' He liked that.

He gazed out of the window and watched the lush green vegetation of the rice paddies flashing past. The Americans might think they were clever, being able to steer a typhoon towards him, but *Krakatau* was a better weapon. It wouldn't be long now before they'd realize just who they were dealing with. *Krakatau* would make Indonesia a major player in the Pacific – and after that no one would dare to resist them. And, with the source of *Indera* finally in their grasp, his country would be on the path to rapid growth. They would become the richest and most powerful nation in the world, and he would be like an oil sheikh – how often he'd dreamed of that.

7.30 a.m.

The door to the upper room crashed open. A Chinese man dressed in a tatty running vest and dirty slacks carried in a large rectangular plywood box and thumped it down close to Nicole's feet. He had a faded black Mercedes hat pulled down over his gaunt face. He began to lever off the lid with a large screwdriver, the wood squeaking in protest before the plywood finally snapped and clattered to the floor.

Nicole gazed inside the box and saw a squat three-foot-long dark green tube; trigger and sights scabbed onto the sides.

Freddy heaved in a second box and dropped it loudly next to the first.

'LAW80,' explained Freddy. 'Anti-tank. One shot – bang! – throw it away.'

'Where the hell did you get that?' demanded Rykhlin.

Freddy looked up: 'Hey, no say – you know that.' He grinned enthusiastically. 'You ever use one of these, Mr Rykhlin?'

'Sure!'

'What about you, Missy?'

Nicole bent down and ran her hands gently along the smooth outer tube, trying to recall her training in Belize. 'If I remember rightly – remove the end caps, pull out the extension, and lock it into position. That flicks up the sight. Then simply pull the trigger, OK?'

'No, Missy! Select "arm" first, before fire. This lever here.' Freddy bent down to show her. Nicole felt her training click in. Felt again the confidence and certainty she had in her mission.

She shot Rykhlin a glance. 'Let me do this, OK?'

Rykhlin looked at her carefully. 'If that's what you want. Who'll fire the other weapon?'

Freddy jerked his thumb at the Chinese man. 'Him – evil bastard. He'll take out the armoured car, stop the motorcade.' He turned to Nicole. 'Then you shoot Rahman, OK?'

'Sure!' she said, and stared confidently at Rykhlin, daring him to disagree.

8.00 a.m.

Rahman looked up at the large gilt-edged clock that hung splendidly on the wall of the imposing dining hall and watched the minute hand flick to the upright position. He dabbed at his mouth with a napkin and rose carefully from his seat. A white-coated steward bustled over with a short wooden lectern and moved aside the breakfast things so that it would fit in front of the President.

Rahman looked down at his notes: just a few key words on cards. He knew exactly what he was going to say.

He gazed commandingly down the long table at the assembled military personnel, watched their eyes all swivel in his direction and listened to the quiet buzz of their conversation dying away. The stewards stood to one side as the room hushed.

'Gentlemen,' he began, 'today sees the launch of the Navy's first attack submarine, a submarine that has been wholly designed and built in Indonesia. A great first for our country.' He paused impressively. 'But, in less than twenty-four hours, even this occasion will be eclipsed by the most important event in the whole history of our great nation.' He saw their eyes narrowing, questioning, wondering.

'Before the morning sun next rises above the horizon, Indonesia will have demonstrated to the world the supreme strength of her growing technological might.' Rahman glanced around the room and saw the faces staring up at him.

'We now have in our possession,' he continued, 'a weapon that will put fear into the hearts of all those who seek to dominate us; fear into the souls of all those who seek to steal the fruits of the ocean so carefully won by our great scientists. A weapon, gentlemen, that will make us not only a strong power but a *world* power.' Stares were fixed on him, all around the table, quiet stares – wondering, glinting.

'I know that times have been difficult and that nature has not been kind to us. The environment continues to deteriorate, and great sacrifices have had to be made at home. But now, at last, our time has come. Soon America will face her nemesis.' He felt a tightening in his throat as he reached down and brought up the maroon-covered folder with the gold-block printing.

'This morning, on the historic day we launch our first nuclear-armed attack submarine, I would like to present to you – *Krakatau*!'

8.20 a.m.

Nicole kneeled among the junk piled up by the window. She hefted the LAW80 and felt eight and a half kilos of rocket launcher press down on her shoulder. She looked through the sight and found that she had a commanding view of the street. She aimed at a corner in the far distance, then swung the weapon expertly round to follow the line of the road as it passed below her. She saw how the parked vehicles narrowed it to just one carriageway and then she studied the low wall with the green and stagnant canal beyond.

Her heart thumped heavily in her chest. There was still a stiffness in her right hand, and she flexed her fingers, feeling her palms slick with sweat from the growing heat of the day. It was a perfect ambush. They couldn't fail.

Nicole was suddenly startled by the hollow sound of empty boxes clattering to the floor. She swung round and saw a little Chinese girl standing in the doorway, no more than six or seven years old, slum-dressed, her face smeared with dirt, a grubby naked plastic doll hanging from her hand. Two dark little eyes stared back at her, widening as the girl's gaze ran along the full length of the rocket launcher.

The Chinese man also turned at the sound. 'Mei-Lin!' he shouted. The child turned and fled down the wooden staircase, followed by a scattering of paws as a tatty mongrel followed her across the rubble-strewn floor, its tail curled low between its legs.

Nicole rounded on him in astonishment. 'You know her! Who is she?'

He looked back, eyes dull and staring from sockets deep with exhaustion. 'My daughter,' he explained.

'Then get her away from here!' ordered Rykhlin urgently. 'It's too dangerous!'

The Chinese man shook his head. 'Where I go, she goes.'

'But she could be killed!' exclaimed Nicole.

He gazed stonily back at her, the look of a man grown weary with explanation. 'Rahman took everything I had, lady. Where do you suggest she goes?'

9.00 a.m.

Rahman strode out of the Ministry building, resplendent in his uniform of Commander-in-Chief, medal ribbons bright in the strong sunlight now pouring down onto the palm-studded expanse of Merdeka Square. Bodyguards swarmed around him, machine guns at the ready, scrutinizing the crowd, peering up at nearby windows.

The traffic had been stopped and Rahman's motorcade stood ready: first an armoured car rumbling gently to itself, then the President's white limousine, door swung open to receive him, and behind that the black cars of the *Bakorstanas*, freshly polished and gleaming. A helicopter thumped and whined somewhere overhead.

Rahman acknowledged the salutes of his generals and then progressed unhurriedly towards his car.

9.01 a.m.

Freddy dropped the mobile phone. 'OK! He's leaving the square. Six minutes!'

He made a grab for his own sub-machine gun, tossing the second one towards Rykhlin. Rykhlin caught the weapon out of the air, checked it and reached down into the ammo box to pick up two thirty-round magazines.

Nicole watched Rykhlin as he took up an aiming position. She felt confident, knowing that he was there. They would look after each other, slip through the coming dangers together.

She checked out the Chinese man and saw him poised in the adjacent window, the launcher on his shoulder, his black Mercedes hat pulled close down over his eyes to shade out the morning sun. Then she turned her attention back to the street, knowing that out there were other fighters hidden in the jungle maze of the *kampung*, waiting.

On the road, nothing moved.

The trap was set.

In the quiet of the moment, she pulled a small plastic tube from her pocket, fingered out some yellow foam plugs, and stuffed them into her ears. She re-shouldered the launcher and aimed it carefully at the street corner.

Her fingers felt for the lever, pushed it down to 'arm', and then rested lightly on the trigger.

She waited, listening to her own heartbeats echoing heavily inside her sound-deadened cocoon. She felt an itch of sweat running down between her shoulder blades. She breathed steadily in the cloying heat of the stifling room, muscles taut with anticipation.

Down on the street, a solitary dog trotted out and began to sniff at the bags of rubbish. A grubby little child ran after it and went down into a crouch, holding out an arm to beckon it back.

Nicole saw the movement, saw the possibility of unfolding tragedy. Saw an echo of her son, of the little children Rykhlin had left behind on the road to Pristina. Was this the way it was going to be, then? A life for a life?

She swallowed hard, her throat raw with anxiety.

9.05 a.m.

Rahman was startled by the limousine's sudden swerve. He looked up and saw traffic cones blocking the road, a jumble of construction vehicles. Why hadn't he been warned about this?

The armoured car in front kicked up some dust as it turned off the main highway and barrelled into a long, narrow side street. He saw the long white bonnet of his own limousine obediently following and, glancing behind, saw the black cars of the *Bakorstanas* coming round too, like the coaches of a train.

He turned to face the front again . . .

Good God! They were inside the *kampung*, among the stink of the poor. What were the fools doing? He plucked nervously at the tightness of his collar and felt his body begin to sweat despite the air-conditioning. He reached quickly for his car phone as fear gripped tight at his belly.

9.06 a.m.

Nicole saw the helicopter, like a predatory insect against the smoke-tinted sky, saw it bank sharply as it shadowed Rahman's convoy, rotor blades smacking the sultry air. She could see the sinister barrel of its chain gun swinging threateningly below the 'chin' of the cockpit.

Then the armoured car lurched into view. Swirls of dust boiled up against the grubby white walls of the cramped houses alongside. She could hear the roar of its engine, the whine of its tyres.

Down below, the little girl still crouched in the street, staring impassively at the approaching convoy.

The Chinese man shifted his position. Nicole was instantly alert: had he seen his daughter? Would he break cover for her? A black shadow seemed to spread across the tarmac. In her mind she saw again a dark canal among reeds, the bloated bodies of children floating high in the water . . .

She blinked the vision away. *Forget it. Forget the past. Think about Peter – this is for him, this is his future.*

The convoy thundered towards her, dust and debris billowing up behind the speeding wheels. The helicopter chopped down low over the canal. The little girl stood up, drawn by the spectacle of the approaching convoy.

Nicole glanced across at the Chinese man, saw his attention riveted on the oncoming target, staring down his launcher at the lead vehicle.

Forget the girl. She had to forget the little girl.

She had to concentrate and watch them coming. Watch them grow large in her sights.

A thin line of smoke streaked out from one of the houses and curved tightly across the brown haze of the Jakartan skyline. She followed it with her eyes. Too soon! Too soon for a missile's sensor to lock on to the heat of the chopper's well-shielded exhaust. She watched, fascinated, waiting to see if the helicopter would erupt in a searing explosion. The missile screamed straight past its tail and angled steeply away – impotent, useless.

The little girl was running now, running back towards the shelter of the house.

The Chinese man fired! The hot blast of the ignited propellant slammed against Nicole's face. A sudden dull roar made its way through her earplugs. Dust swirled, fumes swept into her nostrils. Then the man was swinging round, yelling in fury, chucking the spent launcher to the floor.

The rocket detonated against the front of the armoured car with a bright orange flash. The vehicle seemed to stagger, then veered right, ploughing into a nearby house. Bricks cascaded across its front as black smoke boiled out of the driver's hatch and small flames licked around the turret ring.

The Chinese man was thundering down the stairs, yelling for his daughter, yelling in despair for all that he had left in the world.

Rahman felt the thud of the explosion and was thrown forwards as his driver hit the brakes. He grabbed at the seat, looked up – and was amazed at the way the armoured car in front seemed to *swell* as white-hot metal sprayed into the hull, igniting the ammunition, incinerating the crew. Smoke erupted from every vent. Debris scattered across the road.

'Go through! Go through!' he screamed at his driver.

He reached for his side arm and drew the weapon from its leather holster. His knuckles whitened as he gripped the seat in front of him. His teeth were bared in fear and his neck muscles bulged; his eyes were round with shock. The limousine surged forward and began to lurch across the wreckage.

Black smoke billowed down, smothering the windscreen.

Nicole caught a flash of white coming through the smoke.

Rahman's car!

She *felt* the evil now. Felt it crawling through the veins in her body. She lowered the sights over the target and felt the hard strip of the trigger beneath her finger as the car accelerated out of the smoke, coming towards her at high speed.

Wait! Let him come.

Let him get really close.

Giant hammer blows slammed into the wall just above her head. Dust and debris cascaded from the floor above, shards of tile and brick scythed through the air. She flicked her gaze upwards and saw the helicopter, hovering over the canal now, sparks erupting from the chain gun as it hosed hundreds of rounds into the house that she was inside.

Someone was shouting at her, 'The car! Get the car!'

Her gaze flicked down again. *Concentrate! Don't be distracted.*

Line up the target. Be certain.

Wait until it's almost beneath the house.

My God! She could see him now. She could see Rahman sitting in the back. Leaning forward, medal ribbons gleaming, looking up at her. She could see him! She could see his fear.

Her skin crawled. The bastard knew!

She could see right into his eyes, and he knew.

NOW!

The missile leaped from the launcher.

There was a blinding flash as the motor ignited. A wave of heat and orange flame blossomed like a lethal flower over Rahman's car. The limousine reared up, twisting in the air, its roof peeling off and spinning away into the canal. The vehicle became a hurtling tangle of black and white wreckage; oily smoke boiling up as it crashed back to the ground. Black limousines slewed to a halt behind it.

Swarms of people came running out of the adjoining houses, sub-machine guns blazing, firing into the burning wreckage, hosing it down, magazine after magazine. Others surrounded the black cars, filling them full of bullets too. Glass crazed and shattered, sugaring the road like snow; rubber window seals coiled out like snakes.

The gunship hovered over the canal, chain gun silent now, unable to fire in the confusion between friend and foe.

Then the personnel carrier was spewing out troops who started firing at the terrorists. People began to fall awkwardly, arms and legs jerking.

9.07 a.m.

Someone was bellowing at Nicole and tugging at her shoulder. Nicole pulled out her earplugs, let the roar of the battle fill her ears. 'Drop the weapon! Get out! Get out!' She was yanked back into the middle of the room by Freddy; saw Rykhlin in the corner, grinning at her triumph. He was loving every minute, loving her, revelling in the excitement. He let out a war whoop of triumph.

'Right!' he yelled. 'Let's go!'

She sensed they were in real danger now. She threw the empty rocket tube to the floor, then picked up the Chinese man's discarded sub-machine gun, pushed in the stock, checked the magazine and twisted the safety.

'Come on!' yelled Rykhlin from the top of the stairway. 'Merdeka Square! We can do it!'

They stumbled, half running, down the stairs behind Freddy – and came up against a body in the doorway; its feet twisted, blood running from the sliced-open head that was now a mess of torn tissue and bone, exposing the pale rubbery flesh of the brain beneath. She put out a hand to stop their headlong rush. A dark red pool was spreading swiftly through the dirt on the floor. A black Mercedes hat had been flung into the street outside.

Nicole stared down at the horror, then looked up and saw the big Toyota parked up against the canal wall, a plastic doll lying stiff-limbed by the front wheel.

She turned to Rykhlin. 'My God, the girl! She's still out there! Under the car!'

Rykhlin's gaze was firm. 'You'll be killed,' he said simply.

'But we can't leave her,' she cried.

Rykhlin sensed her determination. He operated the slide on his pistol to put a round in the chamber. 'OK, but we go together,' he mouthed.

They raced side by side for the vehicle. There was a loud thumping of helicopter blades overhead. She looked up, saw the gunship turning towards them, skidded to a halt and aimed up, shooting from the hip, letting rip with a burst of fire that made the gun feel alive in her hands.

The angry response of the chain gun came instantly. Cannon shells ripped into the tarmac, chewing it into tiny pieces that peppered her face.

'Get back!' yelled Rykhlin. 'For Christ's sake, get back!'

They scuttled back to the safety of the buildings. 'Where's Freddy?' she shouted.

'Gone!' Rykhlin shouted back, pointing out the door. 'Joined his friends! We're on our own. Go and get the girl. You can talk to her. I'll cover you.' He grabbed her weapon, took up position by the dead father, and began firing from the kneeling position – short bursts so as not to overheat the barrel, trying to disturb the aim of the helicopter gunner.

There was no time for her to think.

She made another dash for the big Toyota. Feeling totally exposed now, naked to the gaze of the helicopter crew. She expected an explosion of cannon shells at any moment.

Out of the corner of her eye she glimpsed another thin line of smoke arcing across a pale blue sky. Flares shot away from the helicopter as it dropped its nose quickly to evade the missile and accelerated across the canal, turning fast.

Again the missile screamed past . . .

Nicole slammed into the side of the big Toyota and crouched down to peer into the gloom beneath the car, the din of battle all around her. She saw a slim little body laid out flat, eyes wide with fear.

'Mei-Lin!' she shouted in Mandarin. 'Come on!

Quickly!' The little girl slithered across the tarmac. As Nicole scooped her up, Mei-Lin clung to her neck, wrapped her legs tight around her, and stretched down for her doll. Nicole reached out to grab it and thrust it into the child's hands. The girl buried her head hard into Nicole's shoulder, her bony limbs quivering with fear.

Nicole made a run for the house, the weight of the child awkward against her chest, thin legs banging against her thighs. She could hear the staccato clatter of Rykhlin's covering fire.

Keeping the child's gaze averted from the mess that had once been her father, Nicole pushed right on through the house until they were in the yard at the back. She found dark walls stained with moss, along with great piles of junk. Rykhlin was beside her now. She knew his strength and thrust Mei-Lin into his arms, took her weapon back, and looked desperately for a way out.

The roar of the helicopter returned, the steady beat of its rotor blades seeming to fill the enclosed space. The yard was now a killing ground, a death trap.

'Over the wall!' shouted Rykhlin.

They clambered up a junk pile, scraps of metal sliding around beneath them, then dropped down heavily into the courtyard beyond.

'Watch out!' yelled Rykhlin.

He had his face turned up anxiously towards the sky. The helicopter was hovering right above them, its chain gun swivelling downwards. The muzzle spat flame. Tiles ripped off the house and dust billowed around them.

Nicole looked round frantically and saw an alleyway leading into the next street. 'Out and left!' she yelled.

They ran down the alley and pounded into the road. All traffic had stopped. Cars lay abandoned, doors swung wide. Bicycles had been dropped at random. People were cowering in doorways, their brown faces turned up fearfully towards the throbbing airborne menace.

Nicole's feet pounded the tarmac, three kilos of stubby sub-machine gun swinging from one hand. Rykhlin was beside her, Mei-Lin slung easily over his shoulder. Nicole had trained for this, and she felt fully confident. *Run. Target! Down. Shoot! Up. Run.*

'Chopper coming back!' yelled Rykhlin. She glanced behind and saw it cranking round in a tight turn, coming down low along the street. There was a dark passage to her left.

'Alleyway, left!' she yelled.

They dodged along it, protected by a canyon of high walls, and heard the withering sound of chain-gun fire spraying the road beyond. There were screams from terrified people, wailing from children. They stopped, backs against the wall, chests heaving, recovering their breath.

Nicole looked across at the little girl and saw how Rykhlin's hand covered Mei-Lin's head, pushing it protectively against his chest, at the same time cupping her ear to shield it from the noise. A little black eye, round with fear, stared back at her.

Rykhlin was no coward.

The sound of the helicopter became a throbbing beat

in the narrow street. She knew it was hovering somewhere and craned her neck, but couldn't locate it.

There!

The gunner, in his cockpit, was peering down the narrow slit of the alleyway, the gun barrel slaved to his sights and swivelling round towards them. She aimed her weapon again . . .

But Rykhlin grabbed her arm, 'Come on, move!' he yelled.

They sprinted on down the narrow passageway and out into the stark daylight beyond, turned right, and pounded along tarmac again, hidden by a line of shops and houses. She kept looking behind, expecting the machine to reappear at any moment. They weaved among the abandoned vehicles, managed to reach the end of the street unseen, and skidded round the corner.

To see the helicopter straight ahead of them.

Hovering low like some carnivorous insect, just above the tops of the abandoned cars.

'For Christ's sake, shoot!' yelled Rykhlin.

Nicole brought up the sub-machine gun and aimed at the gunner. Her bullets ricocheted off his armoured plexiglas screen. The machine lurched sideways and swerved away, blades slapping the air, the downdraught whipping up a maelstrom of litter and dust that stung their eyes.

And then, from out of nowhere, a white smoke-trail connected violently with the helicopter.

The machine erupted in a blinding orange ball of fire. The shock wave of the explosion slammed against their faces, forcing them to duck. The helicopter spun violently to earth and hit the cars below it, rotor blades shearing and flicking away wildly into the trees as the main wreckage disappeared in a searing ball of exploding fuel. Debris rained down around them, and people ran screaming from the chaos. One woman, her clothes on fire, staggered a short distance before collapsing onto the grass of the central reservation nearby.

A jeep skidded to a stop beside them, a yellow flag with the black silhouette of a buffalo draped over its bonnet. Thameena's mob! The vehicle contained three young Indonesians, two men and a girl, wide-eyed and glossy with sweat. The girl was brandishing an empty missile tube, grinning wildly with excitement. Spare rounds rolled casually to and fro in the back of the vehicle. The driver studied them, looked at the kid with her arms wrapped around Rykhlin's neck, and then shouted across in Indonesian. 'You going to the barricades?'

'No, Defence Ministry!' yelled Nicole.

'OK!' He gave a wild victory sign, intoxicated by the excitement. They clambered aboard, Nicole in front, Rykhlin swinging up behind, hanging on to the little girl as if she was a fragile china mannequin.

They set off with a violent lurch and began to weave at high speed between the abandoned cars, bouncing over the kerbs and dodging desperately scattering crowds.

Nicole clung to the dashboard. Above the sound of the revving engine she could hear the chatter of gunfire, the loud *crump* of heavy mortars. More plumes of smoke smudged the horizon between the tower blocks. The whole of Jakarta must have erupted with the excitement of Rahman's death, igniting fires of rebellion that would burn their way to the very heart of the President's corrupt regime.

9.32 a.m.

The Defence Ministry was in utter chaos. Commandeered vehicles littered the broad highway outside. More yellow flags hung lazily from the windows, their black buffalo silhouettes waving gently in the breeze. Steady streams of uniformed and civilian workers were being expelled from the building, their hands on their heads. People were being kicked and thumped into line and made to sit in rows on the broad swathe of grass at the front of the building.

Adrenalin pumping through her system, Nicole leaped from the jeep and rushed up the steps to the front entrance, taking them two at a time. A thickset Indonesian, broad-faced and with eyes as hard as stones, barred her way. 'Where the fuck are you going?' he snarled.

'Room 061 – Operations!' she replied.

A sarcastic smile spread across his face. 'Shouldn't you be on a barricade somewhere?'

Then Rykhlin was there too, pushing his way forward, Mei-Lin dragging back on his hand. He eyed the M16 swinging from the man's brawny grip. 'Why don't you radio Thameena Rahman?' he said briskly. 'Give her our names.'

A deep rumbling laugh issued from the man's stomach, disbelief and contempt darkening his expression. He began to open his mouth to say something, but Rykhlin had already spotted his rifle's empty magazine slot and registered his sloppy carelessness. He rammed the barrel of his pistol hard into the man's flabby belly, making him grunt in pain.

'Just do it!' Rykhlin growled. 'She'll be in the RRI building. Do it – *now!*'

The man eyed them uncertainly till Rykhlin dropped Mei-Lin's hand to operate the slide on his pistol and shoved its muzzle back even harder into the man's gut. The Indonesian saw the menacing look on his face and got the message. He unclipped his radio and spoke into it, but kept his eyes fixed on them all the while. There was a long exchange in Indonesian, a heated argument. Then he asked for their names.

'Rykhlin and Tai-Chung.'

The man repeated the names and listened to the reply. His eyebrows lifted in surprise.

He put down the radio and eyed them suspiciously. 'OK, you can go in.' Then he shouted after them: 'Just don't get in the fucking way.'

9.58 a.m.

The Defence Ministry had been ransacked. Carpets were covered in shattered glass that crunched underfoot. There were papers scattered all over the floor, and bodies lay awkwardly in dark pools of blood. People were still being led outside.

A plaque on the basement-level door read: Operations Room. Red lights on the ceiling flashed an alert and there were signs of violent struggle everywhere – PCs lay wrecked on the floor, a body was slumped across a keyboard, peripheral equipment had been smashed.

Nicole wandered round the large room, studying the rows of control positions. She examined some of the screens that still functioned and began to type at a keyboard to see if she could break through into the software, find out more about *Krakatau*. But this proved useless – everything was protected.

Then Rykhlin shouted to her.

Leaving Mei-Lin perched quietly on one of the desks, she went into a smaller side room and found rows of metal bookshelves lined with black box files, each one neatly labelled and numbered by hand. Rykhlin was in the process of running his fingers along the ranks of spines, reading their alphanumeric codes. 'There might be something in here,' he suggested. 'It's some sort of records room.'

Nicole stared round at the ranks of files, beginning to feel out of her depth. She had no idea where to start – even if this was the right place to start. She walked slowly along a row of shelves, thinking it might be better to go back and take a chance on finding something on one of the computers . . .

Then she stopped.

A name had caught her eye.

She peered back along the row of labels. Had her mind played a trick? No – there! On one file's spine, in neat handwritten felt-tip – KRAKATAU.

An icy hand clutched at her stomach. 'Rykhlin!' she called.

With a shaking hand, Nicole pulled the box file from the shelf and flicked it open. There were scientific papers inside – a whole bundle of them.

'Rykhlin!' she yelled again, excited.

He hurried down the aisle to see what she was holding. 'Hey, that's good,' he breathed. She pulled out the top handful of papers, leaving the rest in the open box down by her feet, and began to leaf through the titles:

On the estimation of tsunami energy, IUGG Monograph no. 24.

Human behaviour during the tsunami of May 1980, Science 133.

Proceedings of the 30th International Symposium on Tsunami Research, Honolulu.

With the next document she suddenly stopped and stood gazing at it. 'You won't believe this,' she said, and held it up for Rykhlin to see: *Tsunami devastation on Lanai, the catastrophic results of long run-out landslides emanating from the Hawaiian Islands. A PhD dissertation by Nicole Tai-Chung.* 'They've even got a copy of my thesis.'

'Why would they want your doctoral work?' asked Rykhlin.

'I don't know – but I'm getting a bad feeling about this.'

Nicole flicked through the word-processed pages, enveloped by a growing sense of unease. She recognized the familiar text and diagrams, photographs and maps as if she'd written them only yesterday. But some of her work had been heavily annotated in Indonesian. She peered at the pencilled notes but couldn't make any sense of them. They were in some sort of shorthand she didn't understand.

Rykhlin bent down and picked up another handful of documents:

Landslide-created tsunami and the devastation of the Minoan civilization on Crete.

The dynamics of long run-out landslides.

Then:

The potential for slope instability on the north flank of Molokai, Hawaii; Dr J. Akimas; Centre for Deep-Ocean Studies.

'Bingo!' he muttered under his breath.

She turned round to read the title.

'Look!' he said, 'It's by Akimas – one of Rahman's top scientists. I think we might be on to something.'

She watched as he searched on through the document. There was a cross-section diagram through the Kamakou volcanic cone, showing layers of lava and seasonal ground-water levels. A sketch of the cone broken along various slip-surfaces. Maps of resulting landslides. Computer predictions as to how far the mass from each would run out into the Pacific. Rykhlin glanced at the maps, leafing through them, studying the figures.

'Jesus!' he breathed. 'Some of these slides he's predicting. They're big. Very big.'

'How big?' Nicole asked urgently.

Rykhlin fixed her with a gaze. 'How about cubic miles of the stuff?'

She tried to imagine that much material sliding into the sea – like half a mountain – and found it difficult.

'I had no idea he could do this,' muttered Rykhlin, his hand shaking slightly as he continued to leaf through the evidence. 'Nicole – I think they're planning to drop one whole side of Molokai right into the ocean.'

She took the document from him. 'You mean it's not one of those trench systems off the American West Coast?'

'No, this is all about a huge landslide slicing away part of Hawaii.'

'Rykhlin, we've got to warn Washington.' Her voice was tight with anxiety. 'Landslides like these have generated some of the worst tsunami ever, real killer waves.' She became visibly more distressed. 'My God, Rykhlin, they're going to use an idea from my thesis – against my own son!' She stared up at him, panic in her eyes.

He grabbed her shoulders: 'Hey, hold on there. You're

not to blame for this. We're in this together, OK? We're going to stop it.'

He continued to leaf through the papers. 'Look, there's something here I don't understand.' He was looking at a map of the North-East Pacific, curved lines advancing across the ocean to show the spread of the tidal wave. 'Can you explain this to me?' He showed her. 'It doesn't make sense.'

Nicole peered more closely at the map. 'What doesn't?'

'Remember Noble's briefing? The submarines were heading north, up the Marianas Trench – Hawaii lies to the east. If they were Rahman's submarines, then they weren't intended for this operation.' She watched him put the papers back in the box, then snap the lid shut and tuck it under his arm.

'We don't know enough,' he declared. 'This is just background stuff, that's why it's all on open file. We now know it's Molokai, but we still need to know more – such as when and how.'

'I think we should tell Washington straight away – about Molokai.'

'Tell them what? We don't know the details yet.'

'But what about my son? I want him out of there.'

'Trust me, we've got to do this properly. We don't know enough yet. We've got to get it right first time. We can't afford to make any mistakes.'

He was right. Make a mistake, and Peter could end up in even worse danger.

Suddenly Nicole realized what she had to do. She had to hack into the computer network, like she'd done once before, and get the facts they needed as quickly as possible.

But last time it had nearly led to her death.

'OK,' she said calmly. 'I'll need a workstation and an external line.'

Rykhlin looked puzzled. 'The computer files,' she explained. 'They'll be secure. I need to download the software again, so that I can break in.'

They searched around the Operations Room till they found another side office containing two computers displaying Internet icons. Neither had been damaged.

Nicole clicked on the screen and typed in a set of commands to bring up a site. The title page said: BLACKNET.

Blacknet – a Cold War hangover, now supercharged for the following century. A secure Internet web for spies.

She began entering various commands and passwords, but the system refused her entry. Her hands froze on the keys.

'What's wrong?' asked Rykhlin.

'They've removed my passwords. I don't exist any more.' She stared at the screen – defeated.

'Just a minute,' said Rykhlin.

'What?'

'Wait here. I'll get you access.' He grabbed his handgun from the table and dodged out of the room.

Nicole carried on typing ineffectually at the keyboard, but still nothing worked – ACCESS DENIED.

She got up from the keyboard and turned round to check on Mei-Lin.

The girl had gone. The desk was empty.

Nicole suddenly felt very concerned. In her mind she saw the little girl running out into the street, bewildered by all the noise and chaos. She walked quickly into the Operations Room, calling out to her, listening for an answer. It was as if Nicole was in a dream: she kept seeing that huge wave in her mind, dark and forbidding. She wanted to warn her son about what might happen, tell him to get himself out of there. She didn't want to waste any more time messing around here. She just wanted to find the little girl and go.

There was a shuffling sound, and something bounced and clanged onto the floor. Nicole turned and walked carefully back the way she'd come. She spotted Mei-Lin hunched tightly inside the dark footwell of a desk. Nicole squatted down to see better. The little girl looked so tiny and frail in there, shivering arms wound tightly around her knees, her eyes wide with lack of understanding. Nicole's heart went out to the tiny creature, sensing the trauma coiled inside her head.

'Hi!' she said gently.

The girl stared back silently.

What did you see? thought Nicole. *Did you see your father being smashed to a pulp in the doorway? Oh God, no – did you see that?*

Slowly she stretched out her arm invitingly, like one would with a cornered animal. Mei-Lin retreated instantly, pushing further back against the wall behind her. Nicole reached out to touch the child's doll, but the little girl snatched it away.

There was a scuffle in the corridor outside. Nicole looked up and saw Rykhlin frogmarching one of the uniformed prisoners into the room. He had his pistol pressed hard up against the base of the man's skull.

'This fellow works in the Operations Room. He's just "volunteered" to get us into the system.'

Rykhlin shoved the man down onto a chair in front of one of the workstations. He thumbed the catch on the butt of the Glock-17, dropped out the magazine to show his captive the neat row of seventeen rounds, then palmed the magazine back in. He pulled back the slide to put a round in the chamber, then shoved the barrel hard into the side of the man's throat.

'Right!' he barked. 'I want the *Krakatau* file.'

'Rykhlin, you're scaring the little girl – she's hiding under the desk.'

Rykhlin ignored her.

The man did nothing. He just sat there, looking at the keyboard, limbs visibly trembling. He knew he was staring death in the face.

Rykhlin took the pistol away from the man's throat, moved it up close to his temple, and fired.

The pistol jerked. The round slammed into a monitor, exploding the tube. The prisoner almost leaped out of his seat with fright, and began to whimper. The pistol went back against his throat.

'OK, translate this for me,' Rykhlin shouted to Nicole. 'Tell this guy that thousands are going to die unless he finds me that file. Tell him I'll kill him and fetch someone else if he doesn't cooperate.'

Nicole stared open-mouthed at Rykhlin – a different Rykhlin. She couldn't believe the anger that was driving him now.

'Go on, tell him!' he shouted again.

She translated quickly into Indonesian.

The man typed obediently at the keyboard with quivering fingers. He brought up the front page of a program, then a menu. He typed a password, and a new front page appeared – entitled KRAKATAU.

'OK,' breathed Rykhlin, scanning the short menu that came up: 'Dynamics, Logistics, and Operations – which do you want?' he demanded.

'Dynamics?' suggested Nicole.

As the man's fingers hesitated, Rykhlin rammed the pistol harder into his neck. He yelped. 'Do it,' Rykhlin commanded.

The prisoner's hands moved to the keyboard. Nicole came closer to watch. A whole new menu appeared. 'Which one now?' asked Rykhlin.

'Let's get the height of the wave first.' She looked down the list, found a suitable simulation and told the Indonesian to access it.

The machine loaded and ran the program. First it drew graph axes of height and distance; then it ran a simulated wave coming in and showed it slowing and steadily increasing in height as the water shallowed. Tiny digits scrolled on the crest of the moving wave, recording its growing height in metres. Nicole watched the numbers as the wave swelled. They went through ten metres, then twenty metres – surely they must stop! – thirty, forty, fifty, sixty, 60.96 metres. Then the wave broke and ran a long way inland before sweeping slowly back out to sea again.

Rykhlin stared at the screen, a look of total incredulity on his face. 'Jesus! A tsunami can do *that*? That was almost 200 feet, travelling at over one hundred miles per hour. OK, we need more. We need to know when and where this is going to happen. Tell him we need more.'

Nicole spoke quickly in Indonesian. The man shook his head. 'No more! Is no more!'

'Tell him to try Logistics!' urged Rykhlin, and she translated. More tapping at the keyboard: another long menu.

Nicole ran her gaze down the list and found a familiar name. She pointed. 'Look – it mentions the *Ibn Battuta*.'

'OK, go for it.'

The soldier accessed the file, and the computer began to construct a wire-frame diagram of a submersible lowering a canister into a hole drilled on the sea floor. Nicole examined the diagram and studied the shape of the submersible – a familiar shape.

'Those are the submersibles from the *Ibn Battuta*,' she exclaimed.

'So they're using their survey ship to plant the bomb,' breathed Rykhlin. 'Well, that just makes it easier for us to find them. Now we need to know *when*. Ask him. Ask him when they're going to do it.'

Nicole spoke. The soldier said nothing, just looked down at the keyboard. Rykhlin prodded the barrel of his pistol harder against the man's neck, which resulted in a rapid stream of Indonesian.

'He says it's not in the program, for security reasons,' translated Nicole. 'But he thinks the explosion might be due today, or tomorrow, to coincide with the submarine launch.'

Rykhlin took the weapon away from the man's neck, and looked at her, stunned.

'My God, we need to warn Washington. They've got to find that boat immediately.'

'What about all those people living on the West Coast? Will they be safe?'

'How long does it take for a tsunami to cross the Pacific from Hawaii?'

'About five hours.'

'So if we contact Washington right now, give them a warning, they'll have at least five hours to evacuate people to higher ground.'

Nicole grabbed her sub-machine gun, 'Unless it's already started! We've got to get across to the RRI building, try and link up with Washington from there. Perhaps Thameena can recall that boat for us.'

Rykhlin crouched down in front of the desk and held his arms out to the little girl. But she didn't react. The soldier at the computer barked something in Indonesian.

Rykhlin turned to Nicole, looking for a translation – but the girl had already caught the meaning of his words and was scrabbling past him to cling to Nicole's legs.

Nicole lifted her up. She nodded at their prisoner, still sitting stiffly at the keyboard. 'What about him?'

Rykhlin took the rifle from her.

'Leave him,' he said.

11.10 p.m. Eastern time: the White House

Gilbert Byrd looked up from his desk as James Cordrey, Secretary of Defence, slipped into the Oval Office. Byrd nodded towards the TV in the corner, which was running news footage of jubilant scenes on the streets of Jakarta that were taking place amid sporadic fighting with troops still loyal to Rahman.

'You seen it?'

Cordrey was dressed in jeans and sneakers, a red baseball cap crammed on his head, the word 'Boss' inscribed on it in large white letters. 'Yeah, they really did it,' he grunted approvingly.

Byrd thumbed the hand controller and blipped off the TV. He eyed Cordrey's rig. 'Did I catch you in the middle of something?'

'One of my boys is pitching for the high-school team. Promised I'd be there.'

Noble hurried into the room, still dressed formally for

work. 'Mr President.' His eyes flicked across to Cordrey. 'James.'

Byrd leaned back in his chair and put his hands behind his head. 'OK, so what've you got for us, Greg?'

'We've had a phone call from Jakarta. Tai-Chung was right about *Krakatau* – it's for real. And it's due at any moment.'

Byrd let out a low whistle. 'Well, I'll be damned!'

'But she glitched on one thing. It's not a slide off the continental slope. This thing's coming at us from Hawaii. It's a big slide off the north coast of Molokai.'

The President's eyes rounded. 'Good God!' He swung round in his chair, reached for the large globe beside his desk and spun it on its axis. His fingers slid across the globe's surface as he braked it to a stop on reaching the centre of the Pacific Ocean. He tapped thoughtfully at a cluster of tiny islands. 'When?' he asked.

'Sometime within the next twelve to twenty-four hours.'

'Jesus!'

'And it's not what quite what we thought, either. It's not submersibles. They're using that survey ship of theirs – the *Ibn Battuta*.'

Byrd looked over at Cordrey, and their gazes met. 'I want you over in the War Room, James. I want the *Ibn Battuta* stopped.'

Cordrey looked puzzled. 'Sir?'

'The *Ibn Battuta* – it's carrying the damn bomb, or whatever it is. It must be hovering around Hawaii somewhere.

591

Board the bloody thing. Shoot it out of the water if you have to. You've got satellite surveillance! Go and find it! Then destroy it!'

Cordrey gazed at Byrd for a moment, opened his mouth to say something, and then changed his mind.

Noble watched Cordrey's retreating back, waiting till the door of the Oval Office shut quietly behind him. 'James is worried,' he explained. 'Thinks you should come clean on this one. So does Walter.'

Byrd ran his hands through his mop of hair and sighed. 'Yeah, I know.' He paused. 'Sit down, Greg.' He motioned with his hand. 'You ever been to Molokai?'

'Yes, Mr President, as a matter of fact I have. You know, with the family.'

'Took my kids there too, did the educational thing.' Byrd twirled a pencil between his fingers. 'Rahman's done his homework – the whole north slope's one thick slab of lava, twelve square miles of it, just ready to slide off into the Pacific.' He demonstrated with a slow swoop of his pencil.

'Yeah, another turn of the wheel,' muttered Noble.

Byrd looked at him quizzically. 'What do you mean?'

'We've been here before, Mr President.'

Byrd was aghast. 'You mean we were planning to do something like this?'

'Project Seal, against the Japs. Went the wrong way, though. Leech was an engineer, Aukland University. He thought about using explosions, but couldn't find a bomb big enough to trigger the wave. Even considered a nuke – I think we took him to Bikini.'

'My God!' Byrd's eyes were round with shock.

The large antique clock on the Georgian mantelpiece ticked loudly in the silence that followed. Byrd felt that the elaborate timepiece was counting down the seconds to some sort of retribution.

'You going to tell 'em, Mr President?'

'Who?'

'The state governors – are you going to warn them? We need to pull all our population back from the Pacific coast.'

Byrd swung round in his seat, turned his back on Noble for a short while and watched the darkness outside.

'How long before the wave gets to the West Coast?' he asked.

'Rykhlin said about five hours.'

'Hawaii will issue an alert as soon as the slide lets go. We don't need to broadcast a warning till then.'

'I think you should warn them now, Mr President. We've got to start getting people out of there.'

Byrd spun round. 'No! I'm not going to cause any panic, Greg, not yet. We might be able to stop this thing before it gets started.' He paused. 'How big did Rykhlin say the wave would be?'

'He didn't – his call went down before he'd finished. I think Tai-Chung said thirty feet when we talked with her.'

'Thirty feet – that'll do. We don't want to start a panic.'

'I still think you should issue a warning, Mr President.'

Byrd looked up at Noble. 'Look, we're going to find the *Ibn Battuta*, Greg. Then it'll be as if this never happened.' He pushed forward earnestly against the edge of his desk. 'If I press the panic button, they'll start asking questions in Congress. Why did I do this? Why did I do that? Then someone will squeal about Typhoon Anna, and I'll go down as the first President who's used the goddamned environment to make war.'

'Not the first, Mr President. There was Vietnam, remember?'

'Yes, but did Johnson know about that? Did the CIA tell him anything?'

Noble shrugged.

'I'm up to my neck in shit, Greg. And if any of it sticks on me, you won't see me in this office for much longer.'

'What about Tai-Chung's kid? He's in that institute, isn't he, right on the coast? Are you going to get him out?'

Byrd shook his head. 'They'll get the warning like everybody else. I can't give him preferential treatment. I won't panic the whole population just for one kid.'

'Did you tell Rykhlin that?'

Byrd doodled on his pad irritably. 'What do you think?' Then he caught Noble's gloomy expression and looked him straight in the eye. 'Greg, it's a tsunami – an act of God. Nobody's going to expect me to predict a tidal wave, for Christ's sake!'

SLIDE

Nicole watched Thameena Rahman coming out of the recording studio. A soldier wearing a yellow armband held open the heavy glass door for her. She looked tired and drawn, and there was concern etched onto her face. 'I can't contact the *Ibn Battuta* for you,' she said grimly. 'They seem to be running in radio silence.'

Nicole's heart sank.

Someone had brought in a tray of coffee and set it down on the low table among the litter of styrofoam beakers and sticky coffee stains.

'We've tried everything,' Thameena continued. 'They're just not answering. We don't even know where the ship is. Did you manage to get through to Washington?'

'Yes, they're going to try and find her themselves,' Rykhlin said. 'It shouldn't be too difficult – she can't be far off Hawaii.'

'Will they intercept her in time?' asked the new head of state.

Rykhlin shrugged. 'Who knows?'

'Are they evacuating your people?'

'They assured me the evacuation would start straight away.'

Thameena sighed. 'There's still hope, then. If the American Navy can't find the *Ibn Battuta*, at least you've had plenty of time to move your people to safety.' She turned and eyed the tiny figure of Mei-Lin sitting quietly on Nicole's lap. 'I see you've picked up a stray.'

595

'She belongs to one of your men who got killed,' answered Nicole. 'He brought her along to the killing ground. She's lucky to be alive.'

'I could arrange to have her taken off your hands and placed in an orphanage,' suggested Thameena.

Nicole looked down at the little girl clinging desperately to her and thought about what had happened over the last few hours – the trauma, the torture and the confusion that must lie behind the child's blank stare.

'We'll look after her,' she replied quietly.

Then she suddenly felt a prickling on the back of her neck. Felt evil crawling across her skin like electricity.

She spun round to see Lukman standing in the doorway, a lit *kretek* in his right hand.

'Miss Tai-Chung, how charming to meet you.'

She shot up immediately, catching the table with Mei-Lin's tiny foot, sending beakers of cold coffee splashing to the floor.

Rykhlin reached out to take Mei-Lin into his arms, his gaze fixed on Nicole, whose face had turned deadly white.

A thin smile curled the edges of Lukman's lips as he let his cigarette fall to the floor and ground it out with a slow scrape of one leather shoe.

Nicole felt anger surge through her body. She turned to face Thameena. 'I want this man arrested!'

Thameena stared at her with eyebrows raised. 'Why?'

'Because he's a torturer, a murderer!' Nicole snarled.

An arrogant smile smirked upon Lukman's lips. 'Such harsh words . . .'

Anger pounded in Nicole's ears. She leaped forward, sending the coffee table spinning across the floor. She advanced on Lukman, as if intending to reach out and grab him by the throat . . . but her hands were brought up short as they encountered something hard and metallic. The soldier was suddenly there, stony stare fixed on her face, his rifle raised to protect Lukman. Nicole grabbed at the weapon and tried to pull it away from him, but his grip was like a vice . . .

'Stop this!' Thameena's icy voice rang out in the studio.

Nicole spun round. 'Don't you understand? He's one of Rahman's henchmen. You can't trust him. He's a liar, a cheat, a sadist . . .'

'Perhaps you should know that it was Colonel Lukman who enabled you to escape from Arguni,' answered Thameena sharply. 'He had to serve time in a labour camp for having ensured your freedom.'

Nicole stared at her, couldn't believe what she was hearing. 'No, that can't be right. He had me beaten. He wanted access to Hendra's computer files.'

'That's enough!' commanded Thameena. 'I think your job here has finished, Miss Tai-Chung. Perhaps it is unwise for you to stay any longer.'

Rykhlin rounded on Thameena. 'Now wait a minute—'

'I'll have a plane waiting for you at Don Muang Airport.'

'So that's it then, is it?' demanded Nicole. 'You were quite happy for us to do your dirty work, get rid of your husband, put you in power. Now you want us to go so that you can work alongside this scum . . .'

'I think you'd better go and wait downstairs until I can arrange for someone to escort you safely to the airfield,' said Thameena sternly. Lukman and Thameena stood side by side now. 'Your work here is finished, Miss Tai-Chung. Just go home.'

'But what if they can't stop the *Ibn Battuta*?' demanded Nicole. 'What if they don't stop the tsunami wave? What then?'

Thameena stared at her coldly. 'Miss Tai Chung, I cannot be held responsible for my ex-husband's actions.'

Chapter Forty-eight –
the following day

Midnight: 150 miles off the coast of Hawaii

The gold leaves that edged the captain's cap gleamed red in the dim lighting that bathed the bridge of the *Ibn Battuta*. The night-vision binoculars were heavy in his hands as his gaze slowly swept the horizon. Through the lenses the ocean glowed dark emerald, and the stars shone as bright patches of light in a glass-green sky.

He saw no ships, no navigation lights of incoming aircraft, nothing.

He dropped the binoculars. 'Speed?' he barked in Indonesian.

'Twenty-eight knots, sir!'

The captain looked briefly at his watch. Another thirty minutes before he could break radio silence and inform the President of their success.

He stood quietly on the bridge, listening to the heavy throb of the big twin diesels, feeling the gentle tug as the ship's bows cut through the Pacific swell. An electronic chime pierced the hushed atmosphere. He reached for the receiver: 'Captain.'

'Radar, sir!' returned a clipped voice. 'We have jamming on all frequencies.'

'Thank you, radar.' The captain kept his voice calm. He replaced the receiver and thought for a moment.

So, now they were being blinded. Someone out there was trying to catch them. Well, he'd give them a run for their money.

'Sound action stations.'

An urgent high-pitched electronic beeping rang throughout the ship. Men tumbled out of bunks; marines grabbed their weapons and ran on deck to take up their pre-arranged positions. The captain moved out to the starboard wing of the bridge and swung his binoculars along the horizon again, still detecting nothing.

So where were they? *Who* were they? If they were Americans, perhaps it would be best to get rid of the evidence for a while. He walked back to the centre of the bridge and picked up a handset. 'Operations? ... Captain ... Launch the submersible.'

Then he punched two keys on the keypad and let his voice ring out through the ship. 'This is the captain. Unidentified hostiles closing in. Stay alert. I say again, stay alert.'

He replaced the handset and saw the helmsman shifting his feet nervously. 'Maintain your speed and heading,' he said firmly.

SLIDE

The captain could hear it now, a deep-throated roar through the window glass on the bridge. He peered out, still trying to spot something – but he saw nothing.

A powerful searchlight suddenly pierced the night sky, flooding the foredeck with light. They – whoever 'they' might be – were directly above him. Then he could see it, edging down: some sort of helicopter, indistinct in the darkness. But he could just make out that it carried the black star and bar of the United States, the ramp at the back lowered. He grinned. He'd play with them, delay them just that little bit longer.

'Hard to starboard!' he rapped.

The helmsman looked startled.

The captain reached across and gave the chrome wheel a violent tug. 'Starboard!' he shouted.

The *Ibn Battuta* shuddered, then heeled over. The captain braced himself against the increasing angle of the deck as the bows swung. The Americans slipped away, their searchlight now stabbing uselessly down over the water. Immediately yellow flashes lit up the night, and a necklace of red tracer rounds streamed across the bows.

The navigation officer looked across at the captain, expecting another order. The captain shoved the peak of his cap further down his forehead. 'Hard to port!' he said carefully.

The wheel spun again. The *Ibn Battuta* shuddered,

began to right itself, then heeled over in the other direction. The captain grinned. Cat and mouse – he was enjoying himself.

More lights flashed in the darkness. Blobs of red raced towards them and hit the bridge with what sounded like a thousand rapid hammer blows. Glass shattered everywhere. Sparks flew. Metal smashed and tore jaggedly. The navigation officer fell to the floor, screaming and clutching at his leg.

The captain looked down at his colleague writhing on the floor and realized that now he had no choice.

'Both engines stop!' he barked.

0.14 a.m.

The captain was content to watch as the drama continued to unfold. A rope snaked out from the helicopter's loading ramp and soldiers streamed down, abseiling onto his deck.

He waited quietly, as if aloof from the pandemonium outside.

The door to the bridge crashed open and a young US Marines officer burst in, black camouflage streaked across his face. More soldiers pushed in from behind.

'Captain Salim?'

The captain stood still and said nothing. The young officer pulled a card from his combat dress and read it. 'Sir, your ship is currently sailing in the territorial waters of the United States of America, and has been seized in our belief that your transit through these waters is prejudicial to the peace, good order, and security of the United States territory of Hawaii.' The young officer folded the card away.

The captain looked at him, looked at his smooth well-fed flesh. To Salim he looked no more than just a kid. 'Get off my ship,' he growled.

But his hands were pulled roughly up behind his back, and he felt the cold steel of handcuffs snapping around his wrists.

'Sir!' barked the officer. 'We intend to search your ship for contraband of war.'

The marines handcuffed the rest of his bridge crew and hustled them out through the door. 'You will remain here, please,' said the young officer. The captain glared at him, resenting his authority – and his youth – and slowly, deliberately, turned his back on the young man.

0.26 a.m.

'I want medical attention for my navigation officer.'

'Sir?'

The captain nodded towards his colleague, who'd propped himself up against the aft wall of the bridge. He was nursing his leg, grimacing with pain, the sweat glistening on his skin. 'My navigation officer, he's wounded. He needs medical attention.'

The young officer spoke into his microphone, then

looked back at Salim. 'A medic will be along shortly . . .
sir,' he said, insultingly.

The captain grunted.

0.29 a.m.

A marine sergeant clattered onto the bridge and
approached the young officer. He saluted breathlessly. 'We
need the key to their armoury, sir!'

Salim spun round. 'We don't have an armoury. This is
a research vessel.'

The young officer was getting nervous and impatient.
'The key to the armoury, Captain. Or we'll blow the
fucking door off!'

The captain glanced up at the ship's chronometer:
00:29:15

The officer followed his gaze and looked suspicious.
'Medication,' explained the captain. 'I have a strict routine.'

'The keys to the armoury, sir – NOW!'
00:29.30

'I believe the keys you want may be in the key safe.'
Salim nodded over to the far corner where a small steel
cabinet was bolted to the bulkhead. 'I'll have to operate the
combination for you.'
00:29:40

They took Salim to the other side of the bridge and
removed his manacles. He stood by the side of the safe and
glanced up again at the chronometer.

00:29:50

He could feel his heart pumping in anticipation. He began to turn the dial. 'Left six – right five – left nine ... No, I'm sorry, I think I might have that wrong ...'

A gun came up and jabbed him hard between his ribs. 'Don't bullshit me, Captain.'

00:30:00

The blinding light of a thousand suns flooded into the shattered bridge. The captain saw the shock photoflashed onto the young man's face.

Then the light slowly dimmed.

Far out across the Pacific beyond the horizon, a fireball the size of a pumpkin was growing, rolling up into the night sky, trailing a long stem of incandescent gas.

The captain laughed, and recited: 'And I dreamed that I was on the wing of a huge bird ...'

The officer spun round, levelled his weapon. 'What did you say?' There was fear in his eyes.

'I was quoting Ibn Battuta himself, my friend – the Prince of Travellers. A description of his dream before he set out across the known world. I think our dream might have just begun, don't you?'

The young officer stared at the captain. 'Dream? What fucking dream? Your President's dead, Captain! And right now – you're going nowhere.'

0.30 a.m., the island of Molokai, Hawaii

The north-east coast of Molokai is a rugged and isolated place. Great slabs of rain-soaked lava jut precariously into the Pacific Ocean, forming cliffs over 2,000 feet high. Inland, the ground rises gently up to the lush, wet, rain-forested slopes of Kamakou – an ancient volcano whose summit towers almost a mile above sea level.

Forty seconds after the explosion, the first shock wave reached the north slope of the island, slamming into it with the force of a Magnitude 5 earthquake. Three cubic miles of rock were jolted upwards. Then it rocked and vibrated in the aftershocks. Groundwater, trapped between the ancient lava flows, penetrated the hairline joints and filled them with a microscopic film of incompressible water. It began to act as a lubricant. For a moment, nothing happened. Then, imperceptibly, millimetre by millimetre, a huge section of rock the size of Long Island began to slide off the mountain.

In the darkness of the dripping forest, great fissures gaped open, like mouths. Ferns, bushes and trees trembled as the ground moved beneath them. Roosting birds woke with alarm, and screeched flapping out of the forest canopy. Waterfalls lurched drunkenly.

Energized by the sheer mass of moving material, the immense piece of land quickly began to break up. Slabs of rock the size of office blocks separated, slowly rolling and tumbling. The slide gathered speed down the incline and began to sweep over the contours of the land like a flood. Huge fountains of dust spurted out; tree trunks and rock debris were thrown high into the air.

The slide roared off the upland plateau and found itself channelled into narrow canyons that cut their way down through towering cliffs to the ocean. Now one-hundred-foot-high bow waves of rock and earth banked and curved through the steep valleys, slamming blast waves ahead of them, snapping off trees like matchsticks.

A small group of teenagers, camping on the narrow floor of the Pelekunu, heard the thunderous roar and felt the ground start to tremble beneath their feet. They turned away from the spectacle of the distant fireball and saw the dark shadow of the oncoming slide as it swept round the corner of the valley. They yelled out in fear and ran for their lives. But the shadow was too fast. It reached out for them, smashed them to the ground, buried them instantly under millions of tons of debris.

Travelling at well over a hundred miles an hour, the slide then leaped out of the valleys and slammed straight into the Pacific Ocean. The blast wave hit first, forcing the water back with a smack of its giant hand. Then the slide itself, like a huge piston, rammed out into the ocean, instantly displacing billions of tons of water and ploughing on and on . . . for over a mile.

Finally the slide stopped and the water lurched back violently. Vast waves slopped eight hundred feet up the side of the cliff. Breakers surged high into the narrow valleys, sweeping out rocks, boulders, trees, and the fragile, twisted remains of what few people lived on this remote part of the island.

Then more waves came back and did it all again … and again … until finally the ocean began to calm.

A huge pulse of energy was now spreading out across the Pacific from the coast of Molokai, like ripples moving away from a stone thrown into a pond.

But these were not normal waves: they were shock waves. From crest to crest they were separated by hundreds of miles; they sat only a few feet above the ocean's surface, and travelled at the speed of a jet airliner. They passed, harmless and undetected, below vessels in the shipping lanes.

But in five hours' time they would reach the West Coast of America, and there they would become a very different animal. They would rear up out of the shallow coastal water, and come crashing down onto the land in a savage fury of death and destruction.

They would become raging beasts of waves.

They were tsunami.

They were the nemesis that Rahman had bequeathed the world.

0.36 a.m.: Honolulu

Six minutes after Salim's nuclear blast, the shock wave reached Hawaii's capital – Honolulu.

In the Pacific Tsunami Warning Centre, computer screens went suddenly wild, scrabbling frantic lines onto the seismographs. Warning bells were triggered automatically, and staff came running.

Almost immediately they heard the rolling thump of a huge detonation. They looked at each other in alarm and hurried from the control room. They stared out at the eastern horizon and watched, horrified, as the distant fireball painted the quaint streets of Honolulu a gruesome shade of pink.

They were obviously under nuclear attack!

As sirens began to wail over the city, they scrambled back into their bunker. Frantic hands tapped at keyboards, but they couldn't get the machines to function properly. They found that programs had crashed, screens stubbornly refused to move. Some machines had gone down completely.

The controller grabbed the telephone and tried to get through to Civil Defence – but he found the line dead. He searched, panic-stricken, on a shelf and took down a thick blue manual. His hands shook; he couldn't take this in. The nightmare of his childhood: a pre-emptive nuclear strike.

But by whom?

And why?

Trained for a tsunami, the scientists suddenly found themselves fighting for their own lives, their delicate electronic equipment a victim of electromagnetic pulse – energy that had flashed unseen out of the explosion and thrown most of Hawaii back into a communications Stone Age.

6.42 p.m. local time: Jakarta

Thameena's limousine was making its way slowly south from Merdeka Square towards the Parliament Building. The streets were lined with people waving yellow flags, shouting and cheering. Flowers were being thrown at the car, mounding up against the windscreen. Occasionally the crowds spilled onto the highway and brought her to a halt, engulfing Thameena's entourage in a wave of hysterical humanity.

The window was down; hands were thrust in for shaking. People jogged alongside just to be near her. Out in front, a jeep tried to clear a path through the ecstatic masses and loyal soldiers rode shotgun.

On the seat next to Thameena was a pile of electronic equipment from the radio station. It warbled for her attention. The aide sitting with her picked up a mobile and spoke briefly before passing it across to Thameena: 'The President of the United States, madam.'

Thameena raised her eyebrows coyly and smiled. She assumed she was about to be congratulated.

Byrd's voice sounded synthetic through the receiver:

'Ms Rahman? We've just had reports of a nuclear strike on Hawaii!'

The joyous excitement of the moment was instantly forgotten. A chill wind of reality blew icily through Thameena's limousine. She leaned back and crouched a little to stem the noise from the ecstatic crowd, putting her free hand up against her ear. She spoke to the President. 'Is that the tsunami attack?'

The aide turned around on the seat and looked at her in alarm.

'You tell me!' replied the President. 'NORAD have just reported a detonation off Molokai, but no incoming missile track. I need your immediate assurance that Indonesia has not launched a pre-emptive nuclear strike on the United States.'

'We've not launched any attack.'

'A dissident group, maybe? Someone still loyal to your husband? I need to know.'

'No, Mr President. The missile control room on Palau is now safely in the hands of your marines. This *must* be the tsunami attack you've been talking about.'

'The Chinese are getting jittery. I want them reassured. You must telephone Hung and explain what's going on. I'll get in touch with the Western Alliance.'

'Mr President, have you warned your people about the tsunami?'

There was a pause in the conversation.

'Ms Rahman, I don't think I need any advice from you as to what I should do.'

'How big is this tsunami? What's Hawaii predicting?'

There was another pause.

'The Warning Centre at Honolulu is off the air. It's a civilian system – it's not hardened against a nuclear strike.'

'You don't understand tsunami like we do, Mr President. They can do great damage, cause huge loss of life. Do your people realize the danger they're in?'

Byrd ignored her point. 'You gave me no time to evacuate my people in Hawaii, Ms Rahman. I'm expecting a large number of casualties.'

'I didn't understand that the *Ibn Battuta* would be armed with a nuclear device. I regret that.'

'My country has asked for an emergency session of the Security Council, Ms Rahman. You have just committed an act of war.' Then the receiver went dead.

Thameena looked out of the window. She saw the dancing adulation of the crowds outside, but even in death Amir's shadow still stalked her. 'Thank you, Mr President,' she said quietly, and slowly returned the mobile to the seat beside her. Only hours into her presidency, not even formally inaugurated, and already she was having to face up to the might of the United States. She was walking a political tightrope.

Thameena turned to her aide. 'Get me President Hung, please.'

Then she continued to wave to the crowd and shook the hands that were being thrust in towards her. But somehow the edge had been taken off her enthusiasm: her triumph now somewhat hollow.

1.30 a.m.: Pacific Ocean

Cruising eight miles high above the Pacific, Rykhlin lay collapsed on the comfortable leather couch of Rahman's Gulfstream V – and slept. He slept the deep dreamless sleep that comes with exhaustion, hovering between two states of consciousness. A hand shook his shoulder – a persistent hand that wouldn't go away. He grunted irritably and shifted his position.

'Rykhlin, wake up!'

'What?'

'Something's happened. You've got to wake up.'

Reluctantly, he clawed his way up through blankets of darkness, and wrestled to focus his attention.

'We've been diverted.'

He struggled to understand the words and opened his eyes, squinting in the soft cabin light.

Nicole was crouching down beside him, clutching an aeronautical chart in her hand. The gentle light played across the soft skin of her face, but there was anxiety in her tired eyes. 'They've closed all the airports around San Francisco,' she was saying. 'We've been diverted to Sacramento.'

He struggled upwards on the couch, feeling the stiffness in his neck. His throat was dry, and his head felt hung-over. He yawned, blinking back the tears of fatigue in the corners of his eyes. 'Why?' he croaked.

'It's started.'

He began to grasp what she was talking about. 'What?'

'The bomb's exploded.'

'When?'

'Half-past midnight – their time. It's only an hour since we refuelled at Honolulu.'

He looked at Nicole's face and saw something hovering behind the mask – something she wasn't telling him.

'And . . .?' he prompted.

Nicole looked back at him, eyes searching. 'It was nuclear.'

His stomach squirmed in fear. 'Jesus!'

'The pilots can't raise Honolulu any more,' she continued. 'They think all the communication systems have gone down. Some military traffic's operating – but they're not talking to us.'

'Christ! The whole side of Kamakou must have gone. When did you say it exploded?'

'Half-past midnight – their time.'

Rykhlin did a simple calculation. 'That means the tsunami will hit the West Coast . . . at about half-past five. What's the time difference?'

'Two hours.'

'So that makes it half-past seven in California. When are we due in?'

'About five a.m., local time.'

'Jesus! That's cutting things fine.'

Nicole started to unfold the chart. 'Let's find this diversion airfield.'

Rykhlin studied the map with her and found Sacramento north-east of San Francisco. It took only a moment to realize the implication. He jabbed his finger at the chart. 'It's too far from the coast – it won't give us time to get him out.'

Nicole looked horrified. 'But you said they were going to be evacuated. All the people along the coast. You said they'd be safe.'

Rykhlin stared back at her. *Christ!* She'd believed it! She'd believed what those creeps had said. But he'd been around people like that for a long time – people like Noble and Simes. Weak people, little people, cowards – career men whose only concern was to find the next fall guy. There was no guarantee that anyone would be safe in the apocalypse that was about to hit the Californian coast.

He looked at her carefully. 'I don't think we should trust those bastards any longer, do you?'

She faltered. 'No, but . . .'

'Right, we do it ourselves. I'll radio Sacramento, tell them we're running short of fuel. That should get us clearance into San Francisco.'

'Can we do that?'

'Nicole, we can do anything if we set our minds to it. I'll go and talk to the pilots.'

He reached across for his jacket and slid out the Glock-17. It felt heavy and reassuring in his hand. He got up and squeezed between the seats, heading for the curtained door of the cockpit.

'What are you doing?' Nicole called after him uncertainly.

He turned awkwardly in the confined space of the aisle. 'Just a little persuasion,' he said. Then he turned back and continued forward to the cockpit.

4.00 a.m.: Pacific Heights, San Francisco

The exclusive Victorian neighbourhood of Pacific Heights stared disdainfully across the undulating blanket of cold grey fog that hung over the Bay. Street lights burned in the half-light of early dawn, but few windows were lit. Cable-car tracks snaked silently up the inclines.

Amongst the dark, wet, leafy woodland of the Presidio, a long-forgotten tower looked down on a solitary early-morning jogger. Slowly, the rusty vanes of its siren began to turn. A phantom wail rose slowly above the lush landscape of the north-west corner of the city, gathered in strength, then fell gently – only to rise again, louder still.

The sinister sound was taken up elsewhere. It began to fill the streets. It echoed around the Transamerica Building, bounced off the Federal Building, rolled across the middle-class suburb of Haight Ashbury.

Lights flicked on nervously behind the heavy curtains of Pacific Heights. In one of the late-Victorian row houses that made up Clay Street, a blind flicked up in a tall bay window and a young man's face peered out into the early dawn.

Gogi Scaglietti pushed some strands of his long greasy

black hair away from his smooth tanned face, and scowled at the noise. 'Fuck's sake, give me a break, man!'

He stumbled back into his bedroom and sat, yawning, on the devastation of his bed; then leaned across to slap his radio into action:

'This is KDIA, on-line for soul, at the early-listening hour . . . And the news is: we have an alert this morning!

'The State Governor's Office of Emergency Services has issued a warning. Yes, folks, following a major explosion that sent Hawaii into chaos in the early hours of this morning, a big wave is now heading our way . . .'

'No shit!'

'Now this release tells me it's a Magnitude 3 tsunami wave!'

'OK, that's at least a thirty-foot swell, running in at 7.30 this morning, so low-lying land around the Bay is simply not a safe place to be right now! The SFPD are telling me that anybody living down there has to get up and get out this morning, move to higher ground . . .'

Gogi's eyes glazed over. He looked longingly at the surfing poster on the wall; saw the muscle guy, his arms out, threading the needle, creaming his board out from underneath a curling double-overhead.

A thirty-foot swell – right here, right into the Bay! Wow!

He reached under his pillow and, yanking out his mobile, punched in some numbers. 'Hi – Lewis? Gogi! . . . Yeah – I heard it too . . . Yeah, cool . . . Get your board out . . . What? . . . No, man, the 9–8 – the biggest you got, OK?

... Tell Gina and Mark, meet me in the truck ... twenty minutes!'

5.00 a.m.: San Francisco International

The white pencil shape of the Gulfstream V emerged out of the early-morning fog that was rolling in off the chill waters of the Bay, and touched down lightly between the lights of Runway 19-Left. The twin thrust-reversers clapped down, and a steady roar from the Rolls-Royce turbofans swiftly braked the speeding aircraft. Landing lights blazed in the murky pre-dawn light as the machine turned off the runway and taxied swiftly in towards the brightly lit terminal complex.

The place was in chaos. Closed to incoming traffic, the authorities were trying to get as many aircraft out as possible. Most of the big jets had already cleared the terminal. The biz-jet flight line was frantic with activity – tankers refuelling, engines starting, aircraft taxiing out.

Rykhlin descended the air-stairs with Nicole, cramped and stiff after the tedious twenty-hour flight across the Pacific. He stretched to ease his knotted muscles, and watched a bright yellow Jeep Cherokee rolling fast down the taxiway towards them, amber lights flashing on its roof bar. The vehicle swerved round the back of the aircraft, tyres screeching on the tarmac, and braked hard beside them, engine still running. A man leaped out, a fluorescent safety jacket thrown over his business suit, a radio in his right hand. 'Kramer – Airside Manager,' he shouted at Rykhlin. 'Look, we got one hell of an emergency on here. What's your problem?'

'Fuel!' answered Rykhlin.

Kramer's look said it all. Said he wouldn't suffer fools gladly, especially on a cold crisis-ridden morning like this one. 'Well, dumb-shit! What sort of fucking outfit are you? I want this aircraft out directly you finish, OK? And you'll have to wait for your slot with the tanker like everyone else.'

Kramer set off towards the air-stairs to chew out the pilots, then threw back over his shoulder: 'And don't piss me around. When this surge comes in, we're under thirty feet of Pacific. So I want you out.'

Kramer's number instantly registered in Rykhlin's mind.

Thirty feet? That wasn't enough!

'Kramer?' he shouted.

The fluorescent jacket didn't stop moving. 'Yeah?'

'Did you say thirty feet?'

Kramer turned around on the aircraft stairs. 'Just get your fucking aircraft out of my airport, OK?'

'Who told you it was only thirty feet, Kramer?'

But Kramer had already gone, taking the steps two at a time. Rykhlin saw Nicole standing there, hands thrust into her jacket pockets, staring at him. She was looking distraught. 'But you told Washington, didn't you?' she shouted. 'You told them how big it was.'

Rykhlin looked across at Kramer's bright yellow truck,

its door open, engine running, a mobile on the seat. Right now Kramer was talking with the pilots, and his bluff was about to be called at any minute.

Rykhlin went over, picked up the mobile, dialled 911 and asked for Civil Defence, gaving his status as CIA.

He looked back and saw Nicole hunched against the morning cold, saw her trying not to think the unthinkable.

Someone answered: Rykhlin asked when the warning had been issued. By whom? What height had they said the surge would reach? .

Slowly he replaced the mobile on the seat and turned back towards Nicole. She stared at him anxiously. 'Governor's Office didn't issue a warning until four o'clock this morning,' he said slowly. 'And Kramer's right – thirty feet.'

He'd known it all along, he'd just known that was what they'd do. Play it down – save their own skins. *The bastards!* He kicked at the door of the Cherokee.

'No, that can't be right!' Nicole shouted at him. 'You told them, didn't you? You told them what to really expect.'

'Yeah, I told them. They'll try and push people further back from the coast.'

She ran across the tarmac towards him. 'For God's sake, Rykhlin – the Institute, it's right on the cliff edge. Peter could still be there!'

A film ran vividly in Rykhlin's head – a huge wave coming in over the cliff at Gazos, crashing down onto a complex of white buildings, smashing them open, scattering beds, equipment, people, sucking them back into the ocean. A young boy in the water, struggling . . .

'We've got to get him out!' Nicole yelled at him, wild-eyed, determined. '*Now*, Rykhlin! We've got to go *now*!'

He gazed across at the yellow Jeep, the engine running, the door open, the inside still warm from the heater. And Kramer would be clambering out of the aircraft at any minute.

'Get Mei-Lin off the plane,' he said. 'We're going.'

The vast bulk of the *Pacific Conveyor* soared high into the swirling fog as it lay tied up at the side of Pier 13, Oakland Harbour. Wet rail tracks glistened on the empty wharf. A huge yellow crane stood sentinel, legs towering out of sight into the wet blanket of gloom above. Huge walls of stacked metal containers loomed out of the grey mist.

Captain Vince Ryan was in his bunk, sound asleep, staying with the ship as he always did when he was on short turnaround.

The rising wail of sirens drifting across the vast open expanse of the container terminal had not penetrated the steel walls of his ship.

Ryan slept on.

Stephen Glantz and his girlfriend, Nina Hoffman, parked their blue classic VW Beetle in the Golden Gate Visitor

Centre car park and walked hand in hand towards the dimly lit toll-booths that led onto the Bridge.

Butterflies fidgeted restlessly in Nina's stomach. Stephen was her new lover, exciting and impetuous. Late home from the nightclub, they'd made love at his place, away from her parents; and now here she was, going to watch the sunrise from the Bridge. So romantic! She huddled closer into her jacket, felt the warmth of Stephen's hand in her own.

Strangely there was little traffic on the bridge, even for this early hour. As they walked out, she could feel the deck gently sway and bounce as if it was alive beneath her feet, alert to every movement of air and water around it.

From far below on Marine Drive came the rising wail of a convoy of police sirens. It made the flesh at the back of Nina's neck creep.

6.00 a.m.

'We've got to come off the freeway at the next junction!' shouted Nicole. She was in the passenger seat, maps cascading over her knees. 'Follow the signs to Half-Moon Bay.'

'Yeah, I know!' shouted Rykhlin.

He shoved his foot hard down on the accelerator and got the big V8 in front bellowing out. The airport hack wasn't used to such treatment. It rattled and thumped over the bumps, trying to wander between the lane markings.

Vaguely worried about traffic cops, Rykhlin glanced in the mirror and caught sight of the tiny figure of Mei-Lin on the back seat, curled up in a blanket, cuddling her doll close to her face.

'How long?' shouted Nicole above the din in the cabin.

He looked down at the speedometer – the needle was nudging ninety-five. 'Just over an hour if we keep this up.' He looked at his watch. 'We'll make it, no problem.'

But he wasn't that confident.

The big red Chevy pick-up snarled its way down the street, four youngsters crowded into the front. Gogi braked hard and swung the vehicle sharply across the traffic streaming up from the waterfront. Something clattered across the bed of the truck and Lewis had to grab at the open window to steady himself. 'Hey – mind them boards, will yah!'

They saw a large black sedan parked across the road ahead of them; white door shining in the dawn light, red and blue lights strobing from its roof. The cop turned as he heard the throaty burble of the truck and strode towards them, hand held high, radio swinging from his hip.

'Cops, Gogi!' breathed Gina.

'Yeah – OK, OK!'

They drew level with the black-shirted police officer. He poked his nose into the vehicle, the eyes behind his tinted shades flicking from one youngster to the next. 'Where do you kids think you're going?'

Gogi went all sycophantic. 'Got to check out my daddy's boat, sir. He's left important stuff in the locker. Reckons it might not be there after the wave hits.'

The officer eyed the surfboards, all bagged up, lying flat in the back of the truck. He chewed at his gum. 'You kids wouldn't be reckoning on riding this thing, would you?'

Gogi's eyes opened wide. 'Hey, man, chill out. You think we crazy?' A gale of laughter rose from the cab.

The officer eyed the boards again, then stood back from the vehicle. 'OK, but don't be long now. I'm checking you in. Expect you back in thirty minutes – OK?'

'Sure, man!' Gogi gunned the engine and let the truck burble off down the deserted city street – then he opened up its engines with a roar as he swung down towards the brightly painted boats and Italian restaurants of Fisherman's Wharf.

Vince Ryan felt a rough hand shaking his shoulder.

He dragged himself out of a half-sleep and opened bleary eyes on the brightly lit world of his cabin. He saw the long face of his chief engineer. 'Yeah, OK, I'm awake.'

He swung his legs out and sat fully clothed on the edge of the bunk, wearing a navy-blue jumper with gold rings at the shoulder. He coughed phlegm from his chest. 'What's up?'

The engineer studied him for a moment, waiting for

him to focus. 'We got a wave coming. Do you want to try and get the ship out?'

Ryan's befuddled brain struggled to take it all in. 'Wave? What wave?'

'Tidal wave – a big bastard.'

'Jesus!'

Ryan swung down from the bunk, rubbed at his eyes. 'When?'

'07.30.'

Ryan looked at his watch. 'Just over an hour.' He coughed. 'How many men have we got?'

'Enough.'

'Are we unloaded?'

'Mostly. Dry side's all been evacuated, in any case.'

'We'll need a pilot.'

The chief engineer shook his head. 'No pilot – we're on our own.'

Ryan looked at the man and narrowed his eyes. 'You think we can ride this thing out – in deeper water?'

'Sure!'

'Then let's do it.'

Stephen looked down at Nina, his whole face radiating the warmth of an early dawn reflecting up from the blanket of fog shifting uneasily beneath the Bridge. 'You OK to stay? Watch the wave coming in?'

A warm surge of love thrilled through Nina's body. She

pressed up close to him and squeezed his hand. 'If you think it's all right.'

'We're two hundred feet above the water. Got the best view in the city.'

Nina looked along the length of the Bridge and saw that he was right. She could see a crowd gathering on the sidewalk, people walking hand in hand along the now deserted freeway. She looked over the parapet. The fog was beginning to disperse and she caught a glimpse of Fort Point far below, its brickwork shining warmly in the sudden sunshine. There were cars parked down there too, people crowding along the walls. Someone had dressed up in a clown suit and was swooping along on a skateboard. She tugged at Stephen's arm and pointed down. They both laughed.

Two police cars cruised into the fort, lights flashing. The warning drifted up towards them. '*Please vacate the fort now! Please assemble in the Golden Gate Visitor Centre car park, where you will be safe. It is a Federal offence to ignore this warning. You must vacate now!*'

7.00 a.m.

Highway 1 was a nightmare.

The scenic route wound its way south, along the Pacific coastline. The last time Rykhlin had followed this road it had been when he was a boy. The road had been almost deserted then, like a country road. Now it was clogged with traffic that slowed them badly.

A big Buick ambled along in front, waffling around, looking for somewhere to park. 'Sightseers – Christ! They've got no idea what's coming.' He rammed the palm of his hand against the horn to force his way through, bouncing the big yellow Cherokee along the verge to get past. The Buick driver leaned out of his window and shouted abuse.

Nicole said little. She just stared straight ahead through the windscreen, sometimes glancing down at the clock on the dash.

Rykhlin worked hard to push the Jeep through the clogged traffic. He had their route already pictured in his mind, remembering each of the landmarks, every one they passed edging him closer. Nicole stared down at the map, her features taut with anxiety. 'We've only got another twenty minutes.'

'Don't worry. It's not far now.'

He hit the horn button again and kept his hand there, pulling out to force his way down the centre of the highway, scattering the oncoming vehicles. He edged the speed up again and started taking the bends too fast, hoping it would be clear on the other side.

The sweeping lines of the sixty-foot motor yacht *Peppina* sliced easily through the light chop in San Francisco Bay.

Gogi stared up at the looming Golden Gate Bridge and saw people far above him, hanging over the rails, staring down, waving and cheering. He grinned mischievously and sounded the air horns, then pushed hard on the throttle levers to urge the twin diesels to even greater efforts. Streamers floated down towards them. He could make out people clapping as he disappeared beneath the broad span of the arch.

Gogi, rich daddy's playboy, was having the coolest moment of his life.

'Stupid bastards!' muttered Ryan. Through the high-power lenses he watched the tiny white cruiser speeding under the huge arch of the Golden Gate, and saw what he thought must be half of San Francisco lining the railings above. He let down the glasses to check on the smaller boats jostling for space in the Bay and threatening to get under his bow. Then he bent forward and sounded a long blast on the siren, hearing it echo back off the cityscape around him.

Nina waved at the smart cabin cruiser as it emerged from under the Bridge, thrilled at the sight of the white water streaming back from its bows. She saw youngsters on board, surfboards stacked on deck. A muscular young man with long dark hair turned and waved up at her. She waved back.

A long blast sounded way back in the Bay. Stephen

turned and pointed out to her the red shape of a big container ship rounding Alcatraz. She smiled up at him, lovingly, rose up on her toes and kissed his cheek. He bent down and took her head between the warm palms of his hands, pressing his soft lips up against hers.

7.22 a.m.

'Rykhlin, look!' Nicole pointed urgently to their right.

He glanced over and saw the dark blue of the Pacific, long ribs of waves marching slowly in, white surf creaming against the rocky cliff-line. He jerked his gaze back to the speeding road. 'What?'

'The water – it's coming in. It's beginning to cover the rocks. Look at the people down there, they're running back from the edge.'

'Just the initial surge,' he said. 'Means we've still got about twenty minutes before the big one.'

She looked across at him, uncertain. 'You know something about tsunami?'

'Sure! Used to live in Hawaii.'

He was lying – to protect her.

He floored the throttle and the automatic transmission kicked down with a thump. The engine bellowed as he forced up the speed and swung the big yellow Cherokee brutally at the steep curves, feeling the front wheels tug hard at the steering. The tyres squealed in protest, scattering gravel up into the wheel arches.

He glanced over at the Pacific again and saw the ocean pushing in, drowning the rocks down by the shore, pressing up against the cliff as if to test its resolve.

The *Peppina* wallowed in the gentle swell of the Pacific. Three of the young surfers had peeled off their clothes and were laughing and giggling as they began to wriggle into their wet suits. Gogi unzipped his bag and started to wax his favourite longboard with loving care . . .

Then the *Peppina* squirmed uneasily beneath their feet. They felt her lift, carry back for a short distance, then stop.

Their horseplay stopped abruptly. They looked at one another.

'All right, crazy guys!' said Gogi quietly. 'Let's go rhino-chasing!'

'Pacific Conveyor, Pacific Conveyor – *Coast Guard, Coast Guard. Over.*'

Ryan reached up for the receiver, pulled it down on its long black coil of wire, and thumbed the switch.

'*Pacific Conveyor.* Go ahead.'

'Pacific Conveyor, *state your intentions, over.*'

'Getting the hell out of here! Over!'

'Pacific Conveyor, *we advise you stay in harbour. We have a tsunami warning – imminent . . . Over.*'

'Shit!' Ryan looked across at the impassive chief engineer.

'Can you give me an e.t.a. on that? Over.'

There was a pause – the sound of static from the loudspeaker.

'*Offshore tide-monitors recorded first surge about one minute ago. Suggest you have fifteen minutes to the next wave. Over.*'

'Thank you, Coastguard. We copy that.'

Ryan gazed out of the bridge window, saw the vast span of the Golden Gate Bridge now looming ahead. 'Maintain speed and heading,' he ordered.

He began to tap his fingers against the window. But, as he did so, he felt the huge bulk of the ship falter. He saw the bows rise gently above the horizon, then drop slowly down again.

The two men looked at one another. Not a word passed between them.

Ryan began to whistle tunelessly through his front teeth.

Nina yawned as she stared over the railings. She sensed a quietening among the large crowd jostling and chatting around her, and noticed something happening down by the fort. Water was surging around its stonework, streaming past like a fast incoming tide. She tugged at Stephen's arm to attract his attention.

Together they watched the water level rising steadily and saw it reaching up towards the top of the wall. There were tiny people still standing there. Some panicked and began to back away. She stared dizzily down from the Bridge, watching the muddy water pouring into the Bay at freeway speed. All along the sidewalk people began to laugh and clap.

07.37 a.m.

As he rounded the headland, Rykhlin was doing between eighty and ninety on the narrow road. He could see the tarmac ahead swinging down towards a small pebble cove, a clump of cypress trees beyond silhouetted against the blue of the early-morning sky. He saw that the water was unusually low in the bay. The ocean had pulled right out, and stranded fish were flicking among the glistening mud and rock. He'd read about this and knew what it meant. Knew that the next wave was now pounding in towards them.

He pushed down firmly with his right foot. Felt the pedal go hard against the stop, felt the big Jeep gathering speed.

'Rykhlin.' Nicole's voice was low and urgent. She was pointing to one side.

His gaze followed her arm and looked out across the ocean. Where he saw the wave approaching.

It had come in quickly, catching them unawares, and was already drawing slowly up out of the water. It was about the height of a two-storey house; a huge scalloped wall of steel – cold, grey and menacing – running smoothly in towards them, already breaking white along the crest line, spray whipping back in the slipstream.

Rykhlin willed the Jeep forward, pressing hard on the throttle. He knew that he had to outrun it, knew that their speed had to get them through.

But the wave was coming in fast.

For a moment it seemed to hover just offshore, the morning sun glinting off the great curve of its glassy face. Then it broke suddenly, and water cascaded down, thumping with a roar onto the beach, throwing up a vast welter of foam and spray. Deep surf swept violently up towards the road, boiling with thrashing shingle.

The Jeep hit the flood at speed, and water planed out to either side, roaring up into the wheel arches. The vehicle was braked hard by the water, jerking the occupants forward against the safety belts. Mei-Lin gave a shrill scream and scrabbled for something to hold on to. Rykhlin felt the steering go light in his hands, felt them being pushed sideways by the raging brown surf as it spun them round like a top. Then the wheels caught at the ground beneath, bounced briefly, and caught again.

Rykhlin hit the brakes and wrenched the vehicle to a stop.

He leaned forward on the steering wheel, arms and legs shaking uncontrollably, a sick feeling in his stomach. The sea began to cream back beneath the Jeep. He could feel the tyres settling into the soft ground and he stamped on the throttle. The engine roared, the wheels finally caught, and forced them, lurching, out of the hole.

Rykhlin kept them moving forwards slowly as the water drained away.

The wave had lifted them up and dropped them a hundred feet away from the road. He couldn't believe they were still upright. He turned in his seat to check out their tiny passenger and saw her wide-eyed stare, her little hands held up high clutching the grab-handle in the roof. He wondered if she would ever survive their wild journey.

As he drove back onto the road, he noted the muddy water in the Bay still churning. He watched as the level dropped away eerily. It was beginning to suck slowly back.

For the Big One.

Nicole caught his arm. 'Look!'

He followed her gaze and in the far distance caught sight of the thin white tower of a distant lighthouse, Pigeon Point, a tiny needle of hope on the horizon, the last landmark before reaching the Institute – and Peter.

Maybe they were going to do it!

Maybe they were goddamned well going to do it!

Gogi sat upright on his surfboard, drifting and waiting.

The cold water of the Pacific smacked against his body and made his hands burn. He checked around him, saw the others bobbing in the water, and shouted encouragement.

They'd been waiting.

They'd been waiting for a long time.

Then at last he saw it: a thin grey smudge of a line stretched right across the horizon.

Gogi's heart beat frantically in his ribcage.

He shouted again, lay down on his surfboard and began to paddle with his hands towards the oncoming mass of water. The wave seemed to grow in size as it approached, like a long mound rolling in towards him. As it came near he began to make out shreds of foam that rose swiftly up the face of the huge swell before dropping away over the lip.

So – it was just him and the wave now.

He sized it up, estimating its height as at least a fifty-foot overhead. A monster, the mother of all waves – a tsunami. He turned and began to paddle towards the shore, running with the wave and he felt it start to lift him . . . up . . . up . . .

He grabbed the sides of his board and jumped.

Standing, he looked down the steep face of the wave, and watched the water sliding up towards him. He wavered for a moment, then felt the board grip, and got his balance. He had it! He was cutting down the face of a huge wave, dragging a fantail of white behind him. He was radical. He was his own hero. Knees bent and body leaning forwards, he was Holua, the cool Hawaiian guy who'd ridden the fifty-foot tsunami into Minole Bay.

The wind roared in his ears and his long black hair began to whip back in the slipstream. Spray stung the raw skin of his face. *Ecstasy!*

Gogi looked around for his friends and made out Lewis some distance further along. Couldn't find Gina. Then he saw the vast span of the Golden Gate in the distance. *Yeeeeeesss!* he thought. Through the Bridge and into the Bay, this was going to be the ride of his life.

He sensed the wave was already tugging at the lessening depth, could feel it growing and steepening as it neared the shore. He glanced sideways along the line of the giant breaker, and saw the outer part beginning to peel, white foam cascading down its steep face, spray hissing back over the thick lip ... then he was in the tube himself, the turquoise outer wall sweeping low over his head.

He bent down and creamed fast through the tunnel of water. But not fast enough ...

Niagara slammed down on top of Gogi. Tons of water jackhammered him into the depths of the Pacific.

The wave had eaten him up, wiped him out.

He held his breath as he went under and felt the strength of the whirlpools grabbing at his body. Felt his board tugging violently at the leash, then breaking free from his ankle. He rode the turmoil, waiting for it all to stop, waiting to break through to the surface.

But the breakthrough never came.

Instead, violent currents continued to pummel painfully against his body. He opened his eyes to check, and saw only dark green, tumbling and moving around him.

He began to strike out for the surface, chest bursting for air, lungs bruising with pain. He had to breathe, he had to take something in ...

The pain grew quickly, became intense . . .

His chest heaved.

Water flooded inside. Cold solid water that hung heavy in his body.

Gogi stopped thrashing and calmed. He could feel the weight of the sea dragging him down. He let the darkness close slowly around him and, strangely, he felt no panic. Instead, he thought back to his moment of triumph, and quietly let the velvet blackness take him into its arms.

Ryan saw it in the distance through the span of the Bridge: a dark line growing on the horizon. He raised his binoculars. God, the wave must be fifty feet or more – breaking at either end as it entered the shallows. The speed of the thing was phenomenal. He could see spray whipping back over the crest as it ploughed towards him.

'Slow on both.'

The engineering officer pulled back on both levers.

'Engine room reports slow on both.'

'We'll ride this sucker out. Keep it straight on to the bows.'

Nina screamed as the wave hit the fort with a tremendous thump. Sheets of water spewed vertically for over a hundred feet, tossing tiny-looking cars into the air.

Then the whole bridge shuddered as the wave slammed against the towers and rushed beneath them through the narrow strait. It spread out into the Bay beyond, scything through the waterfront buildings as it went. She saw restaurants, shops, boats all being caught up in the maelstrom and tossed in the air, debris tumbling and spinning before crashing back down into the churning white foam.

7.42 a.m.

'Rykhlin, look!'

He was driving hard for the Point, the yellow Jeep bucking and pitching on the undulating road, thankful to see the familiar row of white houses huddled on the rocky promontory not far ahead of him.

'Rykhlin!' Nicole repeated.

He caught the urgency in her voice and glanced across at her. 'What?'

She pointed again.

His gaze travelled across the uneasy surface of the Pacific and made out a dark line smudged onto the horizon.

He knew that line. He'd read about it but never thought he'd actually witness it.

A huge rolling mass of ocean. Wild, unstoppable, uncontrollable – a great solid wall of water, hundreds of feet high.

The third wave.

The Big One.

You either outran it – or you died.

Fear gripped Rykhlin. He floored the accelerator and the Jeep lurched sideways as the wheels scrabbled for grip on the gravel-strewn road. He raced past the houses, seeing people running back inland from the cliffs, all shouting and pointing. A woman screamed at him above the roar of the engine.

He reached a fork in the road, the place where the Institute was signed off to the right. And, in that split second, he hesitated.

Fate had just dumped him in the same place for the second time.

He'd been here before, in Kosovo, facing the same ghastly decision.

To him, there was no point in going for to the Institute for Peter. If the boy was still there – he was already dead. If there was to be any future, they had to save themselves, save the little fugitive on the seat behind them.

So he ignored the turn and drove straight on, heading for the mountains.

Nicole screamed – a desperate animal howl of hate and anger.

Rykhlin kept the Jeep pointing up the road. They had to climb; they had to get to higher ground.

She flung her hands on top of her head, tearing at her hair. 'No! No! No!' she screamed. Then she beat at him with her fists, tears streaming down her face. Her lips drew back and a primeval scream roared from the depths of her body. 'You bastard, Rykhlin! You yellow bastard! You coward, go back! Go back! I'm not losing him now!'

The Jeep took a dip in the road too fast, lost contact with the ground. The engine raced, then the vehicle jerked as the wheels caught the road again. He had to get away. Death was coming fast. He felt the pain of his guilt.

Nicole battered him with her fists, fighting him for the steering wheel. The noise confused his mind. He was back in the chopper, heard again the thump and shriek of cannon, the *whomp* of helicopter blades, the roar of powerful engines. He glanced in the mirror and saw Mei-Lin's small face, her eyes tiny and round with terror. Saw again the haunting eyes of the dead he'd left behind. And behind the child, on the distant horizon, a great mountain of water stretched way up into the sky, hanging impossibly over the tiny cluster of houses down on the Point.

People were pulling back from the railings, running down the freeway, trying desperately to get off the Bridge.

Nina felt panic rising up inside her. She started to run like she'd once run as a kid, trying to escape the unimaginable horror now looming on the horizon. The crowd surged around her, ignoring her, pushing her out of the way. She lost Steve in the confusion.

She turned towards the ocean and gaped at the mountainous wave coming in straight towards her. Hundreds of feet high, a vast wall of water – ugly, yellow-brown, with debris lifting rapidly over its speeding face. And in her ears the sound of it: a steady roar, the heavy thunder of water on the rampage.

'Steve!' she screamed.

The crowd was now in a blind panic. People tripping and falling in their haste to clear the bridge were getting trampled by those behind, all stampeding for the safety of the mainland.

It was almost upon them, its roar drowning their screams of terror – billions of tons of water, a vast and powerful mass, a huge fist of power. It thudded against the concrete piers. Huge fountains of water soared into the air. The Bridge shuddered under the hammer blow. The foundations held for a moment, then the south pier slowly tipped. Suspension cables as thick as tree trunks tugged alarmingly at their huge anchorage points. The deck jerked and swayed drunkenly. People were slammed to the tarmac and rolled across the roadway like skittles.

Nina lost her footing and was thrown to the ground. She felt the deck shudder beneath her, felt it rise and fall like a ship at sea as pressure waves passed along the length of the bridge. She could hear the shriek of tortured metal as the deck tipped alarmingly. She began to roll and couldn't hold herself back, fetching up against the guard rail. As the deck continued to sway, she hung on tightly, looking down dizzily at the huge wave surging on into the Bay.

Then the Bridge gave another lurch – and the rail Nina was clinging to peeled out over the water. She hung on, terrified, as she was swung out into space, hundreds of feet above the surging water. The rail jerked suddenly. Nina lost her hold and fell, dropping through the air like a sand-filled dummy, smacking into the water with as shattering an impact as if it had been concrete.

'Holy Mother of God!' Ryan was staring out through the bridge window of the *Pacific Conveyor*. He watched the great mountain of water pass under the Golden Gate and come straight on into the Bay. He saw one tower waver, the deck sagging under the impact. He watched the wave as it surged towards him: huge, fast and ugly.

The Bridge disappeared from sight behind the tsunami's swelling bulk. He could hear it now, like the steady roar of a thousand jets. He clung, white-knuckled, to the control panel. No time to be frightened! The vast bulk of the *Pacific Conveyor* shuddered as her bows began to lift.

Something came loose and crashed against a bulkhead.

Still the ship's bows lifted.

Ryan felt hammer blows passing through the ship as some of the massive containers were ripped away from their mountings.

Still the bows climbed: up . . . up . . .

Ryan clung on to stop himself from sliding. Books and charts tumbled out of their racks and cascaded around him.

Now they were moving backwards. They were caught on the wave and moving backwards. The whole ship, all 120,000 tons of her, surfing a 200-foot wave, backwards, across the Bay.

Perhaps he could save her. If only he could get to the

engine controls, he might just be able to push her over the other side. He clawed himself upright, clung to the console. Caught a glimpse of the wave exploding across the San Francisco waterfront. Buildings shattering, towers toppling, debris being thrown upwards in a great welter of tearing foam.

'The bows are swinging!' yelled the engineer. 'We're broaching!'

She was going side-on to the wave, beginning to heel over.

Ryan grabbed at the ship's wheel as he felt the deck tipping beneath him.

'*Whoaaaa . . .*'

Glass shattered. More containers ripped loose and plunged off the ship.

Then slowly, majestically, the *Pacific Conveyor* rolled . . . 120,000 tons of marine scrap iron smashed at high speed into the industrial city of Oakland, bouncing and rolling with the wave for over half a mile, flattening warehouses, factories, hotels, railroad stations, entire neighbourhoods beneath its vast bulk.

Then the wave reached its zenith and the ship lay still for a moment, stranded among the debris – before the powerful backwash lifted her up and took her back the way she had come, scraping the devastated area clear of debris, and finally dumping her onto the scoured surface of the container terminal – just a few hundred feet from the place where she had started.

Chapter Forty-nine – 8.30 a.m.: Gazos Creek

Rykhlin pressed the toe of his boot into glutinous mud and watched the wetness oozing out. He smelled the sharp freshness of salt inside his throat as he looked across at the Pescadero Cancer Institute – or, at least, the place where the Institute had once been.

Where well-manicured lawns had undulated smoothly down towards a picturesque cliff top, there now lay huge drifts of mud and gravel, deeply etched by miniature ravines. Where once had stood proud modern buildings, all glass and architect-designed, there now stood only the flat concrete rafts of foundations, swept clean as if by some giant hand.

Rykhlin lived again the last few moments of their escape – the frantic speed of the Jeep, the wave towering wall-like behind the lighthouse, Mei-Lin's screams, Nicole's fists beating relentlessly upon his body.

The situation had been hopeless – surely she could see that? They would never have made it. They didn't even know whether Peter had still been there when the wave struck. Maybe he was safe. They really didn't know.

But if he'd driven on to the Institute. If he'd done that. Then the wave would have wiped them all out and rolled them to oblivion inside the tumbling wreckage of the Jeep. And left Peter – if he *was* safe – without a mother, Mei-Lin without a life.

It had been the right decision.

Surely Nicole could see that.

Rykhlin gazed around the alien landscape and saw how the wave must have hit it with unbelievable force. Saw how it had overwhelmed this tiny community, smashing it to fragments, rolling the wreckage inland for over a mile, then sucking it all back out again – taking with it boulders, trees, and rubble. Only wreckage was left now – drifts of broken masonry, shards of twisted metal, the pathetic fragments of sodden clothing. The erratic deposits of a cataclysmic flood.

At the bottom of the cliffs the ocean still heaved, water fountaining into the air as smaller waves continued to drive onshore. But the third wave had already done its work – there was nothing left to take.

Nicole stood propped against the side of the yellow Jeep, hands thrust deep into her pockets. She was staring at a small group of figures in the far distance, workers who'd arrived from somewhere. Rescuers now, their bright yellow jackets smeared darkly with mud, soil-caked trousers flopping heavily around their ankles, their metal rods probed the soft earth.

A call carried on the thin wind. The group huddled together for a moment, then worked to heave another victim from the sucking ground. They dragged the body heavily towards the small pile of corpses arranged like logs on a stretch of water-washed shingle.

Nicole had checked each body when they'd first arrived. He'd watched her, stiff-backed and numb with grief, turning them over carefully, making their limbs flop heavy and lifeless on the gravel.

Now she just watched. And waited.

The wind caught at her hair and blew it across her face as Rykhlin walked back to where she stood. He wanted to comfort her, to stand by her, to give her strength. But her face was a mask, her eyes hard and distant. She had withdrawn inside herself.

Then she turned her back on him.

They stood like that for some time, rigid and awkward.

The silence was broken by the steady beat of a helicopter's rotors. Rykhlin looked up and saw it flying slowly along the coast. He watched as it rounded the headland and turned towards them. It circled noisily overhead, then came back in over the sea to land among the waste. It was a military chopper, camouflaged, searching for survivors.

A National Guardsman stepped out of the open door and walked across the mud and gravel, splashing through sheets of water that still wept back into the ocean. He carried a blanket, brilliant red against the steel-grey mud.

'You folks OK?' he asked. 'You want to come back to the Evacuation Centre?'

Rykhlin nodded. Where else would they go now?

The Guardsman looked at Nicole, then back at Rykhlin, finally handing the blanket to her. She opened the passenger door of the Jeep and took Mei-Lin into her arms. She wrapped the blanket protectively around the little girl's slim body – then tried to pass her to Rykhlin.

But he wouldn't accept the child.

He knew consciously, then, what he already felt in his heart . . .

That Nicole wasn't coming with him, that she wasn't going to leave this place.

The Guardsman shrugged and told Nicole that another chopper would pick them both up later. Then he began to delve into his pockets to find some candy for the kid before they left.

As they took off, Rykhlin watched the bright yellow Jeep drift slowly away below the helicopter's open doorway. Nicole was still standing there, hunched against the vehicle, hair torn back from her face by the powerful down-draught, hugging the little girl close to her chest.

And he was alone in the cabin, cold and numb.

He felt hollow, a husk, unable to believe what had happened, unable to believe that her son had perished. Surely Peter would have been evacuated, taken to higher ground. As soon as the helicopter landed at the centre he'd make a few calls – there were people he knew, people with resources. People who could help him.

He gazed across at the Guardsman sitting quietly in the doorway, legs dangling, scanning the swathe of devastation that ran along the coast.

Rykhlin wasn't going to give up easily – on either of them.

Chapter Fifty – 4.00 p.m.: Santa Cruz

The shadows were lengthening by the time Nicole's helicopter finally came in to land, swooping low over a patch of ranch land to the north of the city. She could see a tent city that was being hurriedly erected by the National Guard. It was a hive of activity, and a line of big trucks was parked to one side. She saw uniformed soldiers heaving off dark green bundles, and watched as they carried them over to neatly taped-off squares of ground.

A Guardsman helped her as she lifted Mei-Lin out of the helicopter. An earnest young man was hurrying over to meet them. He hadn't had time to shave that morning. He wore sneakers and jeans, and his dark blue jacket had large bright yellow letters on the back – FEMA.

'Hi! I'm Ed Daugherty, Federal Emergency Management Agency.' She saw that he had a clipboard and computer printout in one hand, a pen in the other. 'If you would come this way, I'll try and sort you out with some accommodation.'

'It's my son!' she said hoarsely, her eyes sore and red-rimmed.

He turned to her with an enquiring look on his face.

'He was at the Institute,' she continued, 'Gazos Creek. I don't know . . . I don't know whether . . .'

'And the little girl, ma'am?' he enquired. 'Is she yours?'

Nicole, her emotions bludgeoned by the catastrophe, struggled for an easy explanation.

A smile crossed his concerned face. 'It's OK,' he said kindly. 'We'll see what we can do.'

Nicole waited with Mei-Lin inside a large army tent, sitting on plastic chairs among a growing flow of bedraggled survivors – some weeping, some just quiet. A gentle wind tugged and flapped at the canvas. The sun had shone brilliantly all that day and had made the inside of the tent warm, releasing the sweet smell of new-mown grass.

A small crowd of high school children bundled in. Some were laughing and chattering, excited by their adventure; others looked pale as they were ushered in by fussing teachers. Rucksacks were shrugged off and stacked in a corner.

She stared at the boys in the party and found herself wondering if somehow Peter might be among them. She listened to their young excited voices, listened to them broadcasting their youth, their joy at being alive.

But in a dark recess, in a place where she did not dare

to look, there flitted the shadow of Peter's body: broken and awkward, entombed in debris, maybe lost for ever.

When Ed came back Nicole searched his face intently, looking for some sort of clue, some sort of sign. He stopped in front of her. His gaze flicked up from the piece of paper tagged to his clipboard. 'Where did you say he was staying?' he asked cautiously.

She heard a distant voice answering, her voice. 'The Pescadero Cancer Institute, Gazos Creek.'

'Gazos Creek . . .?' Ed frowned.

He sucked at his lower lip, shaking his head. 'As I understand it, most of the Pescadero people were evacuated last night.'

Hope exploded into Nicole's mind!

Thank God! Peter might still be alive! Relief surged through her like a drug and a smile unfolded across her face.

'Yeah,' Ed continued, 'they've got their own lodge up near Big Basin, right inside the Redwood State Park . . .'

'How do we get there?' she asked anxiously, her body sagging under the weight of Mei-Lin.

Ed studied her carefully over the top of his clipboard. He, too, looked tired. 'Well, I guess I can take you up there now, if you like. We've got to account for them all anyway.' He paused. 'If that's OK with you?'

It was dusk by the time Ed's jeep finally rattled and slithered its way along the wet stony track that wound its way up through the giant redwood trees. Nicole sat in the back with the little girl, a protective arm around her bony shoulders. She watched the low sunlight flash through the black-branched canopy, her body filled with anticipation and excitement.

They had passed a sign: Pescadero Institute Vacation Camp – Private.

Nicole's anxiety was intense now, her expectation high, and the pain inside real.

Low timber cabins came into view. 'That's it,' Ed called out from the front. He brought the vehicle to a halt, got out and slammed his door.

Nicole gathered up Mei-Lin and felt hot little hands reach up to clutch at her neck. She shut the rear door of the jeep and stood there, not sure what to do.

Ed looked at her across the vehicle's roof. 'If you stay here, I'll go and check it out.'

She watched as he walked over to a group of people in the distance. Saw them pointing something out for him.

He headed off towards one of the cabins.

She wandered round to the back of the vehicle and tried to kill time. She kicked at loose stones in the dirt road while Mei-Lin clung to her shoulder. She felt some relief now that they'd arrived, thankful that someone had had the good sense to evacuate the patients, reassured that Peter was in good hands.

From somewhere nearby she could hear the laughter and shouting of excited children. She couldn't wait much longer.

Ed came back across the clearing with a member of the Pescadero staff: a small round man, his grey hair in tight curls above the fur collar of his anorak. He held out his hand. 'Miss Tai-Chung? I'm Dr Hamblin – consultant.'

Nicole put Mei-Lin down and stared at him, waiting for him to tell her about Peter.

'I'm afraid your son's not here.'

The world suddenly closed in around her, all movement stilled. The sounds of the children receded. 'Where is he, then?' she asked, her voice wavering.

'There's no easy way of saying this, Miss Tai-Chung.' Hamblin was watching her eyes. 'We haven't been able to account for all the children . . .'

From out of nowhere a sharp pain sliced savagely through her gut. She sagged, reaching out for the side of the jeep. 'No, no,' she stammered, 'that can't be right.'

Ed's arm came up to steady her.

'We tried to get in touch with you at the Evacuation Centre,' continued Hamblin. 'It was very difficult . . . you know . . . under the circumstances. We tried our best.' He looked at her, his face impartial, professional, and controlled. 'I'm very sorry,' he added.

She'd failed her son.

Maybe she'd killed him, as sure as his cancer would have.

Hamblin shuffled awkwardly, uncertain of his ground. He coughed nervously. 'You must understand, there wasn't much time. We had to evacuate quickly, take our most serious cases first.' He gave her a haunted look. 'He was in one of the end vehicles, and they were late getting away, in the chaos . . . I still don't know . . .'

But *she*'d known! Known all along that she might lose him.

Abruptly Nicole turned and walked away from Hamblin. Away from Mei-Lin and Ed and the jeep. Away from the laughter of the children.

She headed off down the track, reaching out for the sanctuary of the darkening forest.

And they let her go.

Nicole became aware of the forest gathering around her, and let it close in and envelop her like a womb. She felt the cool wetness of its damp air as it softly embraced her, smelt the cloying sweetness of rotting vegetation on the forest floor – heard the evening calls of birds in the canopy above, the quiet rattle of stones as they scattered beneath her feet.

And as she walked, pictures formed in her head: her father . . . her brother . . . her former lover. All dead.

And now – her son?

She looked down at the steady tread of her feet, watched the blur of the gravel passing below . . . and became aware of a faint answering scurry from behind, tiny footsteps treading the stones, a small hand reaching up into hers, little fingers poking into her fist, two tiny eyes staring up at her – eyes bright with innocent hope.

It was Mei-Lin!

She smiled, and reached down to gather the warmth of this little body up close to hers, wanting to feel again the answering embrace of a child's arms.

And she knew. Knew as clearly as day follows night, that if there was a God, that if there really was life after death – then maybe this was it, in the warmth of this little person, this little scrap of life who had nothing to share with her but her love and her trust.

They stopped and stood for a moment on a small ridge, cheek to cheek, looking out across the growing darkness of the forest. Two people with no one but each other. Together they watched the final flash of the sun come slanting down through the trees, and listened to the chill evening wind as it came soughing through the pines.

Presently they heard the dull roar of a hard-working engine: a truck labouring its way along the rough track towards them, tyres scrabbling for grip on the damp stones. Nicole watched as it lurched into view: a blue pick-up, large cab at the front, bright yellow letters shining in the gloom – FEMA.

Nicole strained forward as it came closer, searching for a face in the cab, but the low sunset bounced vivid reds and oranges off the window glass, making it difficult for her to see inside.

A shadow passed across the vehicle and for a moment it extinguished the reflections. She glimpsed a cheek pressed up against the glass, and children's faces in profile, smeared with the dark mud of chaos.

Then they were gone.

For a moment she stood there, staring at the red tail lights as they flickered into the distance.

My God! She'd seen her son, her son's face through the window.

Then she was running, wild, shot through with adrenalin. Shouts of laughter poured out of her, went rolling away among the trees as her feet pounded the gravel. She reached out desperately towards the camp, Mei-Lin heavy against her chest, the wind sighing through her hair – desperate to see him, desperate to touch him, to have the feel of her son tight against her body.

At last she was complete – *this* was what she'd been fighting for.

This was what really mattered.

BBC Television
Transcript of News Broadcast

June 28

In this special extended edition we present a report on the extent of the damage caused by the recent tsunami weapon that has left the people of the United States reeling in shock. We also examine the implications now reverberating around the world.

San Francisco bore the brunt of the attack as the wave funnelled through the Golden Gate and then swept on into the Bay, creating a huge swathe of destruction all around the rim. Oakland and Berkeley took the giant two-hundred-foot wave head-on. It swept inland for over a mile, flattening docks, piers, harbour buildings, cranes, shipping, freeways, and whole neighbourhoods as it went – all replaced by billions of cubic yards of mud and debris. Several large fires are still burning, caused by the wave punching open oil and gas storage tanks.

The tsunami struck Los Angeles some thirty minutes after reaching San Francisco. More low-lying than the area around the Bay, here the tsunami was able to

sweep well inland. The entire dockland area of Long
Beach has disappeared, along with most of the buildings in the commercial heart of the city. The devastation is total, and bears frank witness to the frightening
power of this weapon. The area from Malibu to
Redondo Beach has been especially badly hit, as have
the high cliffs of Pacific Palisades, a desirable residential
area.

Valdez in Alaska is no stranger to seismic sea waves,
and many people remember the great earthquake of
Good Friday 1964, when thirty-two people died. Here,
the tsunami was funnelled up Prince William Sound
and grew to an unprecedented height as it was compressed by the land to either side. Damage has been
reported as high as four hundred feet above sea level.

The wave then swept on around the Pacific, reaching the coasts of Japan and Mexico some two hours
later, exposing the wild and indiscriminate nature of a
geophysical weapon. Even though it had become far
less powerful by then, serious damage has been
reported in these countries also. Yet, thanks to United
States and British intelligence officers operating deep
inside Indonesia, American Federal Agencies and various national governments had received warning of the
attack, and the number of deaths around the Pacific
coastline has been kept remarkably low.

Outright horror at and condemnation of Indonesia's extraordinary pre-emptive strike, designed to
deflect the United States' attention away from Indonesia's illegal mining of ocean-floor resources, has been

widespread. Many people now see the world as sliding towards a completely new type of warfare.

Geophysical weapons are terrifying. They give a potential enemy the ability to control and manipulate the environment, enhancing its own position by visiting horrific and indiscriminate destruction upon a rival population, yet striking its foe without any warning.

But quite what the Indonesians have discovered on the ocean floor that merits such a violent response remains a mystery.

Epilogue

Saturday, late August

Nicole watched as the wave came sweeping in and saw it curl as it hit the shallows, then break as it ran over her feet. She wriggled her toes as sand streamed past in the backwash and felt the grit flow softly around her ankles.

Turning, she began to tread the wet sand towards the steps that led up to the cliff top, past the slender-limbed Mei-Lin playing quietly in the soft sand, past the hollow sound of Peter's bare feet kicking a coloured beach ball.

The wooden rail felt warm beneath her hand. It smelled of tar. She took the steps steadily, hearing the shriek of the gulls, the rhythmic sigh of the surf breaking far below, the squeals and shouts of other children in the waves.

She stepped off the top and made her way towards the brick café where families downed Cokes and ice creams and Union Jacks fluttered in the breeze.

'Nicole!'

She looked up sharply.

The big grey BMW dominated the front row of the car

park. Simes had one hand held out in greeting. He looked so out of place here, in his well-cut city suit.

'Shall we sit down?' His voice was as polished and well-rounded as ever.

A moment of panic swept through Nicole – a memory of a Washington briefing room, of icy words from a man called Rykhlin that had cut deep into her consciousness.

She backed away. 'I thought we'd finished, Simes.'

'Please,' he gestured, waving towards one of the wooden patio tables outside the café. 'If you wouldn't mind.'

Nicole hesitated, uncertain, then sat down, feeling the warmth of the polished wood under her naked thighs. 'Why are you here?' she demanded.

He sensed her fear. 'It's not what you think, Nicole. I'm not here to harm you. After all, it's in the public domain now, all in the past. But I had wondered . . . the details. Whether you might ever be tempted . . . as a journalist perhaps . . .?'

She turned away from him, gazing out to sea to watch the sunlight sparkling like diamonds on the water far below. 'I know the rules, Simes,' she said carefully. Then she studied his face for a moment. 'Is that the only reason you came here?' she asked. 'To warn me? To keep me in line?'

'No, there was something else. *Indera* – I thought you should know: it was just a Fool's Gold.'

'Fool's Gold?' She stared back at him without comprehension.

'The Americans brought up a sample, had it analysed. It's not a superconductor – it never was.'

Nicole struggled with this new absurdity. 'You mean, all that misery, all that death – for nothing?'

Simes shook his head. 'No, not for nothing. You rid the world of another dictator.'

Nicole laughed, a harsh laugh that turned faces. 'I'm not naive, Simes. We simply replaced him – with Thameena, and with that worm Lukman. Just another evil dynasty.'

Simes slowly got up from the table, his well-dressed figure silhouetted against the cloudless summer sky. The big BMW started up as if in response and began to whisper gently to itself in the car park.

'You may be right,' he said. Then he reached into his pocket. 'I thought you might like this – as a memento, something to pass to your son one day.' It was clenched in his fist. He placed it on the table.

She looked down and saw a fragment of rock, its chipped end sparkling with little flashes of gold, bearing a tiny handwritten code in red ink.

She knew that rock.

She picked it up like one might pick up a favourite keepsake, felt it heavy and cold in her hands, and turned it over and over, her mind far away.

She heard Simes get up from the table, and listened to his soft tread as he returned to the car, heard the sound of an opening door. 'Rykhlin was no coward,' he called out.

'He simply did what was right. I think you should know that.'

Then came a heavy click as the door shut, and the quiet crunch of tyres on gravel as the BMW eased out of its parking slot. She waited for the purr of its engine to die away, then, with a flick of her wrist, she sent the stone spinning into the car park, where it bounced and rattled to a stop. One stone amongst so many.

Slowly, Nicole got up and walked back to the cliff top to stare down at the beach. She saw a young boy and a little girl running and tumbling into the sea, splashing side by side in the surf, white foam kicking up around their feet. Their innocent shrieks of laughter carried up towards her on the wind, and made her smile.

She turned back towards the steps, but then hesitated, catching sight of a slip of paper wedged beneath the planks of the picnic table. It flapped and quivered in the breeze. She moved forwards to pluck it from its prison.

On it was pencilled, in Simes's neat copperplate handwriting, a telephone number.

A private number, with United States national and area codes.

And beneath it a single word: Rykhlin.

Rolling dice
and tiger's roar.
Reaching out
the tiger's claw.
Fear the tigers' strike
when *Korinchi* stalk the night!

In a world dominated by growing population pressure and environmental decline, a situation will arise one day when a nation will wage a secret war against its neighbours in order to try to gain control of an essential and valuable resource – water, perhaps, or oil, or maybe some important mineral. For the aggressor nation the environment would make a useful weapon. The strike could go on for years, frequent attacks doing great and indiscriminate damage, but the truth remaining hidden amongst the normal random violence of nature. Neighbours would not even know that they had been deliberately attacked.

Perhaps they already have been.